A
SELLSWORD'S
RESOLVE

Book Three
of
The Seven Virtues
by
Jacob Peppers

This book is a work of fiction. Names, characters, places and incidents are either the product of the author's imagination or are used fictitiously. Any resemblance to actual persons, living or dead, or to actual events or locales is entirely coincidental.

A Sellsword's Resolve
Book three of the Seven Virtues

Visit the author website:
www.JacobPeppersAuthor.com

To my wife

Without whom...

Well, we really don't have that much time.

Sign up for the author's New Releases mailing list and get a copy of *The Silent Blade,* the prequel for The Seven Virtues, FREE for a Limited Time!

CHAPTER ONE

They were coming. The night was dark and moonless, filled with an almost preternatural silence, the silence of ancient things and long forgotten places, and they were coming. The great trees loomed overhead, monolithic shadows that watched the scene play out before them, thinking their strange, alien thoughts. Those who came were not of the forest, but intruders in this place who cared nothing for the world of men and its doings. Each metallic shift of their armor rang like clarion bells in the near silence. Each heavy footfall was loud and somehow profane.

Aaron waited, silently crouched in the shadowed nook of a tree and its branch some fifteen feet up from the base of the trunk. He waited, his hand on the hilt of the sword at his back, and listened as the intruders drew closer.

Aaron had grown up in cities, his life spent surrounded by shops and taverns, criminals and whores, a world very different than the one in which he found himself, yet there were similarities, if a man looked closely enough.

The Downs, the slum of Avarest, may not have been filled with trees, but buildings and trees were not so very different in the darkness. Vague, shadowed outlines that served to conceal predators and prey alike. In the woods, such predators were wolves and bears, creatures of claws and teeth that hunted to survive. In the Downs, there were predators too, more, in fact, and though these did their hunting with knives and swords, with clubs and shivs, they too hunted for their survival.

Still, Aaron had to admit that he'd learned a lot from Wendell, his new sergeant. The man was a gruff, irreverent bastard with a jagged scar across his face—not that he'd have won any beauty contests anyway. Unlike the majority of Perennia's soldiers who'd been born and raised in the city, Wendell had grown up in a small forest village and his father taught him much of what it took to survive—and fight—in the woods. He, in turn, taught Aaron and those men under Aaron's command. Or, at least, he'd tried. The failure of many of the men to learn the sergeant's lessons was evident in each snap as they stepped on a twig, in each metallic scrape of armor against the forest's undergrowth.

Aaron kept his eyes wide in an effort to pick up any light the night held, peering into the darkness where the sounds were coming from. He could have used his bond with Co to see the men clearly, locating them by the many emotions that were no doubt roiling through them, but he was determined to win or lose based solely on the things Wendell had shown him. And anyway, he thought he knew well enough what emotions he would find should he hunt for them. There would be exhaustion, mental and physical, annoyance more than likely, and some small bit of fear as was always present when a man finds himself in the deeper, darker places of the world, places that felt, if not malevolent, certainly indifferent. Such places cared little for men and their concerns.

Aaron, too, was weary, and he wanted to rub his eyes, to shake his head in an effort to clear vision that was blurred from lack of sleep, but he fought back the impulse. In the deep silence of the woods, the smallest sound could give away a man's position.

Three days they'd been at it this time. Three days and only four men left besides Aaron. Wendell himself, of course, and three others, two of which were the owners of those unmistakable footfalls down below. At least one of the others—not Wendell, he was sure of that—he heard coming from the other direction, the men doing what they could to pen him in and leave him no room to flee.

It would have been a clever enough strategy, Aaron supposed, except that he was not the type of man who often looked for a way to flee. Things that fled were chased. Things that fled were prey and left a scent in the air that all predators could detect and pursue. No, fleeing had never been the idea.

The two were drawing nearer now, and he judged that it would take them no more than five minutes to be underneath him. The other was closer, hidden somewhere in the darkness by the oak sentinels, but easy enough to track by the sound his steel boots made on the forest floor.

Aaron eased himself down the trunk of the tree, taking his time, acutely aware of the unavoidable sounds he made as he clambered down the tree. He let go a couple of feet above the ground, his own leather boots making little noise as he landed on the blanket of grass beneath him. There had been dead leaves lying about the oak he'd chosen, but he'd moved them away before he climbed, all too aware after Wendell's lessons of how easily such oversights could give a man away. He stayed crouched low, sliding the dulled sword he'd brought out of its sheath, his heightened senses wincing at each scrape the blade made against the leather before it was free.

He waited then, watching and listening for any of the tell-tale signs—whispers, rapid footfalls—that would indicate that he'd given away his position. The lone man was almost on him now, the other two a few minutes away, or so he suspected. The forest did strange things with sound. Still, he knew they were close and that was enough. He crept forward, keeping the trees between him and the sound of the approaching man, his eyes studying the forest floor below him, so that he might avoid any fallen twig or leaf that might give him away.

Soon, he was close enough to hear the sound of the man's breathing. Shallow breaths, caused as much by anxiety, he suspected, as exertion. Being in such a place, on such an errand, had ways of awakening a primal fear, no doubt a remnant of times before men learned to cultivate, to build, back before they had learned—for better or worse—how to shape the world around them to their liking instead of being forced to be part of it as it was.

Aaron propped his back against the trunk of a tree, waiting until the man passed, and he could see his breath pluming out before him in the chill night. Then he glided forward, clapping a hand over the man's mouth from behind even as he brought his sword up to the soldier's throat.

The man grunted in what would have been a scream had Aaron not clamped his mouth shut, and his body went rigid in the darkness. "You're dead," Aaron whispered in his ear, "go and be with the other dead men." The man slumped but nodded quietly enough before turning and starting back in the direction he'd come. Aaron thought he saw something almost relieved in the man's posture as he walked away, and he frowned at his back for a moment before stalking back into the woods toward the other two.

He didn't have much trouble locating them again—a blind man would have found them well enough for all the noise they were making. Gritting his teeth, Aaron crept toward them, concentrating on keeping his own breathing under control and stepping only on the balls of his feet—a task that had grown more difficult as exhaustion threatened to give way to carelessness. He'd had little sleep the past three nights. Almost none, in fact, and his body felt each movement all the more for his weariness. Still, he did not mind the loss of sleep as much as he might have. Whatever was happening with his bond with the Virtue, whatever magic brought on the terrible rages in which he lost control of himself, it had not stopped since he'd thrown Owen—or Boyce Kevlane, that was—from the queen's balcony. In fact, the rage had gotten worse, following him even into his dreams.

They were red dreams now. Dreams of blood and pain and screams, and it was not the dreams themselves that scared him, at least not as much, but the fact that each night he woke from them, he found himself less frightened, less unnerved. Found, instead, that he was well rested, rejuvenated and, if not happy, exactly, possessed of a certain satisfaction that he did not care to investigate further. The important thing was that it—whatever it was—was getting worse. Over the past weeks, he'd found himself getting angry at things that normally wouldn't have bothered him and furious at things that he might once have only considered a small nuisance.

Things, for example, like the careless noises the soldiers were making. As he drew closer to them, he found the anger growing within him, a creature rousing from a troubled, fitful sleep and baring its teeth within him. They though themselves soldiers. But not Aaron and not the building rage within him. They were butcher's meat, cows with bells wrapped around their necks, signaling an easy meal to all within earshot. Sacks of blood waiting only to be pierced so that they might spill their contents onto the forest loam. Had they listened to nothing the sergeant had taught them?

He tried to slow his breathing, to get a grip on his rising anger, but with each sound the fools made he found his rage growing. He waited until they moved past him—unmindful of his presence— before he abandoned his position among the shadowed trees and charged forward. He planted a boot in the lower back of the first, and the man cried out as he went sprawling. The second got his sword—already drawn—up in time to block Aaron's blade, but he grunted, stumbling backward under the force of a blow that had been delivered much harder than Aaron intended. Blunted blades or no, it had been a dangerous blow and aimed at the man's neck.

The man, a youth really, no more than nineteen or twenty years old, was much bigger than Aaron, but his sword came back surprisingly quickly, just managing to block Aaron's follow up strike. It was a good parry or, at least, would have been but the man, Bastion by name, was gripping the sword's handle tightly in his surprise. Too tightly. All too aware that the man behind him would find his feet any moment, Aaron swung his sword again, this time with both hands and aiming for the young giant's sword. The youth's tight grip on the handle kept his wrists and arms from being able to flex and shift to absorb the shock as they should. Instead, his sword went wide, and Aaron lashed out with his own blade. In his anger, he wasn't sure what was going to happen until the tip of the steel stopped an inch away from the big man's throat. Bastion grunted, his eyes wide with shock, but he nodded in acknowledgment of his defeat.

Aaron hardly noticed the nod though, for he was already spinning, sweeping his leg out and kicking the feet out from underneath the other soldier who'd only just risen. The man landed on his back in a clanging of metal, and his breath exploded from his lungs. Before he could try to rise once more, Aaron stepped forward and rested the tip of his sword inches away the soldier's throat.

The man wheezed a curse, going for his own sword, and Aaron growled, the blade darting closer until it pierced the skin of the soldier's throat. Aaron watched the trickle of blood slide down the man's neck and, for a moment, the only sounds were the soldier's wheezing breaths, and Aaron's own, ragged and shallow in his anger. A part of him wanted to drive the blade through, to finish what he'd started. What good was the man, anyway? He was loud and careless and of no worth. Better to kill him. Better to—

Aaron, Co spoke into his mind, and her voice sounded strained as she spoke past the anger that she and Aaron shared, *don't. He doesn't ... don't.*

Aaron's sword hand started to tremble. Small, almost imperceptible tremors, but enough to draw his attention, and he studied it, remembering the way it had looked covered in a glove of crimson blood after he'd killed the slavers and the men in the tavern back in Baresh. He remembered the feeling, too. Savage joy, a satisfaction at sating some bestial hunger, but he closed his eyes and took a slow, deep breath. "You're dead," he said, then slowly, he brought the sword away. The soldier nodded, apparently unaware of how close he'd come to being killed.

"So are you," came the words at his back, and Aaron spun in time to have the tip of a sword at his throat. He followed it with his eyes to see Wendell standing in front of him. The sergeant was grinning—seemed to always be grinning, in fact—and the expression did ugly things with the scar on his face.

Aaron grunted in surprise. "You quiet bastard. How long have you had me?"

The scarred man winked, "I guess maybe an hour or two, no more. Wasn't sure it was you—wasn't sure it was anybody, really, up there in that tree. You're gettin' better, sir, and that's a fact. 'Course, there's some children of eight years or less in my old village could sneak up on you and steal your virtue without you knowin' it, but you're gettin' better anyway. Didn't know it was you, not till you came down from that tree, anyhow. Heard your boots."

Aaron frowned, glancing down to see that the sergeant was barefoot, his calloused feet nearly black with dirt and covered in pieces of leaves. "And then?"

The sergeant shrugged, "Well. Figured I'd let you take out these others, save myself the trouble."

Aaron nodded, biting back a curse. "Well done, sergeant."

He glanced back at the two others, frowning, then put his fingers to his mouth and let out a loud whistle. "A fire, sergeant." Wendell nodded, motioning to several of the soldiers who set about gathering wood and soon they had a fire going, a big enough blaze that it could be seen for a great distance in the dark woods. Then they waited in silence.

Soon, men began to appear on the edge of the light like revenants rising up from the darkness. They shuffled toward the fire, their exhaustion evident in each step they took, and the scarred sergeant kept count as they appeared. After a time, Wendell walked over to stand beside Aaron and nodded, "That's all two hundred, sir."

Aaron nodded, studying the men gathered in the firelight. For a time, he only stood there regarding them in silence, and they began to fidget anxiously. "Two weeks," Aaron said finally. "Two weeks we've been at this and for what?"

None of them answered, their eyes cast on the ground like children being chastised, and Aaron felt himself growing angrier. "Two fucking weeks," he growled, "and what have we got to show for it? You men clomping around in the woods like a bunch of fucking sheep waiting to get their throats cut. You," he said, jabbing a finger at one of the men closest to him, "Adney, isn't it?"

A middle-aged man who'd been sitting slumped with his arms over his knees glanced up at his name, "Yes sir?"

"You have any family? Kids? A wife?"

"Yes sir," he said, a confused look on his face, "Got a wife, Emily. The kids, Fran and Sarah."

Aaron nodded, pointing at another man, "And you, Gerald?"

The man—a gray-haired veteran—seemed to know well enough what was coming judging by the shamed expression on his face, but he nodded, "Yes sir. A wife."

Aaron nodded again, glancing around at the gathered men. "Well, who looks forward to telling little Fran and Sarah that their father got killed because he's too fucking loud? Who'd like the privilege of letting Gerald's wife know she's a widow now because her husband thought stealth meant only whistling some of the time? Anybody?"

All of the men were silent, glancing around at each other as if wanting someone else to answer but no one did. "No?" Aaron said, "no one? Then what is it? You, Bastion," he said, glancing where the giant youth stood studying his feet, an ashamed expression on his face. "What about you?"

"S-sir?" The youth asked.

"I want you," Aaron said, forcing himself to remain patient, "to explain to me why it is that after two weeks of training, you're all still walking around the woods like you're on a holiday."

"Sir," the youth said, "I guess ... maybe, we're not used to fighting this way. Sneaking up on folks in the dark and all ... well, it seems sort of ... dishonorable, I guess."

Aaron studied the man for a moment then glanced around at the others, "Is that right?" He said, "Does it seen dishonorable to you all as well?"

There were sullen murmurs of agreement as the men nodded their heads in support. Aaron let it go on for a moment then spoke, "Adney. Tell me, what happens to little Fran and Sarah if you end up dying? How, do you suppose, they're going to have food enough to eat?"

"Sir?" Adney asked, "I don't—"

"What about you, Gerald?" Aaron went on. "That wife of yours. Think she'll do okay without you at home?"

Gerald let out a nervous laugh, "Sir, forgive me, might be she'd be happy enough at the news."

"Aye, that she would," someone shouted, "but I'll keep her bed warm for you, Gerald, you can count on that." The men broke out in laughter then, but not Wendell standing at his side or the youth, Bastion, who was watching Aaron's expression growing darker with each moment.

"That's funny," Aaron said, and the men grinned, glad to have him in on the joke. "Real funny. You know what I think's funnier though?" He said, smiling.

"What's that, sir?" The man who'd spoken asked.

Aaron let his smile fall. "Watching dead men laugh."

The laughter cut off abruptly, and Aaron glanced around at the men. "What? You don't want to laugh anymore, is that it? Not funny anymore? No, go on laugh. And as for being honorable," he said, turning to Bastion, "well, I guess you can tell Salen all about it while he leads you across the Fields of the Dead. From what I hear, the god's not much of a conversationalist but, hey, what do I know?"

"General, sir," The youth stammered, "I didn't mean—"

"Never mind what you meant," Aaron said. "What you men don't seem to understand is that Belgarin's men will be here. Soon. And the men that come will come to kill not just you but your families. They will come and kill any who oppose them. Do you understand? And if you're not ready—if we're not ready—all the jokes and laughter in the world won't save us. There's nothing honorable about leaving your wife without a husband or your children without a father, and it's my job to keep that from happening."

"When they come, these men, you kill them however you can. If you can drop a boulder on ten of them, if you can catch one of them pissing or shitting and slit his throat for him, then fucking do it, because that's one less man, one less chance that you don't go home to your families. When the fighting starts, either chivalry dies, or you die. Your choice."

"We ain't murderers," one man muttered sullenly, "we're soldiers. Not criminals."

"No, you aren't murderers," Aaron said, meeting the man's eyes, "I can see that well enough. The ones the murderers practice on, maybe. You men need to stop and think about why you're here. You tell me you're not criminals, what I'm hearing is that you're not survivors. You understand me? Say what you want to about criminals—they know how to survive. Now, I tell you what. How about we discuss this more on our jog back to the city."

"Jog, sir?" One of the men asked, his voice incredulous.

"That's right," Aaron said, "let's go." They were up and jogging then, each of them struggling to put one foot in front of the other, weary from three days and nights spent in the woods in the mock battle. Aaron was weary too and wanted nothing more than to lie down and sleep for a week, but he forced himself to keep pace in the front, concentrated on the breath coming in and out of his lungs as they began the two-hour run back to Perennia.

You were awful hard on them, Co said into his mind.

Aaron glanced at the men jogging beside him, their faces set in grim expressions as they forced their weary bodies forward. Two hundred of what Wendell said were the best of them. The most clever, the best fighters. If this was the best Perennia had to offer, then gods help them all. Too hard on them? He thought back, no, firefly. Life's hard—it's dying that's easy.

CHAPTER TWO

She sat on the porch in the chair her husband, Franklin, had given her so long ago. Franklin had been gone for ten years, but the chair was nearly as good as the day he made it, and she rocked back and forth, watching the boy, humming a quiet tune to herself as she did.

The boy's hands were grubby and dirty from digging in the yard, creating a trench for his toy soldiers to fight over, maybe. She smiled, but it was a sad one. It seemed to her that boys started playing at war just about as soon as they could walk, and they never really stopped. The difference was that the wars of children left dirt and laundry to be done where those of men left blood and ashes. There was a little shovel she used to garden from time to time in the shack out behind the house, and she thought of telling him to get it, thinking maybe the shovel would keep him from getting quite so filthy, might even save the trousers and shirt before it was too late, but she stayed silent. Sometimes a body had to get their hands dirty to get a job done, that was all. She'd learned that at a young age, and she'd not forgotten it.

Besides, she was loath to take the boy's fun from him. The gods hadn't been kind to him, she knew, his mother and father murdered when he was barely more than a babe. The only person left to him in the world a dried up old woman whose hands were steadily growing into claws from the stiffening sickness and who could tell when it was going to rain by the ache of her knees in the morning.

She heard them coming before she saw them, half a dozen men, maybe more, the rattle of their chain mail and the swords in their scabbards loud in the near silence. The early morning sun shone bright in a cloudless sky, its light cutting through the trees surrounding her home, spilling onto the ground in golden patches, and the wind was cool and sweet against her skin. A good day for it, if any day could be. And despite what she'd expected—no, old woman, don't kid yourself. You knew what was coming, as sure as you knew anything, you knew that—she found herself growing afraid, saw the cup of tea trembling in her hands. She thought of Hannah, her daughter, of how the boy looked so much like her, then she pushed the thought away, wiping a withered hand across her tired, moist eyes.

She looked at the cup again, at the hands holding it. She watched them tremble for a minute, studied the wrinkled, stick-thin fingers, once so sure and deft, now old and frail. Then she sighed and sat her cup down on the table. The woods around their small secluded cabin grew quiet, no birds chirping, no squirrels chattering in the trees. It was as if they knew what was coming, as if they'd been waiting for it. And why not? She'd known, hadn't she? As for waiting ... well, it seemed like she'd been doing that just about all her life.

"There's still time," a familiar voice says, "You know there is."

She considered it, not for herself, though. The truth was, she was tired, seemed like it was all she ever was. Went to bed tired and woke up tired. Tired of all the memories, of all the ghosts where her family had once been, tired of looking over her shoulder, of getting out of bed each morning and wondering if today was the day. But, mostly, she was tired of waiting. Still, she did consider it. For the boy. He'd be alone without her. Such a small little thing and the world such a big place. Big and cruel, like a bull gone mad from pain.

She'd seen one, once. A big draft steer her husband had named Palder. She thought it a might presumptuous of a name for an animal spent its days pulling a till across fields but, then, Franklin had loved that steer, and it had seemed, to her at least, that the steer had loved him. Right up until it got bit by some coyote wandered on the property. Franklin chased the thing off with a torch, and they'd seen to the bite as best they could but that didn't stop it from becoming infected. A few nights later, Franklin went out to check on him only to have Palder, the thing he loved more than anything else in the world save her—and sometimes she'd wondered about that one—come charging at him with violence on his mind. Franklin had made it out and over the fence, but not before the mad, thrashing steer got in a good stomp on his knee.

He never did walk the same after that, and she remembered kneeling in the darkness wondering how she was going to get her screaming man up to the house with a leg that was clearly broken. And, the whole time she was doing it, that damned steer was ramming into the fence over and over again until it was bleeding across the face and still didn't stop. Just kept right on trying to get through, mad with the need for it, deciding maybe that it was either the fence or him, not stopping no matter how much she yelled or screamed, not stopping until she grabbed a crossbow from the shack and put a bolt through its heart.

The world, Beth figured, was a lot like that bull. All bent on destroying, not much caring what it was it destroyed just so long as it did. A world that made a mockery of things like love and trust, a place that thought the only answer to any question was blood and more of it.

"You can't think that way. It's not all bad, anyway."

"No," she said, laying her head back and closing her eyes for a moment, feeling the sun on her face, "not all bad. But what ain't is spoilin' in a hurry."

She sighed, rubbed at her knee where a cold ache was beginning to settle as she stared up at the clear sky. "There's a storm acomin', I reckon."

"It's been coming for a long time now. But there's still time, just a little. We can get out; we can run. You and me and the boy."

Beth sighed again, shaking her head, "And what then? Run for the rest of our lives? Run until that's the only thing the boy knows? Never how to stick, only how to run? I did it with Hannah, and how'd that turn out? Franklin told me we ought to stick, but no I insisted we run and so we did, and now she's dead and gone. So's he, and I'm still here. Lingerin'.

"You would have died."

She nodded but did not speak.

"Please," the voice said, desperate now, "there's still time."

"You know there's not," she said. She considered taking another drink of tea, looked at her trembling hands, and decided against it. "Anyway, I couldn't carry him. Once, maybe, but not now. It's just about all I can do to carry myself, these days. Besides, could be we're wrong. Could be something altogether different."

"We're not wrong."

"Yeah. I know it. Still. Could be."

The approaching sounds faded for a few minutes, enough so that she could almost convince herself that they'd never really been there at all but, soon, they were back, louder than ever, the clank of armor, and the nickering of horses. They'd gone around the bend where the road curved, then. Another five minutes, no more than that, and they'd be in sight. "Michael, honey," she called, "why don't you go on in the house and wash up? Be time for lunch 'for long."

The boy turned from his mock battle, an earnest look of concentration on his face. "Aw, nanna, do I have to? I was just gettin' to the best part."

"Yeah, I guess you'd better."

The boy sighed, a world of wishing in it, but he got up and walked to the porch, kissing her on the cheek. "Okay, Nanna. I love you."

"And I love you," she said, watching him walk in the house. A good boy. Despite everything else, a good boy, and she was proud to have been a part of that. "Well," she said once he was gone, "Why don't you come on out for a spell? I think maybe I'd see you one last time."

She felt some of the warmth leave her body, felt the aches of old age settling deeper as the glowing yellow orb coalesced in front of her. It swayed back and forth sporadically, the yellow light of it shifting and swirling.

"My, but ain't we a fidgety thing today?"

"Of course I am. You know why. You know what they'll do."

"Yeah. Well, I expect I do. What are you worryin' yourself for anyway? Ain't as if they can kill ya."

"It's not me I'm worried about."

She smiled widely then, and the smile transformed her wizened face, setting back, for a moment, the ravages of time, showing the girl she'd once been. "Well. You're a good one, Davin. Been a pleasure to know ya."

"The pleasure's been mine, ma'am." The voice said, sad now, bordering on desperate.

She laughed, "Ma'am, is it? Well, 'spose I'm old enough, anyway." She thought she caught the shimmer of something metallic through the trees, and her laughter faded. "Alright, then. Reckon you'd better make yourself scarce, just now. Might be we can fool 'em."

The orb vanished, and she felt the warmth fill her body once more, pushing back some of the aches and pains of old age. "We can't."

She didn't have an answer for that, so she stayed silent, watching as the first of the soldiers appeared on the path leading up to her house, twelve of them, all on horses, their helmets obscuring their features. It could have been anyone there, beneath that metal, anyone or no one. Behind the twelve rode a thin man, so thin as to appear almost sickly. His face, too, was thin, and coupled with his pale skin it gave him the look of a corpse. A jagged, puckered scar started below his left eye and ran diagonally across his face, ending at the underside of his right jaw.

Riding on his large war horse, the man looked like some dying pilgrim suffering from starvation and depravation. He smiled as he approached, but there was no humor in it, and the expression looked strange and unnatural on that wasted face. There were dark circles under his eyes, but it was the eyes themselves that caught her attention; there was madness there, she thought, and again she found herself reminded of her husband's bull. Palder had much the same look in his eyes before the crossbow bolt struck home. Somehow, she didn't think this would prove that easy.

The man rode to within a few feet of the porch and then waited, silently, as the others fanned out in the yard, two circling around to the back of her small house. He seemed to expect Beth to break the silence, but she did not. If waiting was what was required, she would wait. She'd had a lot of practice at it, over the years.

They sat in silence that way, regarding each other for several moments. Finally, the man's face twitched irritably, and his smile faded. "Hello, mother. You're well, I hope?"

Beth shrugged, "Bout as well as one of my age can expect, I 'spose. Now how about you tell me what matter brings men with swords and crossbows to an old woman's door, disturbing her rest?"

The man smiled again, and despite herself, Beth felt a shiver of fear run through her. There was something not quite human, she thought, about that smile. "Oh, not so old as that, I think, and I believe you know well enough why I'm here."

Beth shrugged, "Can't say as I do, stranger. We don't get many folks up in these parts. Pretty far away from the cities with their wars and their soldiers all dressed up and looking for somethin' to poke. Anyhow, I ain't got much, but if it's a meal you're after, I reckon I might be able to feed all of ya, just so long as you aren't countin' on seconds. If you're here for anythin' else, to steal an old woman's virtue, maybe, I have to tell you that ship sailed a long time ago, and it weren't no great matter when it did." She cackled at that, thinking maybe it would be alright, after all. Hard, sure, but she'd lived a long time, and she'd seen hard, had dealt with it before. Buried a husband, a daughter too. Yeah, her and hard were old ... well, not friends, maybe, but acquaintances, that was certain.

The man's smile widened, "Did you say 'we?'"

She cursed herself inwardly, gods but she was an old fool. No reason to draw attention to the boy; still, it would be alright, she thought. The boy had nothing they wanted, nothing they could want. "Just me and my grandson is all. His mother died shortly after he was born. Caught the fever, if you'd believe it."

"No," he said, the smile still there. And gods but it's a cold thing. "No, I don't think I do."

She shrugged as if it made no difference one way or the other, reaching for her cup of tea once more. "Well, that's as may be," she said, proud of the calmness in her voice, though she wasn't able to keep her hand from trembling as she took a sip of the tea. Luke warm now and mostly tasteless, but it was something to do, something to hold on to.

The man watched her, his grin widening as he motioned to someone she couldn't see. She turned and felt her heart gallop in her chest, an old, worn out horse who'd thought its racing days long done. Two of the armored men walked around from the side of the house, each of them holding one of her grandson's arms the way guards might drag a condemned man to his execution.

"Nanna?" The boy asked, his little chubby features trembling, on the verge of tears.

"It's alright, baby," she said, forcing down the tremor in her voice, "everything's okay."

"Sure it is," the man said, smiling at her wider than ever before kneeling down and looking at the boy, "Michael, isn't it? Come here, Michael. Why don't you come visit your uncle Aster."

The madness was in the man's eyes again, not dancing beneath the surface this time, but showing itself in full, and Beth felt a shiver of terror run up her spine. "No," she said, up and out of her rocker before she realized it. "You just stay, honey. Ain't no need for you to be comin' over here." She turned back to the man, Aster, her heart racing in her chest, the first real fear coming on now, tearing at her with small, cruel claws. "Please," she said, hating the sound of her voice breaking but unable to stop it, "Leave him be. He's just a child; he's got no business with you."

"Oh?" Aster said, rising, "Well, Beth, I'd say that's up to you. Are you going to give me what I want?"

"I told you," Beth said, "I don't have anything. I'm just an old woman doin' her best to look after her grandson, okay? The boy's got nothin' to do with you and neither do I."

"Is that so?" Aster said, his fingers tracing the scar on his face. He stared at Beth for several moments, and she forced herself to meet his eyes, to face the madness there. Finally, the thin man sighed and shrugged, "Well, guess we got the wrong place. Suppose we'll just be getting out of your hair now."

He turned and started toward his horse, and Beth let go of the breath she'd been holding, feeling a flicker of hope. "Just one more thing," Aster said, turning back, a cold, wooden smile on his face like the ones she'd seen in shop windows when she'd been a girl, "I don't believe you." He turned and motioned to the soldiers holding her grandson, "Kill the boy."

One of the men reached for his sword, but before his hand could so much as clasp the handle of the blade, something blurred across the yard and fallen leaves flew into the air as if carried on an aberrant wind. The guard didn't have time to make a sound before Beth's knife took him in the throat. Blood poured over his armor, staining it crimson, and he crumpled to the ground, dead.

Beth stood in front of him, panting, staring at the bloody knife she held in shock, gasping, her face pale with what looked to be pain. "Impressive," Aster said. He motioned with his hand and the remaining five soldiers drew crossbows from their backs, aiming them at Michael. "Truly, a marvel. I wonder, Beth, just how fast are you? Fast enough to stop five crossbow bolts, would you say? I only ask because you look as if something pains you. Old age, perhaps? Well." He shrugged, "I suppose there's only one way to find out."

"Wait," Beth said, holding up her hands, "Please. Leave him be. I'll do whatever you want."

Aster nodded, "I know. Now, drop the knife."

She hesitated, a look of anguish on her face then, finally, she let the blade fall to the ground. Aster nodded, "Take her." Something struck Beth in the back of the head, and her vision exploded in a brief flash of light before darkness settled into her thoughts. She fell, heard her body hit the ground as if from some great distance, and didn't feel it at all.

"What of the boy?" She heard one of the men ask as unconsciousness crept over her.

And the last thing she heard before the darkness took her was Aster's voice, cold and pleased. "Bring him."

CHAPTER THREE

Leomin grabbed his mug off the bar's counter and drank the last of the ale. "Thanks," he said to the tavern keeper, a man with the unfortunate name of Destrian, a name that made Leomin think of a horse. Although, to be fair, he supposed that might have had something to do with the fact that the man's front teeth were considerably bigger than was strictly necessary. The tavern keeper smiled, and Leomin only just managed to hold back a shudder. You'd think he'd have learned not to smile a long time ago, Leomin thought. "Another ale, if you would, Darren."

The man laughed, "It's Destrian, sir. Remember?"

I try not to, "Of course, Darren, of course." The thin man only shook his head, a grin still on his face as he and his teeth turned and poured another ale.

He set the mug down in front of Leomin before going off to see to another customer, and the Parnen was just about to take a drink when something brushed against the side of his face. He turned in surprise at the unexpected touch to see a woman sitting down beside him. "Well, hello there," she said, and Leomin found his eyes wandering down to the woman's chest. If the job of dresses, he thought, is to keep things covered, then this one is very close to failing in its duties. He forced his eyes back to her face to see her giving him a smile that said his attention had not gone unnoticed, "My name is Emma."

"Good evening, Emma," he said, clearing his throat, "I am Leomin, but you may call me ... well, Leomin."

She laughed as if he'd said the funniest thing in the world and suddenly her hand was on his thigh. "So," she said, "I don't think I've ever seen your handsome face in here before."

"I would be worried, if you had, dear Emma," he said, "for I can say with some confidence that the rest of me has never been to this particular establishment."

She cocked her head at him, a confused smile on her face, "You're funny," she said, "I like you."

Her hand traveled further up his thigh, and Leomin swallowed. "Yes, well," he said, "I like me too, so thank you."

Gods, but these women have no decorum whatsoever, Aliandra said into his mind, her voice prim and proper and full of disapproval.

Not decorum perhaps, my dear, Leomin thought back, but I must admit that there is something about these western women that I find most ... distracting.

Yes, the Virtue of Charisma answered, I suspect it's their breasts.

Leomin cleared his throat, forcing his eyes back up to the woman's face once more. "And, if I may ask," he said, "what brings you to this particular establishment?"

The woman smiled, leaning forward, the motion doing considerable things to improve the already pleasant view, "Oh, I just thought I might get out for a bit. Have some fun. Do you have any ideas where I might find some?"

Overgrown hussy, Aliandra thought, it's a wonder she doesn't tip over. What good are those udders, anyway? It's not as if she can fit into any dress correctly.

Yes, yes, Leomin thought back, that was my concern as well. "Forgive me, Miss Emma," he said, reluctantly, "on a normal night, I'm sure that I could find something to interest you."

"I'm sure you could," she said, her hand moving further.

Leomin's eyes went wide, "Yes, well," he said, "the thing is, you see, I have some business to be about, just now."

"Business, is it?" The woman said. "Are you sure?"

Leomin opened his mouth and, for a second, no words came out. Then he took a breath and tried again, "Yes, I'm afraid," he said, "I am quite sure. This business, you see, is not the sort of business a man can forget about."

"Oh?" Emma said, "and just what business is it?"

"Ah, that," Leomin said, "Right. Well, suppose I would say it is the business of being married."

The woman's expression turned into a pout. "Married? And just how married are you?"

"Quite," Leomin said hurriedly, catching her hand before it could travel any further—not that it could travel much further. "Yes, yes, and a lovely lady she is too. As you yourself are."

She met his eyes, studying him, "You're sure?"

Leomin sighed, "Alas, I must be. For I am many things, my dear Emma, but unfaithful is, unfortunately, not one of them."

The woman nodded, and rose, "Well," she said, "if you change your mind."

It's already changed, Leomin said, as her impressive breasts came to sit inches away from his face.

"Wait, Emma, I—"

Leomin, Aliandra interrupted.

He forced back a sigh, The things I do for the good of the world. "That is, I wanted to say goodnight," Leomin said.

The woman shrugged as if to say it was his loss—and with the dress she wore, that shrug communicated the fact clearly enough—then turned and walked away. Sauntered really. It was much more of a saunter. Perhaps, Aliandra said once the woman was gone, you should turn it down a little. This is getting ridiculous. Go much further, and they'll have you on stage, auctioning off pieces of you to the crowd.

I have in mind the piece that our dear Emma could make use of, he thought back.

Leomin, Aliandra scolded, honestly. We're here for a reason or have you forgotten? And that's the third woman in less than an hour.

Leomin sighed and was just about to get up and take matters into his own hands when the person he'd been waiting for came up and sat beside him. A young woman, slim but in a very appealing way, and he couldn't help but notice several men glancing away from their women of the evening to admire her. Not that he blamed them as the dress she wore contrived to be thin and tight enough so as to leave very little to the imagination. "An ale, please," she said.

Destrian—gods but it was a horrible name—turned and nodded, smiling wide so that his teeth nodded along with him. "Ale it is, ma'am, coming right up."

Leomin took a drink from his own glass and waited. "Nice night, isn't it?" The woman asked.

He turned and nodded his head, "So it is. I'm Leomin."

The woman smiled offering her slim hand, "Bella."

"Ah," Leomin took the offered hand, kissing it, "and have you been in Perennia long, Mrs. Bella?"

She laughed, a warm, pleasant laugh which, coupled with her appearance, made it clear enough why she had been chosen. "Oh, not so very long, Leomin. And please, just Bella. I have come to visit this fine city and hope that I might be lucky enough to steal a look at the queen. I wonder, is she really as beautiful as they say?"

"Ah, queen Isabelle," Leomin said, "her beauty, yes. It is ... quite ... bountiful. That is to say there is very much of it ... her beauty." He paused, frowning and shaking his head, "Anyway, is that the only reason? For your visit, I mean?"

She ran a hand through his long dark hair, paused to jingle one of the bells hung from it, a small smile on her face and, in that smile, a promise. "No, not only that. Let's call it business, and I do hate to talk of business—it has such a way of spoiling things."

"As you wish," Leomin said.

"The queen ... I wonder, Leomin, if you wouldn't think me too bold if I asked—is she as beautiful as me?"

"Oh, not so beautiful as that, I'm afraid, and I think few are, if you don't mind me saying so. Still, she is quite ... riveting, in her own way."

The woman nodded slowly, her smile still in place, "And yourself?"

He shrugged, "Less riveting, I'm afraid."

She gave that throaty laugh again, "No, I meant what is your own reason for visiting Perennia? It's not often you see a Parnen so far north. Have you been here long?"

"Not so long," Leomin said, meeting her eyes and calling on the powers of the bond. "I came much for the same reasons as you yourself, I suppose. To see the queen."

The woman's eyes grew wider, and she let out a quiet, nearly breathless moan. At the same time, several of the women in the tavern turned in their chairs to stare at Leomin with a hungry look in their eyes.

Easy, Leomin, Aliandra warned. Unless you want to spend the week here.

Leomin was about to answer when the woman leaned in, her slim-fingered hand resting on his leg. "Tell me, Leomin," she said, her voice near a whisper, "what are your plans for this evening?"

"I must confess that I hadn't had any," he said, "thought that perhaps I would have a drink or two then go to my room."

She nodded slowly, "And you've a room in this inn?"

"Yes," Leomin said, "I find that it is the wisest course, of course, to do my sleeping in the same place in which I do my drinking."

"A clever thought," she said, "so, you were going to get a drink and then go to your room. Well," she glanced at his nearly empty glass, "it would appear, to me, that you've had your drink. That only leaves one thing left to do, doesn't it?"

Leomin smiled, rising and offering her his arm, "So it would, my lady, so it would." He tossed a coin on the counter, and Destrian walked over and grabbed it, shaking his head in something like wonder. Leomin turned and began leading her toward the stairs. "And what of your friends?" He said, as if it was of no matter, "surely, they will be upset that I have absconded with you and left them alone?"

"Friends?" The woman said, and there was the slightest narrowing of her eyes.

Leomin called on the power of his bond and smiled, "Yes, for I doubt a woman such as yourself would ever spend an evening unaccompanied. If it is a man, well, perhaps I'd best know him, so that I can avoid his company in the near future and if it is a woman ... well, it really is quite a large bed."

She laughed, her eyes dancing, "Oh, but you are wicked, aren't you? Anyway," she said, nodding her head at a man sitting at the bar, two empty stools separating him from the next closest patron, "that is my friend there, and you've nothing to worry about from him, I assure you. He cares for little besides his ale, at any rate."

Leomin glanced where she'd indicated at a man of average size sitting at the bar, his back to them. "The blonde one, then?" Leomin said, "well," he turned back to her and grinned, "he doesn't look particularly fast."

She smiled, "Let's hope that you're not. Now, lead on before I pick you up and carry you."

"Very well," Leomin said, bowing his head, "as my lady commands, so it shall be."

He turned and led her up the stairs. The door to his room had only just swung shut when she was on him, kissing him, her hand dropping below his waistline. "Out of curiosity," he gasped, finding it hard to concentrate, but focusing so that the power of his bond colored his words, making her want to tell him the truth, "from where did you come?"

"Baresh," she said in between kissing his neck and pushing him back toward the bed, somehow contriving to pull off his shirt as she did.

Leomin's knees struck the bed, and suddenly he was sitting. "Baresh, I see," he managed, "um ... that is ... you're really quite good at that. Anyway, that is a far way to travel, isn't it, for only one man and woman?"

She pulled back and smiled at him then as she slid the straps of her dress down over her shoulders, "Oh, I can take care of myself as can my companion, I assure you."

"That," Leomin said, "I do not doubt. Still, it seems—"

"Enough talk," she said, her voice a low growl as she threw him back on the bed and straddled him. "Now, it's my tur—" she cut off, as suddenly the door swung open, slamming against the inner wall. She spun and jumped to her feet as four soldiers in the queen's white uniforms filed in, their blades held in their hands. "What is the meaning—"

"By order of Queen Isabelle," one of the guards said, "we are here to place you under arrest for suspicion of being a spy of Prince Belgarin."

"That's ridiculous," the woman said, glancing nervously between the guards and Leomin.

Leomin sighed heavily, "It really is ridiculous. Surely," he said, glancing at the soldiers, "you four men wouldn't mind coming back later? Say ... twenty minutes?"

The soldier who'd spoken glanced at Leomin, raising an eyebrow, "Is she a spy or not, Parnen?"

Leomin winced, "Well, the thing is ... we would want to be sure of such a thing, wouldn't we? I really think that some short time for me and the lady to ... talk would be exactly what is needed for us to determine with a certainty that she is, in fact, working for the prince."

The soldiers glanced at each other before looking back to him, "Is she or isn't she?"

Leomin sighed, "Yes, fine. She is. Her companion is downstairs—blonde man, sitting at the bar, three stools from the left."

The soldier nodded and in another minute the woman's hands and ankles were manacled and the soldiers were leading her out of the door. The one who'd spoken hesitated, glancing back at Leomin, "Good job, Leomin. That's one more criminal to fill the dungeon."

The Parnen captain shook his head sadly, "Spying is not the only crime that has been committed tonight, of that I assure you."

"Oh?" The soldier asked, raising an eyebrow.

Leomin frowned, glancing at the empty doorway, "It really was a nice dress."

The man grunted, "So it was. But relax, Parnen. Most folks have to get dressed to go to their jobs. You're the only one I know gets to take his clothes off."

"Yes," Leomin said, unable to keep the bitterness from his voice, "Dress and undress, yet what I seek now is redress, soldier. And that dress. "Still," he mumbled, "a job well done all around, I suppose."

The man grinned, "See you around, Leomin."

In another moment, he was gone and Leomin sighed, laying back in the bed and closing his eyes. Why not? After all, he'd paid for the room, and he was already undressed.

CHAPTER FOUR

Aaron showed the summons to the two guards posted outside the queen's audience chamber, and they read through it before bowing and opening the door.

Walking in, Aaron saw Leomin, Captain Brandon Gant, Adina and, of course, the queen herself were already seated. "Sorry about the wait," he said, "I was out working with the troops when I received the summons."

"Well," the queen said, favoring him with a smile, "considering that you saved my life, I suppose I can accept you being a few minutes late to a meeting. And how are the troops anyway, General Envelar?"

Aaron grunted, "Another few months, I might trust them to butter a piece of bread without cutting themselves."

Isabelle laughed at that, a rich, genuine laugh that was completely at odds with the childish giggles she'd shown when he'd first met her. He had to admit that since the attempt on her life, the queen had been a lot easier to deal with. But, then, he supposed that having a few thousand years old wizard break into your quarters with murder on his mind had a tendency to make a person reprioritize. "Charming as always, general," she said, motioning to one of the empty chairs, "please, have a seat."

Aaron did, glad for the chance to be off his feet. He'd been working the men and himself hard. That, coupled with the fact that he was lucky to get three or four hours of troubled sleep a night because of the dreams meant that he was perpetually exhausted. "I have called you all here," the queen said once he was seated, "because I have had some news I would like to share with you. We had only begun to speak on it when you arrived, general."

Aaron took a quick glance at the others seated at the table. Captain Gant looked as if he'd swallowed something sour. Adina's face was etched with worry and even the normally affable Parnen seemed troubled. Aaron frowned, "Whatever the news is, it doesn't look good. What, did somebody die?"

Leomin coughed at that, and the queen winced. "Please, captain," she said, turning to Brandon, "speak your piece first."

Brandon grunted, rubbing at the gray stubble on his jaw, "Well, Aaron," he said, "to answer your question, yes. Somebody did die. General Vander."

Aaron glanced between those seated at the table, "As in the man who was taken prisoner for conspiring with Kevlane to kill the queen?"

Brandon nodded, "The same, I'm afraid."

Aaron raised an eyebrow at that, "How could that happen? Did the questioners get too eager in their duties?"

The captain shook his head slowly, "Sadly, no. The general was found dead in his cell this morning, his throat cut from one end to the other, a bloody dagger that was no doubt the tool he used lying on the cell floor beside him."

Aaron's frown deepened, "I'm assuming you're not in the habit of giving blades to your prisoners here in Perennia?"

Brandon heaved a sigh, "No, General Envelar, we are not. The truth is, we don't have any idea how Vander got hold of a blade. I've got several men looking into it, investigating anyone who visited Vander since his incarceration but, so far at least, no luck."

"Shit," Aaron said. Obvious enough, then, why the others seemed so troubled. The general had been arrested along with Captain Francis for conspiring with Kevlane to assassinate the queen. Captain Francis had been questioned thoroughly, and it had been determined that he knew nothing more than his own role in the plot before he was executed. The general had been their last remaining link to Boyce Kevlane, their last hope of gaining any insight into what the ancient wizard wanted or what his plans might be. "Shit," he said again.

"Yes," Brandon said, nodding slowly, "and there is more. The general left a ... note, of sorts."

Aaron rubbed at his grainy eyes, "I don't guess he decided to tell us the whereabouts of Boyce Kevlane, did he?"

Brandon shook his head, "Not quite. It was found on the floor of the cell it read, and I quote, 'You cannot kill a god.'" The captain met Aaron's eyes, "he wrote it in his blood."

"So," Aaron said, sitting back in his chair, "we've not only got a man who is pretty much unkillable out to get us, we've also got someone on the inside helping him."

"I wonder, captain," the queen said, a glint of hope in her eyes, "is it not possible that, perhaps, General Vander had the blade on him when he was imprisoned?"

The older man shook his head slowly, a grim expression on his face. "I'm afraid not, my queen. I arrested and searched the general myself before imprisoning him. Wherever the dagger came from, it was not on his person when he was put into that cell—of that I am certain. As for the possibility of someone on the inside working for him, my men have interviewed the dungeon guards and, as of yet, they have found nothing to indicate that any of them might be a traitor. Nor have there been any visits that were out of the ordinary."

"Still, it's Kevlane," Adina said, her own voice troubled as she looked at Aaron, "it has to be."

Aaron sighed, "Yes, Kevlane or someone that works for him. I'd like to think that if dropping hundreds of feet to a stone street doesn't kill him, it would at least put a hitch in his gait. And judging from what I saw when we fought, the man is able to heal but it takes time. The more wounds he healed, the slower the magic seemed to work, I'd like to believe that having pretty much every bone in his body broken would preclude him sauntering into the dungeons and handing the general a weapon to kill himself with."

"Yes," the queen said, "and so I think we would all like to believe. But there is no way to be sure."

Aaron sighed, "No there isn't. And anyway, it'll be damned near impossible to figure out who might be working for him. Shit, your own general and captain were, that much we know at least, but nearly anyone could be."

"Not a particularly comforting thought, Mr. Envelar," the queen said.

"I find that the truth rarely is, Majesty."

The queen nodded slowly, "I still cannot believe that this could be the very Boyce Kevlane from the stories. I will confess that I had thought them nothing but that, would even still, had I not seen his ... abilities with my own eye. To think that the Virtues are real, that men with such power walk among us ..." she shook her head, "it is most troubling, indeed. No men should possess such power."

Aaron and Leomin shared a furtive glance but were saved from the uncomfortable silence by Adina. "As worrying as all this is, there are other matters we need to focus on. It's been nearly two months since we fled Baresh, and I don't think it will be much longer before Belgarin decides to bring the weight of his armies against us."

Captain Gant nodded, "As to that, our dear resourceful Leomin," he said, winking his one good eye at the Parnen captain, "has found us some information that may be of use. Recently, thanks in large part to Leomin's efforts, we were able to apprehend two of Belgarin's spies. Luckily, they were captured quickly before they could send any messages back to their master."

"Too quickly, some might say," the Parnen captain grumbled.

Brandon grinned, having heard of the situation at the tavern from one of his men. "Yes, well, we all have our sacrifices to make, Leomin, and I'm sure we are all very thankful that you made yours. I still am amazed by how easily you were able to coax the identity of the woman's companion from her. I find it ... curious."

Leomin cleared his throat, "Yes, well, what can I say, captain? My questioning of the subject was most thorough."

Brandon raised an eyebrow, "Though not so thorough as some might have hoped, I suspect."

Leomin frowned at that, and in the following silence, the queen spoke, "Yes, well, very good work, Captain Leomin. Now, Brandon," she said, turning to the older man, "what information did you find from these two individuals?"

29

The sergeant nodded, "Right, apologies, Your Majesty. The spies were reluctant to speak, and your royal questioners are not done with their work, but they did report to me that, according to what they've learned, Belgarin's army will march within three months."

The queen let out a hiss of frustration that was mirrored in the faces of the others around the table. "I had hoped for more time."

"Yeah," Aaron agreed, "I myself was hoping for maybe another fifty, sixty years but, then, tyrants have a way of being unreasonable."

The queen arched a perfectly shaped eyebrow, "I find, Mr. Envelar, that while I am within your company, I must often remind myself that you are responsible for saving my life. Please, tell me, how do the men fare?"

"Well," Aaron said, "my queen, I'll say that nobody has accidentally stabbed themselves for a while, so we've got that going."

"Quite. And will they be ready, do you suppose?"

For dying? Aaron thought, sure, but one man can do that as well as the next, I think. "As ready as me and the captain here can make them, Your Majesty."

The queen nodded, "Very well. Now that those things are out of the way, I would like to get to the primary reason for which I summoned you all here. We have received word from Ellemont."

They all sat straighter at that, turning to study the queen. "What did he say?" Adina said, and Aaron couldn't help but wince at the excitement he heard in her voice. From everything he'd heard of Ellemont, he didn't hold out much hope of them being able to convince him to fight alongside them. "Is something wrong?" Adina asked.

Isabelle smiled, shaking her head, "Nothing is wrong, sister. The messenger only rode ahead of Ellemont so that we might prepare for his master's coming. He and his retinue are no more than a week away from Perennia, if the messenger has it right."

Adina's eyes went wide, "You mean ... Ellemont's coming here? I'd thought—"

"Yes," Isabelle said, "you thought the same as I. I had expected our brother to bid us come to him. It is, I must admit, surprising that he should venture here, so far away from his place of power."

"Well," Adina said, smiling, "that must mean he is serious. It's … it's fantastic."

"So it is, so it is," The queen agreed, motioning to a servant who moved forward from the side of the room and filled each of their glasses with a light amber wine. "Now, I do believe this calls for a toast." She raised her glass into the air, eyeing them each in turn. "To siblings—excepting the one who intends to kill us, of course."

There was laughter at that from everyone at the table except for Aaron who frowned looking around at the others. Even Leomin was smiling as he tipped the glass back and drank its contents down in one swallow.

What's wrong, Aaron? Co said in his mind, this is good news—you should be happy.

It is good news, firefly, he thought, too good. I learned a long time ago that anytime good news comes unexpectedly, there's some bad following closely on the end of it.

The virtue scoffed, Honestly, Aaron. I don't know why it is that you think everyone is out to kill you.

Because, in my experience, firefly, most people are.

So? What, you think that Ellemont is plotting to betray us and, therefore, has traveled away from his own seat of power, completely putting himself under Isabelle's control? A funny strategy for a man seeking to betray us.

I spoke with a sailor once, years ago while I was out drinking in a tavern. The man told me an interesting story about a snake he'd seen on one of his trips. The thing wasn't the biggest snake, nor was it particularly fast. It couldn't hunt down its prey like some of its cousins, but the man claimed that the snake ate better than all others, anyway.

Alright, Co said, her tone humoring, I'll bite. How?

See, this snake, Aaron thought back, it's got a tail that looks like a worm. So what it'll do, the thing hides in the sand and the dirt, leaves nothing but its tail sticking out. It'll sit like that for hours, the man said. Then, sooner or later, some hungry animal—

a frog, maybe—comes along thinking it has found its dinner. Only it's the one that gets eaten.

So you're saying that Ellemont is the snake?

I don't know if he is or not, firefly, but if he is, I can damn sure tell you who's the frog. He glanced around at the smiling faces as they laughed and talked amongst themselves, excited at the news of the prince's visit. And, I think, we may have just been shown the worm.

CHAPTER FIVE

Boyce Kevlane, the man who'd once been High Mage of an entire kingdom, the most powerful wielder of magic ever to walk the face of the earth, lay in a bloody mass of flesh and bone in the dark cave that now served as his home, nursing thoughts of revenge as his shattered body slowly reknit itself, a process that was both agonizingly painful and—when there was as much work to be done as there was now—terribly slow.

He did not think of himself as a man—had not for a thousand years or more, for what mortal could claim to have lived for centuries upon centuries, his body weathering even the most grievous of hurts? Still, as he laid there, his broken body ever so slowly reshaping itself, a very mortal agony ran through him, making him shudder and sweat and whimper from the unbearable pain. It was this whimpering that enraged him the most, such a mortal thing, not fit for a god—for that was what he was, what he had become—yet he could not hold it back under the tidal wave of pain that rushed unceasingly through him.

For weeks, he'd lain in torment, the gift and the curse that was the bond with the Virtue of Adaptability working its slow and laborious magic, slowly pushing and pulling on tendons and bones, forcing them back into place. Yet even now, he knew, he was monstrous to look upon, could see it in the eyes of Captain Savrin as he brought him his meals. Aaron Envelar. The name had been on his mind for every waking moment since his fall from the castle.

The man who had caused all of his suffering. Sometimes, he thought of what he would do to the man when he recovered, not just to him but to everything he had ever cared about, and it was enough to bring a smile to his wretched, disfigured face—at least, for a moment. The pain never let such things last for long.

His was a world of torment, of anguish no man or woman had ever or could ever experience. He broke his fast upon it in the morning and laid down with it at night, a mistress that would not let him sleep, that insisted on being known and being recognized, until there was little else in the world but the pain and the hate and, of course, the hunger. And perhaps that last most of all. For there was power in the bond, power to reshape his limbs, to reknit his flesh, yet such power made its own demands and no matter how much his broken body consumed, there was always that terrible, desperate hunger, as bad, if not worse, as the pain itself.

A particularly powerful wave of agony swept over him as if to contest his thoughts, and he would have screamed, if he could have. His voice had long since gone hoarse, and when he spoke, his words came out as little more than a wet, gurgling croak, barely intelligible even to himself.

He remembered little of what had occurred since his fall from the tower, his memories no more than jagged images that drew blood when touched. Memories of flesh and bone and blood and all of it in the wrong places, of being thrown into a sack, a sack for the gods' sake, memories of his limbs, twisted and bent and shattered, of agony beyond what any mortal might experience. For in their fragility they also held release—such pain that cannot be endured, is not endured, for death has its say, finishes the story when words to describe such agony do not and could not exist. For mortals, death served as an answer, an ending, pain and suffering only its prelude but not for him. Not for gods. "It is no great gift," the thing lying shattered in the corner croaked, "to be a god."

He knew that he was mad, had been driven insane by what he had suffered. First, at the hands of Caltriss and the barbarian hordes and then at the hands of Aaron Envelar, but he was not overly worried. The sanity of the gods had ever been in question, and they need not concern themselves with it as mortals might—a god was a god, after all.

Over his whimpers and cries, he heard the cloth flap that served as a door move at the entrance to the cave and turned his one good eye to it. Good, of course, was relative. It was a bulging, blood-coated thing, though it was in much better shape than its companion, smashed into little more than jelly by his fall and not yet healed. It had been too much, too fast, that was all. First the wounds he'd taken by the guards and then by the sellsword and then from the fall. Too much even for the magic to heal quickly and completely. It would be another few weeks, months, perhaps, before he could so much as venture into public without eliciting screams. And, once he was able, there would be screaming enough. Once he found Aaron Envelar, tracked down those the man cared about, there would be screams enough to deafen the world.

"Master, I've brought food."

The thing in the corner watched with its one good eye as Captain Savrin stepped inside, two dead chickens in his hand. The man tried and failed to disguise the wince of disgust that came over him as he came into the cave, and Kevlane would have laughed, had he been able. He did not blame the man. The parts of him necessary to detecting smell had begun to heal, and he knew the odor well enough. It was the smell of a charnel house, a butcher's storeroom gone spoiled and rancid in the sun. It was rot and blood and filth—yes, that too, for despite the fact that he was little more than a puddled heap of broken bones and shattered cartilage, his flesh doughy and misshapen like a sack filled with a conglomeration of rocks and sticks, despite all of that, his body still found a way to expel the waste of that which he ate, and so he lay in it, a puddle of his own filth, lacking even the ability to move himself away from it.

The thing watched the captain, but he did not speak. Words were pain. The world was pain, and he did not speak, only watched the captain with that red eye, filled with blood, and though he needed the man, though he'd served him well, he found that he still hated him. Hated watching him walk in on two legs, his own bones and tendons and veins all in their proper place, hated the way he so casually held the two chickens, a feat that would have been impossible for Kevlane, just then, and that he would have experienced incredible agony in the attempting of.

The captain swallowed hard as he stared into the corner in which his master lay. He could see little in the dark cave, the only light what weak moonlight made its way past the draped cloth, but what he could see was more than enough. The glisten of blood-slicked flesh, the blood black in the moonlight, the pale, ghastly white shards of bones sticking out of the mass of flesh, the man not a man at all but some cruel god's fashioning. A thing with little discernible shape or form to it, only sloughing, doughy skin and the sharp twisted angles of bones broken and shattered. There was no hand to put the chickens in, and no functional stomach to digest them even if there were, so the captain did as he had done the previous nights and only threw the chickens—feathers and all—onto the mass of flesh.

He saw the shadowed figures of the dead chickens slowly, painstakingly begin to disappear in that mound of flesh, as if they were somehow being absorbed by it. He fought back the urge to vomit, swallowing hard. Savrin had seen corpses before—had made more than a few himself. He'd seen injuries caused from battle and war, but the thing lying pooled in the corner of the room was unnatural, and he found that his stomach had its limits. "I'll go get some more," he managed. The creature in the corner was insatiable, he found, eating more than ten normal men, if eating it could still be called. He suspected that the meat and the flesh he brought it were used with the dark powers it possessed, used as some means of healing, but he did not think of it often. Or ever, if he could help it.

He turned to go, wanting, needing to get out of the cave, away from the smell of offal, the sweet sickly odor of rotten meat. He waved a hand at the flies buzzing maddeningly in his face and reached for the cloth hanging.

"Wait."

The words were deep and jagged and hoarse, not sounds that should ever be made by a human throat, and Savrin tensed, turning slowly to look at the creature. "Master?"

"Send word. Aster. In Avarest. Tell him to take the woman. And the others."

Savrin nodded hurriedly, his gorge rising despite his efforts. "Yes, master." Then he was out and into the woods, his breath coming hard and fast, the forest air cool and damp on his fevered face and hands.

The thing in the corner watched the flap fall, and its disfigured face twisted into a mockery of a smile even as its flesh pulled the dead chickens further and further inside it. "Oh, Mr. Envelar," it croaked, "you will learn the meaning of suffering." It tried a smile again, but just then some bone flexed and re-broke with agonizing slowness as it sought to find its proper form and function, and the smile vanished in an instant, and there were only the screams. Always the screams.

CHAPTER SIX

Aaron jerked awake with a scream on his lips, not one of terror—or, at least, not only that—but one of rage. He clenched his teeth, managing to keep it in, but only just. He sat there in the darkness of the room, his naked chest and back covered in sweat, his breathing ragged. He didn't remember what the dream had been about, knew only that it was a dream filled with rage and fire and blood. A red dream. A dream where he had not controlled himself, only been a helpless bystander to whatever it was that drove him onward, whatever creature or impulse carried him along in its wake.

I am Wrath.

Aaron swallowed hard, rubbing a hand across his dry mouth. The voice that had spoken had not been Co's, nor had it been his own thoughts, but he felt that he knew it anyway. Co? He thought, are you there?

I'm here, Aaron, the Virtue said, and her voice sounded small and helpless and afraid, a child sitting in the dark, knowing something hunted her but not knowing what it was or what shape her terror might take.

What ... what was that? Aaron said, struggling to get his breathing under control.

I don't know, the Virtue responded, I only remember ... anger. Rage.

Yes. And blood. He remembered that, too. Aaron glanced to where Adina lay beside him, sleeping peacefully, her own expression smooth and at rest. *Does she not know what she lays beside?* Aaron ran a hand through his sweat damp hair and saw that his hand was trembling. *Is … is someone else there?*

The voice, if it had been a voice at all and not his imaginings, some last vestige of the dream lingering before dissipating upon waking, did not answer. Aaron eased himself out of the bed, careful not to rouse Adina, and walked to where his shirt lay on the floor, discarded carelessly in the night's passion. He pulled it on along with his cloak then slipped into his soft leather boots and stepped out of the room, easing the door closed behind him. He walked the hall aimlessly for a few minutes before coming upon the doors to one of the castle's balconies.

Perennia was a port city and this high up the sea breeze would be cold. Just the thing he needed after visions of fire and burning. Aaron stepped out and was surprised to see another figure standing there in the darkness of the balcony, gazing out over the city stretched out beneath them. The figure turned, and the hood of his cloak blew off in the wind. Aaron let out a grunt of surprise as the light of the moon showed him the face of Captain Leomin staring back at him.

"Ah, Mr. Envelar," the Parnen said, smiling and displaying his too-white teeth, "or should I say general?"

"Not unless you want to get thrown off this balcony," Aaron said, walking up and propping his arms on the balcony railing beside Leomin.

"Ah," The Parnen said, "Well, I suppose there is a precedent for that."

"Sure." Aaron said, "Also, I've done it before."

Leomin laughed, "Ah, Mr. Envelar, you really do your best to hide your own cleverness, don't you?"

Aaron grunted, "I'm not feeling particularly clever right now, Leomin."

"No? And what, then, are you feeling?"

Aaron shook his head, finding that, now that they were speaking of it, he was having difficulty putting it into words. "I feel … assaulted. Worried, sure, about Belgarin, Kevlane, shit, even Ellemont. But more than that I feel assaulted. Like a mountain that's slowly being chipped away at by thousands of men swinging thousands of picks. And angry. I feel that most of all. I'm always angry, Leomin."

The Parnen frowned, "I noticed, Mr. Envelar, that you did not tell the queen or the others about that thing which you possess."

Aaron raised an eyebrow, though whether the Parnen could see it in the moonlight or not, he didn't know, and he didn't much care. "Neither did you. I'm not the only one with a pain in the ass ball of light following me around, captain."

Pain in the ass, am I? Co demanded.

Sorry, you're right, Aaron thought back, massive pain in the ass.

He glanced at Leomin and saw the Parnen's brow knit in concentration, no doubt having to assuage the anger of his own Virtue. "Anyway," Aaron said, "point is, you didn't seem particularly forthcoming about your own secret."

Leomin nodded, "It's true, Mr. Envelar. If my experiences have taught me anything, it is that a reckless man often becomes a dead one. Although, I'm sure we can trust Queen Isabelle and Adina's brother Ellemont, I find myself reluctant to divulge such information when it is not strictly necessary that I do so."

"Do you?" Aaron said, "Find them trustworthy?"

Leomin met his eyes, frowning, "Well, Mr. Envelar, you saved the queen's life, after all. As for Ellemont—"

"As for Prince Ellemont," Aaron interrupted, "we don't know anything. And for a man who's supposed to be a coward, it seems rather strange to me that he intends to travel here to see us."

"Surely, though," Leomin said, "if the man meant us harm, he would not put himself in such a situation as to be powerless, would he?"

Ooh, tell him about the snake, Co said.

Maybe another time, firefly. "I hope you're right, Leomin," Aaron said, staring off at the city, at the buildings beneath them where men and women lived and worked and died. From this height, they seemed no more than ants or bugs, busily constructing their nests, blind to the giant foot that would inevitably crush them all beneath its heel.

Cheerful today, aren't we?

"I hope you're right, Leomin," he said again, "but, then, hope isn't what's kept me alive for this long."

"No?" The Parnen captain asked, "Then what is, Mr. Envelar?"

Aaron sighed, shaking his head, "Never mind. Ellemont will be true, or he will not, and there is little I can do about it just now either way. Anyway, he's not what's bothering me. Tell me, Leomin, when you first received your Virtue, did you ever experience anything ... odd?"

The Parnen captain cocked his head, raising an eyebrow, "By odd do you mean homicidal urges that send men fleeing and screaming for their lives in the night?"

Aaron cleared his throat, "Something like that. Yeah."

"Not as such, Mr. Envelar, not as such. Although, for what it's worth, I will say that the late Mirmanon posited, in his works, that the Seven Virtues, created as they were by the twisting and shaping of great magic and the death of what very well may have been the world's best king, were possessed of both good and evil. Mothered by life and fathered by death, Mirmanon believed that each of them gave the man who wielded them a gift and a curse."

"A gift and a curse," Aaron repeated, his gaze wandering to the pale moon up above, shedding its weak light on everything beneath it. "Well, if you've been cursed, Leomin, I'm not seeing it. Unless, perhaps, you've been cursed to never stop talking but that seems less a problem for you and more for those around you, if you ask me."

Leomin laughed at that but his expression quickly sobered, "There can be ... difficulties in being so bonded with such powerful magic, Aaron. Think of it like this—you use a sword, yes?"

Aaron frowned, "If this is about to be some puzzle, Leomin, I might be inclined to use a sword right now. It's late, and I've little time for riddles."

The Parnen smiled but there was little humor in it, "Forgive me, Mr. Envelar, but let me ask for your patience. I only try to make you understand."

Aaron sighed, "Go on."

"Well, why do you carry a sword at all, Mr. Envelar?"

"Because it's a damn lot easier to cut a man with a sword than with your bare hands."

"Yes, but why the need to cut any man at all?"

"To protect myself," Aaron said, "and not just me. Others too, people I care about."

Leomin nodded slowly, his gaze meeting Aaron's, "Just so, Mr. Envelar. But a sword, in the hands of a novice, can be as dangerous to the man wielding it and those he tries to protect as to those he tries to protect them from, can it not?"

It took a moment for Aaron to parse through that then he nodded. "What's your point, Leomin?"

"My point, Mr. Envelar, is that as the bond with your Virtue strengthens, so will the gift it gives you. And the curse."

"Great," Aaron said, "And just how much worse can it get? I killed those slavers, Leomin. Nothing I haven't done before and nothing I'd lose much sleep over. Except ... I enjoyed it."

The Parnen nodded, his expression troubled, "Yes, Mr. Envelar. Compassion is more than just the feeling of another's grief or an understanding of another's feelings. According to Mirmanon, true compassion, the real ability to be able to understand a person's grief, not just to sympathize but to understand it, starts with kindness. It is only that, only in man's essential goodness, that he finds the ability to know compassion, to truly feel what another feels. Kindness, Mr. Envelar. All the Virtues are double-edged. What, then, do you suppose is the opposing edge of such a sword?"

Aaron frowned, "Hate."

"As you say."

"And what of your own sword, Leomin?"

The captain's gaze got a far-away look to it, his eyes unfocused as they stared into some memory that lay behind him, that he would, no doubt, have preferred to leave there. "A year after receiving the power, one of the priestesses tried to kill me." He said, his tone matter of fact. He turned so that his back was to Aaron then pulled his cloak aside and lifted his shirt.

At first, Aaron didn't see anything, the pale illumination the moon provided a poor light, but he looked closer and then grunted in recognition. Half way up the Parnen's back, there was a puckered scar, the kind that was familiar to Aaron, as he'd had occasion to see them before. A knife made such scars.

"I was knelt in prayer within my room at the castle of the priestesses," Leomin said, his voice empty and lifeless, "when I felt the knife's bite. I screamed, but the others were long since asleep, and I knew they would not make it in time. You see, they changed shifts, the priestesses, one staying up to pray with me while the others slept each night. I screamed, and I fled to the opposite end of the room, turning around in shock."

"The priestess was one of the younger of them, a pretty thing, if slight, and kinder than most all of the others. It's funny, Mr. Envelar, but I would be lying if I told you she were not my favorite. She would bring me treats, from time to time, sneak them past the others and into my hands. In fact, it seems that I remember expecting such a treat after the finishing of my prayers. In that lonely place, the woman had become like a mother to me."

He paused, letting out a slow, ragged breath. "Still, when I looked at her standing before me, I saw none of the woman I'd come to know, for where her features had once held kindness and understanding, now there was only a hate and rage beyond anything I had ever seen before. She screamed when she came at me—I will never forget the sound. Within that scream was rage and hate and madness. You understand, Mr. Envelar, she went mad with her desire to destroy me. Insane with it."

"Damn," Aaron breathed, as the Parnen let his shirt fall and turned to stare back out at the city with eyes that saw only the past, only the face of that woman whom he'd loved.

"I had lost my family, Mr. Envelar, my home and my friends, but I did not want to die. When she came at me, I fought her. She scratched and clawed, and I kicked and scratched and somehow I got hold of the knife. I did not feel relief or satisfaction when the blade went into her heart, only shame and revulsion for myself, a hatred that was, I suspect, similar to the one she'd felt. I knelt there, weeping, covered in the blood of the woman who had shown me kindness, and I considered turning the blade on myself. Finally, I did not. As I told you, I did not want to die. It is a memory that has been with me for nearly all of my life, one that will follow me even unto death, and if your Salen is real and comes to collect one such as I, then it is a truth I would hide even from his cold touch, if I could. I was six years old."

"Damn," Aaron said again as he watched a glistening tear wind its way down the Parnen's cheek.

So much pain, Co said, and he could hear the sorrow in her voice. Poor, poor Leomin.

"The curse, then," Aaron said. "The opposite of charisma. Revulsion, hatred. Leomin," he said, putting a hand on the man's shoulder, surprised by how thin and frail it felt beneath his fingers, "the woman, the priestess. I'm sure that she cared for you. It was the curse, that's all. If the gift is to be loved and revered by those you meet, then it follows that the curse is to be hated and reviled. It was not your fault."

"Wasn't it, Mr. Envelar?" Leomin said, turning to meet Aaron's gaze, his eyes watery. "Oh, I've said such words to myself often enough, so much so that their meaning has been lost, and that they have become but a mantra, words used as a shield against the shame and the revulsion that always follow in my footsteps. Words I use to find sleep at night, and words I use to awaken myself in the morning, to drag my body from its bed when I want nothing more than to stay and let the world forget about dear Leomin. But you see, it was I who had the gift and the curse, and it was my job to control them. I did not, and a woman died for my mistake. The scar I carry is no more than I deserve, and, in truth, I think it quite less."

"Gods, Leomin," Aaron said, "you were six years old. Did these priestesses of yours not foresee this? Had they not learned of ways to deal with it?"

Leomin shook his head, "Something that you must understand, Aaron, is that the bond between a Virtue and its possessor is not constant from one pairing to the next. It is the same with people, after all. It is not something that can easily be understood, cannot be quantified or measured, for the bond is different for each man or woman."

Aaron frowned, "So you're saying what? That some of the others who paired with Aliandra, your Virtue, didn't have the same problem?"

Leomin turned to meet his eyes, "I'm saying that none of them did, Mr. Envelar. My people have guarded this Virtue for hundreds and hundreds of years and not even in our oldest records had anything like it ever been mentioned. Aliandra and I, we have a strong bond—as you and your own Virtue do, for I have seen it working in you. Such a bond, such a connection strengthens the lines through which the bond's power is carried. And power, Mr. Envelar, is neither wholly good or wholly evil."

"Power is just power," Aaron said.

"Not quite, I believe," Leomin said. "It is my belief, Mr. Envelar, that power is both good and evil, only it is these things at the same time. There is no such thing as true evil power or true good. Imagine, if you will, two starving men fighting over a loaf of bread to feed their starving children. One man will be the victor and one the loser. The loser will die then or later, his children along with him. The winner will bring home this loaf of bread to his family, and they will eat and perhaps grow strong. But tell me, Mr. Envelar, is such a thing good or evil?"

Aaron frowned, considering the man's words, but Leomin was not finished. "Power, by its very nature, is a thing of good and evil tied together so tightly that one cannot be separated from the other. That blade you carry? That is power, Mr. Envelar. The skill with which you use it is power."

Aaron grunted, "It's training, is what it is"

"Ah, Mr. Envelar," The Parnen said, giving him a small smile, "I do so enjoy our talks. Consider how much the man whose life that blade takes cares of your training, of the years spent in sweat and strain and soreness for you to know it as well as you do. It matters not to him how you obtained such power, only that you have it. And who," he said, frowning again, "can be blamed if that power is used wrongly but the one who wields it?"

Aaron decided to leave that bit alone for now. He'd have to do some more thinking on it but, just then, something else was bothering him. "What of the other priestesses, Leomin? What did they do?"

Leomin sighed. "They did what any would do, in such a situation. They believed her to be crazed, somehow—I believed much the same, I'm sorry to admit. You must understand, Aaron, this thing had never happened before. These women spend their lives protecting this power, bent in prayer over it, chanting their chants and singing their songs. They knew it, or so they thought, as well as they knew themselves. Better, in truth."

He paused then and, for a time, there was only silence, yet Aaron did not speak, for he felt that the Parnen was not finished. "The next attack came a year later," he said finally. "I had since grown accustomed to keeping a knife on my person, hiding it from the priestesses. I slept with that knife, Mr. Envelar, I woke with it and went to bed with it. I practiced at swinging it when there were none of the others around. It was a poor thing, really, but it pierced the second priestess's flesh well enough, found her throat and let loose a flow of blood that would not be stopped until whatever internal reservoir it came from was emptied and withered in its emptiness."

"Gods," Aaron said. "How many?"

Leomin would not meet his eyes, staring off into the darkness, his jaw rigid, his body tensed as if for flight. "Five, Mr. Envelar. Five souls who meant only good—misled as they might have been—five souls who had dedicated their lives to honoring the gods in the best way they saw fit. Five souls that I drag behind me with each step I take."

"How then, Leomin? How did you fix it?"

"Fix it?" Leomin asked. "No, Mr. Envelar, it is not a broken chair or a wobbly door to be mended. The power the Virtues offer is a knife thrown into the air, flipping end over end until it falls back to the earth. The working of that power is you catching the knife before it strikes the ground, grasping the handle and not the blade."

Aaron frowned, "What if you miss? What if you grip the blade?"

Leomin shrugged, and there was something frail and weak about it, "Then someone dies, Mr. Envelar. You, perhaps, but more likely one of those you care about. It is those we keep closest to us that the blade finds first."

Aaron thought of Adina, of the way she'd looked lying sleeping peacefully next to him, untouched by the visions of rage and madness that haunted his dreams. "How long?" He said, his own voice coming out harsh and raspy, "How long have you been able to catch the knife?"

Leomin nodded, "Nine years and seven months, Mr. Envelar."

"Ten years," Aaron said, "well, gods, Leomin, you've beat it. If it's been that long—"

"You do not understand," Leomin snapped, and some powerful emotion, anger, perhaps, danced in his eyes. "This thing is not a thing to be beat. It is no swordsman, and this is no duel. The power of the bond is like a pit beneath your feet, one that you must cross. Sometimes the pit is no more than a foot long and easily stepped over. Other times, it is a great chasm, one that requires all of your strength and energy to cross. And I grow tired, Mr. Envelar. I grow so very, very tired."

Aaron found himself staring at his hands. There was no blood there, he knew there wasn't, yet he saw it anyway. "So there's no solution."

Leomin sighed beside him. "None that I have found."

Aaron nodded, staring off at the city below him. He hadn't truly expected one. The world, after all, was always taking, that was all. It was what the world did.

"Still," The Parnen said, "it is not all bad, Mr. Envelar. The bond cannot be controlled, not truly, but it can be ... managed."

"What do you mean?"

"Two men with the same advantages, the same training regimens, compete in a race. One would think the outcome would be obvious—a tie—but it so very rarely is. Why is that, do you think?"

"Leomin, how in the shit should I know?" He was frustrated just then, frustrated and without hope. Even now, he could feel the rage, the fury growing within him, and he didn't have the patience for the Parnen's riddles. The anger was a kettle left too long over the fire. It was not a question of if it would explode—only when.

"Will, Mr. Envelar. The difference between one man's victory and another's loss is will. You have shown, in the time that I've known you, a great will, one that few might match. I would argue that it is this, more than your blade, that has allowed you to conquer your enemies, to survive."

Aaron grunted, "I think the dead would probably disagree with you, if they could."

"Perhaps, but it would not make them right. There is a fire burning within you, Mr. Envelar. You may not extinguish it, but you may create breaks for it. You might gather piles of dirt and rock to slow its spread. That is within your power."

"How?"

The Parnen shrugged, "The same way that men accomplish anything in this world. First, you must believe that you can. And then you must do it."

Aaron rubbed his temples where he was beginning to get a headache. "Forgive me if that sounds a bit too simple, Leomin."

"The answers to any problem are rarely complicated, Aaron. They are usually simple enough; it is men who complicate such things when they do not like the answers. I speak truthfully, you can hold it back. Not forever, perhaps. But for a while."

They stood in silence after that, and though their eyes stared out at the city, it was the pit Leomin had spoken of that they saw stretched out before them, and they wondered if this time would be the time that they fell. And what would happen when they did.

CHAPTER SEVEN

Aaron crouched with his back against the trunk of a tree, his practice sword, with its dulled edges, lying over his bent knees. The night was alive with the sound of crickets and birds, of squirrels rushing from branch to branch. The moon was high and full, and its light, filtered through the trees, fell on the forest floor in patches and beams.

It was their first night out on another training exercise and so far he had run into no one. He needed to piss, had needed to for the last hour, but he didn't dare do it. The woods had plenty of noises in them, but none that sounded like a man taking a leak, so he held it, and he waited, cursing the woods and the damned trees.

Crouching there, resisting the urge to slap at the bugs that landed on him, he realized that he missed the Downs, missed the simplicity of it. Sure, there were people there—Hale and Grinner, the two most powerful crime bosses among them—who would be happy to see him dead, who would be happy to help him along if they found the opportunity, but it was home just the same. It was a place he understood, full of predators that he understood. These woods, though, they would no doubt have predators of their own—Wendell had mentioned wolves and bears—and such creatures couldn't be reasoned with, couldn't be bought. And anyway, he had to take a damn piss.

Just then, he heard footsteps not too far ahead of him. Quiet, trying for stealth, but not quite getting there. There were more, too, coming from behind, and he realized that he was surrounded. He could not tell how many were in front or how many were behind, for the forest had a way of distorting sound, but it was an easy enough thing to guess. He'd paired the men up in twos except for him and Wendell. That meant that, most likely, there were two groups, one ahead of him and one back somewhere further in the trees. Both, it seemed, were heading in his direction.

He cursed the brightness of the moon. In such light, if both groups continued on their path, they couldn't help but see him, and he would find himself trapped in the middle. Only one solution then. Attack.

Aaron, something's wrong ... I feel them but—

Don't, firefly, he thought back. I need to learn how to do this without you.

But Aaron—

I said don't. He glided forward, wincing at the sound his footfalls made on the dead leaves littering the forest floor. Still, there was no help for it, and he hadn't been moving for a minute, maybe two, when he caught a glimpse of the two men, two shadows moving purposefully in the night. He worked his way around behind them, using the trees and undergrowth of the woods for cover, then rushed out into the open. The two soldiers were studying the woods in front and to the sides of them, their blades held ready—this, at least, he was glad to see—and so they did not see him until he was nearly on them and a dry twig snapped under his foot in his haste.

Cursing with surprise, the two men turned, but Aaron was already on them. He spun, his foot lashing out and sweeping the legs out from under the first man, his own dull-edged sword flying up in time to parry the attack of the second as he turned. There was a brief exchange, but the soldier overbalanced, putting all of his weight on his back foot, and Aaron stepped to the side and planted his foot in the man's knee. The soldier's leg buckled beneath him, and he went down. Aaron put his practice sword first at the throat of one, then the other. "It was much better done," he said, "but you're dead."

"Not this time," a voice spoke from behind him, "This time, you're the one that dies."

Aaron whirled to see six more soldiers facing him, and he frowned. "I won't say it isn't clever, teaming up, but it isn't in the rules either, boys. The point is to get used to working in pairs against even odds."

The man who'd spoken—Aaron realized as he stepped into a patch of moonlight that it was Adney—grinned, a blade in his hand.

Will you listen to me now? Co said, these men, they have evil in their hearts, Aaron. Darkness.

Aaron glanced behind him and saw that the two men he'd dropped were on their feet, their own swords held at the ready. They'd backed up several paces, and Aaron saw the edge of one of their blades glistening in the moonlight. Not dull at all, then. And, he suspected, the same for the rest. "That's how it's gonna be, is it?" He said, turning back to Adney.

The man shrugged, his smile still in place, "You said yourself, general, I've got Emily and the kids to think about. Ain't none of us here stupid. We all know well enough how it'll go once Belgarin and his army get here. An army several times our size, an army that will have overwhelming numbers even if that chicken shit Ellemont does decide to combine his troops with ours, and I think I've got a better chance of wakin' up a prince than that happening, don't you? What kind of chance does any of us have against an army like that? Might as well try to stand against a whirlwind. The result'll be much the same."

"I'm no prophet," Aaron said, the anger roiling in him now, the kettle hot and steaming and threatening to boil over. "And I don't honestly know what chance we have. Not good. Not that you need worry about it, Adney as you won't be alive to see it one way or the other."

Adney hocked and spat, "I'm going to enjoy this."

The anger flared up in Aaron suddenly, fierce and bright and alive, and his eyes narrowed, his muscles tensing. The fury screamed and howled in him, demanding release, but he forced himself to take a deep breath, to wrest control of himself back from himself. Not stopping the fury, not making it heel like some placid dog. Instead, in his mind, he threw a long rope about its neck and pulled it fast. The beast still kicked and fought and struggled, but, for now, at least, it would only go in the direction he led it. Just then, that wasn't a particularly hard decision. "Enjoy it?" He said, a smile coming to his face, "No, I don't think so."

The men rushed him then, and Aaron bellowed an inarticulate sound of rage and pleasure combined, charging forward toward the six approaching soldiers. Their eyes went wide, and they hesitated, apparently not having expected him to charge. It wasn't much of a hesitation, a few moments, no more, but it was enough for him to close the distance between him and the first two. The first soldier didn't even have time to raise his sword before Aaron was on him, swinging his fist into the man's stomach. The soldier doubled up, the air leaving his body, and before he could recover, Aaron struck again, his fist taking the man in the temple, and the soldier crashed to the ground, unconscious.

Something rustled behind him, and he ducked his head just in time for a sword to go flashing past where his neck had been a moment before. With a growl, he turned and lunged, his own sword, dull or not, tearing into the man's midsection and exploding out of his back in a shower of blood. Aaron had time enough to see the surprise in the soldier's eyes, to hear his scream before the sound of steel whistling through the air came from behind him. He leapt to the side but wasn't fast enough to avoid the blade dragging its way across his right arm. The pain was intense and immediate, and he only just managed to keep hold of his sword as he took several more quick steps away before turning to see Adney and the other five remaining soldiers watching him, their own swords held ready. The other two were sprawled at their feet, but they paid them no attention as they moved closer.

Gritting his teeth at the pain, Aaron transferred his sword to his unwounded left hand and looked down to see blood running freely from his arm. Not a fatal cut unless it was left untended, and he thought that the thing would be decided, one way or the other, long before he need concern himself about that. "You're a tough bastard, I'll give ya that," Adney said.

Aaron was just about to answer when there was a crashing in the undergrowth, and he turned to see the giant youth, Bastion, wander into the small clearing off to Aaron's left. The youth took in the two men lying on the ground and frowned, a confused expression on his face. "What's going on?" He said, glancing between Aaron and the others, "I heard a scream."

"Bastion," Aaron started, "run—"

"Oh, just a training exercise is all, big lad," Adney said as he walked closer to the young soldier, "nothin' to worry about. There was an accident, you see," he said, putting an arm on the confused youth's shoulder, "Darby took one in the gut. We need you to fetch a healer quick, before he bleeds out."

The giant hesitated, his gaze moving to Aaron and his blood-coated arm, "Sir?"

"Bastion, get out of—"

Before he could finish, Adney drew a knife with his free hand and rammed it into the big youth's back. Bastion grunted in shock, took two stumbling steps forward, but remained on his feet. Adney followed him, ripped the knife free and plunged it in again. Bastion grunted and fell to his knees, producing a tremor Aaron thought he could feel in his feet. "You fucking bastard," he hissed. He started forward but the two soldiers that had been behind him moved to block his path, and he was forced to watch as Adney plunged the knife in one final time. He ripped it free, and the youth sprawled on his face on the forest floor, his mouth working soundlessly.

"Sorry, big fella," Adney said, looking down at the man as he replaced the knife in the sheath at his side. "Weren't 'spose to be like this. You should've done like I told you and fetched a healer. We could have taken care of business and you none the wiser." He shook his head sadly, "What a fuckin' waste." He looked back at the others and held up his hands in frustration, "Well?" He demanded, "What the fuck are you lot waiting for? Kill that bastard," he said, motioning to Aaron.

As if they'd only been waiting for the order, the five soldiers followed Adney forward, and Aaron retreated into the trees, backing into them as he looked around for some advantage. The first man rushed forward and swung his sword in a horizontal blow that would have split Aaron in two, but he dodged behind a tree trunk, and the soldier cursed as his blade stuck deep into the tough bark. The anger bucked and leapt within Aaron, and he exploded forward, his sword taking the man in the throat before he could free his weapon. He only just got his sword around in time to block the next soldier's strike, but the others had circled around his side, and he was forced to abandon any chance of a counterattack as he leapt backward, narrowly avoiding their strikes. "Just die, you fucker," Adney said as he came around the other side, and Aaron continued to back up, watching as the men encircled him.

Five more, he thought, struggling to get his ragged breathing under control. The problem, of course, was that five was too many. He was tired already, and the wound in his arm was stealing his strength. Soon now, they would come at him as a team, and he would be out of options. Some small part of him couldn't help but be grimly amused by the fact that he would die because of the very lessons he'd been trying to teach them. He found himself reaching out to the bond with Co, not entirely sure what he was doing or how he was doing it, acting on some instinct that it seemed he'd always had, one that he'd only forgotten for a time.

He reached for the power and it was there, waiting, a blade ready to be grasped, and understanding burst in his mind. Suddenly, he knew these men, understood everything there was to understand about them. He felt their fear and their worry, their shame, and their anger, all of it. "You know this is wrong," he said. "All of you know it." Wrong or not, though, the men kept moving closer, all except one who hesitated, looking uncertain.

"You," Aaron said, locking gazes with the man, "Roger, isn't it?"

"Yes si—err ... yes. That's my name."

"Don't pay 'em any fuckin' attention, Rog," Adney said, walking up to stand beside the man, "he'll say anything he can to keep his heart beatin'."

"You know that this is wrong, don't you, Roger?" Aaron said, ignoring Adney as he called upon the power of the bond, taking the measure of the man's fear and shame, pulling out the name that floated within that storm of emotion, "what would your sister, Clara, think? Do you think she would still be so proud of her brother, the soldier, if she saw you now?"

The man's eyes went wide, "How do you know—"

"Never mind that," Aaron said, still backing up as the others moved closer, "it's not as hopeless as these here would have you believe, Roger. We can beat Belgarin's army—we can keep your sister and her children safe. You can be the hero."

Roger lowered his sword to the ground, and Aaron felt, knew, that the power of the bond was working, "Maybe he's right," Roger said. "It doesn't have to—" his words turned into a gasp of pain as a sword erupted from his chest, and Aaron stared in shock. He'd been so focused on the man, on the bond, that he hadn't noticed Adney creep up behind Roger as they'd spoken.

"We're doin' this thing, Roger," Adney hissed from behind the man, "with our without you." He ripped the blade free, and Roger crashed to the earth. Through the power of the bond, of the connection he'd formed, Aaron felt as well as saw the man die, felt each memory of his sister and his nephew and nieces as they crumpled and vanished as if set aflame until there was nothing but darkness.

He stumbled, suddenly disoriented and barely managed to keep his feet as he felt something—whatever force had claimed Roger's life—reach out and grasp at him with icy talons. He fought against it, but the force was too strong, and he screamed as he felt some part of himself being ripped away. Then Co was there, a comforting presence in his mind, I'm here, Aaron, she said, and with those words, he felt his own strength, his own will swell with power. Growling, he tore himself free of whatever force held him, lurching drunkenly before he could find his balance.

He shook his head to clear it and looked up in time to see one of the other soldiers rushing him, swinging his blade in a two-handed downward slash. He got his sword up in time, but he didn't manage to brace his feet beneath him, and the impact of the blow drove him to his knees. The soldier pressed down on his blade and, arms straining with the effort, blood pumping thick and hot from the cut he'd taken, Aaron struggled to hold the sword at bay. The soldier hissed, spittle flying from his mouth, as he tried to force the blade down and slowly, ever so slowly, it crept closer to Aaron's throat.

Aaron strained for all he was worth, and he managed to keep the blade at bay, yet he knew it meant little difference. He could hear the others circling around him now, drawing closer. He could not turn to fight them, or the man's sword would finish its work, yet if he stayed as he was, they would kill him just the same. Two options, then, and both leading to death. Adina, he had time to think, I'm sorry. The anger flared up in him again at the thought that she would be left alone with no one to protect her and that decided him. He might die, but he'd take this bastard with him, at least.

He let his right hand fall away from his sword's grip. Immediately, the sword began to move toward him more quickly, and he reached out and clutched the handle of the knife on the soldier's belt, ripping it free. The man grinned at the weakened pressure, too distracted to even notice that Aaron had taken the knife until he rammed it into the inside of the soldier's thigh. The man grunted in surprised pain, but Aaron was not finished. Growling, he ripped the knife further down, severing the artery, and hot blood fountained out of the wound. The man let out a final wheeze then collapsed to the ground.

Gasping, Aaron lurched to his feet, expecting to be cut down at any moment from an attack he never saw coming, but nothing happened. Instead, gaining his feet, he turned to look around him and saw that two of the soldiers lay dead behind him. Confused, he spun to see a figure holding a blade at Adney's throat. For his part, the soldier's eyes were wide and terrified, his mouth open in shock. "M-Mister," he said, "whoever you are, this man's got it comin' I swear. The gods know it's true. I ain't got no quarrel with you."

"Has it coming does he?" Said a familiar voice, "Well, I might have to agree with you there, but whenever it's coming, it's not today."

Aaron stared at the figure with its back to him in shock. The moonlight filtered through enough for him to see that the man had long gray hair and, when he turned, Aaron saw the cool, blue gray eyes that he remembered. "Darrell?"

The old man tilted his head, smiling so that the skin around his eyes crinkled, "It's me, lad. And it's good to see you."

Aaron glanced around at the corpses littering the forest floor then back to the man who'd taken him in when he'd been an orphan on the street, the man who'd been a family to him when his own had been murdered. And, of course, the man who'd just saved his life. "It's good to be seen."

The old man winked, "Now, what of this one?" He said, nodding his head at Adney whose eyes were locked on the length of steel at his throat.

Aaron was moving forward before he realized it, the anger slipping its leash. He stalked toward the man and Darrell, his old swordmaster, brought his sword down and stepped away. Adney held up his hands as if to show that he was unarmed and stumbled backward, "Now look, general, sir, you have to understand—"

Aaron struck the man backhanded in the face, and Adney cried out, reeling backward under the force of the blow. Adney looked up at him with eyes full of terror, his mouth bloody. "W-wait," he stammered, tears in his eyes, "m-mercy, please—"

But the anger roiling in him knew nothing of mercy, and it did not care for waiting. He braced his right leg and pivoted as his left foot flashed up, catching the man in the stomach.

Adney flew backward from the force of the kick, rolling end over end until he finally came to a stop on his back, a wheezing, blubbering mess. The soldier had made his way to his hands and knees by the time Aaron reached him, "P-please," Adney blubbered, "m-my family—"

"Will get over it," Aaron said. He grabbed a handful of the man's greasy, lanky hair and jerked him up, the edge of his blade coming to rest at the man's throat. He hesitated then, some small part of him working its way past the anger and the rage. He should question him. See what he knew. It was the right thing to do—the smart thing. Still, the wrath demanded release, and Aaron shook with the need to drag his sword across the man's throat, to watch the blood pour from his ruined neck, an answer for the youth, Bastion, and for Roger. An answer of blood and death, the truest kind. He wanted to kill him, needed to kill him, yet still he hesitated, the sword wavering.

It is manageable. Leomin's words rang in his ears. *It is a matter of will.* Gritting his teeth so hard that his jaw ached, Aaron told his arm to let the sword fall. At first, it did not. Then he exerted his will greater still, his body shaking with the force of the battle raging within it, and, finally, his arm fell loose, and the sword dropped to his side.

"No," he gasped, feeling like he'd just fought the worst battle of his life. "You won't die today—I won't be your executioner. There will be questions first, Adney. And there will be answers."

"Y-you're not gonna kill me?" The man whimpered.

"Not me," Aaron said.

"Oh gods, thank you," Adney said, "thank you so much, general." He scrabbled forward on his knees until he was embracing Aaron's calf. "Gods bless you, sir. My wife and children, you understand. I didn't have a choice."

Aaron saw the attack coming, he suspected, even before Adney realized he was going to do it himself, the magic of the bond a powerful thing warning him, so it was no real trial to catch the soldier's wrist before the knife hit its mark in his side. Then he pivoted and brought his knee into Adney's face. The soldier's head snapped back, and he collapsed to the ground, unconscious.

"I had thought you meant to kill him, lad," Darrell said as he came up to stand beside him, both of them staring at the unconscious man at Aaron's feet.

Aaron shook his head slowly, "I am more than just a killer," he said, though whether the words were for Darrell or himself, he wasn't sure. Suddenly, he was overcome with exhaustion, and he stumbled and would have fallen had the swordmaster not caught him.

The bond, Co said into his mind, it takes its toll. But, Aaron, you beat it. We beat it.

For now, he thought. For now, firefly. He lurched to where the youth Bastion lay, flipping him over. He was surprised to find that the youth's eyes met his own, full of pain but full of life, too. "G-general," the youth said, blood leaking from the corner of his mouth, "I'm sorry. I should have known—"

"Hush now, lad," Aaron said. "You aren't to be blamed here." But the youth did not seem to hear him as his eyes closed, his body slumping. Aaron felt his neck and was relieved to find a heartbeat. Not dead then, only unconscious. He started to rise but suddenly a bout of weakness came over him, and the next thing he knew he was sitting on the ground.

Darrell rushed forward, "Are you alright, lad?" He studied Aaron and seemed to notice the cut on his arm for the first time. "Gods, Aaron, that's a deep one. It needs to be seen to and now."

"Never mind that," Aaron said, his own voice sounding distant and strange to his ears, "I'm fine. Now, help me with him."

He started to rise again, and the swordmaster put a hand on his shoulder, "Aaron, I really don't think that's a good idea. Your arm..."

"I'm fine, Darrell," he said, "really. I appreciate it, but Bastion's in far worse shape than I am." Grunting, he pushed himself to his feet, swaying dangerously, "we'll see to him first then you can fuss over my arm to your heart's content." It was a good idea, a good plan, and the swordmaster seemed to agree. At least, that was, until Aaron turned to grab Bastion's arms and suddenly found himself falling, the darkness taking him even before he hit the ground.

CHAPTER EIGHT

Aaron came awake with a gasp, his heart galloping in his chest like a frightened horse. He lay there for a moment, his breathing ragged and shallow, his eyes closed as he tried to shake off the last vestiges of whatever his dream had been about. He didn't remember it, but that was little comfort. He knew well enough what its substance must have been. Rage and fury and blood. His hands ached, and he glanced down at them to see that they were clenched into fists, blood leaking from them onto the bed linens. Wincing, he opened his hands and saw that he'd dug his nails into the meat of his palm while he slept.

The dreams are getting worse, he thought.

Yes, Co answered, his worry echoed in her tone. Aaron, I'm sorry. It has never been like this before.

Never mind. He thought back, not wanting to talk about it. After all, talking wouldn't change things, wouldn't keep the pit from rising beneath his feet. He sat up, wincing at a pain in his arm and noted that the wound had been freshly dressed. He looked around him and saw that he was in a small room with no furniture but a bed a nightstand and a single chair in which Adina sat, bent so that her arms lay on the bed, her head buried in them.

Aaron reached out to shake her awake but hesitated, realizing that he didn't want to wake her. Realizing that, just then, he could think of nothing he'd rather do than sit and listen to the sounds of her peaceful breathing, to forget about the world for a time and hope that it would forget about the two of them. The problem, of course, was that the world never did, and those he and his companions faced would not sit by idly. Belgarin's army would march sooner or later—sooner if Aaron's instincts were true. Boyce Kevlane hadn't struck him as the type of man who took being thrown from a balcony in stride. He was out there somewhere, healing and plotting and thinking his dark thoughts. Captain Francis and the general had worked for him, and neither was a concern any longer, but that meant little enough. A man who had lived for thousands of years, a man who could shrug off fatal wounds as if they were nothing, who could turn his hands into fucking claws and make spikes rip from his body to impale unlucky castle guards, would no doubt have other friends, other allies. And what dark allies might a creature such as that find? And, more pressing still, how many?

Aaron sighed. He stretched his left hand out, surprised at how weak he felt, and rested it on Adina's hair. "Adina."

She stirred slowly, her mind apparently reluctant to remove itself from whatever world it had created in her sleep, but finally she raised her head to look at him and her eyes went wide. "Aaron, you're awake!"

He smiled, but it quickly turned to a wince as she pulled him into a tight embrace, oblivious of the bandages on his arm. Still, pain or not, he was glad to have her beside him. "We've really got to stop meeting like this," he said.

She must have heard something of the pain in his voice, for she released him, "Oh, gods, Aaron, I'm sorry. You must hurt terribly."

Aaron glanced at his bandaged arm and gave her a half shrug. "I've been hurt a lot worse."

She studied him, her expression worried. "Darrell told me what happened. He said that some of the soldiers tried to kill you but that you fought them off."

Aaron grunted a laugh, "That old bastard loves giving someone else the credit. No," he said, sobering, "the truth is, Adina, if Darrell hadn't shown up when he did, I'd be dead right now."

Adina shook her head, running a hand through her hair, "Aaron, maybe you were right. Maybe we should just go to

Avarest, let the world take care of itself. I've lost count of the times you've almost died. We could just give it up—find somewhere, maybe, in Avarest or out in the country. Get a house and just live. We could live, Aaron. We could go anywhere, do anything."

Aaron met her blue eyes, saw the tears gathering there, "We could, Adina. But we won't—we both know that. I could live with myself. I could leave it all behind, leave the people to whatever fate awaits them and just go—the gods know I've done worse. But you?" He shook his head, "Could you really do that, Adina? Could you live your life knowing that people were suffering and dying and that you weren't doing anything to stop it?"

"I could try, Aaron," she said, and the tears spilled over then, winding their way down her cheeks, "For you, I could try. I don't want to lose you. We've done what we could. Someone else—"

"There is no one else, Adina," he said, grabbing her hand in his, "you know that. And anyway, I don't want to lose me either. I'll just have to be more careful, that's all. We both will."

She let out a ragged sigh, "More careful," she said, sarcasm filling her voice, "maybe we can try to be a little more conservative, reduce it to what, say only one assassination attempt a week?"

Aaron gave her a small smile, "Let's not be too optimistic."

She tried a smile of her own, but it quickly turned to a worried frown. "Are you sure you're okay? You were twisting and turning a lot in your sleep, making noises."

Aaron frowned, "Noises?"

"They were ... well, they sounded like growls."

Aaron nodded slowly. An image from his dream, something fleshy and slick with blood, tried to surface in his mind, and he forced it down with a will. "I'm okay, Adina. Really."

She studied him for several seconds as if unsure, "It was only a bad dream then?"

Gods, I wish. A bad dream, sure, but not only that. Bad all over. Bad sleeping and bad awake and both of them getting worse. "Just a bad dream."

"Does it," she glanced around, ensuring herself that they were the only two in the small windowless room, "does it have anything to do with what you told me before? About ... what you thought you were becoming?"

He could see the worry in her face, and he hesitated. He did not like the idea of lying to her, but the truth would do nothing but give her something else to worry about. Leomin's words from a few nights before echoed in his mind, the way the Parnen had described the trouble with the bond, compared it to a pit at your feet, sometimes big and sometimes small. Aaron thought the man hadn't got it fully right. Sure, some days were worse or better than others, some days the pit was smaller or larger, but what the captain hadn't mentioned is that it grew. It was always growing, that pit, a hole ready to swallow his whole world.

How long, then, before it was too far to make it across? How long before he fell? And, when he did, what would happen? Would there be anything left of him at all, or would he be nothing more than a man turned into a furious animal, a beast that killed for the pleasure of it, that reveled in death and pain and despair. "It's nothing, Adina," he said, waving it away, "to be honest, I've already forgotten what it was about." A lie, that, but he thought that maybe he could make it true, if he tried hard enough. At least for a time.

Adina watched him for several seconds then apparently decided to let it drop. "What brought Darrell to Perennia anyway? I hadn't expected to see him since Leomin said he sent him to Avarest. I'd thought he would have gone to May and the others."

Aaron frowned. He'd been so busy fighting for his life—and being unconscious, there was that—that he hadn't stopped to think of the swordmaster's unlikely appearance at such a fortunate—for him, at least—time. It was strange, to say the least. They'd sent a messenger to Avarest carrying a letter for May and the others, but he doubted if it would have reached them by now and, even if by some miracle it had, there would have been no time for Darrell to have made the journey all the way to Perennia. Once, Aaron might have been able to tell himself that nothing more than coincidence had led the swordmaster to Perennia, but being reunited with a friend he'd thought long dead and then having the same friend turn out to be an insane mage that should have died thousands of years ago had a way of making a man lose faith in coincidences.

He didn't think Darrell would ever do anything to harm him—after all, the man had taken him in when he was young. If he'd wanted Aaron dead, all he would have had to do was leave him on the street as a young child. The Downs would have taken care of the rest. Still, he hadn't thought Owen would have been a maniacal figure of myth bent on destroying the world. *Shit has a way of surprising you sometimes.* "You know," he said frowning, "I think I'll have to ask him about that the next time I see him."

"Well, as to that," Adina said, "you can see him whenever you're ready. He's just outside the door—he's been there since they brought you back. You should have seen him, Aaron, carrying you by himself as if you weighed nothing, screaming for a healer. I think he probably woke up the whole castle, doing it. I never would have thought he'd be so strong."

Aaron frowned, thinking again of Owen, of the creature he'd been, thinking that he'd been best friends with the same being that had murdered his parents. It had worn a different face then, sure, but it had still been Owen. "People have a way of surprising you, I guess," he said distractedly, the words the creature had spoken before he'd thrown it from the balcony ringing in his mind. *Your parents died because of a choice your father made.*

"Speaking of," Adina said, "I can't believe I nearly forgot. Healer Malakson asked me to fetch him if you happened to awaken. I'll be right back."

Before Aaron could speak, she was already out the door and gone. Aaron stared after her, his mind whirling with a dozen different emotions until finally settling on something akin to shame. *She deserves better than me,* he thought.

So be better, Aaron Envelar, Co said, *if you are not what she deserves, then become it.*

Aaron grunted. He was tired, and he thought it wasn't just the wound but his use of the bond that had left him feeling so exhausted. Still, there was too much that needed doing to rest, and he had an inescapable feeling that time was running out. He decided that he would let the healer see to his wounds then he would get up, tired or not, and get to work. Decided, he let his heavy eyes close. Not to sleep but only to gain what small rest he might while he waited.

When he opened his eyes again, an old man in a white robe was standing over him, squinting through thick eye glasses as he raised Aaron's wounded arm, removed the bandage and studied it. The man made a noise in his throat, nodding to himself. "I see. I see."

You ought to, Aaron thought, wearing lenses thicker than some shields I've seen. "You don't mind me asking what you see, do you?" Aaron said, glancing at the raw, jagged wound on his arm. As many times as he'd been hurt, it was always somehow surprising to see your body different than the way you'd left it last. There was something disconcerting about the impermanence of it. How much could a man's body change, after all, before he didn't recognize it anymore? How many scars could he acquire before that's all he was?

The healer started as if surprised by hearing his patient speak. He met Aaron's gaze with eyes that seemed impossibly large behind the lenses he wore and blinked several times in quick succession before turning back to the arm. "Ah, forgive me, young man," he said, "I am Healer Malakson, and I've the pleasure of being Queen Isabelle's personal healer. She insisted that I come and see to your wound myself."

Pleasure, is it? "Well?" Aaron said when the man didn't offer anything else, "how's the arm? Is it going to rot off anytime soon because, if so, it might help for me to be prepared for it."

The old man shook his head slowly as if seriously considering Aaron's words, "Rot such as you speak of is very rarely found in a wound as fresh as this, assuming it has been cared for which, of course, it has. Still, I suppose there is always the chance. I read an account once of a youth that stepped on a sliver of glass from a broken window and ended up losing his leg from the knee down. Still," he said, smiling in what Aaron took as a failed effort to comfort him, "such things are rare."

"Great," Aaron said, "well, at least I'll still be able to walk around if it does fall off, it just being my arm and all."

The doctor nodded thoughtfully, rubbing a thin, wrinkled hand over his pointed chin, apparently oblivious of Aaron's sarcasm, "Yes, that is the way to look at it, young man. Just so. Still, I must confess that, according to the account, the boy passed during the procedure to remove his leg. Such procedures can be

65

quite difficult under the best of circumstances and with his body already in such a weakened state ... well, I'm sad to say he didn't make it."

"Fantastic," Aaron said, shooting a look at Adina who only shrugged helplessly.

The old man favored him with a smile then but it was one that seemed more than a little self-congratulatory, as if he was proud of his bedside manner and ability to set his patient at ease. "Now," he said, removing a vial from the inside of his white robe, "this is a mixture of several different plants. Many of which, actually, are quite rare. It should help the wound to heal faster. Did you know," he said, pausing to lean conspiratorially forward, an eager expression on his face, "that one such vial as this costs more than most men pay for a horse?"

The older man studied Aaron expectantly, so Aaron offered him a one-armed shrug. "Shame to waste it," he said, joking.

The doctor nodded, his expression sober, "True. That is very true."

With that, he turned the vial up so that what couldn't have been any more than three drops of the liquid fell into one of his hands. Immediately, the room was filled with a pungent, acrid odor that made Aaron's eyes water, and he coughed, unable to help himself as the smell clung to the back of his throat. The old man paid no attention as he rubbed the mixture into Aaron's wound. Immediately, a cool numbness seemed to spread over it, covering the pain that he'd felt only moments before.

"Ah," Aaron said, "that's not so bad." From his experience, being healed of wounds and sicknesses was never fun. In fact, it seemed to him that more often than not, the cure was worse than the disease, but he had to admit that whatever mixture of herbs the man had used on his arm made it feel better than he'd thought possible when he'd woken to the pain of it. The healer might be strange, and he might also just happen to be the absolute worst at comforting his patients, but Aaron found himself smiling anyway at the cool, comfortable feeling suffusing his arm. "Usually, I always regret visiting a healer, typically think it'd be better to bleed out than to go through what a lot of your colleagues put a man through but I feel ... better. Thanks."

The old man smiled, "It is, of course, my pleasure," he said, carefully stoppering the vial and tucking it in some hidden pocket in his robes. "Now, there's just one more thing." He turned and grabbed a glass Aaron hadn't noticed from the small nightstand beside the bed and offered it to him.

I should have known, Aaron thought, wincing and taking the glass. The liquid inside was thick and green and chunks of something floated inside of it. The smell reached him, and he nearly gagged. "Let me guess," he said, swallowing his gorge, "this will help me heal faster?"

"Hmm?" The old man asked as if his mind had been elsewhere. "Oh, oh yes. Your body has lost a fair amount of blood. This brew will help you to replenish it more quickly. Most likely."

Aaron cocked his head at that. "Wait a minute. What do you mean?"

The healer blinked his owlish eyes, "Mean? Oh, only that the body can take some time in producing new blood. Until then, your symptoms would include dizziness, loss of balance, and several others that—"

"No," Aaron said, "I meant what did you mean by 'most likely'?"

"Ah, that," the old man said, "well, you see, there have been studies but none, unfortunately, have been as my colleagues and I would like. Still, I am fairly certain that it should help, and it certainly will not hurt."

Won't hurt? Aaron thought, grimacing as he studied the drink, you sure about that?

"Well," the healer said as he wrapped a fresh bandage around Aaron's arm, "I will leave you to get your rest," he paused, glancing at Adina, "and to speak with the princess, of course. Only, please do make sure that you drink all of the glass's contents."

Aaron was just about to tell the man that, if he had to drink the whole glass, he was fairly certain the only contents he'd be considering would be those of his own stomach, but the old man moved with a surprising speed for one of his age and was out the door before Aaron had the chance. He glanced at Adina who stood on the far end of the room near the door, "You can come back over here, you know."

She grinned at him, and he felt what little worry had remained about his dream vanishing at that expression, "No thanks. There seems to be a bit of a smell coming from that side of the room," she said, nodding her head at the glass, "I'd hate to distract you from what you need to do. Probably, it would be better if you finished that before I come over."

Aaron frowned, "And what kind of smell do you think I'll make, if I die trying to drink this poison?"

She laughed at that, "You know, for a man who has spent the majority of his life with people trying to kill him, you sure can be a baby about some things."

Aaron sighed and did his best not to breathe as he turned the glass up and took a drink. His stomach heaved as the foul liquid went down his throat. It wasn't as bad as he'd thought it would be. It was worse, and he only just managed to keep it from coming back up. "Gah," he said, wiping his arm across his mouth, "it's like every healer goes to the same damn torturer for training."

Adina grinned, "Remember he said to drink it all."

Aaron sighed, "You might as well send Darrell in. I'm sure the bastard's plenty smug enough, and if I'm already going to be miserable, there's no reason to wait."

Adina winked at him, "I'll be right outside."

In another moment, Darrell walked in. The old swordmaster saw him and smiled widely. "Ah, it is good to see you awake, Aaron. You gave us all quite a scare."

"I'm fine," Aaron said, glancing at the drink he still held and swallowing hard, "For now, anyway."

"Ah yes," Darrell said, "I myself have had to suffer through such potions and cures in my time. Good reason, if any was needed, to try to avoid getting stabbed or cut by sharp metal items. Like, say, swords. Wouldn't you agree?"

Aaron scowled at the man, "It wasn't as if I exactly planned it, and anyway there were eight of them. I think I did okay."

"Oh, do you?" Darrell asked, his eyebrows drawing together as he nodded as if in deep consideration. "Well then, as long as you think it, I suppose that's something. Still, what would have happened, do you suppose, if I had not been there?"

Aaron sighed, "I guess I would have died."

The swordmaster nodded again, "Died, is it? Well, now, you tell me, Aaron. Knowing that, would you still say that you did 'okay?'"

"Damnit, Darrell, you saw how many there were. It wasn't a fair fight anyway."

"No, it wasn't," Darrell agreed, "but, then, when was the last fair fight you've been in, Aaron?" When Aaron's only answer was a scowl, the swordmaster smiled, "Ah, I see. Yes, fights are rarely fair, whatever people may think. Oh, they love to cheer their favorites in the tourneys, love to hoot and holler when their heroes knock a man from his horse in the jousts, but rarely, I find, does the man who has to pick himself up from the ground think it fair. And, in my opinion, he's probably right. Oh, maybe his horse isn't quite as brave or as fast. Maybe his arms aren't quite as long. The gods know, some men have really long arms, and what's a man to do with—"

"I get it," Aaron interrupted, "Fine. Anyway, thanks."

The swordmaster smiled but did not speak, only bowing his head to Aaron instead.

"Now that you're done gloating," Aaron said, "tell me, what of Bastion?"

"The youth that looks like he could crush bricks in his hands?" Darrell asked, "Oh, he's fine, Aaron, I wouldn't worry on that score. He's been awake since noon. Three hours faster than you I might add, and he really did have some serious injuries. Almost makes me wonder if you're not milking it a bit, taking the opportunity to take a rest in a comfortable bed and drink ... well," he said smiling as he glanced at the glass in Aaron's hand, "perhaps that's not the case."

"Good," Aaron said, deciding to ignore the man's jibes. Since he'd been a child, Darrell had always told him that he had a bad temper and that he needed to learn to keep it in check. To that end, the man had made a game of teasing and taunting Aaron whenever he could. Aaron wondered idly what his old swordmaster would think if he knew the sort of anger problems Aaron had been dealing with of late. "I'm glad he's okay," he said. "I'll want to see him later."

Darrell nodded, "Of course."

"And Adney?"

"Locked in the queen's dungeons, safe and sound. No one has spoken to him yet—they all seemed to have the idea that you would want to be the first."

Aaron grunted, "Well, the bastards were right about that. Adney first and then Bastion. I've got to figure out how far this thing with Adney and the others went before I end up with a knife in my back." He put the glass and its vile contents down on the nightstand and rose from the bed. He wobbled uncertainly, and Darrell was there in an instant, holding his arm to keep him steady.

"I'm fine," Aaron said, "really. Just had to catch my balance, that's all."

Darrell nodded, releasing him, "Very well."

Aaron stared at the swordmaster for several seconds, remembering Adina's words about him showing up in Perennia. "Why are you here, Darrell?"

"Hmm?" The older man asked, grinning, "I'm here because my one-time apprentice seems to have an affinity for getting himself wounded. I suppose, that must be some sort of failing on my part, though the gods know I tried to teach you which end of the sword was the pointy one."

"No," Aaron said, refusing to be distracted, "I mean why are you here, in Perennia. The last I heard, Leomin had put you on the Clandestine and sent you to Avarest. That's a long way from here, Darrell."

"You aren't wrong in that, Aaron," the swordmaster said, "I traveled it myself. And, as you well know, I have never been particularly fond of ships."

Aaron only just managed to suppress a laugh. Darrell liked ships about as much as most men liked getting kneed in the fruits. In both instances, someone ended up bent over whatever was handy, trying their best to keep their heaving stomachs from ejecting their breakfasts onto the ground. Still, his betrayal by Owen was too fresh in his mind for him to let the matter drop so easily. "You still haven't given me an answer."

Darrell sighed, "If someone had asked me, I would have told them there was no way the man you would become could be any more suspicious than the youth I found in the streets so long ago.

Or, perhaps, more accurate to say the youth whose hand I found as it tried to relieve me of my coin purse."

Aaron grunted, the subject still sore after all this time. "It was a good lift. If you hadn't happened to glance back when you did—"

"Relax, Aaron," Darrell said, grinning, "you may keep your fancies, if you'd like. I was not able to disabuse you of the notion that you had been caught for being careless and nothing more when you were a youth, and I don't suspect I'll be able to do so now."

"Fine," Aaron said, "then tell me why you came here, Darrell."

The older man smiled, "Well, Perennia is as nice of a place as any, I find, and their university is quite impressive. There are few places in the world as nice. Of course, I can tell you why I've come, lad, but I had thought that you had expressed some degree of urgency in the need to speak with this Adney fellow," he said, raising an eyebrow.

Aaron grunted moving toward the door, "Fine. Adney first then Bastion and then you. We will talk, Darrell."

"Of course," the swordmaster said, "I do love our chats, boy. Still, I think that you've got the order slightly wrong."

Aaron frowned, "What do you mean?"

"Well," Darrell said, grinning widely, "You said Adney first, but I don't think that's right. It seems to me," he said, glancing meaningfully at the nearly full glass sitting on the nightstand, "that there is one thing that needs to be done beforehand."

Aaron narrowed his eyes, "Fine, damnit. But if I die drinking that piss, I hope they make you general."

CHAPTER NINE

May sighed, reclining in the chair at her office desk, enjoying a brief, uncommon moment of solitude. Lately, it seemed that there was always someone about. The chamberlain was one such, the man always hanging around as if he expected a message from Adina at any moment. May liked the man well enough—he was one of those people it was impossible not to like—and didn't even mind the question, at least not much. The problem was that, in between asking after any message from the princess, the chamberlain passed his time by critiquing everything May did. If she had to hear one more word about the fact that she held her wine glass in a manner not befitting a lady, she was quite sure there would be violence.

It was as if the man needed someone to look after, to tutor, and had decided that May would be his project in his mistress's absence. Not something she was particularly fond of. She had always believed that the things that separated ladies from harlots had little to do with the way they held wine glasses or how much they drank and a lot more to do with what they did when the wine was gone, and they'd drunk their fill.

If it wasn't the chamberlain, it was Balen, Leomin's first mate, coming to see if she'd had any word from his captain. The man— possibly the most direct person she'd ever met, save Aaron himself—trying his best at the social niceties, trying to be casual and ask about how things were going with Grinner and Hale and how the club was doing but all the time May could see the question in his eyes as clear as if it had been written there.

Thom, too, was proving a distraction, though one that she enjoyed more than she would readily admit. There was something about Festa's first mate that made her feel much younger than she was; a woman of nineteen or twenty years instead of one in her early forties who would soon, she suspected, catch the first signs of gray in her red hair. She had been glad when Festa had decided to stay over in Avarest for a time, giving his men a break as he supposedly worked to procure merchandise to sell in other ports. From what May had seen though, the temperamental captain had accomplished little of that in the weeks that he'd been in Avarest, and she was careful to not entertain the hopes that such thoughts often brought to her mind. After all, she thought that, before much longer, she and the others might have need of ships, if things went well with Hale and Grinner. Not that there was much sign so far that they would.

You're stalling and you know it, she thought. Sighing, she withdrew the letter from where she'd hidden it underneath a stack of ledgers in one of the drawers of her desk. A messenger had brought it two days ago, and she had yet to tell Balen or Gryle of its existence, had not even told Thom. If the things Aaron had written in the letter were true—and the sellsword was many things but never a liar, not to her—May suspected the letter's contents would do little to assuage whatever fear Gryle and Balen felt. Boyce Kevlane. A name from myth and legend, a story told to children before they lay down to sleep.

The problem, of course, was that, according to Aaron, the man wasn't just a story at all. Not just some legend or fable for children, to be heard and then put away like so many other children's stories. And the Seven Virtues real also. All things May had believed nothing but fiction, yet they were real anyway. It was not a comforting thought for a woman who made her living—no, not just made it, but kept on living—because she made it her business to know more than everyone else.

The door to her office swung open, and May was so engrossed in thought that the sound startled her, and she jumped, giving out a small cry. The letter flew from her hand, sailing on a draft across the desk to land at the feet of the figure in the doorway. "Oh, gods, forgive me, madam, it was not my intention to frighten you."

May let out a heavy breath of relief when she saw that the figure standing in the doorway wasn't dangerous—not some assassin sent by Hale or Grinner, not this time, at least—but instead Adina's chamberlain, Gryle. The heavy-set chamberlain rubbed his hands together anxiously as if he expected her to yell or scream or maybe throw one of the books that cluttered her desk at him. Not that she wasn't tempted—she did not like to be scared. Still, the chamberlain was the most nervous man she'd ever met, and she tried to take into consideration everything that he'd been through. He'd been nearly killed half a dozen times since meeting Aaron and most recently had been forced to sail away on a ship without his charge, Princess Adina.

All things that made a nervous man more nervous still. If it got much worse, the man would most likely shake so hard his clothes would come off, and May would spare herself that. Besides, in the Downs, the prim, proper man was as far removed from his life in the castle as a fish in the desert, so she took a slow, calming breath and forced herself to smile. "It's alright, Gryle. Still, I'm quite sure that it is proper etiquette to knock before entering a woman's quarters. Though, I suspect, a castle chamberlain might know more of such things than I."

The man's face turned red with embarrassment, and his eyes grew so wide it was a wonder they didn't pop out of his head and go floating to the ceiling, "Forgive me, please, my lady. I can assure you I meant no offense. It is only ... as you know, I have been gone for three days now dealing with several of the city's merchants and seeing to our provisions for the journey."

May nodded. She knew that well enough. It had been her, after all, who had given the chamberlain the task. His was a mind made for bartering and discussing prices with merchants as well as it was made to lecture young princesses about which fork to use during dinner. Of course, sending him had held the added benefit of getting him out of May's hair for a bit. "Yes," she said, smiling, "I thought it a task well suited to your particular skills. So, how does it go?"

The chamberlain shrugged self-consciously, and May could have sworn that he ducked his head further into his neck, a turtle retracting into its shell at the first sign of danger, "It goes well enough, I suppose, Miss May, though I must admit I think myself ill-suited for the task. I know little of dealing with such men as these and the prices they try to charge. Why, it ... it's criminal. I think ... I think that, perhaps, I am not up to the negotiations. I'm embarrassed to say that I might be ... being taken advantage of."

May considered telling the man that her name was May and only May, but decided against it. She had done so before, many times, and it seemed that if the chamberlain had his way, she would become a miss regardless of her own wishes. She raised an eyebrow, "That isn't what Celes tells me. According to her, you're the best trader and negotiator she's ever seen save, perhaps, for Leomin and even there she's unsure."

The most damning thing about it was that it was true, and that Celes had said much more than just that. Almost like some wizard, she'd said, casting a spell over men until they're nearly paying him to take their wares. Gryle, though, was one of those types of men who was blind to the good in himself and, May suspected, always would be. "In fact," she went on, "if the ledgers that Celes has brought to me are correct, you're practically stealing all that food and clothing."

The chamberlain swallowed hard, "Miss May, I assure you, I would never steal. It ... well, it's wrong," he said in a tone of voice that seemed to imply that no one would ever even think of doing anything that was wrong. "As for the accuracy of the ledgers," he went on, "I swear on the gods that I would never deceive you, nor hide anything from you in my accounting. Still," he said, studying his feet now, a child called out for misbehaving, his body stiff, "if you wish it ...." He paused, his body visibly tensing as if he'd just been dropped at the feet of an executioner with a real love for his job, "I will resign my position. I know that there are others far more qualified than I to—"

"Enough, Gryle," May said, shaking her head in wonder, "I don't think that you're being deceitful—gods, don't be ridiculous!" The truth was, she couldn't imagine this nervous, self-deprecating man ever swatting a fly or walking outside in unwashed clothes, let alone conspiring to rob or lie to her. "And I mean what I said—

you really are exceptionally good at this. I've known a lot of the men and women you're dealing with for half of my life, and I've never gotten prices as good as what I've seen in the ledger."

He bowed his head, the ashamed expression still on his face, "It is kind of you to say so, ma'am." He said, as if she was only being gracious. The man really was quite infuriating.

"Truthfully," he said, "I have been met with some difficulty in finding everything you asked for in the quantities needed. If it were only your people, that would be fairly straightforward, but with Hale and Grinner's mixed in ... it has been taxing. Still, I can assure you, ma'am," he said, screwing up his courage and meeting her eye for a moment before his gaze drifted back down to his feet, "I will see that all of the men have food and provisions, as well as weapons for the journey should the princess and Mr. Envelar need us."

"I'm sure that you will," May said, "of that I've no doubt." She snorted, "Assuming, of course, that Hale and Grinner actually come, along with their men. For myself, I have my doubts."

Gryle frowned in confusion, "But ma'am, you said at the meeting that they agreed."

May ran a hand through her hair, wanting a drink. "Yes, Gryle, I did. And they did agree. But, you see, Hale and Grinner—along with the men that follow them—are criminals. And criminals, among their other less savory qualities, have been known to lie on occasion."

"But ... why would they lie, mistress?" He said in the confused, doubting tone of voice of a man speaking of a concept completely foreign to him. "I mean ... forgive me, that is to say, what would motivate them to do such a thing?"

May shrugged, "The same sorts of things that motivate men to do most of the bad things they do, I imagine. Men such as Grinner and Hale have made a career out of doing whatever would serve their own interests with no regard for what was right or proper, chamberlain. They lie, sure. They cheat and steal and kill if they think it'll benefit them."

"But ... surely you trust them?"

May noted the seriousness in the man's expression and she laughed, a true, hearty laugh, and it felt good. The chamberlain's face grew even more confused at her laughter which, of course, caused her to laugh harder until there were tears leaking from her eyes. She couldn't remember the last time she'd had a real laugh and that was strange for a woman who prided herself on always finding the humor in the world. It wasn't even particularly funny, in truth, but the world hadn't been offering up many jokes of late, and a woman had to take them where she could find them. "Gryle, you are a sweet man but never sit down at a table of cards, alright? You see, I trust Hale and Grinner to be Hale and Grinner. Which is to say that I trust neither of the plotting bastards any further than I can throw them. Less, really."

The chamberlain frowned, "Then ... perhaps, they are not the best of allies?"

May smiled, "Perhaps not, chamberlain. But if there is a line of people out there waiting to be interviewed as potential soldiers in a war that we will almost certainly lose, I must have missed it."

Gryle glanced back at the door as if he might see such a line through the walls of the club, "Forgive me, mistress, but I did not see any line when I came. Still, I suppose it's possible that they may have gathered lat—"

"My point, Gryle," May said, searching in herself for patience and her hands very nearly coming up empty, "is that a starving man doesn't complain about the meat he's given. He doesn't claim that it's under cooked and throw it away. A starving man eats. Sure, if the meat is undercooked enough, it might kill him. But eating nothing certainly will. Do you understand?"

The chamberlain nodded, looking down at his feet again, "I believe I'm beginning to. Oh, mistress," he said, bending down and grabbing the letter off the ground, "You must have dropped this."

Damnit, May thought, the letter. You forgot the damned letter.

Gryle glanced at it, moving toward her desk to hand it to her then paused, his eyes going wide, "Mistress," he said, meeting May's eyes, his excitement enough to override his normally sheepish behavior, "this ... this is a letter from Aaron and Adina!"

May sighed, "Yes."

May watched in dreaded anticipation as the chamberlain read the letter, learned of the man, Boyce Kevlane, learned about Belgarin's armies soon to be marching and Aaron and the others being thrown in the dungeons before nearly being killed. The man's eyes grew wider and wider as he read, his mouth working soundlessly, and May cursed herself for a fool for dropping it, for then letting the chamberlain's annoying self-deprecation cause her to forget about it entirely.

I've not slept enough lately, she thought, not nearly. And that had to be it. Communicating back and forth with Hale and Grinner and worrying over everything had robbed her of most of her rest, and she rarely got more than a few hours of sleep a night, less when Thom managed to extricate himself from Festa's command long enough to pay her a visit. Not that she was complaining—such visits had become the high point in a series of very low, very tiring days.

Once he was finished, Gryle looked up at her, his hand shaking where he held it. When he spoke, his voice was tight with worry, "Mistress. The princess ... she's in danger. She needs me. Did this arrive only just now?" He shook his head, confused, "I don't ... I didn't see a messenger when I came, but I suppose—"

"No, Gryle." May paused to take a deep breath, "I have had the letter for some few days now."

The chamberlain looked more confused than ever, "But if you had the letter ... then why ...."

"Because I knew that you would want to go to them, Gryle," May said, "that's why. Aaron and Leomin and the princess have enough to deal with right now, and you wouldn't do anybody any good rushing to them."

The man recoiled as if struck, "You mean to say," he said, swallowing, "that I'm worthless. That I would only get in the way."

"Of course you're not worthless, Gryle," May said, "you are capable of making a tremendous difference, don't you see that? Gods, man, you are making a difference. Here. If we are to bring an army to them in Perennia, we will need food for the voyage. We will need weapons and clothes and ships to take us across the sea—all of the things which you have worked so tirelessly and so efficiently at procuring. Stay here, Gryle. Stay where you are of so much use—there is no reason for you to endanger yourself on a voyage when there is nothing you can do for your princess even if you make it there safely."

The chamberlain considered that for a moment then slowly shook his head, meeting her eyes. "No. I'm sorry, mistress, but it was wrong for you to keep this from me. You were wrong just as I would be wrong to let Princess Adina go without what small support I might offer. Perhaps I cannot make any difference," he said, "I know what people think of me. I know what they see when they look at me." He paused, taking a deep, steadying breath, "I am a coward, it is true, and I know nothing of the arts of war, but I will not let my mistress come to harm, if I have even the slightest chance of stopping it."

"Gryle, please—"

"I thank you," the chamberlain said with affected dignity, "for allowing me to stay in one of your rooms, for giving me a chance to do something useful." He walked toward her desk, not an anxious, nervous man now but one with the confidence that can only be found in making a decision and making it firmly. He lay the letter on her desk, "If you have not told Balen," he said, "I believe that you should for what it's worth. He would be glad to know that his captain is alive." He nodded and bowed his head slightly, his body stiff with anger or perhaps worry, May wasn't sure which. "Good day, mistress," he said, turning and starting for the door.

"Gryle, wait," she said, "let's talk about—" but he was already gone, out the door and closing it behind him. May leaned back in her chair, shaking her head in frustration and exhaustion. "Damn, but I need a drink."

***

Gryle walked the streets of Avarest, unsure of where he was going, knowing only that while he'd spent his days talking to merchants and sleeping in a comfortable bed, his mistress had been fighting for her life, nearly being murdered by a wizard out of legend.

He was so distracted by his shame and worry that he'd made it down several streets before he realized something. It was dark outside, and he was alone. He was not usually a man prone to fear of the dark, had overcome his belief that grotesque monsters lurked within the cloak of night, waiting to pounce on the unwary when he was still a little boy. The problem, of course, was that, in the Downs, the monsters were real. May had made sure to tell him as much when she'd warned him never to venture into the Downs alone, particularly at night. Criminals, she'd said, behaved like other predators, shying away from the revealing sunlight, choosing instead to conduct their dark business beneath the cloak of darkness.

Even as he had the thought, he heard a scuffling sound in an alleyway off to his right and froze, his breath catching in his throat. He turned, his body tensing as he peered into alleyway, but if there was something lurking in the shadows, he could not see it.

Another noise sounded behind him, and he spun, his heart galloping in his chest to stare down the street behind him where a filthy cat rooted in a pile of garbage. He should have felt some relief then, but he did not. His forehead had broken out into a sweat, and he removed a kerchief—he always kept one handy— from his tunic and mopped his sodden brow.

He was just telling himself that it was nothing, to relax, when the night's silence was broken by the sounds of shouting. He tried to tell himself that the sound had come from several streets away, that it was no doubt the drunken call of some man deep in his cups, but his feet were not convinced and soon he was running.

He ran for a time, unsure of where he was going, but worry for Adina and Aaron cut through even his fear, deciding him. He would go and see Festa. It would not be a terribly long trip to the docks—half an hour, no more—and the captain might be persuaded to take him to Perennia. Or so he hoped.

Gryle rarely ran and, as a result, his side soon began to ache, and he slowed to a panting, hurried walk. His eyes roamed the streets around him, his hands sweaty and clammy with fear, and he'd not gone far when he heard another sound in a nearby alleyway. Panic rose up in him, threatening to override all rational thought, and he forced himself to stop, closing his eyes. Just another cat no more than that, he told himself, or a dog, perhaps, looking for food. It wasn't either of these things, though, and the last image he saw before the darkness took him was of something rushing toward his face.

CHAPTER TEN

The guards on duty at the dungeon didn't even ask how they could help Aaron when he came down the stairs, trailed by Adina and Darell, both of which had refused to leave his side no matter what he'd said.

"Glad to see you're alright, sir." The first one said.

"He's the fifth cell on the left, general," said the second, "There's a chair sat out for you, but we didn't know you'd have guests."

"Thanks," Aaron said, not slowing, "and don't worry about it. This shouldn't take long." He led the others to where the two guards had indicated and stopped outside of the cell, peering in. Even in the dim light provided by the torches spaced in intervals along the dungeon's corridor, he noticed that Adney had several bumps and bruises that he had acquired since the last time Aaron had seen him. Apparently, the guards had been efficient in their duties but not particularly kind. Aaron found that he didn't mind much. "I'm guessing you've probably seen better days, Adney."

The man was hunched in the corner of the dirty cell, his clothes torn and filthy, and he looked up at the sound of Aaron's voice. "General?" He said, surprised, real fear coming into his eyes. "You ... but I thought ... from what I overheard from the guards' conversation, I thought that you had died."

Aaron shrugged, "Sorry to disappoint you, Adney. I suppose I've got a habit of doing that. Now, why don't you tell me who hired you to kill me."

"Hired?" The prisoner said, and he let out a mad, cackling laugh, "As if someone was going to pay me? Is that what you think?" He broke into laughter even as tears coursed their way down his dirt-grimed face. "You have no idea what's going on." His laughter cut off in another moment and turned to sobs, "Gods why couldn't you just die? It would have been better. Now ... my family...." He trailed off, his head drooping between his knees, his body shaking with his grief.

Aaron frowned, "What are you talking about? Are you trying to tell me that Belgarin threatened you?"

"Belgarin?" the man said, looking up at him once more and there was such fear and grief in his tortured expression that Adina let out a small gasp beside Aaron. "Surely, you can't be that stupid," the man said, spit flying from his mouth as he did. "Do you think I'm worried about some royal half a world away? Fields take it but you're a fool. I don't care, general. Do what you want to me—torture me, kill me, it doesn't matter. You've killed my family already."

Aaron frowned, "What the fuck are you talking about? If Belgarin didn't hire you then who did? Who do you work for?"

"My family," the man spat, "they're the only ones I've ever worked for." He laughed then but there was little humor in it, only bitterness, "he'll come for them now. Just like he'll come for you, in time. He hates you more than any other."

Aaron frowned, striding closer to the cell, grasping it with his hands, "Who are you talking about?"

The man grunted, "You know well enough of whom I speak. Did you think you had killed him, general? Is that what you thought?" He laughed then, and there was more than a little madness in the sound of it as it echoed in the dungeons, "You cannot kill what is immortal, Aaron Envelar. You cannot kill a god. He will come for you and all those you care about, just as he will come for me and my family now. You have killed yours and mine both, general."

"You speak of the Endless." Darrell said, his voice tightly controlled.

Aaron turned to look at his old swordmaster, his eyes narrowing slowly. "Darrell," he began, but his words were drowned out as the man in the cell laughed, a shrieking, piercing sound that seemed to dig into Aaron's mind.

"The Endless," the man wheezed between laughter, "Boyce Kevlane. The Ancient, the Everlasting. The god. Oh, you know something of him don't you, old man," he said, his body shaking with mirth and madness, "then you know well enough what is coming. You know well what he is capable of. He told me of you—oh yes, he knows of you and the others. You and your kind can do nothing to stop him. You never could. Yours is a life that will be filled with pain. Because," he hissed, "of the choice you made."

The man's last words echoed in Aaron's mind. Because of the choice you made. When he'd fought with Boyce Kevlane, Aaron had thought he worked for Belgarin, but when he said as much, the creature had laughed, had told him that his father had not been murdered because he followed Eladen, one of Belgarin's rivals to the throne. He'd laughed and grinned that insane, too-wide grin. Your parents died because of a choice your father made.

Aaron studied the swordmaster for a second, but Darrell was too busy staring wide-eyed at the man in the cell. Aaron turned, feeling the rage boiling in him now and grasped the bars of the cell so tightly that his hands ached. "What choice?" He rasped, "Tell me."

The man grinned at Aaron for a second before turning to Darrell, "Your friend here doesn't know, does he? He doesn't know what you are."

"What choice?" Aaron yelled, and the power of the bond came upon him unexpectedly and unintentionally. Suddenly, he felt every emotion the man in the cell felt. As might have been expected, there was fear but not so much as one would have thought. There was anger too, but mostly there was just resignation and a sort of grim satisfaction about him.

The man, too, must have felt some of Aaron's own emotions, for his eyes went wide, and he recoiled as if he'd been slapped. "Such rage," Adney said, "oh, but you are an angry one. That beast you carry within you will break free of its chains soon, I think. The Seven always have their way."

It was Aaron's turn to feel Darrell's questing gaze on him, and he glanced over at the swordmaster's wondering expression only to turn back to the man in the cage. The prisoner cackled another wheezing, screeching laugh, "Oh, you are both fools, and you will die for it. And you, general, will have to find some other target for your wrath, for it will not be me."

Aaron, Co said, I'm feeling something from him, something's not right.

Aaron squinted at the man and noted, for the first time, a shadowed shape sitting on the dirt floor beside him. A beaten tin cup, one that the guards used to bring the prisoners water. "Shit," he said, and the man grinned wider. Aaron moved to the door lock only to realize that he hadn't got the keys from the guards. "Damnit," he hissed, "call the guards. Now."

"Aaron," Adina said, "what is it—"

"It was in the cup," Aaron growled, "it was in the fucking cup."

"Guards!" He yelled, "To me, now!" He looked down the hallway, seeing the two men rushing toward him. "The key," Aaron said, "give me the damn key."

The guard holding the key ring hurried forward, unclipping it from where it was attached to his waist and handing it over. Aaron was looking through the keys when wet, gurgling coughs came from inside the cell, and he spun, staring back into the cell. Adney was not laughing now. His body was convulsing in terrible fits, seeming to tense with back breaking force every two or three seconds. Blood coated the man's chin and stained the front of his shirt, more coming out with each jerking convulsion. "No, damnit," Aaron said, fumbling at the keys. The third one he tried fit the lock, and he threw the door open, rushing inside.

The prisoner was on his back now, and Aaron thought he could hear the sounds of ligaments and tendons snapping under the incredible force that gripped him, his back arching impossibly high. "A healer," Aaron said, grabbing the man by the shoulders and trying to force him down even as he looked back at the pale faces of the two guards watching him, "Fetch a healer!"

"Aaron—" Adina began.

"Adina, we need to know what this man knows. We need a healer. Now, damnit!" He yelled, looking at one of the guards.

"Aaron," the princess said again, "it's too late. He's dead."

Aaron looked back and saw that she was right. The man had grown still in his hands, but he'd been too focused on speaking with the guards to notice. "Don't you dare fucking die," he growled, shaking the man, but Adney was long past threats, long past breathing too, and he stared up at Aaron with eyes glazed over in death.

He turned to stare at Adina, and she stared back at him, her expression troubled. He'd told her what Boyce Kevlane had said before he threw him from the balcony, and her expression showed that she was thinking much the same as him. Whatever choice his father had made that had led to his death, Darrell had made the same choice. He turned to look at the swordmaster, his eyes narrowing, and Darrell met his gaze, his own expression troubled.

Neither of them spoke and finally, Aaron turned back to the two guards, "Search the body and the cell but first tell me, who prepares the meals for the prisoners?"

The two guards glanced at each other, "Margaret, my lord. A nice lady she is, too. Always brings a sweet for the guards on duty when she comes with the prisoners' food."

Aaron nodded, a thousand thoughts rushing through his mind, "She stays in the castle?"

"Uh, yes sir. But, sir, I have to be honest, I've a hard time imagining Margaret as any kind of traitor. A sweet lady she is, all the lads would agree. It'd be a real surprise to figure out she had anything to do with it."

"The world is full of surprises," Aaron said, "and in my experience, most of them aren't good. Now, show me to her quarters."

***

Adina followed Aaron and the others through the castle's corridors, her mind troubled. She could see Aaron's mind working, wondering at the prisoner's words before he died, and she wondered herself. She stole a glance at Darrell, wondering what choice the swordmaster had made, but the older man did not

85

meet her gaze, his own eyes focused on the hallway ahead of them, a troubled expression on his face.

He can't be a traitor, she thought, he can't be. After all, it had been Darrell who'd saved her and Gryle back in Baresh when Belgarin's soldiers had attacked them. Still, she could not get the prisoner's words out of her head. You will die because of the choice you made.

The words were still running through her head when the guard led them down a corridor into the servant's quarters and stopped in front of a door. "This is it?" Aaron said, his voice tense.

The guard nodded, stepping aside, "Yes, general."

Aaron stepped up to the door and knocked, and it creaked open of its own accord. Frowning, Aaron turned and shot a glance at Darrell and the guard before sliding his sword free of its sheath. The other two men did the same then Aaron turned back to the door. "Mrs. Margaret?" Aaron called, "It's me, Aaron Envelar. The general of the queen's army, ma'am."

Aaron waited for several seconds but there was no answer, "Mrs. Margaret," he said, holding up three fingers to the others as he spoke, counting down, "are you there?"

Still no answer, but as the last finger fell, Aaron slammed into the door, rushing in behind it, his sword at the ready. Darrell and the guard came in right behind him, fanning out in the room. Adina followed after and the first thing that struck her was the smell, and she held her hand up to her nose and mouth. It was the sour-sweet smell of rotting meat. Inside the room, Aaron glanced back at the men and nodded his head where a head of gray hair could be seen poking over the top of a rocking chair. "Mrs. Margaret?" He said, moving toward the left side of the chair, past a simple wooden table. "Are you alright?

Adina watched as he stepped around the chair and let out a hiss of frustration. "She's dead."

Darrell and the guard moved forward, and the guard let out a gasp of surprise and disgust. "Oh gods be good," he said, clamping his hand to his mouth, his face going pale.

"If you're going to throw up, get the fuck out of here," Aaron said, and the man nodded, swallowing hard.

Adina came around to stand where the others were and goose bumps ran up her back. Mrs. Margaret looked as if she'd been in her sixties, dressed simply in a dress with more of an eye to practicality than appearance. Her gray hair had been tied in a bun that was now in disarray. She looked like someone's favorite grandmother, maybe, sitting there, a knitting needle and an unfinished square of clothe in her lap. Her throat had been cut so deep that Adina thought she could see the white of her spine in that bloody ruin, and she tore her gaze away as her own stomach clenched warningly.

"Sir," the guard said, "the killer might still be here."

Aaron held his hand up, indicating the tiny room. There was the rocking chair, a small bed on one side of the room, and the table and a single chest of drawers in one corner. "And where would he be hiding?" Aaron said, "under the bed?"

Darrell leaned close to the dead woman, reaching out to put a hand on her arm, and if the sight or smell bothered him, he gave no sign. "Cold. And the body's stiff. Still, no signs of rotting yet."

The sellsword nodded, "Half a day to a day probably then. I doubt any more than that." He frowned, turning to Darrell," how long since we arrived back with Adney?"

Darrell shrugged, "You slept a fair amount since then and it took some time to get everything settled. I guess ... eight hours? Maybe ten?"

"Eight," Adina agreed, and Aaron nodded, rubbing his hand through his hair. "That means that whoever killed her did it right about the time we got back. Right about the time they knew Adney had been sent to the dungeons."

"They didn't want any witnesses," The old swordmaster said, and Aaron nodded.

His jaw muscles worked, and Adina could see the anger, the rage building in him as he stared at the dead woman. "She died because of me. If Adney and the others had got their way, I'd be dead and Miss Margaret there would still be alive."

"Aaron," Adina said, putting a hand on his shoulder, surprised by how knotted and tensed the muscles there were, "it's not your fault."

"Margaret here might disagree with you, if she could talk," he said, still staring at the dead woman. "Whatever monster demanded this old lady's death, I was the one that awakened its rage. I'm the one that drew it here."

"You don't know that, Aaron," Adina said, her voice coming out little more than a whisper, "you can't know that."

"Go," Aaron said turning to the guard, whose face was so pale as to look like parchment, "Bring some men, a healer too. I want to know when she died and anything else they can tell about her or the weapon used to kill her. As for the room, I want it searched before the night's out."

"Yes sir," the guard said, and Adina couldn't help but notice the man's relief as he hurried out of the room at a near run.

"This is my fault, Adina," he said, turning to her, "you know that as well as I do. He didn't show up as one of your family or friends, Adina, not Leomin's either. He showed up as mine. He didn't—" Aaron cut off, narrowing his eyes at the swordmaster who was scanning the room then shook his head, not finishing the thought.

Not that he needed to—Adina knew well enough what he would say—He didn't kill your father. "Aaron," she tried again, "you're not to blame for the actions of others. If that were true, then I could be blamed for much of what Belgarin has done. After all, how many have been hurt or killed in his quest to kill me?" She shook her head sadly, "it doesn't work like that. It can't."

***

Aaron heard Adina's words, but he couldn't seem to make sense of them as he stood there staring at the dead woman. A woman who, to hear the guards tell it, had been kind, a woman who'd had her own hopes, her own dreams, but whatever they'd been, now they were just as dead as she was.

She's right, you know, Co said, Boyce Kevlane's crimes are not yours.

But Aaron was barely listening. He was remembering a time, years ago, when he looked down on the bodies of his father and mother. Boyce Kevlane had murdered his parents just as he had murdered this woman here. Perhaps he hadn't done the actual killing, but he was responsible just the same. All because Aaron hadn't rolled over and died like a good little victim. And his parents ... his parents had died, according to the old wizard, because of a choice his father had made. He frowned, remembering Adney's words before the poison had killed him and turned to Darrell. "What choice?"

"Hmm?" The swordmaster said.

"Don't play with me, Darrell," Aaron growled, "you heard the man as well as I. In the past few months, I've been reunited with my childhood best friend only to have him try to kill me and to realize that he wasn't my friend at all—had never been my friend—was instead a creature, a man who was believed to have been dead for thousands of years if he ever existed at all. No matter how many wounds I inflicted, he healed right before my eyes, was able to shape his body into whatever he wanted. Before I threw him from the castle balcony, he told me that he'd murdered my parents because of a choice my father had made. Before, back in the cell, Adney talked much the same about a choice that you had made. Now, tell me what you're hiding!" It wasn't until he finished speaking that Aaron realized he'd been yelling.

The swordmaster said nothing, only stared at Aaron with that impassive expression on his face, and Aaron found the rage bubbling inside of him. "Even now you keep your damned secrets. Fine. Keep them. But I don't want anything else to do with you. Leave Perennia today—I don't want to see you again."

The swordmaster recoiled as if he'd been slapped, "Aaron, what secrets I have kept I've done to protect you."

Aaron barked a harsh laugh, "Oh, have you? And how's that working out, Darrell? Do I look safe? Do any of us?"

Darrell studied Aaron his expression troubled, "Aaron, I never meant ...."

"To the Fields with what you meant," Aaron shouted, "enough lies, Darrell. I've had enough to last me a lifetime. If you can't be honest with me now, if you won't tell me the truth even after all this, then I want nothing more to do with you. I don't have time for someone I can't trust."

The swordmaster narrowed his eyes, "You speak of trust, lad, but it seems to me that your Adney mentioned something of your own secret as well. I am not the only one here who hides things."

Aaron met the swordmaster's gaze and took a step closer to him, ignoring the hand Adina put on his arm in an effort to stop him. He held up a hand with his palm up, inches from the swordmaster's face. At first nothing happened, and he frowned. *Co. Do it.*

Aaron, are you sure—

Do it.

With that, a magenta light blossomed in the air above his palm, Co hovering, the storm of light inside her communicating the fact that she was troubled. For his part, the swordmaster's eyes went wide, and he took a step back, staring at Co with wonder. After a moment, he mastered his expression and nodded. "Which of the Seven is it?"

Aaron frowned, "Compassion."

The swordmaster's mouth twisted as if to suppress a laugh, but he couldn't hold back the smile that came. "Ah, but the gods do have a most interesting sense of humor." Then he grew serious once more, turning back to Co and dropping to one knee, bowing his head. "Evelyn Caltriss, princess most high, it is my pleasure and my honor to meet you."

Aaron grunted, shocked. He turned to look at Adina who met his eyes, his own surprise mirrored in her expression. "Evelyn Caltriss." Aaron repeated.

Co's light grew lighter, somehow communicating embarrassment. "Please rise, sir. The woman known as Evelyn Caltriss is no more. She and her family have been gone for thousands of years. There are few alive who remember them and fewer still who believe the stories they have been told."

"Forgive me, Highness," Darrell said, rising to his feet, "but there are those that do."

"Evelyn Caltriss," Aaron said again, his mind trying to work it through. "Wait a minute. That would mean—"

"Yes," Darrell said, "the Virtue to which you have bonded is Evelyn Caltriss, the daughter of Aaron and Elisandra Caltriss, princess of Palindra and heir to its throne. Possessed of a strength in the Art, it is said, that many believed to be a match even for Kevlane's himself."

"It has been long since I have been called by that name," Co said, her voice sad and melancholy. "As for the Art, sir, it matters little now. Time passes and the world changes. Things fade. What once was a deep well, where one need only dip a bucket to draw from, there exists now so much dust and memory. The world changes. Magic dies."

"Not all magic surely, highness," Darrell said.

"No," Co admitted, "not all magic. But what is left is a shadow of what it once was. And shadows, swordmaster, may only make more shadows."

Darrell bowed his head low in acquiescence, "As you say, highness."

Aaron decided to put Co's identity aside for later consideration. There had been too many revelations in too short a time. This one, at least, didn't seem to be one that would get him killed. Probably. "Now, Darrell," he said, "you know my secrets, such as they are. Will you tell me your own?"

Darrell considered that then finally shook his head, "No, Aaron. I will not tell you. I will show you."

CHAPTER ELEVEN

Gryle awoke to pain, his head pounding as if it would come apart. He quested at it with his fingers and whimpered as he felt the tender knot that had formed. He was lying on his back staring up at a wooden ceiling. Moaning, he eased himself into a sitting position. Dull pain throbbed in the back of his head, and his vision swam as he was overcome with a bout of dizziness. He closed his eyes in an effort to still the internal swaying and the sudden urge to vomit.

"Ah, it would appear that our guest has awakened."

Gryle opened his eyes. He saw that he was in what appeared to be a small cellar. The floor was hard-packed dirt, and he noticed with horror that his clothes were irreparably stained from where he'd lain unconscious. Ruined, he thought, I'll never get these clean. He wondered what the princess would think if she saw him in his current state, and he felt his face heat with embarrassment. His distress was cut short by a sneeze as he inhaled some of the cloud of dust that hung in the air. Out of habit, he reached for the kerchief he always kept in his trouser pocket but realized with a real sense of loss that it was gone.

The cellar appeared to be small—he'd had occasion to see bedrooms that were larger during his time in the castle—and he realized with a stab of fear that he had been locked inside a cell. He turned to the sound of the voice and saw a man sitting in a chair outside of his cell, his legs crossed, relaxing as if at some banquet, a small smile on his face.

The man was dressed in a fine cream doublet and trousers of excellent make that Gryle couldn't help but admire despite the circumstances, and he felt a fresh wave of shame at his own filthy, disheveled appearance. Two big men stood behind the seated one, and the only light in the cellar came from a torch one of them held. It did little to illuminate the rest of the room, only casting it in shadow, so Gryle could not see much beyond the three men. "What ... I'm sorry," Gryle said, "but ... I believe there may have been some mistake."

Gryle could see little of the man's face because of the shadows cast by the torch, but he saw enough to note that his smile grew wider, "Oh? And what mistake is that?"

Gryle swallowed hard. There was something about the man's smile that struck him as predatory. "I ... that is ... I have done nothing."

"Haven't you?" The man said, clearly enjoying the chamberlain's discomfort. "And do you not recognize me, chamberlain? I fear that my feelings might be hurt."

Gryle frowned, squinting his eyes in an effort to make out more of the man's features, but the shadows hid them well. "Forgive me, sir, I apologize but I ... I cannot see your face."

The man shook his head slowly, as if disappointed, "Ah, but you are an interesting one aren't you, chamberlain? After all, it is my men and I that have knocked you out and put you in a cage, yet you apologize to us."

"I ..." Gryle screwed up his courage, lifting his head, "a disagreement is not proper cause for one to lose one's comportment. Manners are the shield civilized society wields against savagery."

"Ah, you quote Thanium," the figure said, his smile stretching wider still, impossibly wide it seemed in the torchlight, "You are an educated man, chamberlain, and I respect that. I suppose I cannot be offended at your lack of recognition, considering that blow you took to the head and the poor lighting. I wonder," he said, motioning the man holding the torch forward with two fingers, "Does this help?"

The big man stepped forward and orange, ruddy light fell on the seated man's face, illuminating a scar that started beneath the man's left eye and stretched in a hook-like pattern to his right jaw. His head was bald, and even in the poor light, Gryle could see that he was thin, almost impossibly so. At first, Gryle could not place who it might be but then the memory came flooding back, and he let out a gasp of fear and surprise.

The thin man's mouth twisted strangely for several seconds as if unsure of what expression he might make then he finally grinned widely, his eyes going large in his face, "Ah, I think you do remember me, after all."

"Y-you're Aster Kalen," Gryle stammered." You ... you attacked us in Avarest and chased us on the Clandestine."

The man's smile suddenly vanished, and his face twisted with an insane rage. He bared his teeth, a hiss issuing from his throat and madness dancing in his eyes. "Yes," he growled, "and you fled like cowards." The last came out in a shriek, and Gryle let out an involuntary whimper, scooting backward in his cage until he fetched up against the bars.

In another moment, the rage that had so transformed the thin man's face vanished, and he was smiling once more. "Ah, forgive me," he said, rubbing his fingers over his eyebrows, "I do sometimes lose my temper. Still, it is good that you remember. It will save us time."

"What ... what do you want from me?" Gryle said, his forehead beading with sweat.

The thin man cocked his head strangely, studying Gryle. He was silent for several seconds then, "We'll get to that soon enough, chamberlain, I assure you. There is something that I will have you do for me. The least you could do, really," he said, his expression twisting into anger again, the transformation all the more shocking for its abruptness, "considering the trouble you and yours put me through. I do not forgive easily, chamberlain, and you have caused me much difficulty."

Gryle opened his mouth to speak and found that his throat had gone dry. He swallowed and tried again, "Sir, I'm sorry for any trouble we might have—"

"Oh, there's no need to apologize, Gryle," the thin man said, smiling once again, "Truly. You see, I have already discovered a way that you might pay me back, and you will pay me back, chamberlain. For now, though, I think that I would like to see you in pain."

He motioned to the big man not holding the torch, and the man stepped forward, producing a key from the pocket of his trousers. "Please, sir," Gryle squeaked as the big man worked the key into the lock, "I don't ... there is no need—"

"Perhaps there is no need," the thin man interrupted, "except that I will enjoy watching you scream. And you may scream, chamberlain, as loud as you like. This cellar is quite sound proof." He paused, winking, "It's the reason why I chose it, after all."

The big man stepped inside the cage, and Gryle gave a cry of fear as the man grabbed hold of his tunic and jerked him to his feet. "Ah, Gryle," the thin man said, producing what appeared to be an apple from the inside of his tunic and taking a large bite, "it is very good to see you again." With that, he nodded at the big man.

The man moved, shockingly fast, and a fist that felt as if it was made of iron struck Gryle in his stomach. The air left him in a whoosh, and he would have collapsed if not for the fact that the big man's other hand held him up. Gryle tried to scream but all that came out was a choked whimper, and the big man struck him in the stomach again. This time, he released Gryle, and the chamberlain fell to his hands and knees, gagging and vomiting on the dirt floor. He was still dry-retching when the man's open hand caught him in the face, a ringing slap that sent him sprawling in the dirt, his ear instantly numb.

"Not in the face, you fool!" Aster screamed, but if the big man responded, Gryle could not hear it over his own gasping wheezes.

He was still trying to get his breath back when strong hands pulled him to his feet, and he cried out as fists began to rain on his body, everywhere except his face. He was struck in his stomach, his arms, his thighs, even in his back, and excruciating pain beyond anything he'd ever known existed—beyond anything he'd known could exist—engulfed him. And soon, breath or no breath, Gryle began to scream.

Before he passed out, he thought he heard a woman's voice screaming for them to stop, but if the men heard, if the voice was even real, they gave no sign and the beating, and the pain, continued. Gryle wept and begged and screamed, but the beating did not stop, and when the darkness rose up in his mind and vision, Gryle welcomed it gratefully.

***

He awoke in agony, each breath sending a sharp pain lancing through his bruised and battered body. He had no concept of what time it was, or how much time had passed since he'd fallen unconscious. He only knew that the dirt beneath his face was cool and soft and welcoming. Some part of him warned that he should get up, should try to figure a way out of his cage, but even the thought of moving was enough to make him whimper. Not just with pain but also a fear of how much more pain he would feel if he did, for that was one thing he'd learned in that interminable length of time when the man was beating him—however much pain a man felt, he could always be made to feel more.

He remembered Aaron Envelar telling him once that life was pain. Gryle had not believed it at the time, but he believed it now. There was no hope of rescue, no urgency to escape. There was only the pain. That and nothing else. All else had been beaten from him. He wondered only why they had not killed him, and some part of him wished that they had. Another part, though, the small, logical part—weak and cowering in a corner as it was— whispered something into his memory. Not in the face, you fool.

The words, at first, seemed to have no meaning, no substance or significance. They were only words, existing far beyond the pain, far beyond Gryle himself. Something was clogging his throat, and he coughed, his whole body convulsing at the agony that lanced through him as he did and some liquid, wet and dark, came out of his mouth to land on the dirt inches from his face. He stared at it with eyes swollen from weeping in confusion for several moments and it took him some time to realize that it was blood. His blood.

He realized then that he'd been a fool, rushing off to save the princess like some knight out of a story. He was no knight, he knew that well. Knew it now even if he had not known it before, and the world was no children's story. The world was not made for knights and such things as happy endings were fancies and no more than that. He found himself weeping then, the tears streaming down his face, blubbering uncontrollably like a child. He was sickened, ashamed of his own weakness and that only made the tears come all the harder.

By the time they stopped, his breathing was shallow and ragged, his body shaking with small tremors. "Gods help me," he croaked.

"My ma always told me, the gods help those as help themselves."

Gryle started at the sound of the voice, and his fear gave him strength, allowing him to ignore the pain for a moment, as he slid across the cage until his back was against the wall. "Please," he wheezed, "no more. Please."

"Easy there, easy," the voice said, and Gryle realized it wasn't Aster's voice, but a woman's and from close by. The same woman, he realized, that he'd thought he'd heard screaming for them to leave him alone. "I'm not going to hurt you, friend," she said, "couldn't even if I wanted to."

Gryle looked at the room, really looked at it for the first time since he'd woken. A torch hung on the wall nearby, its sputtering flame illuminating the cellar in its orange, ruddy glow. On the far end of the room, an old woman in filthy rags sat in a cage identical to his own, studying him. He could see that the woman, too, had been beaten and whatever prohibition had kept the man from hitting Gryle in the face, it had not been extended to her.

Her nose was twisted at an odd angle, obviously broken, and her face was little more than one big, wrinkled bruise. "I ... I'm sorry," He said, holding a hand to his stomach where he thought a rib might have been cracked and flushing with embarrassment, "I didn't know anyone else was here."

"Sorry for what?" The woman said, "crying? Nah, there's no need for that. You weep, if you need to. The gods know I've done it enough. Sometimes, it's the only cure there is."

"I don't ... feel cured."

He couldn't tell for sure in the near darkness, but he thought the old woman smiled at that, "No, I don't expect you do. Neither did I, the times I did it, but I was healing anyway. When my

Franklin passed, I did it. When my daughter Hannah passed too. I recognize the type of cry—it's the weeping of a body that's lost someone or something they thought they'd have forever. So what it is that you've lost?"

Gryle shook his head slowly, "I always thought the world was a good place. There was pain, sure, but not only that. I thought ...." He laughed but there was no humor in it, "I thought that I could help her and the others. I thought that I could be a hero."

"And now?"

"Now, I realize I was a fool. I'm no hero. I'm not strong or smart—the pr—she would be better without me."

The old woman let out a cackle at that, "Smart is it? Strong? How about fast, lad? Many heroes you know fast?"

Gryle frowned, his eyebrows knitting together in confusion, "I suppose so. Yes, there have been tales of men and women with great speed with the sword or the bow. The histories—"

"Aw, let the histories be the histories, boy. All those heroes are dead and gone now anyway. And it isn't speed or strength, makes a hero, lad. It ain't even a fancy sword or how fine he might look without his shirt on. It never has been."

Gryle sniffed, not ready to stop feeling sorry for himself. "It's an easy thing to say," he said, "but that doesn't make it true. I'm useless to her. I can't fight, I can't do anything."

"Sure seems to me you worry an awful lot about this 'her' whoever she is."

"Yes," Gryle said, "it's my duty."

The woman snorted, "As you say. Anyhow, I've got something to show you. I don't make a habit of this, but I don't suppose it matters much now, one way or the other."

Gryle cleared his throat, "Ma'am, please, I appreciate your attempts to soothe me but, truly, there's no need to—"

She cackled again, "To what? What do you think I'm planning on doing, givin' you a look at my teats? Lad, they haven't been worth lookin' at for a long time now. Not exactly the thing you want to show a man, you're trying to cheer him up. Like as not, you'd take your own life right now. No, this is something different, so shut up and let me do what I aim to."

She held out her hand above the floor and suddenly a yellow light appeared, blossoming above her outstretched fingers.

Gryle gasped in surprise, "Gods ... which ... which is it?"

The old woman grunted, "Which, not what, huh?" She peered at him, "Seems to me, you know more about it than I would've expected."

Gryle nodded, "A friend ... well, a man that I would like to call friend has one."

"That so?" The woman said, "well, this here is Davin. A nervous chap, much like yourself but a good enough sort in his own way."

"Nervous?" The Virtue said in a hurt tone, "I don't think that's fair."

"Well," the old woman said, "mayhap it is, and mayhap it ain't, but I'm old enough I'll say what I want."

"You do realize," the Virtue said, "that I'm thousands of years old, don't you?"

She rolled her eyes at Gryle, "It's a good thing he is just a ball of light, otherwise, I don't suppose he'd be able to move, what with that big head of his he'd be lugging around after him."

Gryle found himself smiling at that, the pain forgotten for a moment at the wonder of seeing another of the Virtues in front of him.

"Beth, please," the Virtue said, "we can still try to make it out. The next time they come—"

"The next time they come'll be the same as the time before it," she said, "they've got Michael either way, and we both know well enough what happens, we don't do what they want."

"But ma'am—"

Beth grunted, waving her hand and suddenly the Virtue vanished back inside of her again. "You'll have to forgive him," she said, "a good enough sort, like I said, but he does harp, sometimes."

"Forgive me," Gryle said, "Beth, is it? But if you've got a Virtue then why are you in here?"

She snorted, "I'm here because I've got a Virtue, lad. That's why. Anyhow, back to the point I was tryin' to make. Davin is the Virtue of speed. Means that I'm the fastest old hag you're ever likely to meet. You'd be shocked how fast I can sew a quilt."

"That must be ... amazing," Gryle said.

The old woman, Beth, snorted again, "Is it? How old do you think I am, boy?"

Gryle fidgeted, "Ma'am, forgive me, but it wouldn't be polite to guess."

"Not polite to be thrown in a cage and get the shit kicked out of you either, but here we both are. And keep the ma'am stuff bottled up, you're around me. My teats sag a little more every time I hear it. I'm old enough I don't need reminding. Just call me Beth. Not Elizabeth or Bethany, just Beth. I'm a simple woman with a simple name and that's how I like it."

"Yes ma—" Gryle cut off as she narrowed her eyes and he cleared his throat, "That is ... yes ... Beth."

"Good," she said, nodding her approval, "Might be there's hope for you yet. Now, how old am I? And no more of this hemming and hawing. That might be fine for those noble women spend their time picking out dresses, their noses held so high lest they accidentally see one of us little folk."

"Beth," Gryle said, finding it almost painful to call her by her first name, to go against what he had been taught, "That is ... I would not want to guess wrongly and give offense."

"Lad, you keep goin' down the road you're headin' down, and I think I'll just about have to be offended. Now. How old?"

Gryle swallowed, thinking that the woman was eighty if she was a day. Eighty five or more, most likely. "Very well," he said, "if it is important to you ... sixty years?" He figured that would be safe enough.

The woman didn't appear offended, and he allowed himself to let out a slow breath. "Oh, lad, but you do carry on, don't you?" She said, grinning, "You and I both know I'm as close to looking sixty as I am to being a bird with wings and all the rest. Clever," she said, leaning in, "but not clever enough, I think. I'm forty-five years this winter."

"Impossible," Gryle said, the word slipping out of his mouth before he could stop it, and he gasped. "Forgive me, I didn't mean any offense, truly. Only...."

The old woman nodded, "Only I look like some dried up old carcass you'd be as like to find in a coffin as in a cell? There's no offense there, chamberlain. I know well enough how I look. It's the Virtue, you see. I was a girl of fifteen when I found him—or he found me, I guess you'd say."

"And it ... ages you?" Gryle said.

"So it does," Beth said, "so it does."

"But that ... that's awful."

The old woman shrugged, "Maybe it is and maybe it ain't. Some things, chamberlain, they ain't good or bad, they just are. A body can sit around moping about them, or she can do her best to change what she can and to accept the rest."

"But ... why would you do it?" Gryle said, "Why not give it to someone else?"

Beth laughed, "At first? Well, Davin told me, of course, let me know what would happen. But I was a fifteen year old girl and, like all fifteen year old girls, I thought I was invincible, that I'd live forever. Such a girl, in the flower of her youth, well, she doesn't believe it will ever end does she? It's a hard thing, believing there's such a thing as winter when you're in the middle of summer and every day is hot and bright without a cloud in the sky. Times like that, it's just about impossible to believe there's such a thing as cold in all the world, but winter comes anyway, don't it?"

"Yes," Gryle said, thinking of how comfortable he'd been serving King Markus, Adina's father, when he'd had everything he'd thought he wanted, and he thought about how easy a thing it was for it all to come crashing down around him. "But ... after?" Gryle said, "surely, when you got older...."

"Sure, I noticed," the woman said, "how not? Not at first, mind you. There was a time—more years than I'll tell so don't ask— where I thought I was just about the luckiest woman in the world. You see, I could jog faster than a horse could gallop, could finish the tasks my ma and pa gave me and go off kissing boys behind barns without ever gettin' a sore behind for leavin' my chores undone. I could do things ...." She shrugged, "well, suffice to say, moving that fast ... makes you almost feel like a god, and there are some things I did, I ain't exactly proud of. Never killed nobody— leastways, not then and never unless there was no choice—but I got into mischief, stealing and knowing I was safe to do it. Things such as that. I think any boy or girl would, given such a gift. And it is a gift, never mind the rest. Still," she said, her eyes getting a distant look, "I began to notice ... things."

"Things?" Gryle said.

The old woman shrugged, "Little at first, small enough that I could fool myself into believing nothing had changed, not really. I'd have some hair fall out, sometimes. Not in clumps, mind you, but enough that it would bother me for a bit. Then, I'd tell myself I had a whole head of hair and a few strands made no difference either way. After that, there were more things," she said, her voice melancholy, "my hair, I noticed, didn't shine like it once did—and you should have seen it, chamberlain, oh, how it used to shine. Wasn't long before I'd sneak off to the back of the barn only to find the boy I was supposed to meet had found another barn, another girl. Still, I told myself it wasn't anything to worry about. After all, boys are fickle things, men too as far as it goes, and there could have been any number of reasons why one barn called to 'em more than another on any givin' night. It was around that time I met Franklin, my husband. A good man. He was twenty-seven when I met him, and I myself was nineteen, but you wouldn't have known it. If anything, I figure folks probably thought him the type of man that liked getting along with older women and maybe he even was that."

Gryle stared at the woman, compassion welling up inside of him. He couldn't imagine what it would be like to age so quickly. "I'm sorry," he said.

She grunted, "Sorry, why? I'm not. Sure, I'll be meeting Salen faster than a lot, but there are others never get a chance to live long as I have. And anyway, the gods have gifted me in many ways. A wonderful husband, a loving daughter ...." She paused, wiping at her eyes, "and a sweeter grandson than an old hag like me deserves."

She paused then and although Gryle could not hear it, he could see the tears winding their way down her dry, leathery cheeks. "Your family..."

"Dead, chamberlain. Franklin going on ten years now, my daughter too. "

"I'm so sorry," Gryle said, feeling selfish for having been so worried about himself, about his own troubles.

"Ah, don't be," Beth said, "the world gives and the world takes, chamberlain. It's the way it is—the way it always has been. Ain't no reason to it, just a thing that happens is all. And, my experience, when the world gives a lot it takes it in equal measure. I've been blessed in a lot of ways, more than I ever deserved. Wouldn't be right of me to be angry about losin' something that was given to me despite the fact I didn't deserve it."

"And your grandson?" Gryle asked, hating himself even as the words were out of his mouth.

"Alive," the woman said, and for the first time, there was real sadness in her voice, a despondency that he didn't like but that he sympathized with, that he understood. "Least ways, he was, the last I seen him. I expect they'll keep him so, just so long as it suits them. Guess they figure I won't do anything stupid or reckless, I know they've got him." Her laugh was a dry, humorless thing, "More fool they. I'm too damned old and too damned tired to cause much of a problem now. Bout as reckless as I get is drinking a glass of water before bed time."

"They've taken your grandson?" Gryle said, stunned, "but ... is he here? Isn't there something you can do with...." He trailed off, unsure of how to continue.

"With the Virtue?" The old woman asked. "Oh, sure, plenty of things. Just now, I could run around this cage really fast, I took a mind to. I could also throw dirt at you so fast you'd be buried up to your ears before you knew it, so keep that in mind." She shook her head slowly, "No, chamberlain. This man, Aster, he knows well enough what I'm capable of—it's the reason why I'm here, after all. He only lets me out of this cage to use the privy, always takin' the time to remind me that they've got poor Michael, should I do anything foolish." She sighed sadly, and Gryle wished there was something he could say, something he could do.

But you can't, he said. You're a coward, and you always have been. What difference could a man such as you make? You're no warrior or hero out of the stories. Just a fat old chamberlain that can't even manage to stay close enough to his charge to do his job properly. "I'm very ... sorry," he said, knowing it sounded lame and weak but having nothing more to offer, "about your grandson."

Beth nodded, "As am I, chamberlain. As am I. Anyway, I know well enough why they've got me here. I'm being kept, Davin too, though for what purpose I don't know. Such men as this have been after me a long time though—it's the reason my daughter, gods watch over her, lost her life so many years ago. Still, that doesn't explain you sharing a cage beside me, so what is it? Why are you here?"

Gryle considered that, shaking his head slowly, "I don't ... I don't know."

The old woman grunted, "Well, I expect we'll find out before long. Anyway, seein's as we're cellmates—gods but that's not a sentence I'd ever thought I'd say and that's the truth—can I ask a favor of ya?"

"Sure."

"I wonder ... if you do end up getting a chance, if you could look after Michael for me, get him out, if you can. I don't ask that you try to save me—that'd be about the same as closing the barn door after the chickens are out—and anyway, my fate's been comin' for me for a long time, bought and paid for. I don't begrudge it none. But the boy ... he shouldn't be made to suffer for my mistakes. Do you think you could promise me that?"

Gryle opened his mouth to speak, to tell her of course he would do anything he could for her grandson, but the words wouldn't come. They lodged somewhere in his throat until he thought he might choke on them. Lies, they'd be and nothing more. He was a coward and a fool and of no use to anyone. He remembered wanting to fight back, when the man had been beating him, but he had not. He had only stood or fallen as the blows had demanded, had whimpered and cried and waited for it to stop. That was not how a hero behaved and anything he told her wouldn't even be to soothe her but to soothe himself and so he said nothing.

"That's alright then," the old woman said after a time, and she nodded her head slowly, trying for a smile that nearly broke Gryle's heart, "That's alright."

But it wasn't alright, he knew that. It just was, so he slouched back into the corner of his cell and sat down, let his head hang to his chest, and waited for whatever would come.

CHAPTER TWELVE

"Just where in the name of the gods are you taking us?" Aaron asked.

He glanced over past Adina, and Leomin—the Parnen had materialized from whatever woman's bed he'd been hiding in when they'd exited the dungeons—to study his old swordmaster. Darrell had spoken little since they'd left the dungeons, and Aaron frowned, wondering if he could trust the man. Obviously, if he'd wanted Aaron dead, he could have accomplished it easy enough, needed only to have let Adney and the others do what they'd come to do. Still, you could make a man suffer in plenty of ways without killing him—Aaron's time at the orphanage had shown him that, and he'd learned the lesson better than most.

"Not much farther now," Darrell said, not turning to meet Aaron's eyes. His expression was stiff, his body too, as if in anticipation of something and despite the fact that Aaron knew it wouldn't make any sense for the swordmaster to set them up to be killed now after he'd risked his life saving Aaron as well as the others back in Baresh, he found himself studying the alleyways they passed for any sign of an ambush. Still, he saw no sign of anything suspicious and soon Darrell was leading them down a street where only the richest and wealthiest in the city lived. They walked past houses that couldn't rightly be called houses at all but manses or manors. The massive buildings sat on either side of the avenue, settled among ornately carved sculptures and fountains or gardens that seemed to contain more varieties of flowers and plants than Aaron had ever known existed.

"You said not much farther fifteen minutes ago," Aaron said, feeling out of place on such a street and half expecting the guards that patrolled at regular intervals to stop him and ask him just what it was he thought he was doing in a place like this. They didn't though, and that was just as well. Aaron was low on patience just then, the rage steadily boiling inside of him, and had they asked the question, he felt reasonably sure that they would not have liked the answer he gave them.

"These are truly wondrous gardens," Leomin said, marveling at the brightly colored blooms surrounding either side of a path leading to one of the houses they passed. They'd explained to him what had transpired with Adney as they'd walked—or, at least, Adina had, Aaron had been too angry, too suspicious of his long time teacher to do it—but the Parnen didn't appear to be worried in the least, smiling and nodding at the richly dressed nobles they passed.

Gods help me to keep my patience.

What patience? Co asked.

Aaron scowled, Thanks for that.

Of course, Co said, and he heard the smile in her tone.

"Anyway," Aaron said, "will you at least tell us who you're taking us to see?"

"You will know yourself, soon enough, lad," Darrell said.

Maybe not soon enough to save someone from being strangled, Aaron thought, but he only nodded and followed as the swordmaster led them further down the street.

Eventually, Darrell walked up toward the wrought iron gate of one of the largest, most expensive-looking houses they'd come across. The frame of the gate had been painted gold. Aaron walked up, peering through the slats in the gate, and saw a massive fountain, easily as high as three men standing on each other's shoulders. The fountain had a total of six circular platforms that grew smaller towards its top and water cascaded down it on all sides, the sun hitting it in such a way that it appeared not to be water at all but liquid gold, no doubt the intention of whoever had taken the time to craft such a massive—and massively useless—thing. Tall hedges of bushes lined the walk, circling around the fountain and leading off to the left and right while a third branch leading up to the house itself.

Two house guards stood at the wrought iron gate, eyeing Aaron warily. "So," he said, "your master's fallen on hard times has he? A shame."

The two men remained silent and expressionless, watching him with eyes that didn't blink. "Alright boys," Aaron said, "much more of that, and I'm gonna start thinking the fountain isn't the only sculpture around here and that your master had so much gold burning a hole in his trouser pockets that he decided to get the sculptor to hang around and craft him a couple of particularly ugly statues to stand watch."

The two men gave no indication that they'd heard him at all, only staring at him blankly, and he was about to say something else when Darrell walked up. "Dillon, Royce, how are you?"

The two guards turned and smiled at him. "Darrell," one of them said, offering the hand that had been grasping the handle of the sword at his side when Aaron approached, "it's good to see you again."

Darrell smiled back, clasping the man's hand. "It's good to be seen, Royce. Tell me, how have things been?"

The other man, Dillon, shrugged, "Nothing much has happened, sir. It's all been a bit boring, to tell you the truth."

Darrell nodded sympathetically, "Well, perhaps you'll get lucky and have something to use those swords on before long."

The two men grinned, "We can hope so," Royce said. "Anyway," he glanced at Aaron, "I was just thinking the same thing."

Aaron gave the man a smile, "I'm game if you are."

"Now, now," Darrell said, "enough of that both of you. Royce, we've come to see the master of the house."

The guard raised an eyebrow, glancing at Aaron and the others before looking back to Darrell. "You and your ... friends?"

"Yes, all of us."

The two men glanced at each other, "You're sure?" Dillon said. "Is the master expecting you?"

"No," Darrell said, "but she'll want to see me anyway."

Royce sighed, shrugging, "You're the boss, of course." His expression grew serious, "Challenge: Some men are cold and some are hot, some will freeze and some will not. What is the difference?"

Aaron snorted, "A jacket."

The guard raised an eyebrow but didn't turn away from Darrell. "Perception," Darrell said.

The guard smiled, "Welcome back, sir." He nodded to his fellow guard and soon they were swinging the golden gates open. Darrell bowed his head to the two then began down the path toward the house.

Aaron stared after him for a moment, frowning in thought. "A jacket?" Adina said at his side, and he turned to see her smiling.

Aaron shrugged, "Better than perception. What kind of answer is that, anyway? If I'm freezing, keep the perception and give me a blanket."

Adina shook her head slowly, "Aaron what is this? Who are we supposed to meet?"

Aaron saw that she and Leomin were both looking to him, as if he had some answer. He shrugged. "Let's go find out."

They caught up to Darrell outside the mansion's door as the swordmaster paused to knock. "Perception, seriously?" Aaron said, "What kind of answer is that?"

The swordmaster glanced at Aaron, meeting his eyes, "The only one. The questions change but the answer does not."

Aaron grunted, "Kind of makes them useless as far as riddles go."

Darrell gave him a small smile, "As far as riddles go, yes, you're correct. If it helps," he said, winking, "I liked your answer."

Aaron was about to respond when the door swung open. Two more guards stood staring at them, "Welcome back, sir. Some men are cold some are h—"

"Perception," Aaron said, "now can we move this along? I've got things I'd rather be doing—asking Malakson for another one of his drinks, maybe."

The two guards glanced at each other then back at Darrell. The swordmaster sighed, "I would tell you that my friend here isn't truly as much of a pain as he seems, but I try to make it a habit not to lie. Still—we need to see the master."

The two guards shared a look before turning back to Darrell, "This is highly irregular, sir." One said.

"These are irregular times," Darrell answered.

The guard grunted, "True enough. Come on, we'll take you."

With that, they turned and started into the house, leading Aaron and the others past several more sets of guards positioned at each doorway. Aaron peered inside as they walked by and saw richly appointed rooms that looked as if they'd belong more in a wealthy king's chambers than in a random house. "Lot of security here," Aaron said, meeting a guard's unflinching stare as they made their way down a hallway.

"Yes," Darrell said, but he did not choose to elaborate.

Finally, they took a branching path in the hallway and came to an intersection guarded by two more armed men, their swords sheathed at their sides. "Darrell," One of the guards said, an older man with a salt and pepper beard. "It's good to see you back, sir."

Darrell nodded his head in turn, "I wish I could say the same, Samuel. We need to see her."

The older guard glanced between Darrell, Aaron and the others. "So many?"

Darrell nodded again, "I'm afraid it's necessary."

Samuel nodded, "Very well." The other guard who'd been silent thus far bent and retrieved a wooden bucket that had sat near his feet. "Please empty your pockets into the bucket," Samuel said, "shoes as well."

Aaron frowned, "Shoes?"

"Yes," the older guard said and, by way of explanation, "they make too much noise."

Aaron shared dubious looks with Adina and Leomin, but Darrell was already removing his boots and putting them in the bucket, so he bent down and went about taking off his own. "Now what?" He asked as he tossed his boots in the bucket, "Do you want us to hop on one leg, maybe?"

Samuel looked at Darrell, his face as expressionless as a statue, "He's funny."

Darrell sighed, "I'll take your word for it."

"You picked a good day, at least," the other, younger guard said, "there have been some bad ones lately. Sometimes—"

"Enough of that," Samuel snapped, "that is none of their concern—Darrell here has enough to worry about without you adding to it."

The youth colored but did not speak. Samuel studied him for a moment then nodded, turning back to Aaron and the others, "My apologies. You remember the way?" He asked Darrell.

"Of course."

"Very well." The two guards stepped aside, and Aaron followed as Darrell led them down a long set of stairs that led to another hallway. There were no lanterns hung here, no windows to let in sunlight, so each step took them further and further into darkness. As soon as he concentrated on his feet, Aaron realized that he was walking on the thickest rug or carpet he'd ever felt. His foot sunk into it almost all the way to the ankle.

"They make us take off our shoes, but they don't take our weapons?" Aaron said, "Strange."

"None that mean harm will make it this far without alerting the rest of the manse," Darrell said.

"What if they meant quiet harm, though?" Aaron asked, "From my experience, assassins and murderers don't yell out a warning before they attack."

He was just able to see the swordmaster's smile in the growing shadows of the hallway, "Trust me. They would be heard. Now, please everyone, keep your voices low and be as quiet as you can."

Aaron, Co said, *something is here. Do you feel it?*

Aaron followed after Darrell and the others, considering. The truth was that he did feel something. It was a similar feeling to the one a man would sometimes get when he walked into a room and knew, immediately, that he was not alone. Such a man didn't have to hear or see anything because he felt it. Felt that there was someone else there. *Yes*, he thought back, *there's ... something. What is it?*

I don't know.

Well, that's alright, princess. I guess we'll figure it out soon.

Don't call me that, Co said, I told you, I am not that person anymore.

Right, Aaron thought, not a person at all, really. She subsided into brooding silence at that, and he found himself grinning. They walked on for some time and when they took a branch in another corridor, Darrell lifted up what appeared to be a long drape of black cloth that went all the way from the ceiling to the floor "This way." They walked on, taking several different branches of corridors, seemingly turning at random, the light growing dimmer and dimmer as they did until soon they were walking in complete darkness.

Aaron reached out his hand so that he might use the wall of the hallway as a guide and found that his fingers were running across cloth. The fabric had been hung a few inches away from either wall and the curtains—if that's what they were—continued on without fail. A hand grasped his in the darkness—Adina's—and he held it, surprised by the strength of her grip. It was clear enough that she didn't like this strange journey into darkness, and he squeezed her hand back, offering what comfort he could.

The truth was, he was glad for it, the chance to touch another human. He realized that he knew little of true darkness. He'd spent time enough out at night, sure, in the Downs and in the forest training with his men. But it had been different then. In the city, there was always lantern light spilling onto the shadowed road or the sputtering orange flame of torches moving in the night. Even in the forest, there had been the moon and the stars. Poor light, often faint, but light just the same. Something to mark itself in the darkness, something to allow a man to mark himself.

Here, though, there was only dark, a dark so deep and prevalent that it seemed almost alive with purpose. It was the dark of the grave, a dark which was normally only looked on by eyes glazed over with death, and he found that he did not care for it, not at all. The hanging cloth and the thick carpet almost completely muted their footsteps, too, so that, before Adina had grabbed his hand, it had seemed as if he traveled some path sewed together of shadow, a path that had no beginning and no ending, that was not really a path at all only nothingness. A vast, complete nothingness that stretched on and on, never going anywhere and never coming from anywhere, only existing.

Eventually, Darrell came to a stop—a thing Aaron only learned when he tried to take a step forward and found himself bumping into the man. He let out a grunt, barely managing to right himself, feeling as if all of his limbs existed beyond him in the complete darkness, as if they might, in fact, not exist at all but be nothing more than passing fancies of his imagination. "We're here," Darrell said, his voice coming out in little more than a whisper. "Please, I need you all to speak quietly."

"Darrell," Aaron said, "What the fuck is going on?"

"Do you trust me, Aaron?"

Aaron hesitated for a moment, remembering the man, Boyce Kevlane, remembering how he'd turned into Owen. Of course, he hadn't turned into Owen, not really. Owen as Aaron had known him, had never truly existed at all. He was only a skin, a mask of flesh and bone to be put on and thrown off whenever it suited its wearer. Still, Darrell was not Owen. The man had saved Aaron's life a dozen times or more and the lessons he'd taught an angry youth when he didn't have to teach him anything had saved his life hundreds of times. "Yes," he said finally, "I trust you."

"Good," Darrell said. "Now, let us proceed." The swordmaster held aside a thick drape of cloth and opened the door—Aaron only knowing he'd done it by the accompanying sounds and the shifting of air as the door eased open, quieter than any he'd had ever heard before. They filed behind Darrell into a room—or, at least, Aaron felt as if it was a room—that was as dark as the hallway itself. He couldn't have guessed at the dimensions of it, but he had the feeling that it was fairly small.

"Ah, Darrell," a woman's voice said from out of the darkness, "it is good to see you."

Darrell shifted beside him, and Aaron thought that the man must be bowing. "The pleasure is mine, mistress. But ... were you expecting me?"

"Say that I had a feeling you would be coming soon," the woman said, amusement in her tone. "There are a few perks to being what I am, seeing what others do not is one, of course, as you well know. And anyway, I would have known it was you even without my sight, for I could smell the chamomile on you nearly as soon as you came down the steps."

"Chamomile?" Aaron asked.

"Yes," the woman from the darkness said, "our Darrell here is a very complex, very unique individual. He has found a penchant for using the herb in his baths, and I don't begrudge him it. It is supposed to be good for many things, relaxation chief among them and with times being what they are, we all must find our peace where we may. But I am being rude, forgive me. My name is Tianya Velar. And you, I suspect, must be Aaron Envelar."

Aaron frowned, "How could you know that?"

"Nothing untoward I assure you," Tianya said, "only, Darrell has spoken of you often, and I find that his description is accurate enough."

"Oh?" Aaron said, "Well, don't believe everything he tells you. I'm not quite as much of a bastard as he makes out."

The woman laughed at that, a rich, full sound. "Oh, you need not worry, Aaron. Darrell has nothing but the best of things to say about you."

"Forgive me, ma'am," Adina said, "but why have we been brought here?"

"Ah, yes," the woman said, "and you must be Princess Adina. Truly, the stories of your beauty do not do you justice, princess. It is no wonder, then, that the sellsword loves you as he does."

Aaron cleared his throat, "Um ... if it's all the same to you, I'd just as soon we left my and Adina's relationship out of it."

"Forgive me," the woman said, "I did not mean to offend. It is only ... sometimes, in the act of seeing a thing, of knowing a thing, I find myself expressing it without giving any thought to what such an expression might cause. I apologize and must apologize twice, for I fear I do not know the name of your friend here."

"Leomin, ma'am," the Parnen said, "Darrell has said nothing of me? I am surprised you have not heard of me."

"Yes," the woman laughed, "and I as well considering what it is that you carry." Aaron tensed at that, felt Leomin tense beside him, "Oh, please, relax yourselves," she said, "for I mean you no harm. Just the opposite, in fact."

"I was the one that saved Darrell's life," Leomin said annoyed, and Aaron couldn't stop himself from grinning.

"And we are all very thankful, brave Leomin. Now," she said, ignoring Aaron's quiet snort, "I think I know well enough why

Darrell has brought you here. Two of you, it seems, possess one of the Seven."

"What?" Aaron said, startled, "How could you kn—"

"It is writ plain in the lines across your face, sir," the woman said. "It is only that it is written in a language none but I can speak. Or so it sometimes seems to me. Your friend, Leomin here, carries Charisma, if I am not mistaken. And how is Aliandra treating you, friend?"

"She's ... fine," Leomin said, clearly taken aback and finding it difficult to respond, "that is ... I do enjoy our time together. Mostly."

The woman laughed, "Mostly, is it? Yes, I suspect it is. And you, Aaron? How is your bond with E—your own Virtue?"

"You can say her name," Aaron said, "I know it well enough. Have only just learned it recently, in fact. Anyway, it's fine. Now, why don't you tell me who you are and why we're here."

"Very well," the woman said, "though the telling may take some time. Does your arm bother you? I can call a healer, if you feel the need."

Aaron frowned again, "And how do you know that? And don't feed me any shit about you seeing it—it's covered by my cloak well enough not to mention that it's pitch black in this room. And why exactly is it so dark in here, anyway?"

"Forgive me," Tianya said, "you're right, of course." There was the rustle of movement and suddenly a gray sphere of light appeared in the room, and Aaron took a step back, his hand going to the handle of his sword. The sphere did little to illuminate the rest of the room, but it was enough that Aaron could see the vague outline of a gray-haired woman sitting behind a desk. She appeared to be in her fifties or sixties, though she had aged well, her cheekbones high and pronounced, her hair, upon closer inspection, not really gray at all but a bright silver. Her face bore few wrinkles, and she did not give the impression of being weak or infirm. Quite the opposite, in fact. "This," the woman said, "is Ursel. Ursel is one of the beings that have come to be known as the Virtues."

"Pleasure to meet you all," the Virtue said, but his tone didn't seem pleased at all to Aaron. Indifferent at best.

114

Suddenly, Co and Aliandra appeared in the room, so that there were three balls of light hovering in the darkness, one gray, one orange, one magenta. "Ursel, is that you?" Aliandra asked, the orange sphere floating closer, "my, but it has been a long time. Tell me, what have you been doing with yourself? How has the world been treating you?"

"Fine," the gray Virtue responded in that same lifeless voice.

"Ursel?" Co asked, and there was some emotion in her voice that Aaron couldn't quite identify.

The gray orb turned and somehow Aaron knew that its attention was focused on Co, "Evelyn?"

Co sped forward, a streak of magenta in the darkness until she was only inches from the gray Virtue. "It is good to hear your voice after so long," Co said, her voice charged with some emotion Aaron couldn't identify, "I ... there is so much that I want to say to you. So much that I should have said long ago and never mind my family."

Aaron frowned, watching the two Virtues. The man had clearly been someone important to Co but who? From the way she spoke, it sounded as if they had been lovers.

"It does not matter," Ursel said, and he could have been speaking about the weather for all the lack of emotion his voice expressed, "those times are done."

"But Ursel," Co said, "Please—"

The gray sphere of light shifted, hovering closer to Tianya's face, "May I return?" He asked in that same dull, lifeless voice. Aaron at first thought it was bored, but even that wasn't right. Boredom would have indicated some sort of feeling or emotion.

The woman gave a smile that was almost sad, "Of course, Ursel." The virtue floated toward Tianya's chest and, in another instant, was gone. "You must forgive him," she said, "He is not particularly fond of speaking with people he does not know." She paused then, "Or people he does know, in truth."

"No kidding," Aaron said, finding himself annoyed for Co's sake, "I've seen dead men with more personality."

"Yes," the woman said, and Aaron could hear the smile in her voice, "still, you must understand that the nature of what Ursel is has had certain ... side effects. Though he is not particularly well-versed in social situations—as you might have noticed—he has many gifts. Ursel is a watcher, a listener, and I do not exaggerate when I say that he is the best at both of anyone or anything in the world. He notices things that no one else will—that no one else even can."

Aaron frowned as Co floated closer to him, and through the bond they shared he felt her sadness, a deep well of regret and something like shame. "Are you okay, firefly?" He asked.

"Please, Aaron, if it is okay ... I would rather not speak of it just now."

Aaron nodded, not liking how similar Co's voice had become to Ursel's. "Of course" he said, "whatever you want."

With that, she hovered toward him and, in an instant, she, too, was gone. "Oh, Evelyn," Aliandra said, the yellow in her sphere growing darker and duller, "I am sorry." Then she vanished, and they were left in darkness once more.

"Okay," Aaron said, "just what was all that about?"

The woman sighed, "Old pains, I do not doubt. Understand, Mr. Envelar, that before the Virtues became what they are now, they were only men and women, little different than you or I except in the fact that they could use the Art. Such manipulation of the forces of the world, I'm told, has not been possible for many hundreds and hundreds of years. Even then, it was rare, and such men and women as were found with the ability were carefully protected and schooled in its use. They were allowed to go out, of course, but with such protection as to discourage any who might be tempted to socialize with them, and the Princess Caltriss even more than the rest. It is no great wonder that among them, within such a climate, certain ... relationships may have developed."

"Oh, Co," Adina said in a whisper, "I am so sorry."

"What about your Virtue then?" Aaron asked, "I've got to be honest with you, lady, he seems like a dick."

"He is what he is, Mr. Envelar," the woman said, "it is my belief that in order to deal with his new existence, Ursel was forced to repress his own emotions to such a degree and for so long that they may no longer even exist. A cruel decision, perhaps, but a necessary one. Had he not made it, I suspect he would be much like Melan, the Virtue of Strength, is now. Insane and beyond all reason. It is no easy thing, Mr. Envelar, to notice everything, to hear the padding of a man's footsteps from two blocks away, or to see everything in an eye blink. The world is full of sights and sounds, of smells and sensations even to regular people. For one such as Ursel—or one such as myself who he has chosen to bond with—there are a hundred fold more, all coming at once no matter what you do. Understand, Mr. Envelar, that such a gift is its own curse, for even in sleep what might be imperceptible to most thunders in my—and Ursel's—head like the world's most terrible lightning storm. It is not something that you can ever stop doing— it is not something that you can turn off."

Aaron grunted. Didn't sound like a whole lot of fun, that. Made him almost glad that all he did was get murderously angry over the smallest thing. Almost. "That's the reason then," he said, "for the lack of lights and the cloth drapes everywhere. For why the guards took our shoes."

"Yes," Tianya said, "that is the reason. You see, Mr. Envelar and you others, the darkness here might seem complete to you, but I assure you it is not. I am not even certain that there is such a thing as true darkness, true silence, and if there is, I have never known it. Even here, even with the precautions I have taken, I can still see you as well as you might see each other on a moonlit night. I can hear the rhythmic beats of your hearts in your chest, can feel the movement in the air at each breath you all take."

"That must be terrible," Adina said.

"It is the cost," Tianya said, "that's all. There is always a cost in this world, even in the mundane. Creatures and constructions of magic—such as the Virtues—have their own costs and as they are not natural but an imposition on the natural world, their costs are greater."

"Maybe they're not natural," Aaron said, feeling Co's emotions whirling in him, her sadness gaining strength with each word the woman spoke, "but I'll tell you something, lady. Co might be a pain in the ass sometimes, and seeing a starving dog might be enough to bring me to tears, thanks to her, but she has saved my life a dozen times or more, and I couldn't ask for a better companion."

"You misunderstand me, Mr. Envelar," the woman said, "I do not begrudge the Virtues their existence; I only try to explain the effect that they will have. You and your man there know it well by now, I imagine. The Virtues are creatures of light and darkness

117

both, born from a man's noble sacrifice in an effort to save his people and born from that same man's death as well and the deaths of those mages who tried to assist him. The Virtues give a man or woman great power, but they always take their price. I suspect that you have experienced this, have you not?"

With the woman's last words, a vision of such power flashed through Aaron's mind that he took a staggering step, a hand going to his head as pieces of the dreams that had plagued him for the last several weeks flashed in his mind. Fire and blood and the sweet, cloying smell of cooking meat. Screams of terror and fear and pain but not only that. Somewhere amid that roaring fire that seemed to engulf the entire world, somewhere among it, came an answering voice, this one not screaming in pain at all, but in joy and hunger. His voice.

"Are you quite alright, Mr. Envelar?"

Aaron didn't answer, couldn't have answered even if he'd wanted to, for his teeth were clamped tightly shut, his jaw aching as a pressure began to build in his mind. Suddenly, unexpectedly, the rage flashed up within him, and he narrowed his eyes at the form of the woman, now glowing a faint magenta in the darkness.

He and Adina and Leomin had been dragged here without being told so much as a reason, and now this woman was arrogant enough to force him to remember things he would rather forget. He bared his teeth then, his hand going to the sword at his back. It would be such an easy thing to move forward, to draw his blade and answer her questions in blood. Such an easy thing. Do it, a voice said into his mind, kill her.

"Aaron?" He felt Adina's hand on his shoulder, "what's wrong?"

Aaron turned at the sound of her voice and saw her, too, outlined standing beside him, her expression troubled as she stared into the darkness, not seeing him despite the fact that he was right beside her. As he looked at her, the anger began to fade, leaking out of him like wine from a pierced wineskin, and he let out a breath he hadn't realized he was holding. "I'm okay, Adina," he said. "Really."

"Such anger in you," Tianya said, and for the first time she sounded troubled, "I have never seen its like. Tell me, Aaron, this rage that you feel. Has it been getting worse?"

Aaron winced at Adina's expectant, worried expression. Normally, she would have hidden her worries for him behind a smile, but she did not realize now that he could see her, and he saw her fear writ plain across her face. He wanted to lie, to say what words needed to be said to steal the fear and the worry from Adina's expression. But it would do him no good, in the end, to deny what was happening. This woman, here, was his best chance of learning some way to control it. "Yes," he said, turning his eyes away from Adina, not wanting to see the effect his words caused, "It is getting worse—has been for some time now. I sleep little and when I do my dreams are ... troubling."

The woman nodded, "I see. I have never seen someone so powerfully bonded to their Virtue as you, Aaron Envelar. It means that the gifts the bond gives to you will be greater than any that have come before you. Unfortunately, so will its curse."

Aaron swallowed hard, his palms aching where his fingernails had dug into them when he'd clenched his fists in anger, "Surely there must be some way to stop it. If you know as much about this as you act like, you must know a way."

The woman shook her head sadly, "I am sorry, Mr. Envelar, but if there is a way, I do not know it. The magic always takes its toll. With those for whom the bond is weaker, the cost is less, but it is always there."

Aaron nodded. It had been a poor, weak hope anyway. "And your own bond?"

"You have seen well the way in which I live, Mr. Envelar. I myself sleep little, for sounds make their way even into this place. We have several houses such as this scattered about Telrear and it is much the same no matter which I find myself in. Traveling, though, is worse. We use a covered wagon, the wheels muffled as best we can, but I do not sleep on such trips, and I must take breaks, for to travel in such a way for too long would mean madness. We have been in Perennia for a week and, even still, I am not fully recovered."

"'We,' you say. Tell me, Tianya, who is this 'we' you speak of? And if traveling is so terrible, why have you come to Perennia at all? And lastly, what do you want with us?"

"As for the last," the woman said, "I had not known you and your friend, Leomin, each possessed one of the Seven until you walked through my door. Still, we will get to that. Regarding your, second question of why I have traveled here, I believe you know, don't you? Given what transpired at the castle not so very long ago?"

Aaron frowned, "You heard, then. It was supposed to be kept secret."

The woman laughed at that, "Oh, Mr. Envelar, if what Darrell tells me of your life is true, then you know as well as I that secrets never last. They cannot, men being what they are."

Aaron grunted. "And the other?"

"As for who we are ..." Tianya said, "that will take some time."

"Well," Aaron said, "my swordmaster once told me that the sooner you begin a thing the sooner it's done."

He saw the woman smile at that, "Yes, I suppose you're right. Forgive me, all of you, but to make you understand who we are, you must understand where we came from."

"If you say another planet, I'm walking out right now," Aaron said.

Tianya laughed, "No, not another planet, I'm afraid. I can assume, then, that you all know the story of the Seven and how they were made? Of Caltriss's rise and fall?"

"I know some small amount, my lady," Leomin said.

"Yes," Adina said, and the single word was enough for Aaron to hear the worry in her voice, a worry that she tried to hide. Not that he needed to hear it, really. His bond with the Virtue had been growing stronger, that much was true, and he found that he usually knew the way people felt, particularly, it seemed, those closest to him. Just now, for instance, Darrell felt nervous, and that bothered Aaron. It didn't bode well for what the woman would say.

"Very well," Tianya said, "you must understand, though, that the creation of the Virtues was not discovered until several years later, after the barbarians had conquered and looted and burned, and there was nothing left of Caltriss's fabled city but ash and the echoes of the dead. No, but I am telling it wrong ... forgive me, for I have never had to try to tell the story in one sitting. You see, in Caltriss's time, he had a select group of bodyguards, the best warriors in the kingdom. These men and women would follow him and keep him safe, for the barbarians were savage, true, but they were also clever, devious, and there was no end to their cruelty.

They would send assassins from time to time, men and women whose sole purpose was to see Caltriss dead. Often, those they sent would be individuals whose families were held by the barbarians under threat of torture and death should they fail. Under the guise of refugees, these reluctant assassins would sneak into the city and search for opportunities to murder Caltriss.

"Huh," Aaron said, "Sounds to me like it would make security a real bitch."

"You are correct, Mr. Envelar. As you have pointed out so eloquently, the constant influx of people made many of those closest to Caltriss concerned for his safety as attempts on his life became more and more frequent. At first, his friend, Boyce Kevlane, tried to convince Caltriss to bar the city gates and not allow anyone else to enter. Caltriss, though, would hear none of it. You see, Caltriss was one of those rare men who truly cared for others, a ruler whose concern was not only for his own people— even this is rare enough, I find—but for everyone, and so no matter how much Boyce Kevlane spoke of the dangers, no matter how many daggers came for him in the night, Caltriss would not relent. You must understand that the world loved Caltriss, and Caltriss loved the world, and so he would not abandon it to its fate under the barbarian hordes, would not allow even the threat of losing his own life deter him from his cause."

"Yeah," Aaron snorted, "and he shat rainbows and puked butterflies too."

"I see that you are cynical, Mr. Envelar," Tianya said, "and the truth is I do not blame you. The world does not often make such men as Aaron Caltriss. Still, the things I tell you now are only truths, and you may accept them or not, that is your choice. Would you hear them?"

"I guess," Aaron said, "assuming there's a point coming anytime soon."

"Aaron," Adina scolded, "Please, ma'am, continue."

"Very well," Tianya said, "as I was saying, Caltriss refused to abandon the people to their fates, no matter the danger. Seeing this, Kevlane came up with another strategy. You see, Aaron Caltriss had always had bodyguards, of course, but Boyce Kevlane took it a step further, creating a training and screening process for the men who would protect his friend and king that is said to have been the most difficult ever to be created. Such men were not tested only in their skill at arms—though they were tested in this, and vigorously—but also for loyalty and obedience and any other quality that Kevlane thought important. They were pitted against each other in tests of skill—many of which the men did not survive. They were spied on, their families thoroughly interrogated as Kevlane and his men searched for any possible sign of deceit, even going so far as to use the Art on each applicant to determine their natures and, it is said, to experiment on them. Unfortunately, the histories say that these experiments were not always successful and many men and women died or were mutilated for life in the attempt."

"Experiments?" Aaron said, frowning, "what kind of experiments?"

"As you've surely heard, Boyce Kevlane was the most powerful magi of his age in a time that held the most powerful magi of any age. Caltriss, also, was his best friend. A man with such powers, with such motivations ... there is little he will not do and little he could not. The experiments were small, at first, spells and incantations to make men and women stronger and faster, to make them be able to know if a suspect was lying or telling the truth, things such as that. From everything we know, Kevlane was humane in his work, at least at first. It is said that he only ever worked with those men and women who volunteered and that their families were guaranteed to be cared for should anything happen to them in the working of the Art."

"But as time went on and the assassination attempts continued even as the experiments failed, Kevlane began demanding more from his Art and more from those men and women who volunteered for the experiments. He grew more desperate and, in his desperation, less careful. Men and women died, dozens of them. Abominations were made and then destroyed, and the lucky ones were left mutilated and scarred for the rest of their lives."

"When Caltriss heard of this, of what the men and women who wished to protect him were being subjected to, he grew wroth. The histories say that Caltriss nearly slew Kevlane, and that it was only by the word of Elisandra, Caltriss's wife, that he lived. For, you see, Caltriss's wife loved him deeply, as completely as any one person can love another. She begged Caltriss for Kevlane's life, told him that the mage had only done what he thought was necessary, explained that dozens had died so that Caltriss—and thereby thousands of innocents who relied on him for safety and protection—might live. Finally, Caltriss agreed to pardon Kevlane and those who had assisted him in his endeavors, though Caltriss forced his friend to stop his experiments."

"I have ... I have never heard this story before, ma'am," Leomin said, "and, forgive me, but I have made a study of all of the available histories of Aaron Caltriss and the forming of the Seven."

"Yes," Tianya said, "and there is nothing to forgive, Leomin, for you are right. I do not doubt that you have been most diligent in your mission and have read all of the available histories. You have not, however, read those which are unavailable. Those which are kept only by me and those who share my mission."

"And those people being?" Aaron said, unable to keep the impatience from his voice.

"I ask that you humor me only for a little while longer, Mr. Envelar. I assure you, we are getting to that. Now, as I was saying, Caltriss forced Kevlane and his men to stop their experiments but not before some ... successes had been made. Nothing so grand as what Kevlane had been aiming for but successes just the same. Men and women who were faster and stronger than they had any right to be—not so great that they could defeat armies alone or lift horses above their heads—but enough to set them apart. Some, too, discovered a knack for knowing when they were being lied to."

"What you must understand is that those who survived Kevlane's experiments were men and women who loved Caltriss with a fervor beyond that which normal men and women are capable of. These were people who would have died without question to keep their king safe from harm. The most loyal, best trained group of men and women to ever exist before or since. In the end, though, it was their loyalty that set them so far apart from others, and it was their loyalty that killed them."

Aaron frowned, "Killed them? How's that?"

"You see, being such trusted men and women, they were always near Caltriss, they and their families given rooms in the castle. When the spell that ended up taking his life failed, when the barbarians were at the gates of the city, some few escaped from the castle by means of a tunnel that had been long in the making, one that led out of the castle and into the woods several miles distant. It was through this tunnel that the families of these loyal soldiers were sent—accompanied by a few remaining members of the nobility. The soldiers themselves, however, would not go no matter how many times they were ordered to by the Queen. Of course, the queen also refused to leave. Elisandra's beauty was legendary in those days but so, too, was her love for Aaron Caltriss, her husband. It was a love so strong that she would not leave his body even as it lay broken and growing cold from the spell's failure, even as the barbarian hordes broke down the gates of the city and charged through, killing and committing such atrocities as you could not imagine. Still, she would not leave, and Caltriss's bodyguard would not leave either. They stayed at the castle gates, fighting and killing a dozen men for each one that fell as they bought time for the nobles and their own families to flee. Or so is the reason the histories give, but I believe it is something simpler than that. I believe that these men and women did not want to live in a world that did not contain their king, and that their final stand, though admirable, was ultimately convoluted suicide."

"And what does this have to do with me?" Aaron said, glancing to where Darrell stood, "what does this have to do with a choice my father made?"

"A choice?" Tianya asked, "Was it Kevlane who told you this?"

Aaron shrugged, "Well, as I recall, he was more screaming it at the time. It was right before I chopped his arms off and threw him off the castle balcony. Now, why don't you stop wasting my time and tell me what I want to know?"

"Aaron—" Darrell started, a warning in his voice as he took a step forward, but he paused as the older woman held a hand up.

"It's okay, Darrell," she said, "he has every right to be upset. Now, as I told you before, the existence of the Virtues was not discovered for several years. It wasn't until men and women began to display remarkable ... shall we say, powers, that people began to investigate. Then, slowly, over the course of years, people began to realize that Kevlane's spell had not been a complete failure, after all, but had in fact created beings representative of the very virtues they had been meant to instill within their king."

"By this time, Aaron Caltriss's armies had been destroyed, his people killed and scattered. All, that was, but those few who had escaped from the castle through the secret tunnel. Sons and daughters, wives and husbands of those men and women whose life mission had been to protect Caltriss. Time passed, as it does, and soon those children grew up. Most of them stayed in touch, brought together by the shared tragedy that had seen one or both of their parents killed and when knowledge of the Virtues' existence was discovered, these brave men and women met to decide what should be done. Some, of course, did nothing, arguing that the oaths of their fathers and mothers were not binding unto them. Still others claimed that their parents' responsibility had been to Caltriss, and that whatever obligation they held had died along with him."

"Many left, then, cutting all ties with their past and those who'd shared it, but when the door of the meeting hall closed for the last time, still some remained. These took it upon themselves to protect the world from the magic that Kevlane and Caltriss, in their desperation, had let loose upon it."

Tianya paused to clear her throat, and when she spoke again, her voice was powerful with emotion, "The greatest fear of these, you see, was that one man or woman might gather unto themselves all of the Seven. Whoever did so, they believed, would be nothing short of a god, with powers beyond what, perhaps, even the gods might command. And so it was that these sons and daughters took an oath to watch over the world, to keep it safe

125

from the danger the Virtues posed. Their duty, as they saw it, was to keep any man or woman from gathering together all of the Virtues and to ensure that those men and women who did bond with them did not use them for evil purposes."

Aaron thought of Boyce Kevlane, of the way he'd killed Mirmanon and several of the guards, had tried to kill the queen herself. He snorted, "I hate to tell you, lady, but they failed."

"These men and women," Tianya went on as if Aaron hadn't spoken, "made it their duty to look after the Virtues, to try to keep them safe but, more importantly, to keep the world safe from them, and when they finally left that meeting hall, they were no longer separate men and women, orphaned by tragedy, but a family they called the Tenders. Tenders, you see, because it was they who tended to the dangers that few others even knew existed, and it was they who had carried on their weary backs or in their hands so long ago in a dank, dark tunnel that seemed to stretch on forever, the true account of what had happened with Aaron Caltriss and Boyce Kevlane."

"As time went on, these sons and daughters grew old, and they passed on their secret purpose to their own children, and so it went through the years. Always with fewer of the children willing to take up the mantle of their forebears, to keep the trust and the oath to which their ancestors had sworn. Those of us you have seen as you entered this house and these grounds are the descendants of those men and women who stood guard over Caltriss during his life, those who have chosen to stand guard over his legacy after his death, and we, I'm afraid, are only a ghost of what we once were."

Aaron frowned, "And what does this have to do with Darrell and the choice he made? What does this have to do with my parents' murder?"

"Everything, Aaron," Tianya said, and her voice was full of sadness. "You see, we are what remain of the Tenders. The choice of which Boyce Kevlane spoke is the choice that each of us faced when we were younger—that our children, should we have them, will also face. Boyce Kevlane knows of the Tenders, and it is for this reason that he wishes to see Darrell, to see all of us dead."

"So what are you saying?" Aaron said, the anger roiling in the pit of his stomach, trying to claw its way free, "my father and mother were killed because they were Tenders? Because they—and I—are somehow descended from the people who escaped Caltriss's castle thousands of fucking years ago?"

"No," Tianya said, ", at least, I don't believe so, though I suppose it is possible. After a generation denies the calling, we do not keep up with the family as perhaps we should, yet descended or not, your father was a Tender, Aaron, and your mother also."

"I ... I don't understand," Aaron managed, his voice tight with emotion.

Tianya sighed heavily, "You see, Mr. Envelar, as our numbers have waned over the centuries, we have been forced to turn to recruiting to bolster our ranks and even still, we are stretched thin."

Aaron felt anger and sadness rising in him in equal measure, two serpents warring within him, "You mean that my father and mother died because one of your people decided to try to recruit them?" Adina grabbed his hand, holding it tight, but Aaron barely noticed. His thoughts were on his family home, so many years ago, on the two murdered parents lying in pools of their own blood and the orphaned child kneeling beside them, his head cradled in his hands as he wept.

"You must understand, Aaron," Tianya said, "we approached your father for several reasons. First, he was known as a man of purpose who took seriously his duties and had a reputation for fairness as well as intelligence. Secondly, at the time we approached your father, he was serving in Prince Eladen's army, was his general, in fact, and it became known to us that the prince possessed one of the Virtues, though we were not sure which it was even then. We went to your father and explained all that I have explained to you. He knew well the dangers, yet he agreed to help us, understanding the importance of what we asked of him."

"You," Aaron growled, his muscles tensing of their own accord, "you are the reason why my parents are dead. You might as well have painted a bull's eye on their backs with your offer."

"Mr. Envelar, please," the woman said, and there was real pain, real grief in her voice, but it meant little to Aaron. The rage was building inside of him, pushing and shouldering its way to the fore of his mind, and he felt himself losing his grip of it, felt himself wanting to. "Please, Mr. Envelar," she said, "Know that we took every precaution we could in contacting your father or meeting with him for information, yet, I am afraid, it was not enough. Even now, I do not know how Kevlane and his men discovered your family's involvement. You must believe me when I tell you that I did not mean any harm to befall your parents."

"Well," Aaron said, "harm befell them anyway, didn't it? Say what you want to, lady, but you're the reason my parents died." Before he realized what he was doing, he'd taken a step forward. The room was still completely dark, but through his bond with Co, Aaron could see the woman as clear as if they'd been standing in sunlight, could see the fear in her eyes. Saw it and was glad. He took another step and suddenly a hand fell on either of his arms. He growled, turning to see Adina and Leomin standing beside him, their expressions sad and troubled. "Mr. Envelar," Leomin said, "this is not the way."

"Aaron, please," Adina said, "don't do this."

Aaron stared at her face, his chest heaving with the need to make the woman pay for what she'd done, and suddenly the rage wasn't fighting to break free, but was free, roaring through him, a hurricane of fury, and he jerked his arms away, stalking toward the woman, his hand going to the hilt of the sword at his back.

Darrell moved in front of him and held his hands up, and Aaron could see the man looking around, unable to place him in the darkness. Aaron froze, a horrifying thought coming to his mind. "Tell me you didn't know of this, Darrell."

The swordmaster let out a heavy, ragged breath, sorrow and grief etched into his wizened features, "Aaron, it was me who spoke to your father so many years ago. I told him the importance of what we did, of our mission, and he agreed. He was my friend, Aaron."

Aaron let out a growl of rage and his hand lashed out of its own accord, backhanding the old man across the face. Darrell stumbled but did not fall, instead remaining in Aaron's path, and through his bond with Co, Aaron could see blood trickling from the swordmaster's mouth. "It was you," Aaron said, his body shaking with his rage, "you killed them."

"Aaron, please," the swordmaster said, "your mother ... your father ... they were my friends, Aaron. Do you not think I wouldn't do anything to have died in their place? To have been there, to have happily given my life for any chance to save theirs? My guilt at what I've done is waiting for me each morning I awake. It is a burden I can never set down, nor would I even if I were able."

"Oh, so you feel guilty," Aaron said, his right hand clenched so tightly around the handle of the sword at his back that it ached. "Well, they don't feel guilty, at least, Darrell. They don't feel anything—the dead never do." He laughed a humorless laugh as he realized something, "It was the reason you took me in, wasn't it? The reason why you raised me. All out of guilt."

"Aaron, it wasn't like that," Darrell said, "at least, not after a while. At first, yes, I admit I took you in because of the love I bore your parents. Understand, I had never met you—your father and mother were very particular about ensuring that you were kept apart from it."

Aaron let out a hiss of anger, "A lot of good that did."

"What I mean to say, Aaron, is that, initially, that is the reason for me taking you in, but I grew to care for you, to love you like my own son."

Aaron drew his sword from its sheath, the metal ringing in the silence. "Get out of my way, Darrell. You might have been the one who spoke to my parents, but you did it under her orders. I don't want to kill you—I'd rather you live with the guilt of what you caused—but I will if I have to. Now, get out of my way or draw your sword."

"No," the old man said, "I will not fight you, Aaron."

"Then move."

Darrell shook his head slowly, "I cannot."

Aaron's chest heaved, the rage bubbling up to the breaking point, and the next thing he knew, his fist was lashing out. Darrell did not try to move or dodge, only stood as the blow caught him in the jaw, and he grunted, his head whipping to the side as he stumbled and fell to one knee.

"Aaron, don't!" Adina yelled, but her voice was a small, distant thing, and the need to hurt, to make someone else feel what he had felt for all those years was too great by far. He watched as the swordmaster slowly started to climb to his feet. "Stay down," Aaron said, but the man ignored him, grunting as he stood in front of Aaron once more.

"This is not the way, Aaron," Darrell said, "you're better than this."

"You're wrong." Aaron's fist lashed out again, hitting his old mentor in the stomach, and the swordmaster's breath exploded from him. Before he could recover, Aaron pivoted, and his fist struck the older man in the temple. Darrell let out a grunting wheeze and collapsed to the ground. Then Aaron was moving, images of his mother and father lying dead in pools of their own blood flashing through his mind in rapid succession. His mother had been wearing a blue dress—one of her favorites—but there was so much blood that it could have been any color really.

In another moment, he was standing on the opposite end of the desk from the woman, Tianya, her eyes wide as she stared at him. "Mr. Envelar, please," she said, "I will not beg you for my own life, but our mission—"

"Fuck your mission," Aaron said, bringing his sword up for a strike.

"Aaron, stop! If you care anything for me, stop this madness! You are not a monster!"

He spun at that, his eyes wild with fury and rage, and he could see Adina clearly, could see the fear on her face, fear that he had put there.

He froze, his breath coming in great ragged gasps, his body shaking with the fury running through it. He fought it then, the look on her face giving him strength to push against the anger, but it surged forward again, more powerful than ever, and he felt himself turning, felt his arm raise once more, and the shared screams of Leomin and Adina were distant things, of no real consequence. They rushed toward him, their footsteps thunderous in the silence, but it did not matter. They would not make it in time.

He grasped the handle of the sword in both hands, growling, his teeth gritted. "You killed them," he hissed to the woman sitting staring at him.

He thought that she would beg or cry, argue or deny, but instead she only nodded slowly, what fear she'd shown in her surprise gone now. "Yes," she said, "and they are not the only ones that have died because we needed their help, Aaron. This is no game that we play."

"You deserve it," Aaron said, "I'd be doing the world a favor to kill you now, maybe saving some other child from watching his parents murdered."

"Perhaps," she said, "but I am ready to die, if that is what is required, Mr. Envelar. Better me, better your parents, than the entire world."

Aaron screamed then, a scream of rage and grief, of old pain mixed with new, and the woman covered her ears, her expression twisting with agony as her Virtue enhanced every sound of sorrow, every nuance of anger, and Aaron noticed a line of blood dripping from her nose as he brought the sword down with all his strength. The steel tore through the wooden desk, and there was a great roar of breaking wood to match Aaron's own scream as the desk was cleaved in two and the shattered pieces tumbled to the ground in a heap.

Aaron's chest heaved, his breathing ragged and shallow as he stared at the woman still sitting in her chair. She looked surprised but no more than that. She'd not been lying, then, when she'd said she was prepared to die for her mission. Maybe that would have made some people feel better, but not Aaron.

During his time on the streets, he'd ran into a few people like her, people who believed in something so much that they would be willing to die for it. Priests, mostly, and criminals were not exempt as most all of them believed in their pride, and many of those would be prepared to give their lives for it. In his experience, such people were the most dangerous of all, for there were no limits to what they would do to serve whatever purpose they held so highly. "You really are ready to die, aren't you?"

"If that is what must happen," the woman said, matter of factly, as if she hadn't just been nearly killed, "then yes. Shame about the desk—I was quite fond of it."

Aaron grunted, "You might think it's noble to believe in something so much that you'd die for it, but I've seen it before— seen what people will do to feed such dreams, dreams that in my experience, are only nurtured on blood and pain and death. Belgarin is such a dreamer."

The woman frowned at that, the first genuine show of emotion Aaron thought he'd seen from her. "You may kill me, if you wish, Mr. Envelar. I could not stop you, even if I wanted to, but I will not be compared to such a man as that. You have no idea of the sacrifices that I and those like me have made to keep the rest of the world safe."

"That's where you're wrong, Tianya. I've got a pretty damned good idea of what you and yours will do to get what you want. And what do you think, exactly, that Belgarin wakes up every morning smiling about how evil he thinks himself?" He shook his head, "Don't be a fool. If we mortals hold any power over the gods, it is our ability to deceive ourselves. The murderer always thinks his actions justified, always believes himself to be good no matter how much blood is on his hands. If he thinks of it at all, that is. In my experience, such men do not like to question themselves too much. Fanatics, though, do not even believe that the question exists."

He turned to start away but paused as the woman spoke. "Wait, please," she said. "Mr. Envelar, I know that you do not think highly of me, and that's okay. Hate me, if you must, but hear me now. Boyce Kevlane will not stop until he has acquired all seven of the Virtues, until he has paired with each of them in turn. If that happens, if all of the Virtues are brought together into one man, he will be as a god to us. He will be unstoppable."

"That sounds like your problem."

"No, Mr. Envelar," the woman said, sounding desperate now, "it is all of our problem. It is the problem of any man or woman breathing. He has sought them for many, many years, and he is close now, closer than he has ever been. The fate of the world, of every man, woman, and child within it rests on the edge of a knife. He has the Virtue of Adaptability already, this you know, but it is worse than that. Strength, too, is within his grasp. And, what's more, just recently, the men I had watching over the Virtue of Speed were found murdered in their hideout."

"Could have been someone else," Aaron said, "from what I hear, Kevlane's not the only one looking for the Virtues."

"No," the woman said, shaking her head, "it was him, Mr. Envelar. None other could have done the ... things that were done to my men. I do not ask for your help—it is clear you would not give it even if I did. All I ask is that you leave this place; he is here, and he will not stop until he has taken what you and the Parnen carry. Let my men take you somewhere safe—they will be able to look after you and the princess and the Parnen too, protect you, so that Kevlane cannot get his hands on you."

"Protect us? Just like they protected my parents?"

She frowned at that, her eyes dancing with anger, "Do you think yourself the only one able to feel anger or rage? I have watched for years as men and women I cared about suffered and gave their lives because they believed in what it is that we do. What is it that you believe, Mr. Envelar?"

Aaron studied the others in the room for a second, saw that Adina and Leomin were staring at the sound of his and Tianya's voices, their expressions worried. He saw too that Darrell had picked himself up and was standing now, though one eye was closed shut and blood ran from the corner of his mouth. Aaron felt a pang of shame at seeing the old man so abused and by his own hand. He could tell himself that Darrell had got his parents killed—and it was true, there was no question of that—but that didn't change the fact that the man had raised him, had taken care of him. He wanted to say sorry, but the words would not come, so he turned back to Tianya, feeling more tired than anything else. "I believe I'm leaving."

With that, he turned to walk away, heading toward the door, but the woman spoke on, "Mr. Envelar, you must listen. Adaptability, Strength, Speed, all of these he has, though he has not taken them unto himself yet. Intelligence, too, is missing, though we have not known where it is for many years, and I believe that he is in possession of it as well. He will bring them together, Aaron, the Seven, and when he does, the world will bleed and burn for your choice."

He turned back at the threshold, his hand on the door handle. "The world is always bleeding, Tianya. I would have thought you'd have learned that by now. The world is a decrepit old man suffering from a thousand afflictions. It is not a question of if he will die, only when and which it will be that claims him first."

133

"Aaron," Darrell said, his voice sounding muffled with pain, "please, you have to—"

"No, Darrell," Aaron said, "the time has passed when you were able to tell me what I had to do. After what I learned tonight, it will not come again. I'm done with you." He glanced at the woman, "With you both."

"Leomin," Tianya said, her voice urgent, "please, listen to reason and make your friend see it. Kevlane cannot be allowed to gather all of the Seven unto himself. He will be a plague on the face of the world. Surely you see that?"

"Forgive me, ma'am," the Parnen captain said, "I understand your words, your purpose, and I do not doubt your sincerity. The problem, though, is that in all the time that I have been with Aaron Envelar, I have learned that he is not a man accustomed to running. Not built for it, you could say. And where he goes, I go as well."

The woman sighed, exasperated, "Princess, please—"

"Thank you for your time, Tianya," Adina said, and Aaron saw her slowly making her way closer to the door as she spoke, "and I wish you luck. Perhaps, we will see you again."

"Fools," the woman spat, "when we see each other again, it will be in Salen's Fields, and we will be embarking upon the great journey of death all because you could not be made to see reason."

"Journey of death, huh?" Aaron said as he opened the door wide and let Adina and Leomin through, "Well, at least we'll have something to talk about." Then he turned and closed the door behind him, leaving darkness only to journey into more of the same.

CHAPTER THIRTEEN

Gryle was sitting slouched in the corner of his cell when he heard footsteps descending the stairs to the cellar and raised his head, a shiver of fear running up his spine. He'd been here for days—he couldn't be sure how long as there were no windows in the small cellar, but he knew it had been two days, at least, perhaps three. The only concrete measure he could use to mark the time was how often one of the big men—sometimes the one that had beat him, sometimes the other—came down bringing a bowl of some foul soup, the smell alone enough to make him want to gag.

At first, he'd told himself that he would not eat, that he would starve himself. Whatever Aster and his men had planned, he wasn't stupid enough to fool himself into believing they'd let him walk away after it was finished and, anyway, Beth had told him the man was after the Virtues. Gryle didn't have one, of course, but that was little comfort, for he knew two men—and, even now, he found the contents of the letter he'd read at May's club shocking— who did possess them. Aaron and Leomin. His friends. Whatever Aster Kalen wanted, it would have to do with that, and Gryle promised himself that he would not betray them. Of course, he'd made such promises before and if life had taught him anything, it was that the best lies are the lies a man tells himself.

Starving himself, it had seemed, was the smartest thing, for he knew enough about himself to know that, should the beatings start again, he would do whatever the man asked. In a moment of rare bravery, he had let the guard slide the bowl into his cell and then kicked it over, spilling its vile contents onto the dirt floor. The guard had only stared at him, his expression unreadable, then finally turned and disappeared out of the door and up the stairs.

Gryle had counted it a victory, had been proud in some desperate, perverse way, until the man had returned, the other guard accompanying him. They hadn't spoken, at first. One had positioned himself outside the cell, while the other unlocked it and walked inside. The guard had set about beating him then, hard, rapid strikes in the stomach and the back, the thighs and the shoulders until Gryle had screamed and begged and cried, whatever small sense of victory he'd held drowned in a sea of pain.

Eventually—it could have been five minutes or an hour, for Gryle was too consumed with his own pain to know—the guard pushed him over so that his face fell into the puddle of gruel still lying in the dirt. "Eat." The man had said, and Gryle remembered what followed well enough, the shame of it carved deep into him.

He had not, at first, had shaken his head in denial, the sobs of pain and fear and helplessness too strong for him to speak. The guard hadn't seemed angry or frustrated—that, Gryle thought, was one of the worst things about it. It was as if he was an owner disciplining a particularly stubborn pet. He'd only set about the beating again, his face that same dull, expressionless mask until Gryle had screamed that he would eat. Then the man had pushed him over again so that his face landed in a puddle of the slimy gruel.

The guard watched him, and Gryle hesitated, groaning and wheezing in pain before he began to lap at the gruel like a wounded dog, forcing it down his throat in between gags that threatened to bring all that he'd eaten back up. The two men had said nothing, but they had not left either, not until all of it was gone, until Gryle's throat and mouth were coated in the dirt of the cell floor and the oily, rancid taste of the gruel. Then, they'd turned and, in silence, disappeared through the doorway.

When they left, Gryle had sat in his corner and wept, and the woman, Beth, had tried to speak to him, some quiet words of comfort, but he did not hear them or understand them, too complete was his pain and shame. He did not feel like a human at all now, just some dumb beast who ate what it was given and did what it was told. A beast that had gone wrong and had been disciplined for it, one that had learned its lesson well.

That had been two days ago, he thought, though he wasn't sure. Now, when the gruel came, he rushed to it eagerly, forcing it down his throat as fast as he could lest the guard decide he was being rebellious again. Beth had tried to talk to him some since, but he had not responded and soon she had given up. What difference did any of it make, really? Whether he ate the gruel or not, whether he cooperated or not, he knew enough to know that this ended the same way for him. He was going to die. The only question was how much pain he was forced to endure before being allowed to.

He thought that he had come to peace with that. At least, as much as a man could, but when the door to the cell swung open to reveal Aster Kalen bathed in the light of a torch one of the two guards standing behind him held, Gryle realized that he was wrong. Fear leapt in him, a deer pouncing away in an effort to flee from a predator on its trail. The problem, of course, was that there was nowhere for it to go. The predator had seen to that.

"Why, Chamberlain Gryle, how are you this fine day?"

Day, Gryle said, it's daytime. It made no practical difference, but he felt some small shred of hope if for no other reason that the sun was shining somewhere else. He had not seen Aster since the first day he'd been brought to the cellar, but he remembered well the man's madness. "I'm ... alright," he said, his voice dry and raspy from not speaking for several days. Not words, at least. Only screams.

"Yes, yes, I'm sure you are," the scarred man said as he moved further into the room. "I suspect you have probably wondered why you are here, chamberlain. Is that so?"

"Yes," Gryle said, swallowing hard to try to clear some of the cellar dust out of his throat. A hopeless cause considering that the stuff coated him, was stuck in his now matted hair, was layered over his clothes and face and hands.

"Well," Aster said, "I believe that it is time you find out why I have brought you here, Gryle. Though, I must warn you, I doubt that you'll enjoy it much."

Gryle didn't answer. There was really no point. He would do whatever the man said—he knew that, had learned that lesson clearly beneath the fists of the guards. He would do it and then he would die, and the world would be no worse off for his passing.

Aster sighed, taking in his appearance, "Chamberlain, you really are quite filthy, you know?" He shook his head as if disappointed in Gryle's lack of decorum. "No matter. I've brought clothes, but we might worry about that in a bit. You may not be aware of this, but I have not been in Avarest long, and the Downs even less. I hate it here. It stinks of filth and desperation. If it were up to me," he said, his face twisting with that familiar, irrational anger, "I would burn this entire city and all those in it to the ground." After a moment, his face returned to normal, and he shrugged, "But, then, we all have our tasks."

"What ... what do you want of me?" Gryle said.

Aster smiled a too-wide smile, the madness Gryle had seen before dancing in his eyes, "Good, good. So eager to please, chamberlain, and I'm glad. You see, this May everyone speaks of is actually quite a surprisingly difficult woman to meet. She is cautious and careful. Traits I normally admire but just now, ones that are causing me some difficulty. My master, you see, has tasked me with killing her and those she works with. Oh, do not look so surprised, chamberlain. You must have suspected as much, didn't you?"

"Yes," Gryle whispered, feeling empty.

"Good. Anyway, that is my task," Aster said, "your task is truly simple enough." He reached behind him and one of the big guards handed him a blank parchment and a writing quill. "You will write to this May and ask her to meet you. Tell her what you need to tell her to get her to come—perhaps that you have new information about Aaron Envelar. Yes, I believe that would serve admirably."

Gryle stared at the offered parchment and considered refusing. He liked May. She had been good to him when she had not needed to, had been good to the princess and Aaron also. She was a kind, strong woman, one that did not deserve such a fate. But then, who does? He thought, his mind trying to rationalize what he knew he would do anyway, besides, everyone dies. At least then she will feel no more pain, no more of this desperate hopelessness that I myself feel.

"Gryle?" Aster asked, "Surely, you aren't considering refusing me this simple request. Are you?"

Gryle stared up at the man and saw the danger lurking there in his eyes. Aster Kalen was a man of no remorse and no mercy. He would do whatever it was he felt was needed to get the things he wanted. If Gryle refused, he would be beat, maybe worse, would be drug down into a world of pain and, in the end, he would sign the parchment just the same. His face heating with shame, he reached out and took the quill and parchment. He started to write and Aster Kalen spoke.

"Understand, chamberlain, that I have been patient with you thus far. I will read over your invitation and should I find anything that I feel is made to warn the club owner, I will make sure that you suffer for it. Am I clear?"

"Yes," Gryle rasped, tears of frustration and helplessness welling in his eyes. "I understand."

"Good," Aster said, "you may begin."

Aster walked Gryle through the letter, telling him where to ask May to meet, and Gryle wrote, each move of the quill like a dagger blade in his heart, but he told himself there was nothing else left to do. In the end, the letter would be written either way, he knew that. So he finished and handed the letter to Aster, the tears so full in his eyes that the man was little more than a blur in his vision.

"That's good, chamberlain. That's good. Now," he said, turning to the two large men standing behind him, "Have a messenger deliver this. Also, get him cleaned up and dressed. We want him to look presentable for his meeting, don't we?"

***

A few hours later, one of the guards led him out of the house and into the street, and Gryle winced at the brightness of a sun he had not seen for days. Aster had left the other guard to watch over Beth and so it was only the three of them standing in the street, Gryle's hair still wet from his 'bath'. The men had not been gentle in their cleaning, dunking his head in to a large bucket of water repeatedly until he thought for sure that he was going to drown, but he was still glad to be free of the dirt that had coated him like a second skin and the smell which had been the worst of all.

The street was packed with people and horse-drawn carts. Merchants stood outside their shops or at their stalls shouting about their wares to those in the street and, for the first time, Gryle realized that he was not in the Downs but some other, finer part of the city. Looking at the people passing them in the street, Gryle started to consider screaming for help. Even now, he saw guards interspersed among the men and women of the city, making their rounds and scanning the crowd looking for anything suspicious.

"Whatever thought you are having, chamberlain," Aster said, leaning so close that Gryle could feel the heat of his breath on his neck, "I would be so very careful just now. You see, whatever difficulty you cause me, I will be sure to visit on the old woman and her grandson. She did tell you of her grandson, Michael, did she not?" He smiled, "A sweet boy. A little soft, perhaps, but the world will cure him of that, won't it? That is, if he lives long enough. Which, of course, is entirely up to you chamberlain. The club owner or the child. Someone dies today—the choice is yours."

Gryle's shoulders drooped as the little spark of hope that had kindled in his chest withered and died. The man would do it, he knew. Aster Kalen was not given to idle threats, and the madness in his eyes was proof enough of his words. "I understand," he said, his voice empty and lifeless. "I will do what you ask."

"Very good," Aster said, "That is the wise choice, chamberlain. The only real choice. Now, walk with me. It would not do for us to be late."

Gryle followed as Aster Kalen set off down the street, the guard a shadow at his back. He wished that he could do something, wanted to do something. If he was Aaron, he would have drawn his sword and made use of his skill to escape or, more likely, kill the men holding him. Leomin would have somehow managed to talk his way out, wielding his words as deftly as Aaron did his blades. Gryle, though knew nothing of swordplay and, even if he did, he didn't have one, and he was no Leomin to confound the men with his charm and wit. He had no charm and, had begun to realize over the course of the last few days, what he'd taken for wit in himself was really only a fragile vase of naiveté, waiting for someone like Aster Kalen to come around and show him its flaws.

Thoughts of Aaron made him remember the sellsword telling him that he was no coward. Telling him that there were more important things than being good at killing. Those words had meant much to Gryle when he'd said them, more than he would have wanted the sellsword to know but, now, held captive and forced to betray one of his closest friends, Gryle realized that they were only that. Words. They would do nothing to stop Aster Kalen from doing what he intended and, after May was dead, what would he do next?

He'd made it clear that he worked for someone, and Gryle might be a foolish coward, but it seemed obvious even to him that Aster must work for the same Boyce Kevlane that Aaron and Adina had written of in the letter they'd sent. A man who, according to Aaron, wanted to destroy the entire world. And this man that walked beside him was serving him in that cause. "What will you do with the woman, Beth?" He said, "And her grandson?"

Aster Kalen glanced over at him and smiled, "I would worry less about the woman and more about myself, were I you, chamberlain. You are no hero and this is no story. You could not help them even if you wished it. Not that I expect you would. You are a coward. That is not a judgment, you understand, simply a statement of fact."

Gryle wanted to argue, but found that he didn't have the strength to do it. Besides, the man was right, was only speaking the words that he had so often thought. He was a coward, had proven it time and again, was proving it now, in fact. Still, the thought of the old woman sitting in the cell, not worried about herself but only her grandson, of the child at the mercy of a man who had none, bothered him. "You'll kill them," he said, his voice empty, broken.

Suddenly, the man spun and his hands were grabbing Gryle's shoulders. Gryle squeaked in surprise and then he was being lifted up as if he weighed no more than a child until his feet dangled a good foot above the road. "Hear me, chamberlain," the man hissed, his face twisted with an inexplicable rage, his eyes dancing with insanity, "I have been kind to you thus far, but I will not always be so, if you think to test my patience. Yes, the woman will die, the boy too, as will all those who dare to stand in my master's way. The world will burn, chamberlain, and all in it will burn. I do not think you are so foolish as to believe you will be set free after this. You, too, will die, but if you try me, fat man, you will be amazed at the agony one body can endure before Salen gets his due. Do you understand?"

Gryle's mouth worked and, for a moment, he was terrified that he wouldn't be able to make the words come, that this madman with impossible strength would dash his brains out here in the middle of the street like he was a child's doll that had lost its use. Then, finally, he managed to croak, "No, please, I mean ... yes. Yes, I understand."

The rage vanished in another moment, and the man smiled wide, "Good," he said. Then he let go of Gryle who fell to the ground in a heap at the unexpected abruptness of it. "Oh, do get up, chamberlain," the man said, grabbing one of his arms and pulling him to his feet with such strength, that Gryle felt like it would be ripped from its socket.

A finely dressed man who'd been walking by paused near them, "Is everything okay?"

"Oh, of course," Aster said, "only, I fear that my friend here has had a bit too much drink, more than is good for him, in fact. Isn't that right?"

He glanced a Gryle, a world of meaning in his eyes. Gryle considered screaming for help again, but the thought of the old woman in the cage and the young boy, her grandson, stopped him. "Sorry, sir," he said to the man, bowing his head, "Thanks for your concern but, as my ... friend here said, it is only the ale, nothing more."

The man nodded slowly, glancing between the two of them, "You're sure?"

Gryle nodded, "Yes. Thank you."

The man studied them for another moment before turning and walking back down the street, and Gryle felt what small chance he'd had of surviving the day leaving with him. Aster Kalen, Gryle, and his escort had just started down the street once more when there was a chorus of shouts behind them, and they turned to see a horse rearing up, its owner—who'd apparently been knocked from his saddle—trying and failing to grab hold of the reins.

The horse reared again even as the owner fought to gain control of it and suddenly it burst forward in a flurry of hooves, dragging the small wooden cart it had been hitched to behind it. People dove out of the way shouting in fear, and Gryle's eyes went wide as he realized the horse was bolting down the street in their direction and would pass right by them in a moment. He glanced to the side to see Aster watching the horse's approach with an amused smile on his face.

"You called me coward," Gryle said, the words out of his mouth before he realized he would speak.

The scarred man turned, raising an eyebrow, "So I did."

"You were right," Gryle said, then he lunged forward with what strength and speed he could put into his exhausted legs, charging into the thin man. Impossible strength or not, Aster still weighed what he weighed and, caught off guard as he was, it was no big thing for Gryle—who was easily twice his weight—to bowl him over. The last expression Gryle saw on the man's face was one of shocked surprise, as if he had expected Gryle to go meekly to his death. Which, no doubt, he had. Gryle enjoyed a split second of satisfaction at that before he and the thin man both went sprawling in the street, directly in the horse's path.

Someone screamed, a scream that rang in Gryle's ears but in a moment even that was drowned out by the impossibly loud thundering of the horse's hooves on the cobbles and the screech of the wooden cart as it was dragged behind it. Gryle whimpered and the last thing he saw before he closed his eyes was a descending hoof, then he slammed his eyes shut, raising his hands in what he knew would be a vain attempt to protect himself. For several seconds that felt like an eternity, he knew nothing but the sound of screaming horse and thundering hooves, of the snap and crack of wood as the cart lurched after the panicked beast. He cringed, expecting at any moment to feel the crushing weight of the horse or the cart strike him, but in another moment the sounds of both animal and cart grew more distant, so that he could hear the shouts of surprise all around him and the one man still screaming.

It wasn't until his throat began to ache that he realized that the screams belonged to him, and he clamped his mouth shut, finding himself somehow terrified to open his eyes. A wet, gurgling sound came from beside him, and he turned to look at its source. Aster Kalen, lay in in the street beside him. One of the man's legs was bent at an impossible angle, and his throat had a crushed, misshapen look. He stared at Gryle with malevolent, hate-filled eyes, his mouth working silently.

Panting, wheezing and covered in sweat caused more from fear than activity, Gryle made his way to his feet, staring down at the dying man. "I am a coward, Aster Kalen," he said between gasping breaths, "but even cowards have their limits." He watched as the light went out of the man's eyes, and his body, which had been twitching in minute spasms, grew still.

Then, something emerged from the man's chest, a glowing red ball of light, a vivid hue, and Gryle stared at it in shock for a moment before, abruptly, it sped directly at him. Gryle cried out, stumbling backward as he expected to be struck in the chest, but the orb vanished inside of him, leaving nothing but a slight, tingling sensation where it touched. His mouth fell open, as he stared, wide-eyed at his heaving chest. "Oh, gods be—" his words turned to a scream of surprise as strong hands clamped on his shoulders from behind and spun him around.

"You'll die for that, you bastard," the guard snarled in his face, and Gryle flung his hands out desperately in what he knew would be a useless struggle. But when his hands struck the man, the guard flew backward through the air as if struck by the wrath of some god. He continued to fly backward until he struck the wooden side of a tailor's shop, crashing through it and leaving a man-sized hole as he vanished inside. Gryle stared down at his hands in shock, whimpering to himself. They were the same pudgy hands he'd had since he was a child, hands he'd always hated, for they were hands that would never play an instrument or paint a masterpiece. A servant's hands and no more. The same hands and yet....

Terrified but unable to help himself, Gryle shuffled toward the devastated tailor's shop, waving a hand in front of him at the dust that had been kicked up when the guard struck the wall. He bent down to look inside and, to his shock, he saw that an equally large hole had appeared in the shop's far wall. "Oh gods be good," he whispered.

"Chamberlain," a voice said, and another hand clamped down his shoulder. Gryle spun, but the man jumped backward, holding up his hands.

"Easy, lad, easy, it's me," the man said, and Gryle let out a heavy sigh of relief when he realized that it was Balen who stood in front of him. "Don't hit me with those, will ya?" Balen said, "My back already hurts like a bitch of a mornin'. I don't think bein' thrown through a wall would do it any favors." Leomin's first mate glanced through the broken wall at the wreckage of the inside of the tailor's shop, saw a thin, bald man in spectacles standing behind the counter, staring in slack jawed shock. Balen let out a whistle, turning back to Gryle, "Gods, chamberlain. Remind me not to piss you off, will ya?"

Gryle shook his head in disbelief, "Balen? I don't ... I mean, how did you get here?"

The first mate shrugged, "May's had me out lookin' for ya for two days now. And not just me either—Celes, and Thom, a bunch of Celes's girls. Even Festa and his men been out searchin' on account of May said she thought you'd be goin' to see him, but you never arrived. Shit, chamberlain, I reckon' about half the Downs is out lookin' for you. Still, I bout shit when I saw you tackle that bastard and dive into the road. I'd meant to spook the horse, sure, but I thought to distract them, maybe give you a chance to run for it. I hadn't thought you'd dive in front of it." He let out a laugh, shaking his head in wonder, "Gods, but you're a man that's full of surprises, chamberlain, and that's the truth. Still, the others'll be mighty pleased I found you."

"You all ... went through all that trouble ... for me?" Gryle asked.

Balen clapped a hand on his shoulder, "Well, course we did, chamberlain. You're our friend, ain't you? It's what friends do."

"Friends," Gryle echoed, feeling tears gather in his eyes. Then realization struck him, and his breath caught in his throat. "Balen, we have to stop May. It's a trap. Aster—"

"Aw, shit, Gryle," Balen said, grinning, "she know'd it was a trap the second she seen the letter. You can't put much over on that woman, I'll tell you that much. Almost enough to make a man pity Thom." He winked, "Almost." Balen frowned, looking around them, and Gryle followed his gaze, only now realizing that a crowd had gathered around them in the street, at least twenty or thirty people staring at them like they'd just sprouted horns and prophesied the end of the world. Or thrown a grown man through not one but two walls of a stout, wooden building.

"Right," Balen said, "we'd best get you off the street. May and the others will be mighty glad to see you, but it wouldn't do for you to get arrested right now."

The first mate took Gryle's arm and started to lead him away. Gryle followed for several steps before he paused, remembering. "Wait, Balen," he said, "I thank you very much for coming to my rescue. Truly, I do, but I can't go with you just now."

Balen turned back, raising an eyebrow, "No?"

Gryle took a moment to gather his courage and did what he could to straighten his back. "No. There's something I have to do first."

Balen studied him for several seconds then finally nodded, "Alright then. Lead on."

"Y-you're coming?" Gryle asked, unable to help the tears that gathered in his eyes and the man's unexpected kindness.

The first mate grunted, "Shit, why not? It ain't like the taverns'll run out of ale, now lead on."

CHAPTER FOURTEEN

Aaron stared out from the castle's balcony at the city below, his mind racing with a thousand different thoughts, a storm of emotions ranging from anger to grief to betrayal all raging inside of him, so that he thought he might explode from the pressure. Adina and Leomin, apparently having sensed that he didn't want to speak, had followed him back to the castle without comment. He appreciated them being there for him, had wanted to tell them as much, but the words would not come, could not be forced past the anger and betrayal that he felt.

He had always thought of Darrell as a second father, the man who'd taken it upon himself to raise him when no one else would. To find out now that Darrell was actually the reason why his father and mother had died was almost more than he could take. And that Tianya woman ... there was something to what she said, he knew. Even past the pain and anger, he'd seen that, but there was a danger there, too. Perhaps her cause was just—probably, even—but that didn't change the fact that she was a fanatic. He'd seen such before.

When he'd been a child, the priests of Salen would sometimes walk the streets of the Downs, parading in their black robes, their faces painted in swirling patterns of white and black. When he'd lived on the streets, he and the other kids—even the adults, in fact—would scatter at the somber parade, and not only because the priests served as a reminder of death.

He'd never had a friend after Owen—not until he'd met Adina and the others, at least. He'd always told himself that nothing precious could be taken from you, if you owned nothing that you considered precious, but growing up on the streets, a man—or a child—grew accustomed to seeing familiar faces, faces that were there when you went digging through the trash for something to eat, faces that stood beside you in line during those infrequent occasions when men came to the poor district to hand out bread.

They were not friends, these faces, but they were part of his world, and so when the Priests of Salen finally finished their march and left the Downs once more, he couldn't help but notice that in their wake one or two of those familiar faces did not show up again. Sacrifices, people had whispered, and it had always been in a whisper where the priests of the death god were concerned, dark gifts to their dark god. Yes, he knew fanatics well. Such men could not be reasoned with, could not be argued with or stopped by threat of violence. Such men went on until they could go on no longer. They were the enemy of logic, the knife buried in the heart of reason.

Aaron was sad and upset and angry, that most of all, and a night's sleep had done little to change that. In fact, if anything, it had made it worse. The dreams, too, had been worse this time— the fire so hot that he could feel it burning his skin, the screams of the suffering so loud, so powerful that he seemed to shake with the weight of it, the blood on his hands—not his blood, no, never his— warm and real. He'd woken several times during the night, bathed in sweat, a scream on his lips like a child waking from some nightmare of a bogey man. The problem, though, was that the child woke up to comfort and to the knowledge—shaky though it might be—that the monster was not real or that, at least, monsters never showed themselves in the day time, that such evil as that was left for the darkness when all the lights had gone out and the world of sanity and logic had closed its eyes to wait for the sun.

It was the capability, he thought, to set the monsters aside for a time, to forget them in the warm, morning light that made a child's life bearable. For him, though, there was no setting the monster aside, no forgetting, for the monster was inside of him, and so he carried it with him, always. It was hidden, now, under the bed, perhaps, but it had begun to creep and like the child cowering under his covers, Aaron felt its creeping, its purpose, and was afraid. Hidden now, but not always. Not forever.

Aaron turned at the sound of the door opening to see Adina walking out on the balcony with him. She moved to stand beside him at the railing and, for a time, neither spoke as they gazed out at the city. "I'm sorry about your father," she said finally.

"Be sorry for my mother," Aaron said, unable to keep the bitterness from his tone, "my father's the reason she was killed."

Adina sighed sadly, "Aaron, you can't believe that. You heard Tianya—your mother was as much a part of it as your father was. They did what they thought was right, Aaron, that's all. It's the most that any of us can do."

Aaron nodded, "You're right. I know that. It's just ... I'm angry all the time now, Adina. It seems that's all I ever am."

She put her hand on his shoulder, offering what support she could, "I know, but we'll figure it out. Together."

He turned to meet her eyes, "And if we don't?"

"We will. And Aaron ... about Darrell...."

"I know," Aaron said, sighing, "I know. I was wrong to hit him. Whether I agree with what he did or not, Darrell took me in and raised me like his own. He didn't have to do that."

"No," she said, "he didn't."

"Still," he said, frowning, "there's something about this Tianya that I don't like. When you start telling yourself that accomplishing a goal is the most important thing in the world, it's easy to justify doing whatever you think needs to be done, hurting whoever needs to be hurt to make it happen." He shrugged, "I don't trust her, Adina."

She grabbed his face in her hands and slowly turned him until he was facing her again, "You don't have to, Aaron. You only have to trust Darrell."

He considered that then slowly nodded, "So what do you think, then? That we should run and hide like Tianya suggests? I'll be honest with you, Adina, that doesn't sit well with me. Not at all."

She smiled, "Trusting someone is different than obeying them, Aaron. You know that." She leaned forward then, kissing him, and for a few brief moments he wasn't thinking of the anger or his murdered parents, of Darrell or Boyce Kevlane, hiding somewhere out there, or even of Belgarin's army. It was only him and her and the cool breeze wafting through the balcony. Then, much too soon, she stepped back from him. "Will you come inside?"

"Soon," he said, "I promise."

In another moment, she was gone, and he turned, staring once more out at the city below him. He looked past the city and its walls to the fields that lay beyond it, eventually leading into the woods, woods which Belgarin and his soldiers would come through, sooner or later. And that was only one of their problems. There was Boyce Kevlane to worry about and now Tianya too. And yourself, he thought, don't forget that.

You know, Co said, the stories always paint my father as some perfect man. Courageous, brave to a fault, kind and compassionate. The people knew him as a fearless leader, as a rock that they could lean against when they grew weary, but people are not so simple as that, Aaron. The stories are pretty enough, but they did not know my father, not as I did

They tell nothing of him wandering the castle almost every night, unable to sleep for the stress of the problems he faced. The stories do not mention the fear and worry that would crease his face when he thought none were there to see it, how he seemed to wither before my eyes, aging five years for every one that passed during the war with the barbarians.

To most of those who followed him, my father was a mountain, indestructible. But I was there when the mountain trembled, Aaron, I saw it. He was a great man, my father, but he was only a man. As are you. You cannot take the whole of the world's problems on your shoulders.

Maybe not, Aaron said, thinking of Adina, thinking of what would happen if Kevlane or Belgarin had their way. But somebody has to.

When Co spoke, there was a sad amusement in her tone, My father said that, too.

Aaron grunted, staring off into the distance. The city stretched out before him, thousands living their lives, trusting that someone else would protect them, when the time came. He only hoped that they were right.

CHAPTER FIFTEEN

May sighed, leaning back as she let the parchment she'd been reading drop to her desk, and rubbing at her eyes. She'd spent the last several hours going over reports from her agents in the city and none of them had seen any sign of the chamberlain. It was not like the man to disappear, not at all, and she was surprised by the degree of worry she felt. Frustrating at times or not, the heavy-set chamberlain had become like a family member to her in a surprisingly short time. Sure, he had a tendency of getting on her nerves sometimes—particularly when he apologized when he'd done nothing wrong or, what was worse, apologized for apologizing—but who didn't want to strangle their family from time to time?

"Shit," she hissed, surprising herself. She rarely cursed—it had always been her opinion that cursing was much like yelling, a sign that a person had lost their composure, their objectivity. In her experience, a person who lost her composure, particularly in the Downs and particularly when said person was the leader of a rebellion against the world's single most powerful man, ended up losing much more than just her composure before it was done. Her friends often, and her own life in the bargain.

"He'll be okay, May," Celes said.

May sighed, looking across the desk to where Celes sat having just put down a report of her own. "I hope you're right, Celes, I truly do. I was a fool to let him go off like that, angry or not. Gryle is no more made for the Downs than a fish is made to fly, and I should have stopped him."

"From what you told me," Celes said, "you tried."

May snorted, "I should have tried harder. If only I had convinced him, if only I had told him about Aaron and the others in the first place ...."

"Sure," Celes said, raising an eyebrow, "or maybe you could have tackled him on his way out, tied him up and thrown him in a cage. While you were at it, you could have dressed him in layers, so he'd be less likely to get an 'owie.' Why, you could have even hand fed him to make sure he didn't starve."

May sighed, waving her hand, "Alright, alright, I get it. Gods, but you can be a bitch."

Celes smiled and winked, "It's what you pay me for."

May grunted at that, "Anyway—" She cut off as there was the sharp crack of wood breaking and suddenly the door to her office was ripped free of its hinges. It flew through the air to slam against the wall with a teeth-rattling crash. May and Celes were up in an instant, ready for anything, and both of them let out a shocked gasp as they saw the chamberlain standing in the doorway, his eyes wide, a sheepish expression on his face.

"Gryle?" May said, "What in the name of the gods are you doing here?"

"Um ..." the chamberlain's face turned bright red, "I ... I'm sorry for the door, Miss May. I will, of course, pay to have it replaced."

May laughed, too elated for the moment at seeing the chamberlain alive and well to even consider the door. She rushed toward him, and he had time to let out a squeak of surprise before she buried him in a hug, "Oh, you silly fool," she said, "it's good to have you back."

"The ... pleasure's ... mine," he squeaked, and May relaxed the hug some, the chamberlain gasping for air as she did, though she also noted that he was wiping at his eyes at the same time.

"Now," May said, "tell me where you've been and what happened."

"Well, now, that's a story," a new voice said, and they all turned to see Balen walking in the doorway. The first mate glanced at the broken door lying shattered against the wall and let out a low whistle, "and it might just explain a few things."

May glanced behind Balen, raising an eyebrow as she noticed an older woman and young boy of no more than five years standing a little further back. "Friends of yours, Balen?"

The first mate grinned, "I'd like to think they are or will be soon," he said, winking at the boy who smiled back, "still, you've the chamberlain to thank for the pleasure of their company, not me." He shot a look at Gryle who was staring at his feet, wringing his hands anxiously and saying nothing, "Yeah well," Balen said, his grin widening, "as I said, there's a bit of a story to it. Might be, it'll explain more than a few things."

CHAPTER SIXTEEN

Belgarin stared out the castle window as he listened impatiently to General Fannen prattle on, his mind overly aware of the letter a courier had brought him moments before. It lay now on his desk, unopened, but he had marked the scent attached to it well enough, would have known it anywhere, and just then he couldn't have cared less for troop numbers or their disposition, wanted only to open the letter and read its contents in private.

"So as you can see, Your Highness," the general was saying, "the men will be ready to march in good order come the morning."

Belgarin glanced back at the general standing so straight and stiff in his military dress uniform that a person could have been forgiven for thinking him a particularly ugly statue. "And supply?" Belgarin asked, resisting the urge to turn and glance at the letter.

The general's flat expression changed almost imperceptibly, one lip tugging down a fraction at the corner which, to him, was as much of a reaction as screaming would be to most. Belgarin wondered, not for the first time, what the man's poor wife saw in him, and he pitied her their love life. "Yes, well, Your Highness, Ilryia assures me that all is well in hand regarding supply. Still, if Your Majesty wishes, I would be happy to inquire to more specifi—"

Belgarin waved a hand dismissively, "Never mind that. Ilryia knows her business—if she says that the supplies will be ready then I suspect they will." Ilryia was the new head of the Merchant's Guild since the man, Nigel, had vanished. Belgarin thought it strange for him to have disappeared as he did considering that he was clearly an ambitious man, his successes with the Merchant's Guild having already made him worth more than almost any single person in the city before his thirty fifth nameday. Belgarin had sent men to investigate the young merchant's whereabouts, but his manse had been emptied of anything worth coin and multiple witnesses claimed to have seen him depart in a carriage heading south.

"Anyway," Belgarin said, shaking himself from his thoughts, "how long before we reach the city?"

"I'm sorry, Your Majesty," the general said, "do you mean Perennia?"

"No," Belgarin said, "I mean how long until we reach the Parnen capital city—oh, but I do enjoy their silence."

"Sir?" The general asked, unsure.

Belgarin shook his head, "Of course I meant Perennia, general. I do hope that you show more intelligence on the battlefield than you do in conversation. Otherwise, this will be a long and drawn out war."

The general somehow contrived to look even stiffer than he had before and a flush crept onto his cheeks, "Forgive me, Your Highness. My staff estimates that the cavalry could reach Perennia in little more than four weeks, the infantry perhaps another month and a half on top of that."

Belgarin grunted, "Very well. Be gone."

"But, Your Majesty," General Fannen said, "I haven't finished explaining the disposition of the—"

"Be gone, damn you," Belgarin roared, and the general's face grew pale, his expression tight as he bowed low and then left, closing the door behind him.

"Forgive me, Your Highness," Caldwell said from where he stood near the wall, "but do you think it wise—"

"You too."

"I'm sorry, Majesty?"

"I said get out damn you," Belgarin growled.

"Of course, my lord," Caldwell said, bowing his head and starting for the door.

"Oh, and Caldwell?"

"Yes, Majesty?"

"Has there been any news of Captain Savrin?"

"I'm afraid not, my lord. He is still missing."

Belgarin shook his head, "Damned traitors. Don't they understand what I'm trying to do here? First Nigel and then Savrin ... gods, but how am I supposed to accomplish anything with such ingrates?"

"I do not know, Majesty."

Belgarin grunted, "Get out of here then, and I want you to double your efforts around finding Nigel and Savrin both. If it is true that they abandoned their posts, I want their heads on pikes before the season's out." Why do you always break things? His mother had been dead for years, but it did not stop him from hearing those words echo in his mind with her voice, one that carried weariness and more than a little disappointment. "Wait," he said, and his advisor stopped near the door.

"Yes, Your Highness?"

"If you find them, Caldwell, when you find them, I do not want them harmed. I want you to bring them to me. I would like to hear their reasons from their own lips without any of your ... motivations. Am I clear?"

"Yes sir, my king. It will be done as you ask." Belgarin waved his hand, dismissing him, and, in another moment, the door was closing behind him.

Once he was gone, Belgarin walked to the desk and picked up the letter, taking a moment to savor the scent it held. Her scent. His heart beating in his chest, he tore open the seal and pulled out the letter inside.

Tonight. King's Crest.

-L-

The "L" was stylized, as it always was, that and the smell proof enough of the letter's origins. He smiled, tucking the letter back into the envelope and throwing it into the fireplace, watching it burn down until it was nothing but ash. Watching the fire dance to and fro, he thought of his mother's words as he often did in times when he was alone. Why must you always break things? A familiar shame welled up in him, worsened by the letter's contents and the realization—not the first, of course—that he was not behaving as a good king should. He should not go, he knew that, but he knew just as well that he would go anyway, and his shame was made all the worse for the excitement he felt at the prospect of it.

Besides, he told himself, you will march with the army soon and leave all of the rest behind. You will do your duty, no matter, and if one must be sacrificed for the other you would keep to your duty, always. He would be a good king, the king that Telrear needed. Nothing, no one could stand in the way of that. He would not allow it. Still, there was a smile of anticipation on his face as he left the room, closing the door against the fire and his guilt both.

***

Belgarin, wearing a single linen cloak, the hood thrown to hide his face, walked into the King's Crest inn. A drunken man stumbled into him, and Belgarin hissed as beer spilled on his tunic, the oblivious man walking past, a dazed grin on his face.

Belgarin looked after him, a scowl on his face, "How d—" Belgarin cut off, realizing that he'd very nearly given himself away. It did little good to try to hide your identity as king if you went around scolding people and demanding they apologize.

"What's that, fella?" The drunk said, turning, his smile turning to a threatening frown as he took a step closer to Belgarin.

"Nothing," Belgarin said, promising himself that he would find this fool later, would find him and make him pay for his insolence. "Sorry to bump you, friend, that's all," he said, his face heating in anger.

The man studied him for several seconds then grunted, satisfied, before turning and stumbling away.

Belgarin watched him go, his teeth gritted, then turned back to the common room. The inn was crowded with people dicing and playing cards and several of those nearby had paused to look at him, apparently excited at the prospect of a fight. Fool, he scolded himself. The last thing he needed was to draw attention. Keeping his head down, he hurried to the bar, "I've someone waiting on me upstairs," he said.

The tavern keeper paused where he'd been wiping out an empty mug and glanced up. "Aye, the lady. It'll be the third room on your left." He said, producing a key from his pocket and laying it on the counter.

Belgarin reached for it, and the man grabbed his wrist in an iron grip, "rooms ain't free."

Belgarin frowned, "I had assumed she'd already pai—"

"Two bodies, two payments," the tavern keeper said, "sheets don't clean themselves, friend."

His face heating once more with anger, Belgarin withdrew a gold coin from his tunic and threw it onto the counter. He jerked his arm away from the man's grip, snatched the key off the counter and headed toward the stairs, his teeth gritted in annoyance. The man might not know Belgarin was his king, but he should treat his customers better. And he would—Belgarin would see to it.

He came to the door the man had indicated and unlocked it, letting himself inside. The room was pitch dark but, in a moment, a small candle was lit, its flickering light showing that she waited for him in the bed, her dress and accoutrements lying over the back of the room's only chair.

She smiled at him, the shadows and ruddy orange light shifting on her face, "My king," she said, "I had feared that you would not make time for your loyal servant. I had thought I would spend a night alone with none but myself and my thoughts to keep me company."

Belgarin's building anger melted away as he looked at her, and he moved to the bed, stripping his shirt off as he did. "You know that I would not allow such a thing," he said.

She smiled, reaching her hands out and running them across his naked chest as he stopped, standing at the side of the bed. "I had hoped, of course," she said, "but I could not be sure."

"You were not followed?" He asked, his own foolishness in attracting unwanted attention in the common room fresh in his mind.

"Of course not," she said, her hands going to his trousers, and he grunted as she grabbed hold of him. "My king wishes to keep me his dirty little secret, and so that is what I shall be. Though I must admit that I do wish I could speak of you in the light of day, that we could walk hand in hand and damn all those who would dare cast their judgment. I would be a good queen to you, my love, I swear it. If only you would let me."

Belgarin caught her hands by the wrists, gently but firmly. "Lyla, please," he said, "you know what I face, that there are those in my kingdom who would love the chance to come by such knowledge as this, men and women who would use it against me in any way they could. Were I to make you queen ..." he shook his head, "even I cannot estimate how many I might lose from my cause. It would be ... undignified, and a king must always comport himself with dignity."

She sighed heavily, the motion doing interesting things with her naked breasts as the candle light played over their supple roundness, "Yet, it does not seem that it is so unseemly for you on such nights as this." She shook her head sadly, and he saw the shame in her own face even as he felt its mirror, "What we do ... there is no dignity in it, Belgarin. I am a body on which you might amuse yourself, and no matter how much I love you, no matter how much I would want it to be more, that is all I will ever be. Your whore. Is it that you do not trust me with your heart, is that it?"

"Lyla, please," he said, "stop. You know that isn't true." He fell to his knees by the bed, pulling her hands to him and kissing them softly. "You are much more to me than that. So very much more. And I have trusted you with everything. Does not the fact that I come here, alone, unguarded, with no weapon, not even so much as a dagger to protect myself mean nothing to you? There are those out there, dearest—and their numbers are many—who would celebrate such a chance to take my life, even my own brothers and sisters. Even those closest to me only smile to my face and plot behind my back. You are the only one that I trust. And one day, soon, when I have finished conquering all of Telrear, when none may stand against me, when none would even dare to defy me, then, I promise you, you will be my queen."

"Sweet words," she said, smiling, "always such sweet words. My nursemaid once told me to beware men whose voices are honey, their words soft and pleasing, for honey, she told me, is only proof of bees, and the sweetness is long forgotten when one feels the sting. Still," she said, her eyes dancing with mischief, "I do believe you, my love, truly. Except that there was one thing of which you were wrong."

Belgarin frowned, "Yes?"

"You said that you were weaponless," she said, reaching her hand up and gripping his crotch once more, "but I fear I cannot agree with you. This," she said, and Belgarin let out a soft moan as her fingers tightened, "is the weapon with which you threaten me pain and pleasure both."

Belgarin grunted, having a hard time finding his words, something his own tutors would have no doubt lectured him endlessly about, were any of the old bastards still alive. "I ..." he coughed, "that is, I love you, Lyla."

"And I you," she said, pulling him toward her and onto the bed, "now come and make love to me. It has been too long."

Belgarin was not a man used to taking orders, a man who gave them and expected them to be followed, but in this, he found, he was happy to obey.

***

Sometime later, they lay in the bed, the candle burned down as had their passion. He lay there, listening to the soft sound of her breathing, and felt at peace for the first time in months. In that moment, there was no worry over the coming battle, no fear that he was doing the wrong thing, and even his mother's voice, always present and disapproving, had been silenced for a time. He relished those moments, knowing that they would not, could not last. And, as he'd known it would, soon the shame came, dragging at his heart and his mother's words came with it, Belgarin, why must you always break things?

This will be the last time, he told himself, sunken low in his shame, never again. There are some crimes, some wrongs from which even a king is not exempt. He told himself this, as he had told himself each time before, and even as he thought it, he knew it to be a lie. His thoughts soured now, the pleasant afterglow vanished, he found himself thinking of his council, the stiff bastard General Fannen, the smug woman, Maladine, the representative of the Golden Oars bank who always seemed to be laughing at some inside joke to which she alone was privy. He thought of the fat worthless man Claudius, and of the old priest with his inane blathering as well as his advisor, Caldwell, the man who always seemed to hide some dark thoughts behind that mask of impassivity, and he heaved a heavy sigh. "I do not trust them, Lyla," he said, "not any of them. They would betray me in a moment, if they thought they could get away with it without recompense. I walk through a pit of vipers and how can I be surprised, then, when one decides to show its fangs?"

Her hand, so soft and warm, rested itself on his chest, "You have done much for this kingdom, my love, have sacrificed much, but your reward is coming."

He frowned at that. "Telrear is not a reward, Lyla, not a prize to be won at some tourney or in a card game. It is not my reward—it is my right."

"Of course, my king," she said, her hand going to his chest, "forgive me, I spoke wrongly. Of course, it is your right," she said, kissing him, "you are the rightful heir. And snakes can be defanged easily enough, if you find it necessary. None, after all, may challenge you, for you are the rightful king." She started to crawl atop him, "Now, let us see your snake, my king. I will show you the way."

"Enough," he growled, finding himself annoyed with her now that the beast of his passion had been sated. He grabbed her by the arms and threw her off of him, back onto her side of the bed. "Do you not understand that I speak of the fate of kingdoms?" he demanded, sitting up, "It is no small thing, no matter to be put off or joked about. Why must you insist on acting like a fool?"

"Forgive me," she said, turning her back to him, and though she did not sob aloud or weep, some minute change in her breathing made him realize that she was crying.

"Gods, Lyla," he said, "I'm sorry." He turned to her, put his arm around her, and she tensed as if expecting him to strike her. "Come now," he said, his voice soft, "do not be afraid of me, my love. I do not mean to be angry with you, it is only that I have much on my mind. You could not understand the burden it is to be king."

"There is nothing to forgive," she whispered, and though she tried to hide it, he could hear the tears in her voice.

He sighed then, "When you are my queen, things will be better between us."

She sniffed, turning back to him, "You promise?"

He nodded, "I do. Now, tell me, please, what news?"

"Not so much, truly," she said, running a delicate finger over her eyes to wipe away the tears. "Isabelle reached out to Ellemont to schedule a meeting, as you said she would."

She stopped there, and Belgarin felt a surge of impatience in him again, "And?"

"He agreed, my love," she said, "he is preparing to depart for Perennia even now. He waits only for my return."

Belgarin nodded, considering, "I see. You must not let this alliance come to pass, Lyla. Ensure that Ellemont sees reason. He will be defeated, either way—separate or together, their armies are still no match for my own in numbers or in skill—but it will cause me some difficulty. I may trust you in this?"

"Of course, my lord," she said, "in all things."

"Good. Now, is there anything else of import?"

"Nothing of any particular interest, my love, at least not regarding your royal siblings. Still, there is something I wished to speak with you about."

But Belgarin was already rising from the bed, his thoughts on his two sisters. How dare they? He thought, suddenly furious. It was as if his entire family conspired against him to steal his crown. And now they planned to turn his brother against him as well? As he started to get dressed, he realized that he needed to speak to the Knower. It would not be long before his army began its march, and the Knower might die at any moment, victim to the bond he had with the Virtue of Intelligence. Belgarin did not pretend to understand the Virtues much himself, had always thought them the fancies of children and had been shocked when Caldwell brought knowledge of their existence to him. It had seemed needlessly cruel to him, at first, but he had to admit that though the Knower was repulsive, he had proved far too useful to ignore.

"Do you truly love me, dearest?"

Belgarin felt a flash of irritation as her words pulled him from his thoughts, and he glanced to where she lay in the bed, a sheet covering her now. "A little less each time you insist on asking such stupid, vacuous questions."

She recoiled as if he'd slapped her, "Forgive me, please, my king. Only ... there is something that I wished to speak to you about."

"Later," he said, waving his hand dismissively, "I've too much to do. As do you. It would be best that you leave immediately—it would be a terrible thing should the meeting take place without you there."

"Please," she said, reaching out and grabbing his hand, "it won't take long, I promise. Only a moment, my love."

"Damnit, woman," Belgarin growled, "I'm not your love, I am your king, and I do not have time for your silly fancies." He jerked his arm away and pulled on his boots, suddenly overcome with a sense of urgency. He started toward the door then paused at the threshold. "You will leave tonight," he said, not bothering to turn, "and you will do what I asked of you. There is no time to waste."

There was the briefest of hesitations, and when she spoke he could hear the sadness in her voice, enough so he knew that, should he turn, he would see the tears gliding down her cheeks. "Y-yes, my king."

"Very well," he said, then he was out the door and closing it behind him.

The woman, Lyla, watched him go, a hand on her belly, the tears warm as they coursed their way down her cheeks. Then she rose and began to get dressed. There was, after all, very little time to waste.

CHAPTER SEVENTEEN

"Gods, Pelar, are you going to take your turn before we all die of boredom or old age?"

The man known as Pelar turned his gaze—but not his thoughts—away from the stairs to see the man who'd spoken and the other three young men studying him, their indignation obvious in their expressions.

Not nobles, any of these, but sons of merchants rich enough that they enjoyed pretending at it, actors on a stage, playing out their roles loudly and proudly for any audience who might happen by. The man known as Pelar did not mind. They were not nobles, and he was not Pelar. After all, the world was full of actors, and they each had their part to play. "Forgive me, gentlemen," he said, showing a smile, and allowing it to fade as he glanced down at the significant stack of coins in the center of the table. "Ah," he said, swallowing hard, affecting the nervousness of a man who has found himself very far out of his depth, "It is too rich, I'm afraid, for my blood."

The man after him—a youth of no more than twenty years of age but fat and spoiled from his parents' attention—laughed, carelessly throwing in the coins to match the bet, more than a little satisfaction in his face as he considered Pelar's financial worries. "It's just coin, man," the fat youth said, "there's always more of it."

Repulsion and hatred flared in Pelar at the fool, but he smiled easily enough. Actors on a stage, nothing more. "Sure it is," he said, "but I don't think the baker will feel the same way, should I have nothing to offer him for bread."

One of the others, a gangly, pimple-faced youth that wore clothes more expensive than the houses many people lived in, snorted at that, "You're a funny man, Pelar, but Adrian's right. It's only gold."

Only gold. That was an expression not even used by the grossly wealthy parents of such as these, for the parents understood enough to know that gold might be only gold, but to a starving man, it was life. These, though, had never had to work for anything, and so did not understand the simplest of truths. All things were relative. Gold was only gold and water was only water, but a man in the desert would give all that he had for a single drink of something even while a sailor might grow sick of even the sight of it. All things were relative, the man known as Pelar had found, even goodness. Even principles.

He'd once considered himself a good man, a man of principles. He'd thought himself the luckiest man in the world, a man who loved a wonderful woman and who was loved by her despite the fact that his job as a palace clerk barely paid enough to keep them fed and clothed.

They had been poor, but they had been happy. At least, that was, until his wife had come down with a sickness that brought on frequent fever, delirium, and vomiting. Terrified, he'd taken her to a healer, and the old woman had assured him that his wife's condition was curable. He'd been ecstatic, going so far as to hug the woman before she told him the price of the cure, a price far beyond what any palace clerk could manage.

It was then, when a man came to his door with a small bag full of coins—enough gold to heal his wife and more besides—when the man had asked him if he'd be willing to do certain things that he'd realized the greatest truth there was. All things were relative. Some might look at the things he did and believe them wrong, but his wife was healthy now, and he was able to buy her jewelry and fine dresses, things she'd always deserved but that he'd never been able to afford. In truth, he suspected he was far wealthier than any of those sitting at the table with him.

"Ah, damnit," one of the men said, and the man known as Pelar glanced back at the table to see the fat man raking all of the coins toward him, though all three were smiling widely enough that a casual observer would have been hard pressed to guess who had won and who had lost. After all, he thought, it's only gold.

The next man was shuffling the cards when Pelar saw a cloaked and hooded form make its way down the steps and out the door. He waited longer still, and was in the middle of a hand when the woman came down the steps, her own face covered by an azure cloak and hood. She headed for the door and once she walked out, the man known as Pelar stood and tossed his cards into the center of the table.

"Pelar," one of the men said, "what gives?"

"Yeah," another said, "you can't fold out of turn like that."

"Fuck off," Pelar said, his voice dry and without emotion, and they were still staring at him, slack jawed and speechless even as he walked out of the common room and into the night. He needed to be sure of where the woman went—his master would want to know.

CHAPTER EIGHTEEN

A knock came at her new office door, and May looked up from the reports she'd been scanning. "Come in."

The door opened and Celes walked inside, "Ah, Celes," May said, rubbing at her eyes and trying on a weary smile, "I'm glad that you're here. I wondered if you couldn't go and talk to Gelsey—I know the old bat doesn't like me, but though she'd never admit it, she's a power of her own in the Downs. I don't have to tell you that the women she employs are often trained in fighting and healing more than the city's soldiers." She grunted, "Not that such a thing means much, I suppose, as the city council's priority seems to be finding new, inventive ways to tax people that are already starving instead of training its soldiers for war. Still, the women would be a great help, and, I suspect, we'll have many more volunteers should the city's busiest brothel empty and head for Perennia."

"They are trained, it is true," Celes said, "makes their clients less likely to vent the day's frustrations on the women they choose for the night."

"Though I'll suspect a few still do," May said, "and those, I don't doubt, regret it."

Celes smiled, running a hand through her long blond hair, "It has been known to happen, but most often the women don't have to take care of it themselves. A word to Gelsey and problem clients either cease being problems or cease being clients and more than a few have disappeared without any trace of their whereabouts. It's the reason all the hired women in the Downs are lining up to work for Gelsey."

May nodded, "I can't say as I approve what the woman does. I know as well as anyone that men have needs and some will take what they want whether there's a cost or not, whether they're invited to or not, yet I still find the whole practice ... disheartening. Still, there is no denying the old bat's effectiveness."

Celes shrugged, the tight fitting shirt she wore shifting in a way that May knew would have most men distracted beyond words. Gods, she thought, and not for the first time, if I had a body like hers, I'd rule this city. "Perhaps it is disheartening," Celes said, "but those women work in a place where they know they'll be kept safe, and they go home with full bellies at the end of the night and plenty of coin to provide for their families."

"I understand, Celes," May said, "and I'm not judging you. You did what you had to do—just as those women are doing now. But I can't help feeling that there' something ... unnatural about it. I employ singers, sure, dancers too, and those singers and dancers will often wear dresses that leave very little to the imagination, but the simple fact is that men tip better, you show them a bit of flesh. With Gelsey's girls though ... they're selling more than a look. It just ... it isn't natural."

"Neither is starving," Celes said, "but people do it every day."

May grunted, "I deserve that. I'm sorry, Celes. It has just been a long few weeks." She squinted, studying the blonde woman, "you really are very much like him, you know. I was always surprised that you two didn't hit it off more than you did."

"Are you talking of Silent?" Celes said. She smiled and shook her head, "Aaron is a good man, though he doesn't know it. Anyway, he and I are too similar. We'd end up killing each other or killing ourselves. Besides, he's found his love already."

May nodded at that, a fresh wave of worry rising in her, "I suppose he has."

Celes moved forward and put a hand on her shoulder, "He'll be okay, May. Silent is not the type of man to give up, nor the type to run from a fight."

"That's what I'm afraid of," May said. "If even half the things he wrote me in the letter were true, I'd be terrified. As it is..." she shrugged, "I am not a praying woman, Celes, but I don't mind saying that if things get much worse, my knees will have callouses on them an inch thick."

Celes laughed then her expression sobered and she sat in front of the desk opposite May. "You look tired. You need your rest."

May grunted, "Sure I do and while we're dreaming why not wish for a king's ransom?" She sighed, "There's too much to do, Celes, and too little time to do it in. If I'm not reading Gryle's expenditure reports—and you would not believe what people charge for salted meat and coffee, it's enough to make Gelsey's finest blush—then I'm caught in the middle of what appears to be a war of letters between Grinner and Hale. I swear to the gods those two men argue about everything just to spite one another. Who has the most men, who has the best men. They haven't got around to arguing over who has the most well-endowed men, but I suspect it's only a matter of time. Mark me, Celes, if Belgarin's army showed up tomorrow, those two bastards would argue over who he got to kill first."

Celes nodded, "Sounds like you've been busy, but that's still no reason not to sleep," she said, her tone scolding, "You'll be no good to Aaron or anyone else if you end up sick or worse from pushing yourself too hard."

May sighed, "I understand what you're saying, dear, but my duties have taken up all of my time. I've barely had time to think of eating let alone sleeping."

"Yes," Celes said, raising her eyebrow and smiling, "so I have heard. As I understand it, you do find a few spare moments to go to your bedroom though, from what I understand, you do not sleep when you're there. Anyway, at least you've had help with your duties."

May frowned, "Help?"

Celes's grin widened, "Yes, just so. From what I hear, there has been a certain first mate that regularly drops by to have ... shall we say, meetings with you in your quarters. One can only suspect that they are pivotal, terribly important meetings to require such pr—"

"Alright, alright, damn you," May said, but she found herself grinning back, "It seems that someone has been speaking out of turn. Fine, so maybe I've stolen a few moments for myself, but a woman has needs too, you know. Besides, Thom is a smart man—at least, as smart as any of them are—and he's proven himself quite useful of late."

"Oh, that I do not doubt," Celes said, arching an eyebrow.

May rolled her eyes and waved a dismissive hand, "Alright, away with you. You've had your laugh."

"And you will have your sleep," Celes said, "I need you to promise me."

May sighed, "Fine, alright. I'll make sure to sleep tonight."

Celes shook her head, "It already is tonight, May, has been for two hours or more."

May raised her eyebrows in surprise, "Is it? Well, then," she said, glancing at the pile of unchecked reports and correspondences on her desk, "I will head up soon. Just as soon as I'm done here."

"You'll head up now," Celes said, "and I mean it."

May pursed her lips into a pout, "You know, somebody happening by would be forgiven for thinking that you were the employer, and I was the employee. Or that maybe you were my mother—and if so, you've aged much better than I myself."

Celes smiled the smile that had allowed her to charge her customers a small fortune when she worked for Gelsey, "And they would not be far wrong. Now, come on. There's something you need to see before you go to bed, and it will do you good to get a little walking in, to get out of this office for a little while."

May frowned, but she rose, "I like my office."

Celes glanced around her as if seeing it for the first time, "Yes," she said, "it has a certain dignity to it. I suspect that many would be pleased to have it as their coffin."

"Fine," May huffed, "lead on then you damned miserable woman."

Celes grinned and winked before turning and leading them out of the office and into the club proper.

The club was packed—as it was most every night when the sun went down and single men and those who weren't single but wished they were came to whistle and gawk at women of such beauty that they usually only came so close in their dreams. She noticed that three of the six club's stages were empty and frowned. They were supposed to be fully booked tonight, having expected a busy one.

She clapped a hand on Celes's shoulder, stopping her and nodding to the three empty stages, "You want to tell me what all that's about?"

Celes followed her gaze and sighed, "You're not going to like it."

May grunted, "Best show me now then. I've been having entirely too much fun of late," she said, the sarcasm heavy in her tone, "perhaps this is exactly what I need."

"Alright," Celes said reluctantly, "but don't say I didn't warn you."

She led May to where three of her singers—the same three, in fact, who were supposed to be singing—stood gathered in a small circle with what appeared to be one or two of the serving girls, all bent over something. "Nissa," May said.

The slight girl turned, her eyes going wide as she saw May and Celes standing there, "M-m-ma'am," the girl said, "um ... h-hi."

May frowned, "Don't stutter, girl, and take a breath. You look as if you're about to pass out, like maybe you've seen a ghost, and though I admit to having let my appearance slip a bit of late, I do not think that it so awful as that."

"N-no, ma'am," the girl said, swallowing hard even as the others turned to look at May and Celes, tensing as if about to bolt, "you ... you look fantastic. As lovely as ever."

May rolled her eyes, "I hope that you are better at lying to your man in bed than you are to me."

"Ma'am?" Nissa said, "I don't have a man."

May nodded as if a suspicion had just been confirmed, "And now we know why. Now, why don't you go ahead and tell me what it is you all are doing here that's so important you can't be bothered to get up on stage and do what I'm paying you for?"

The woman's face grew pale, "I ... that is...."

"Oh, just move aside you sprig," May said, "and stop acting like a rabbit when the lion shows up."

The singers and waitresses glanced at each other nervously then shifted to the side to reveal the young boy, Michael, sitting in the floor with a glass of what looked like warm milk. There were what must have been at least half a dozen different toys ranging from small brightly colored balls that a juggler might use in his performance to what appeared to be a small toy wooden sword built for a child's hands lay scattered on the floor around him. The boy glanced up from where he'd been drinking his milk and his eyes went wide as he stared at May.

"Well," she said, smiling, "if it isn't our young Michael. And how are you, dear boy?"

"I'm ... fine, ma'am," he said, "I wasn't doing anything wrong was I? You won't tell my granny? She's not feeling really good, and I didn't mean to be bad, honest."

May crouched down, running a hand through the boy's hair, "It's not ma'am, it's aunt May, okay? And I won't be telling your granny anything as you haven't done anything wrong, alright? Now," she said, motioning at a small doll dressed in soldier's clothes at the boy's feet, "why don't you tell me the name of this fine gentleman?"

"His name's Gryle," the boy said, "after ... after the man that saved my granny. But he's not a gentleman, Aunt May. He's a hero. The best."

May found herself grinning widely then and unable to stop it, "Yes," she said, "I'm sure he is."

"My granny," the boy said, staring up at her with hopeful eyes, "is she going to be okay?"

She glanced back at the other women who were still watching her, smiles on their own faces now. "Well," she said, "seeing as you all have nothing to do, perhaps I can find some work for you in the kitchen with Edna. I'm sure she could always use some more hands for cutting the heads off of chickens or butchering the hogs for tonight's meals."

In an instant, the women started to scatter, "Not you, Nissa," May said, "you stay here."

The singer froze, cringing and turned slowly, "Ma'am, I'm truly sorry. We didn't mean—"

"Never mind what you meant," May said, "I want you to show our dear Michael here around, make sure to keep him entertained. Can you do that for me?"

The thin girl smiled prettily, and May found herself glad that, this one, at least, had come to her instead of Gelsey. She could have done either job well enough, she knew. A voice like an angel and a face to match. "Yes ma'am," the woman said, still smiling, "that is ... if that's what you want me to do."

May nodded, "It is, girl, it is. The customers will just have to survive with five beautiful women singing or dancing for them instead of six. A great sacrifice, but one that I feel I'm prepared for them to make. Now, run along and show our Michael some fun, won't you?"

"Yes ma'am," she said, stepping forward and grabbing hold of the young boy's hand.

"Your granny will be fine, Michael," May said, bending over and rubbing the boy's hair, "you just be strong for her okay? She's had a tough couple of days, and she just needs to rest. That's all."

The boy nodded solemnly, the serious expression on his young face like a dagger in May's heart, "I will, ma'am. I'll be strong. For Granny."

May cleared her throat, "Okay, dear. Now, you run along with Nissa, okay? Maybe she'll even be able to find you some chocolates."

The boy grinned and in another moment they were off. May turned to Celes once they were gone, "This news you have for me. Tell me it's good."

Celes nodded, "It is. The boy's grandmother—she's awake. The healer says that she was malnourished and had been living in terrible conditions for several weeks, but that she would have a quick recovery."

May let out a heavy breath that she hadn't realized she'd been holding, "Thank the gods for that, at least."

"And thank Gryle," Celes said.

May shook her head in wonder at the thought, "Yes, and thank Gryle. I would not have thought the chamberlain had it in him. Well, alright then. Lead on. Let's go see this grandmother."

***

May and Celes walked inside of the door to find the woman, Beth, sleeping. Her face and body had been bandaged from a

173

dozen small cuts and scrapes, the bruises she'd suffered at the hands of Aster Kalen and his men treated with ointment, and she had been bathed, of course. She looked almost like a different person than when May had seen her stumble into her office, and she was glad for the woman and the boy both.

Gryle was seated in a chair beside the bed, his arms folded on the nightstand, and his head buried inside them, snoring so loudly that May was amazed Beth could get any sleep at all. "How long has he been here?" She asked Celes in a quiet voice so as not to rouse either.

"He almost never leaves," Celes said, "he's here every time I come to check on her, and the healer said she had to run him out a few times."

May shook her head in wonder as she stared at the chubby, balding man, "Sometimes, you never really know a person until they're tested."

"Most times," Celes agreed.

"Oh, hello."

They turned to see that the woman, Beth, was awake and easing herself up into a sitting position in the bed.

"Forgive us," May said, having to raise her voice to be heard over the sound of Gryle's snoring, "once we heard you were awake, we wanted to come visit you and see how you were faring."

"Well," the woman said, smiling, the skin around her mouth and eyes crinkling, "I'm still old and still ugly, but I'm alive, and I reckon that's more than I had any right to expect. The healer told me you've allowed me and my grandson to stay here, and I thank ya for it."

May shrugged, suddenly uncomfortable, "No thanks are needed. Not for me, at least."

The old woman smiled, glancing at the chamberlain where he still snored. "You wouldn't believe it," she said, "the gods know I'm having a hard time believing it, and I was there. Your man, there, knocked the door down like it weighed nothing and threw the guard watching us into the ceiling, so that his damned head got stuck." She gave a cackle at that, "the bastard might still be hangin' there, for all I know." She sobered then, and shook her head, "If not for him ... you got to understand, Michael is the only family I got left. If anything had happened to him...."

"But nothing did," May said, "your grandson is fine, and you're fine."

The woman nodded, giving a small smile, "Just about as fine as I get anyway."

"Forgive me, I don't mean to pry," May said, "but Gryle told me that you have the speed Virtue?"

The old woman nodded, "That's right, though 'bout the only speedy thing these bones have done in a while is ache when a storm's comin'."

May wasn't able to stop the full belly laugh that came at that, and suddenly Gryle jerked awake. "Oh, excuse me," he said, and his hands pressed on the nightstand, as he tried to push himself to his feet. The wood of the nightstand groaned and broke apart beneath his hands, and the chamberlain let out a squeak as he stumbled to the side where May caught him saving him from a fall.

"Oh, gods watch over us," Gryle said in a scandalized voice, "forgive me, Miss May," he said, righting himself and dusting off his clothes, "it was an accident."

Just then, the door opened and the healer came rushing in only to glance at the nightstand with a weary expression before looking to Gryle. "Another one?" She demanded, "that's the third one in as many days."

Gryle swallowed hard, "I'm sorry, truly, I did not mean—"

"Think nothing of it," May said, "it's only a night stand. We can find another." She winked at the healer who gave a tired smile before leaving once more, closing the door behind her.

Gryle's face turned bright red in embarrassment, and his mouth began to work without sound, his hands—covered in tiny pieces of wood—rubbing together anxiously.

May was just about to try to tell the man again that it didn't matter when the old woman, Beth, burst into loud, cackling laughter. "Oh, but you are a sight, you are, chamberlain," she managed between her laughter. "The bastard is still probably in the ceiling."

Gryle's look of shocked embarrassment and terror at what he'd done slowly turned into an anxious smile and, in another moment, he was laughing. May realized it was the first time she'd heard the nervous chamberlain laugh, and she and Celes shared a look before joining in.

When the laughter finally died out, Gryle nodded as if to himself, visibly screwing up his courage. Then he walked to the bed and bowed to Beth. "I am very pleased to see that you are well, my lady."

Beth snorted, "I'm no lady, chamberlain, which you know well enough. And anyway," she said, her expression growing serious, "the only reason why I'm alright, me and the boy both, is because of you. Those men would have killed us if not for you."

Gryle looked more embarrassed than ever, "I ... that is, my lady, I do not mean to contradict you, but I am sure you would have found a way out sooner or later and anyone would have done the same thing in my position and done it better and faster too, no doubt."

"No," Beth said, reaching out and grabbing his hand, "They wouldn't have. You saved my life, chamberlain, the boy's life, and I'm in your debt." Gryle started to protest, but she held a wrinkled hand up, forestalling him, "Listen to me well, chamberlain, for if you demean yourself in front of me for this, if you act as if what you did was anything less than heroic, then you had better hope that there is another like you around to save your sorry hide, for I swear I will beat you over the head until you see reason. Do you understand?"

Gryle's eyes went wide, and he cleared his throat, "Yes ma'am."

May shared a smile with Celes as the old woman grunted, "Good. Now that we've got all that nonsense out of the way for a time, why don't you tell me what the plan is?"

Gryle frowned. "Plan, my lady?"

The old woman snorted, "Oh, don't you bandy words with me, lad. I might be old and look a damned sight older than that, but my momma, rest her soul, didn't raise no fools. What fool was in us she made sure to beat out with a good swat to the butt when it showed its face. Now, it's clear enough to me that Aster Kalen captured you for a reason. Considerin' that you didn't have one of the Seven when he captured you and that neither of these ladies here's got one neither, I gotta think it's somethin' else you're doin' our late friend wasn't too fond of. Now, out with it and tell me how I can help."

The chamberlain looked at a loss and glanced back to May who only shrugged. Then, sighing, he turned back to Beth, "Ma'am, Aster Kalen came for me, I believe, because two of my friends do possess one of the Virtues, and they only recently had a battle with Aster's master, a man by the name of Boyce Kevlane who seeks to unite all of the Seven together within himself."

"This," the old woman said, raising an eyebrow, "bein' the same Boyce Kevlane as children hear stories about when they're growin' up? A man said to have been the most powerful user of the Art in his time? The same man who was best friend and confidant to Aaron Caltriss himself?"

Gryle cleared his throat again, "Yes, my lady. That's the one."

Beth nodded, "Alright. So what's our plan?"

"I ... that is..." Gryle glanced back at May again, and she sighed.

"The thing is, Beth," May said, "it isn't just about Boyce Kevlane, not that he wouldn't be problem enough. You see, we are also pitted against Belgarin, the royal prince himself. Even if we were to somehow defeat one or the other ..." she shrugged, "we will do what we can, of course, but it would not be far from the truth to say that the task before us is near impossible."

"Know what's impossible?" Beth said, "a woman running faster than the world's quickest horse, that's what. Or an out of shape chamberlain—no offense, Gryle—picking up a guard that weighed two hundred and fifty pounds, if he weighed an ounce, and throwing him into the ceilin' with one hand with no more trouble than a child would have trying to skip stones across a stream. You don't need to tell me about the impossible, lady. I've been livin' it since I was fifteen years old. Now, do you got a plan or not?"

May found herself smiling at the old woman's candor and no nonsense approach, "Well, such as it is, yes ma'am. You see, we are trying to gather what army we can from the city of Avarest—criminals, mostly, though we've put a case before the council—and we intend to take ships to Perennia, where Aaron and Adina, the royal princess are, along with another of our friends. There, we will try to help them fight Belgarin's army."

Beth grunted, "That's all, is it?"

"So as you can see," May said, deciding to try one last time, for the boy's sake if not Beth's, "we either already have all of the help we need, or we are beyond help. One more person will not make a difference one way or the other."

Gryle started to nod, "She's—" there was a blur of motion, and May and the others lifted their hands to their faces as a gust of wind struck them sending the sheets flying from the bed, "—right," Gryle finished, letting out a gasp as the three of them saw that the bed was empty, the old woman nowhere in evidence.

"I hope you don't mind me takin' the liberty," a voice said, and they spun, recoiling in surprise to find Beth standing in the doorway, three pastries in her left hand even as she took a bite of one she was holding in her right. "I've always had a sweet tooth," she explained, standing in a simple gown the healer had dressed her in and speaking as if nothing unusual had occurred, "still," she said, "I brought enough for everybody."

She offered up the three pastries sitting on a plate to the others, but they all only stared in shocked silence. Beth cackled, "Why, I wish you all could see your faces. Look like a couple of dumb struck calves bein' led to market.

It took May several seconds to be able to make her voice work, "I .... I didn't realize—"

Beth cackled, "Yeah, I looked much the same the first time I done it myself, though in a bit more pain, I imagine. I tell you now, it don't do a body good to trip, goin' fast as that."

"It's ... unbelievable," May said.

Beth grinned, a mischievous expression that would have been more at home on a young teenage girl intending to do something her parents wouldn't like than on a woman that was seemingly in her eighties wearing nothing but a simple white gown. "I'm tempted to tell ya that it gets old after a while, but I try not to lie, when I'm able. Truth is, it never does get old—only I do." She held out her hand and a yellow sphere of light appeared floating above it.

"Hello," came a man's voice.

Celes gasped, and May took an involuntary step back. She'd known from Aaron's letter that the Virtues were real, of course, but knowing a thing and seeing it only a few feet from your face were very different. Priests knew—or at least thought they did—that their gods existed, spent their time praying to them and asking for favors, but May suspected they'd probably all die of shock if their god ever appeared right in front of them, as real as anything was. "H-hello," May managed, and Celes, perhaps not trusting herself to speak, only bowed her head.

The yellow orb floated to Gryle, its light shifting in ever changing patterns even as it came to stop only a foot from the chamberlain's face. "I wish to thank you, sir, for saving Beth and Michael. I have known them both for some time now, and I would not see harm come to them, if it was in my power to stop it. Thank you."

"Um ... your welcome?" Gryle said, his uncertain tone making it a question, but if the Virtue noticed, he gave no sign, choosing instead to float back in front of the old woman.

"You are quite sure of this? What of Michael?" He asked.

"You know I am," she said, "Anyway, you and I both know I've got a year, maybe two on the outside left to me."

"We can't know that," he said.

Beth sighed, "You're a sweet one, and it's been a pleasure to know ya, but lyin' about a thing won't change it. The truth always wins—it's the only thing you can count on in this world, and I don't intend to spend my last days lying in a bed, bitchin' and moanin' about all the aches and pains I've got or feelin' sorry for myself on account of my teats hadn't seen the up side of my belly button in fifteen years.

"Very well," the Virtue said, "as you wish."

Beth raised an eyebrow in surprise, "That it then? You ain't gonna try to convince me otherwise, like when Aster brought his ruffians to the house? Not gonna tell me that there's more time left to me and all?"

"Would it make any difference if I did?" The Virtue said.

Beth grinned displaying several missing teeth as she did, "Naw, I don't reckon it would."

"Well, then," the Virtue said, and May thought she could detect more than a little love for the old woman in the orb's tone, "let us do it. One last mission, one final trick."

Beth nodded, "Aye," she said, "one final trick." She wiped a finger across her eyes then turned to May, "Well? What needs doin'?"

"For tonight?" May said, "We rest. I need it, and I think you may need it more than I."

The old woman grunted, but she didn't disagree, "And tomorrow?"

May sighed, "Tomorrow, we prepare to take on two impossible foes: a wizard of the past that is thousands of years old and a prince with an army bigger than anything we could hope to muster in defense. Tomorrow, we set about a mission that will almost certainly end in all of our deaths."

Beth nodded then gave her a wink, "Alright," she said, grinning, "Well, sweet dreams then."

CHAPTER NINETEEN

The queen was waiting in the dining hall when Aaron, Adina, and Leomin arrived. She was seated on her throne on the raised dais, the same way she'd been seated when he'd first met her. The tables, too, were the same, set up so that they formed a U shape on the floor below the queen's throne. Aaron frowned, remembering the last time he'd entered this dining hall, remembering how it had ended with him breaking the former guard captain's nose, and he and the others essentially being thrown out by Isabelle and confined to their rooms. 'Confined' he'd discovered, was noble-speak for imprisoned. The memory didn't exactly do much to quell the anxiety that was rising in him at the upcoming meeting.

Still, though many things were the same as they had been the last time, there were some notable differences. Namely, there was no arrogant, smiling young captain beating up on a couple of commoners that knew as much about swordplay as they did about dining etiquette when seated among royalty. Which, of course, was to say nothing at all. Another marked difference was the significant amount of weight that the queen had lost in only about a month's time. She was still heavy enough that Aaron would rather have a fight to the death with a professional swordsman than have her sit on his lap, but he thought that the reduction in her weight had probably given the poor throne on which she sat a few more years of tortured life.

Still, though the queen had lost weight, it had not improved her appearance. In fact, in Aaron's mind at least, she looked worse. There were bags under her eyes and the skin of her previously fat, cherubic face now sagged as if somebody had begun the job of melting it but not quite finished. There was a haggardness to her appearance that spoke not of a night's sleep lost but of weeks of it, weeks of restlessness in which what little sleep she did get was no doubt filled with nightmares of the creature Boyce Kevlane and of the attempt on her life that had so very nearly succeeded. Nightmares that left her almost painfully glad to be awake despite the weariness of her mind and body. Aaron understood the feeling well enough, had been living with it for weeks now. The only difference was that the queen's fear was one of what might happen to her, and his was a fear of what terrible things he might do.

Brandon Gant, the new captain of the queen's Royal Guard was already seated at the table, and he nodded amiably to Aaron and the others as they came inside. Aaron nodded back then frowned as he looked around to see that the tables were empty save Brandon himself. He thought of the old scholar, Mirmanon, a man that was known throughout Telrear for his wisdom and knowledge, only recently another victim in Kevlane's war. Not just, Kevlane's he thought, but Darrell's and Tianya's too. Let's not forget them.

You do Darrell an injustice, Aaron, Co said into his mind, *however he came about it, he saved your life by taking you in. Or would you now question that as well?*

No, of course not, firefly, Aaron thought back, *I know well enough what I owe. Anyone raised in the Downs always does. Still, it doesn't excuse what he's done.*

Doesn't it?

Aaron sighed and followed Adina's lead as she bowed to the queen. "I thank you all for coming," Isabelle said, trying a smile that seemed out of place on her weary face. "You may be seated, if you'd like. Ellemont, I am told, will be with us momentarily."

Aaron followed the others to the table on the left side of the room, the same one at which Brandon sat. He stepped over to the older man and held out his hand. Brandon grinned and took it, "Small company," Aaron said as he sat down beside the captain.

"Aye, so it is," Brandon said, "though I suppose there's less chance of someone endin' the meal with a broken nose at any rate."

Aaron grunted, "I'd hoped you would have forgotten that."

Brandon grinned, "I'm old, lad, but I'm not that old. Besides, forget such a thing as that? I've seen few things finer in my life, and it's a memory I'll cherish for years to come."

Aaron sighed, "You need to get out more, captain. Still," he said, glancing at the several chairs on their side of the room which remained empty, "I would have liked to have had the scholar, Mirmanon here. I think he would have proved a valuable asset."

The captain's grin faded, and he scratched at the salt and pepper stubble on his chin, "Aye, he would've. I'm an old man, Aaron, and I'm not made to sit around and talk, to try to convince people of what they ought to already know. I find that the older I get, the less patience I have for such things. Mirmanon, though, that man was the most patient person I've ever met, not to mention the wisest. His is a great loss and one we will feel for some time, I think."

Aaron was about to respond when the two guards who'd been stationed outside of the dining hall pushed the doors open. "My queen," one said, bowing low, "Prince Ellemont and his retinue have arrived."

Isabelle glanced at Adina who nodded before looking back to the guard, "Very well, Gerald, please, send them in."

"Very well," the guard said, "then may I introduce Prince Ellemont, Royal Son of Telrear, and King of the White Mountains, and his queen, Lilliana of house Swainlen, and their personal guards.

Aaron had never seen the prince before, and he was not what he'd expected. After all that he'd heard of the prince's cowardice, he'd thought to see some puny, frightened thing, more a rabbit than a man. Instead, the prince was tall, at least an inch or two taller than he himself, and if he was afraid, he did not show it as he strode, arm in arm with his queen, into the dining hall.

Aaron took a moment to wonder at the prince's choice of clothes. They were expertly made, that was evident enough, sewed and fashioned by a tailor who knew his business. They would have been a shirt and trousers that any noble would have been pleased to own. The shocking thing, though, was that they had both been dyed a bright yellow that put Aaron in mind of some bird.

Aaron glanced at Adina and Isabelle, noting that their own expressions registered the same surprise that he felt, then back to Ellemont to see the prince smiling a small, knowing smile, as if he knew full well what line of thought his clothes invoked and was pleased by it.

Not the first choice I'd make, if I were a known coward, Aaron thought.

The prince, it seems, Co said, is well aware of his reputation and chooses to play upon it.

Aaron nodded, Which tells us much about him. Either he's insane, stupid, or he's got a very strange sense of humor.

Says the man who thinks it's funny to call a legend 'firefly.'

Oh, don't be so sensitive, princess, Aaron thought, everyone loves fireflies. Why, when I was a kid, we used to go around catching them in jars or hitting them with sticks to watch the light explode.

Imprisoned or murdered out right. I'm flattered.

Good, Aaron thought, you should be. Prince Ellemont and his wife moved further into the room, stopping a short distance before Isabelle's throne, and Aaron found himself studying Ellemont's wife. While Ellemont seemed well at ease, walking with the same casualness he might show strolling through the market, the queen moved stiffly, seeming to think of each step and each movement before she made them, and there was something about her that exuded a sort of arrogance, as if she believed herself to be the most important person in the room. The pair bowed to the queen, and Aaron noted idly that Ellemont's own bow was considerably lower than his queen's.

"Ah, it is a pleasure to see you, brother," Isabelle said, "please, rise."

Ellemont did, smiling, though his queen's expression was unreadable. "And it is good to be seen, sister," he said. "And little Adina," he said, turning and bowing to her just as low as he had the queen, "It has been too long. I was very pleased to hear that the rumor of your death was only that."

Adina smiled, "So it has, Ellemont. Far too long, and I might say that I was possibly even more pleased than you yourself at the rumor's falseness."

Ellemont grinned wider, "Always so very clever, sister. It is good to know that some things have not changed."

"Well," Adina said, "We all have our reputations to live up to, don't we, brother? For instance, I have always believed you to be the royal with the most fashion sense." She paused, taking in the bright yellow clothes, "Though I find myself beginning to doubt my own memory."

Ellemont laughed, and it was a rich, genuine laugh that made Aaron want to laugh along with him. "Oh, sister, well, as you say we all have our reputations to live up to. Yellow clothes for a yellow prince. I find that it suits well enough."

Adina opened her mouth, clearly prepared to protest the prince's own self-criticism, but Ellemont held up a hand to forestall her, "Be at ease, sister. I made peace with myself long ago, and there is nothing cruel or self-pitying in knowing the truth and speaking it. Now, let us move on. I would like to introduce you all to my wife, Lilliana."

Lilliana's face was smooth and without flaw as she bowed her head to each of them in turn, her expression unchanging. Aaron got the distinct impression that this was a woman who did not smile often. "It is a pleasure, I'm sure." She said. "I was quite saddened to hear of your difficulties of late, if I may say so, Princess Adina. And, of course, Queen Isabelle," she said, turning to Adina's sister, "I was equally grieved to hear of the attempt on your own life. I am very glad and thankful to the gods that you both are well."

She doesn't seem particularly thankful to me, Aaron thought.

There is something about her I do not like, Aaron.

That so? Aaron thought back, just the one thing?

I'm serious, Aaron.

So am I, he thought, frowning. Ellemont nodded to him, Leomin, and Brandon, "And who are these fine gentlemen, if I might be so bold as to inquire?"

"These are friends," Isabelle said, "Aaron Envelar, the general of my armies, Brandon Gant, the captain of my guard, and ... Leomin."

Aaron shot a look at Leomin to see if he'd noticed the queen's hesitation which, judging by his wide grin, he had. "It is a pleasure sirs, one and all," Ellemont said, bowing once more. "And may I introduce you to the commander of my own army," he said, motioning to a thickly built man that was just now stepping through the doorway, "Commander Hallifax."

The man appeared to be in his forties, and was nearly as tall as the prince himself, his expression as serious as the queen's own when he bowed to the others. "Pleasure," he grunted in much the same tone that Aaron had heard people in the Downs whisper, 'Give me all your coin or die.'

"Please, have a seat," Isabelle said, "we have much to discuss."

"Why, of course, sister," Ellemont said, and he strutted to the other side of the room and eased himself into a chair, draping one leg over the arm of it as if he was relaxing at his home instead of taking part in a meeting that could very well decide the fate of the entire nation. Aaron was prepared to believe the man a coward, but whatever it was that struck fear into the prince, it seemed clear enough that it wasn't impropriety.

The queen and the general followed behind him, taking up seats on either side of Ellemont. "You must forgive my husband, Your Majesty," Queen Lilliana said, glancing at her husband with a complete lack of expression yet somehow conveying disapproval, "it was a long journey, and he has been wearied from it, so much that it is quite taxing for him to follow simple rules of propriety."

Ellemont cleared his throat and, in another moment, pulled his leg off of the chair, visibly straightening his back. "Yes," he said, "I do apologize, sisters and everyone else gathered. The trip was somewhat arduous."

Aaron shared a look with Leomin, the Parnen frowning at him, and it was Adina who broke the uncomfortable silence, "There is nothing to forgive, I'm sure, brother. I have recently been made quite aware of the rigors of travel myself, and I can't blame you. I myself acted much worse, I'm sure, when we finally arrived in Perennia."

186

"Is that so?" Ellemont said, gratitude clear in his expression, "well, thank you, sister."

"I'm sure," Lilliana said, "that the princess is being very kind, and it is appreciated. Still, though we have only just met, I find it hard to imagine you acting in any way other than with complete dignity and composure as befits a noble and member of the royal house."

Ellemont seemed to deflate at that, but Adina looked over to Aaron, her face growing red, and he stifled a grin before she turned back to Ellemont's wife. "Thank you for that, Lilliana, but I must admit that I have never been very good at being what many would consider a proper princess."

The woman bowed her head as if acknowledging a point, "As you say, my lady, but you may call me Lyla, if it pleases you."

"Very well, Lyla," Adina said. "Welcome."

Several seconds passed in which the two women studied each other, and Aaron got the distinct impression that there was some sort of contest going on between the two of them, one in which no man could participate or even understand.

"Well then," Ellemont said into the silence, his grin seeming more than a little forced, "Now that the pleasantries are done, I suppose it's time that we move on to why you have called us here."

Adina glanced to Isabelle, but the queen shook her head, "Tell him, sister. This may be my castle and my city, but in this matter, I bow to you."

Ellemont raised an eyebrow at that, and Aaron couldn't be sure, but he thought he saw Lyla's blank expression tighten for a moment. "As you say, sister," Adina said, nodding her head to the queen before turning back to Ellemont, "Tell me, Ellemont, what have you heard of our brother, Belgarin?"

Ellemont ran a hand through his hair, "What haven't I heard, sister? What was it father used to always say? News travels fast, but bad news travels on wings of darkness? Some such as that, anyway. I heard of Eladen's death, and I am sorry for it. He was the best of us."

"Not death," Adina said, "murder. Belgarin's men tortured and assassinated Eladen under a flag of truce, and Belgarin now claims dominion over Baresh and all of its people."

Ellemont nodded, a troubled expression on his face, "I had heard—"

"We have heard the stories, princess," Lilliana said, speaking over him, "Many would be surprised by just how much we hear in Cardayum," she said, staring meaningfully at Aaron before turning back to Adina. "Still, with as many conflicting stories as there are, who can say for sure what happened to poor prince Eladen?"

"I can," Adina said shortly, "as I was there. So, too, can Aaron."

"Truly?" Lyla said, looking to Aaron, her eyebrows raised in expectation.

Aaron nodded, "Yes, I was present when the prince succumbed to the wounds Belgarin's men gave him."

Lyla nodded, "And these wounds, you believe, were inflicted by Belgarin's men?"

Aaron grunted, "I believe that the sun will set tonight and come up again tomorrow, lady. I don't believe that Belgarin was responsible for prince Eladen's death. I know it."

Ellemont laughed at that, the sound unaffected and sonorous, "Oh, but you are an interesting one, sir, if you don't mind me saying. Truly—" he only just noticed Lyla giving him a dark stare and cut off. "Well," he said, shrugging, "that is interesting to know."

"And just how, I wonder," Ellemont's wife went on, "did you know that it was Belgarin's men? Did they claim as much? Are they somewhere here, now, so that we might interrogate them on the matter?"

Aaron frowned, rubbing at his chin. He felt caught off guard and out of his element. Fight men to death with a sword, sure, try to avoid being mugged or killed in a place known for it, sure, but bandying words like two fencers seeking a touch? It was something he was not accustomed to. "Yeah," he said, finally, "well, I suppose you could ask them, but they wouldn't tell you much."

"No?" The dark-haired woman asked, and he could detect a certain satisfaction in her voice, "and why is that, I wonder?"

"Well," Aaron said, "that would be because they're dead."

"I see," the woman said, smiling, "well, that is most unfortunate as their testimony would have gone a long way to establishing the veracity of your story."

"Bogeymen are stories," Aaron said, "Faeries are stories. What I'm telling you are facts."

"As you say," she answered, inclining her head the tiniest fraction, her tone doubtful, "and, forgive me, but I cannot help but wonder what prince Belgarin would say were he here to defend his own alleged actions."

Aaron shrugged, "Something along the lines of 'give up or die' I suspect. It seems to be quite a theme with him."

"So is that to say," Lyla said, "that as to Eladen's supposed murder, we have no word or proof to go on except for your own observation of events?"

"Aaron is not a criminal to be interrogated," Adina said, and Aaron could hear the sharpness and anger in her tone, "he is a man who I trust with my life and anything else without reservation, and I do not appreciate you speaking to him as if he were some common criminal."

"Forgive me, princess, truly," the woman said, though if she was bothered or regretful, it did not show in her calm expression, "I did not mean to offend. I am only seeking to establish the truth. My husband, you see, is far too ... kind to ask such questions, so I, being his loving wife, must ask them for him."

Aaron got the distinct impression that 'kind' had not been the first word to jump to the woman's mind concerning her husband, and he'd only just met her, but he thought he knew enough to know that she was probably just about as loving as a pissed off bear. "It's fine," Aaron said to Adina. Then he turned back to the woman, "All I can tell you, ma'am is that I know what I saw. In fact, after witnessing the prince's murder, I barely made it out of Avarest with my skin intact for all of Belgarin's men chasing me."

"As you say," the woman said again, but it was clear by her expression and her tone that what she meant was, 'So you say.'

"I feel that I must attest to General Envelar's character," Isabelle said, "as I have only recently survived an assassination attempt due to his shocking amount of courage and integrity. Without him, I would not be sitting here before you today."

"Since then," the queen went on, "We have caught several spies in the employ of Belgarin in large part due to Leomin's efforts." She smiled at the Parnen who bowed his head graciously.

"Ah," Lyla said, "spies is it? And caught by a Parnen no less. And these spies you have captured," she said, turning back to Aaron, "have any of them spoken or admitted their role as spies for prince Belgarin?"

"They wouldn't be very good spies, if they did," Aaron said. "Still, Leomin has found letters on the person of several of the accused, orders written, we believe, by either Belgarin himself or someone high up in his command."

The woman's eyebrows drew down as if considering his words. "'You believe' you say. Forgive me, but what exactly does that mean? Were the letters incriminating or not? Did they bear Belgarin's seal?"

Aaron found himself growing annoyed. No, he thought, that's not right. Not annoyed. Angry. "I don't expect you would have been subjected to such practices before, my lady, given your station," he said, "so you must trust me when I say that, generally speaking, spies do not consider it wise to walk around with fliers bearing their master's name."

The woman frowned at that, and Ellemont held up his hands, "Peace, peace, everyone, please." He said, "We all know well enough what Belgarin is capable of—we've heard enough of the tales to not doubt the truth of them. Lyla knows that as well as anyone."

The woman stared at him for a moment, and Aaron thought that if looks could kill, the prince would be being buried in that yellow suit tonight, an event that would have been unfortunate for them all. Then, finally, she turned back to Adina and the others, "I apologize, of course," she said, bowing her head, "I only seek to fully understand the situation in which we find ourselves. My husband has certain gifts, but I fear that intrigue and strategy are not among them. Nor, as it happens, is combat."

Ellemont grunted as if he'd been slapped, "Well, I have studied the relevant books on strategy, of course, and I do not believe that any of royal blood may be considered a novice in the ways of intrigue, having grown up with it for many years, isn't it so, sisters?"

"I'd say that's fair enough, brother," Adina said.

"Oh, dear husband," Lyla said, running a hand through his hair in much the same way Aaron thought a person might pet a favored animal, "I do not mean to offend you, my sweet. Only, this is no game, but a matter of very high stakes. It is the reason, is it not, that you brought General Hallifax along, so that we might be allowed the opinion of a man who is an expert in such matters?"

Ellemont met her eyes for a moment, and Aaron thought that he would say something, challenge her. Instead, he looked away and down at the table like a scolded child. When he did finally look up, he was smiling once more though the expression seemed forced to Aaron. "My wife is right, of course," he said, "I am no expert in such matters. Still," he said, looking everywhere but at his wife, "the whole of Telrear has heard of the atrocities perpetrated by Belgarin and his men. This, I think, is beyond doubt. I am more concerned with what your plan is."

Adina nodded, "Of course. Our estimates are that Belgarin is capable of fielding a force of around fifteen thousand men, including infantry, cavalry, and archers. An army that he will send to Isalla and then to your own kingdom, brother, once Isalla is brought to heel. Separately, we've no chance of standing against him. Isabelle's army, though well trained numbers only a little fewer than five thousand fighting men."

Ellemont nodded slowly, "My own is not so large as that, I'm afraid."

"And just how large is the army now, general?" Lyla asked.

Hallifax seemed surprised to find all of the eyes in the room on him, and he grunted. "Uh, that is ... we've roughly three thousand men, my queen."

"I see," Lyla said, "little more than half Belgarin's own force. Forgive me, general, for I know little of such things, but how often has an army defeated one nearly twice its size?"

The commander frowned, "It has happened, of course, though it is not common. Aaron Caltriss is said to have taken on armies much larger than his own many times and—"

"Aaron Caltriss," Lyla said, shaking her head, "I do not speak of myths and legends, general, but of real battles and real armies. If we are to base our strategy on a children's story, then why not look for the king of faeries to appear and beguile our enemies before they even take a step from their own castles."

Aaron found himself tempted to bring Co out right then, thinking he'd love to see the woman's face if one of those 'children's stories' appeared right in front of her face, but he managed to restrain himself. For his part, the general only bowed his head to Ellemont's wife, "Of course, my lady. I guess it's enough to say that it doesn't happen often."

"Just as—"

"In point of fact," Adina said, her tone sharp, "there are more than two dozen such instances recorded in the histories—ones with many witnesses—such as my own father's battle for Araleth only fifty years gone." She stared at Lyla, "Or would you believe that no more than a fable as well?"

"Of course not, princess," the woman said, and though her expression remained neutral, Aaron could see the anger in her eyes at being proven wrong, "your father—my husband's father—was truly a rare man and an even rarer commander, one that none living, I think, can hope to come close to matching."

She did not turn to look at Ellemont when she said it, but she didn't need to. Aaron saw the prince seem to shrink a little in his chair just the same. "Perhaps," Adina said, "I loved my father deeply, but he was still only a man. Anyway, the point is moot, for we are seeking another army, one that would give us at least another three to four thousand men."

"Oh?" Ellemont's wife asked, "and where is this army? Not your own, surely, for the way I hear it, those of your kingdom think you dead."

Adina's face turned red at that, and she opened her mouth to speak, no doubt to say something particularly unpleasant, but Aaron spoke before she could, knowing that the princess would not forgive herself if she allowed Ellemont's bitchy wife to keep them from an alliance that could save the realm. "Avarest," he said.

"Avarest?" Lyla said, raising an eyebrow.

"Huh," Ellemont said, "Well," he seemed to consider, rubbing at his chin, "well, now," he paused, grinning, "that just might work.

Everyone knows Avarest and its surrounding towns have a bigger population than any one royal kingdom. Father left it as such intentionally, I think."

"A city of criminals," Lyla said, her tone disapproving, her face twisted as if she'd just eaten something sour, "murderers and pick pockets and worse."

"Sure," Aaron said, nodding, "and if we were planning on playing a game of chess with Belgarin, or maybe having our armies compete for who was best dressed, they wouldn't be the people to call. We're not though, and the thing about murderers is that, generally, they're pretty good at it. After all," he said, smiling, "they've had practice."

Ellemont laughed at that, a loud booming laugh, and Brandon and Leomin joined in. In another moment, everyone in the room had joined in, everyone except Lyla herself whose face turned a deep, angry shade of red. "Forgive me," she said, her tone full of acid, "but I'm not sure that this is the right time to be making jokes."

"Sure it is," Aaron said, "better now than when we're dead. Dead men tell poor jokes, believe me."

That caused another round of laughter, and though he wouldn't have thought it possible, the prince's wife's face grew redder still until Aaron thought her head was likely to explode from the strain. "Oh, but he is a funny one sister," Ellemont said to Adina, "tell me, where did you find him?"

"Avarest." Aaron said, and that started a fresh bout of laughter.

When he'd calmed down, Ellemont nodded, "Fantastic. And tell me, Mr. Envelar, do you believe that you will be able to create an army from these, as you say, murderers?"

Aaron considered that for a moment, "Admittedly, the council of Avarest is known for not being able to commit to decisions. I guess that twelve men and women one chosen from each of the city's guilds seemed like a good idea at the time, but what it actually amounts to is that they never agree on anything and so nothing ever gets done. Still, they'd be fools not to see what's coming, whether they like it or not. As for the greater population of Avarest—that is those who live in the poor district known as the

Downs—there are three major powers among them. One is already on our side, the other two are named Hale and Grinner."

"And what of these two?" Ellemont said, "do you know them?"

Aaron grunted, "Oh, I know them well enough, considering that both of them have tried to have me killed at one time or another."

"That doesn't seem to bode well for an alliance," Ellemont ventured.

"Well, I understand how you'd see it that way," Aaron said, "but the thing is, prince, just about everybody in the Downs has tried to kill everybody else at one time or another. It's nothing personal, you understand—just business."

From your thoughts, Co said, that does not seem to be true. Something about your mother's necklace and—

Never mind that, firefly, Aaron thought back, it's not the time. "Anyway," he went on, "the other, May, is a friend of mine. She's been meeting with them now, over the last few weeks, and from what she tells me, they've both agreed to join their forces with hers."

"Well, that's great!" Ellemont said, grinning and clapping a hand on the table, "So it's settled then."

"Settled?" Lyla asked in a low, dangerous tone.

"Sorry, brother," Adina said, startled, "but do you mean—"

"Yes, yes," Ellemont said, waving his hand as if it was of no significance, "we will help you, of course. After all, as you say, once Belgarin finished here, he would only come for my people anyway. Understand, I know what people think of me, what they call me. Coward, mole, plenty of worse names I'm sure, and they're right, so far as it goes. I am a coward, and although last I checked I didn't have whiskers—truly, you should see me try to grow a moustache, it's pitiful, really—I do enjoy my mountain home. I enjoy the air and the coolness in the summer, even the cold in the winter—and believe me when I tell you that it's cold enough up there that your piss'll freeze before it hits the ground."

"Ellemont," Lyla scolded, but he waved her away, apparently gaining courage in his excitement.

"Point is," Ellemont said, "just because I'm a coward doesn't mean I'm a fool. I don't have to have a horse cart run me over to know enough to get out of its way."

"This cart as you put it," Lyla said, "consists of thousands of men that, even assuming—and frankly, I doubt it—they manage to gather an army from that rabble in Avarest, will still outnumber our gathered forces by almost half again. General, tell him."

The general nodded, "My king, Queen Lilliana is correct. The chances of victory ... Majesty, we must distance ourselves from this."

"Distance ourselves?" Ellemont asked, incredulous, "and what, general, would you have us become moles, in truth? Hiding in our mountain until my brother decides it's time to pull us from our hole?"

"Majesty," the general said, swallowing hard, and Aaron couldn't help but notice the stare the queen had leveled at the man, "what I mean to say is ... we could speak to your brother of peace. There need not be war at all."

Ellemont's eyebrows drew down in frustration, "Peace? Gods man, my brother knows nothing of peace. He won't be happy until he's built a throne from our corpses, can't you see that? You do not make peace with a mad dog, general. You put it down. It's a mercy not just for the people but the dog too."

If the situation would have been different, Aaron would have clapped the prince on the back for that, but his wife wasn't prepared to let it go. "This is no mad dog, Ellemont. This is your brother, and an army that you will not defeat. Don't be a fool. Of course, you will not join the alliance," she said, in a tone that brooked no argument. She stood then, the general rising as well, and she turned to encompass Isabelle and Adina with her gaze, "We thank you for your time, Queen Isabelle. Princess. Now, we will be going—"

"Am I still king in Cardayum?" Ellemont roared suddenly, and his wife recoiled, shocked into silence.

"Well, damnit?" He said, rising himself now, "am I?"

"Of course, my husband," the queen said, affecting a hurt tone, the voice of a loving wife that does not understand why her husband is wroth with her, "of course, you are. I only—"

"I know well enough what you only, Lilliana," he said, turning to the man on his other side, "and you, commander. You would countenance cowardice, but not just that. You would countenance foolishness, and whatever else may be said about me, I will be no man's fool." He turned and narrowed his eyes at his wife, "And no woman's either."

"Ellemont," Lyla said, sniffling, "I swear but I do not understand why you would speak to your loving wife so. I only want what is best for you."

Ellemont sighed, and by the look he gave her, Aaron could see well enough that the prince truly did love his wife. The poor fool. He stepped close to her, taking her hand, "Lyla, I am sorry that I raised my voice at you, but this is the only way. You must see that."

"I'm sorry, Ellemont, but I don't. What if we sent a messenger to your brother. We could ask for—"

"No, Lyla," he said, and though he was not yelling now, his voice was certain and as unmovable as the mountains he called home. "We will not beg for mercy where none will be found. I may not have much dignity left, but I am not dead either. Not yet." He turned back to Isabelle and Adina, "You will have our men, when the time comes."

"Oh, thank you, Ellemont," Adina said, and then she was up and moving toward him, hugging him as he rose, a bewildered but pleased expression on his face "Thank you so much."

They said something else, and Aaron thought he heard the queen's voice as well, but he wasn't listening. Instead, he was focused on Lyla, the prince's wife. While the others—even Brandon and Leomin—laughed and joked, relieved at the prince's decision, she sat stiffly in her chair, her jaw clenched. Aaron studied her, trying to see her thoughts and, before he knew it, the power of the bond surged forward, and he wasn't wondering what she was feeling anymore. He knew.

Anger. Fools, all of them, and Ellemont, her husband, the worst of the lot. How could he be so stupid? There was anger there, anger that he'd raised his voice at her, that he had yelled at her as if she was some castle servant and not his queen. Anger and frustration at the choice that had been made but not only that.

There was also, beneath it, fear. Fear of Ellemont, fear that his standing up in this matter was not a single, freakish occurrence but an indication of some change that had been wrought in him. Yes, that was there, Aaron was sure of it. A fear that she would lose the control she had over him, that he would once and for all become his own man, his own prince. But there was more there, too, a fear of something else, of someone else.

The pressure of using the bond seemed almost overpowering to Aaron, and he found that he was bent over the table, his body tensed with the force of it. Of who are you afraid? He thought. It was there, he thought, buried somewhere in her thoughts and mixed up with such a riot of emotions that he couldn't tell where one ended and the other began.

Straining, not sure how he was doing it, Aaron called on the power of the bond more, summoned it, feeling like a man being crushed under hundreds of pounds of bricks and each fleeting instant added another to the pile. Still, he struggled on, his breath rasping in his throat now, his body covered in sweat, his skin feeling hot and flushed. It was there, the name. So close. Then, just like that, the power of the bond and the name were both gone, vanished, and the terrible weight that had been crushing him was gone along with it.

Gasping, Aaron sat back in his chair and realized to his surprise that everyone in the room had grown silent and were staring at him, all of them, save Lyla, with worried expressions. The prince's wife, however, didn't look worried but suspicious, and she frowned at him as if wondering what he was about. "Aaron," Adina said as she hurried over, "are you okay?"

"I'm fine," Aaron rasped. "Sorry just … had a moment."

She pressed the back of her hand to his forehead and snatched it back as if she'd been burned, "Gods, Aaron, your skin is on fire. Are you sick?"

Aaron hesitated then finally nodded, all too aware of the Parnen studying him from where he sat, "Yeah, that must be it."

"Well, come on," Adina said, taking his arm and levering him to his feet, "we'll get you to a healer."

"I don't need a healer," Aaron said, "just some rest, that's all. Then I'll be good."

"Fine," Adina said, "but if this fever doesn't break soon, I'm taking you to the healer—I'll drag you there kicking and screaming, if I have to."

Aaron took a step toward the door and stumbled, and would have fallen had Adina not caught him.

"He is quite alright, I hope?" Ellemont asked, his voice troubled.

"I'm fine," Aaron said, "just need a little sleep, that's all." But the truth was, he didn't feel fine, not at all. His skin was hot, his vision blurred, and his heart hammered a thunderous beat in his chest.

"I'm going to take him to his room," Adina said, "I'll be back momentarily." She draped his arm across her shoulders and slowly they made their way toward the door.

Aaron stopped as the guards threw it open, turning back to Ellemont. "Prince, I wonder, will you be staying on at Perennia for a few days, or no?"

Ellemont glanced at the frowning Lyla then back to Aaron, "I suspect not, sir. My wife does not care for places so near to the sea—the air, we believe, makes her queasy. Even in our mountain home, there are many large bodies of water and for this reason she, from time to time, takes small trips to warmer, drier climates. The healers say that it is something with her humors and that dry climates are the best answer for such maladies. I myself—"

"Ellemont," Lyla said, "can't you see that the man is ill? There is no need to make him suffer more so that he might know personal details about us that do not involve him anyway."

Ellemont studied her for a moment, his expression blank, and apparently this was not the reaction Lyla was used to, for Aaron saw something like fear flash in her eyes for a moment before it was gone, and she was scowling once more. Without a word to his wife, Ellemont turned back to Aaron, "Still, it was a pleasure to meet you, sir, and may the gods bring you a speedy recovery to whatever it is that ales you."

"Thank you, prince," Aaron said, "and the pleasure was mine. I wish you a safe and happy trip back to your homeland, and I look forward to working with you to end this war. I will, of course, send a man with you to coordinate our efforts."

Ellemont smiled and nodded, but Aaron didn't miss the frown of displeasure that creased his wife's face, "That sounds like a wonderful idea," the prince said, "and I look forward to our alliance."

Aaron gave a half-hearted, sickly smile then allowed Adina to lead him out the door, the guards closing it behind them. "It seems to me," Adina said once they were in the hallway, "that somebody has been studying diplomacy."

Aaron grunted, "Not as such. Tell me, what do you think of Lilliana?"

Adina frowned, "I think she's a pompous ass and a bigger coward than my brother claims to be. Still, though, I am happy for Ellemont, the way he stood up to her."

Yes, Aaron thought, and that will cost him sure enough. They'd only made it a few more steps down the hall when Wendell stepped into view from around the corner, the scarred sergeant's normal smile vanishing as he saw Aaron leaning heavily on Adina's shoulder for support. He hurried forward, looking Aaron over, "What's happened?"

"Nothing," Aaron said, "relax, you ugly bastard. You're not going to get rid of me that easy."

The sergeant grinned uncertainly, "You're sure you're alright, general? I'd hate that anythin' should happen to you, sir. I'd miss watching you do nothing all day—you do it better than any man I've ever seen, and I'm not embarrassed to say so. Sir."

Aaron was unable to keep from grinning as he shook his head, "Gods, but I don't know who got the idea to teach dogs to speak, but I'd like to have a word or two with him and that's sure."

"You two," Adina said shaking her head, "I can't tell if you hate each other or love each other."

"Apologies, princess," the scarred sergeant said, "but does it only have to be one or the other?"

Aaron laughed at Adina's confused expression, "Why don't you go back in with your sister and the others?" Aaron asked her, "You'll be needed there. Wendell can see me up to my room well enough."

Adina was clearly torn, glancing between the two men before settling her gaze on Aaron, "You're sure you're okay?"

"I'm fine," he said, smiling, "nothing that a few hours' sleep won't cure."

"And you don't mind?" Adina asked Wendell.

The sergeant grinned, "Princess, I'm used to carrying the general here's load. I do it everywhere else—can't see a reason why I can't carry him to bed. I do it with my nephew, often enough. He's five, of course, but I don't expect that the doing of the thing is all that different."

"Alright," Adina said, passing Aaron to Wendell, "Okay, but, Aaron, you let me know if you don't get to feeling better, and I'll be by to check on you just as soon as we're done here."

"It's a deal," Aaron said, and she gave him one more worried look before finally turning and heading back through the doors.

Once they'd closed behind her, Aaron straightened, taking his arm from behind Wendell's neck. The sergeant raised an eyebrow in question.

"So maybe I wasn't quite as bad off as I made out," Aaron admitted, "so what? Now, walk with me—there are some things I need to talk to you about."

The sergeant nodded, hearing the concern in Aaron's voice, "Yes sir."

They walked in silence for a time until they had moved up the stairs to Aaron's floor, and he was confident that the hallway around them was empty. "I have a favor to ask you, Wendell."

"Yes sir."

"You're probably not going to like it."

"I'm a soldier, sir—not likin' things is what we like best. Gives us somethin' to talk about around the cook pot at night. There's only so much bitchin' we can do about you 'for it gets old."

Aaron grunted, "Alright. Did you see the prince's entourage? The general and Ellemont's wife?"

"Aye, I saw 'em sure enough. Woulda been hard not to notice her—I hope I ain't speakin' out of turn, sir, but she's an awful pretty thing, though I can't help but notice her face is always twisted up like she just got a whiff of somethin' didn't agree with her."

Aaron laughed, "That's a fair enough estimation, I think. Anyway, the thing is, I need you to go with them back to Cardayum."

Wendell nodded, "To what purpose, sir?"

"Well," Aaron said, "ostensibly to help coordinate the war effort with Ellemont's own troops."

"Ostensibly, is it?" Wendell said, "that's what I like about you, sir, your courage. Never afraid to fight a man you don't know, or use a word you don't understand. Anyhow, that's a good thing, ain't it? Means Ellemont's agreed to the alliance."

"He agreed," Aaron said, "whether or not it's a good thing, I mean to find out. While you're there, I want you to keep up the appearance that you're coordinating the war effort, but I also have another task for you."

"If it's wooing the prince's woman, general, I got to tell you I think I'd probably have a better chance with his commander. That woman don't seem to be interested in anything but how high she can raise her nose in the air."

"Don't worry," Aaron said amused, "you'd be my last choice if seduction was required. No, what I need you to do is to keep an eye on her and the commander both."

Wendell frowned, considering, "An eye, sir?"

"You heard me," Aaron said, "both of them, when you can spare them. There's something going on with her, and I'd like to know what it is. Anyway, she'll try to convince Ellemont to break from the alliance, of that I'm sure, and call it a hunch, but I think the general would pretty much agree with whatever she said. You, of course, can't let that happen. If we're to have a chance of beating Belgarin, we're going to need Ellemont and his soldiers."

"Alright, sir. Consider it done."

"That's it?" Aaron said, "No clever quip? No jokes?"

The sergeant shook his head, "No, sir. I figure there's a time for jokes and a time to put 'em aside. This seems to me like a time to put 'em aside. I'll do what I can, general. You have my word."

"And glad to have it," Aaron said, offering his hand.

The scarred man hesitated for a moment as if surprised, then took his hand and shook it firmly. "You're a good man, sir," he said, "might be there's some hope for you yet."

Aaron grunted, "The prince and his retinue will be leaving soon."

"Aye, sir," Wendell said, "and I'll be with them."

Aaron nodded, "Good luck, soldier."

"And you as well, general," he said, then he turned and was gone, leaving Aaron alone with his own troubled thoughts and a question—who was he? Who was it that Lyla had been afraid of?—that, for now at least, would have no answer.

CHAPTER TWENTY

Aaron yawned as he made his way to the healer's tent. It had been three days since Ellemont and his retinue had left Perennia and each day had been spent training heavily with the troops and going over strategies for woodland fighting. Aaron had known Wendell was useful, but he had not realized just how much until the man was gone. The scarred sergeant had a way of making the other soldiers understand what he needed almost without even saying it, but that wasn't the only reason Aaron regretted sending him away.

The truth was, he was worried for the man. Aaron didn't know what exactly he expected the sergeant to find—intrigue, murder, betrayal—but whatever it was, it seemed to him that there were only two likely options. One, that he would find nothing because there was nothing to discover, and Lyla was nothing more but a stuck up, pain in the ass noblewoman in a world full of them or, two, there was some plot or conspiracy going on in which, almost certainly, the sergeant would find himself outmatched and given the impossible task of ensuring Ellemont's continued support for the alliance against unknowable opposition. Neither, Aaron thought, was a particularly good use of the sergeant's time.

Wendell is a good man, Co said, he'll be okay.

My father was a good man, Aaron thought back, not angry as he usually was when he thought of his father, only troubled, but he died anyway. Good men stand where weaker ones run, firefly. Good men are good at standing. They're even better at dying.

He was still thinking of Wendell when he made it to the healer's tent. The tent was large, bigger than most of the houses he'd ever seen in the Downs, and it was located near the troop barracks and training grounds—lucky that, considering that lately dozens of soldiers had been forced to make a visit for ailments ranging anywhere from broken thumbs to diarrhea caused by eating some toxic plant while training in the woods to just about any other issue he could imagine.

Stepping inside, he was immediately struck by an herbal smell so pungent that he felt as if he could barely breathe. Several of the healers looked up from where they were tending soldiers laid on cots, but once they saw it was him, they only nodded and smiled and went back about their business. No real surprise considering that they'd grown used to his visits over the past several weeks. He made it a point when any man was seriously injured—an inevitability when men started swinging steel at each other whether it was dulled or not—to come by and visit them, to speak with them for a time.

He made his way through the cots, nodding his head at several soldiers on the mend as they shouted greetings until he finally came to the cot he was looking for.

The cots had seemed large enough until Aaron looked down at Bastion lying on one, his legs so long that they hung over the bottom, his shoulders so wide that Aaron couldn't help but think lying there was its own kind of torture. He studied the unconscious soldier, shame and guilt clawing at him. Bastion had been injured because of him, yet he had not even visited him until now. He'd meant to, but it seemed as if something was always happening to pull his attention away, and he had not even been able to visit the healers tents as regularly as he'd liked of late.

The giant youth looked almost peaceful in his repose, and Aaron rubbed a hand at his weary eyes before motioning to the nearest healer. The heavy-set, gray-haired woman smiled as she approached, rubbing her hands on a white cloth that was stained with blood, "General, welcome," she said, "it has been some time since we've seen you here."

"Sorry, Tilda," Aaron said, and he realized as he did that he'd apologized more in the last week than he'd probably done in his entire life, "things have been ... hectic, of late."

"Oh, that I do not doubt," the older woman said, "what with Prince Ellemont's visit—I can't seem to keep the younger women focused on their duties for dreaming about catching the prince's eye."

Aaron nodded slowly, his eyes back on Bastion's unconscious form, "Is that so?"

"It is," the old woman said, "though, general, if I'm being honest, his visit has caused no more than your own do, after you're gone. If things ever don't work out between you and the princess, I imagine you could find yourself a wife right here in this tent, if you were of a mind to."

A wife, Aaron thought, gods help me. "How is he?" He said, nodding his head to Bastion.

"The youth is doing quite well," the healer said, "very well indeed."

"Are there no bigger beds for him?"

The woman shook her head, "Apologies, general, but this is the largest we have."

Aaron nodded, reaching into his pocket and pulling out several gold coins. The older woman's eyes went wide, "Here," he said, "buy him another bed, a bigger one."

"O-of course, sir," she, and she was off in an instant. It wasn't until she was gone that Aaron realized that he must have given her way more than was necessary, so distracted had he been by the young unconscious man before him.

He sighed heavily and slouched into the chair sitting beside the bed. How many will I put in danger? How many others will take knives and swords that were meant for me?

It is not your fault, Aaron, Co said, you know that.

"Do I?" He said aloud, his voice little more than a whisper, "This man—this kid—nearly died trying to protect me, and I'm no step closer to finding the man behind it than I was the day after I threw him from that balcony, and he vanished like some damned street magician. And even if I do find him, what then?"

"Find who?"

Aaron spun to see Bastion blinking blearily at him, rubbing at his eyes. "What's that?" Aaron said.

"Sorry, general, but I overheard you say something about finding someone."

"You're awake," Aaron said, stunned. "But I thought that you were in a coma or dying or..."

"Coma?" Bastion asked, and to Aaron's amazement he sat up with little difficulty. "No, sir, I'm fine. I been awake for a few days now, but the older woman—Tilda, I think—she insists on changing my bandages every two hours, so I figured it'd just be easier to be on hand instead of traveling back and forth between my house so much."

Gods, I'm a fool, Aaron thought. "Smart thinking, soldier," he said, "so tell me, how are you feeling?"

"Better, sir, truly," Bastion said, "Tilda said I was lucky, said that the knife missed all my vital organs."

Lucky, Aaron thought, staring at the shirtless man in his thick bandage, laid on a hospital cot. If this is luck, I want none of it. "Good," Aaron said, "that's good. Anyway," he paused, clearing his throat, "the thing is, well, I wanted to thank you, Bastion. It would have been a lot easier and the gods know a lot less painful to have sided with those men that were trying to kill me."

"Side with them, general?" The youth asked, as if he couldn't even comprehend the thought of doing such a thing, and the most damning part of it was that Aaron didn't think he could.

"Well," Aaron said, "Thanks, that's all."

***

He emerged from the healers' tents a short time later, surprised to find the swordmaster waiting on him in the street. "Darrell?" He asked. He hadn't seen the swordmaster since he'd struck him in Tianya's presence nearly a week gone and had been under the impression that the older man had left Perennia altogether. "What are you doing here?"

"I came to speak with you," the swordmaster said, "if you'll allow it."

Aaron couldn't help but notice that the side of the swordmaster's face was bruised from the last 'talk' they had, and he felt a stab of guilt mix with his anger. "Alright," he said, "but if you're going to tell me to run and hide like your boss, Tianya, recommended, then you're wasting your breath."

The swordmaster smiled, "I told her as much, after you left, and I don't blame you. Tianya is the leader of the Tenders, and she has her own ideas about how to deal with the problem, ideas that I don't always agree with. Still, she only does what she believes to be right."

Aaron grunted, "Your face is looking better." He sighed then, forcing the words out, "I'm sorry I hit you, Darrell."

The older man shrugged, "I think that, perhaps, I deserved it."

"Maybe," Aaron said, "but I'm sorry anyway, and I want you to know that I appreciate you taking me in when I was a kid. Whatever your reason was, you didn't have to, and I think things would have gone a lot worse for me, if you hadn't."

"Listen, Aaron," Darrell said, a pained expression on his face, his eyes glittering with unshed tears, "about your parents—"

"Forget about it," Aaron said, "you may have asked them to join, but you didn't force them. It is a decision that they made for their own reasons. You have to let that guilt go, Darrell. It took someone very close to me to make me realize the truth, but we can't control the decisions other people make, can't be held responsible for them. My father and mother did what they believed was right, and that's all that need be said on it. It was not your fault."

The swordmaster let go a heavy sigh, "Thank you, Aaron. I came here, originally, because of the Virtues, and that is all that Tianya seems to think about, but I see the other dangers approaching even if she does not. I would help you, if I could."

Aaron studied the swordmaster for several seconds, "There is something I need, but I hate to ask it of you. It is no small thing and, frankly, it is dangerous."

Darrell held a hand toward his face, indicating the yellow-purple bruise, "So is being your friend."

Aaron grinned, "Alright then," he said, "let's talk."

CHAPTER TWENTY-ONE

Aaron grunted as his own blade intercepted that of his opponent. His arm shook with the contact, but he managed to knock the strike aside. The man swung again, and Aaron stepped back, this time striking the sword on the outside, using his attacker's momentum against him, so that he spun, off balance from the unexpected blow. He stumbled, and Aaron lunged forward, sweeping the man's leg out from under him.

The man landed on his back hard, and Aaron thought he felt the ground beneath his feet shake, then he moved forward and placed the tip of his sword on the man's throat. "Match," he said, panting.

Bastion grinned up at him from where he lay on the hard-packed dirt of the training ground, "Good move, sir. I didn't expect it."

Aaron grunted, offering the giant youth his hand to help him up. Bastion took it, and Aaron was forced to pull with all his strength and, even still for several seconds he thought that he was going to go spilling over on top of the man, not exactly an image that would inspire confidence in his soldiers, but he strained, gritting his teeth with the effort, and finally managed to pull the big man to his feet. "Well," he said, "I didn't expect you to hit like a damned battering ram either. Gods man what are they feeding you in the barracks mess?"

Bastion's grin widened, "Oh, I don't know, sir. Same as everyone else, I guess."

Aaron grunted, "Save me a spot next time, will you?"

The youth laughed, and his expression was comfortable, excited even. Looking at him, one would have never guessed that he'd very nearly died only a few weeks before, but Aaron couldn't help but notice the way Bastion's free hand rubbed at his back.

"The wound hurts, does it?" Aaron said.

"Not really," Bastion said, but he wasn't able to hide the grimace on his face.

"There's no need to hide your pain, Bastion, at least not to your friends. Pain's a good thing—it lets you know you're still breathing."

The youth nodded, "Yes sir." Then he paused, grinning, "I'm not disagreeing, sir, but if you don't mind me saying, I'd just as soon not feel any of it. It's not exactly pleasant."

"No," Aaron said, "it wouldn't be, but the hardest, most important lessons rarely are. Each pain that we survive is a story, Bastion. A story in the book of who we are and what we will become, and there is a lesson in the scars that we carry with us, in each of them, if only we look for it. Besides," he said, clapping the youth on the back, "women love a guy with scars."

Some of the nearby soldiers had stopped their own dueling matches, and they laughed at that, "Great," one said, "another advantage for the big guy. It's not as if he doesn't already have women flocking around him like he's a puppy dog they want to take home and pet."

"I don't think pettin's what they got in mind, Flynn."

There was more laughter at that, "Shit," the first man that had spoken, Flynn, said, "quick, somebody stab me in the back."

"Don't tempt me," someone else said, and Aaron found that he was laughing too.

Once they finished, Aaron gazed around at the men surrounding him. Gone were the arrogant, useless soldiers in gleaming white armor that looked as if it had never been used. Now, most of the men wore simple linen shirts and trousers, boots of soft leather. Still, it wasn't the clothes that set them apart, Aaron thought. Partly, it was the way they viewed the world but even more than that, it was the way they viewed themselves.

They are no longer dolls to be dressed up and fawned over, Co said, they are soldiers.

If they're not, Aaron thought, they'll do until the soldiers get here. "Alright," he said, "good job, everyone. Now, we—" Aaron paused at the sound of an approaching horse and turned to see a figure riding toward him, his horse lathered with sweat, its rapid breaths creating white plumes in the air. The man reigned up only a few paces from where Aaron stood. Now that he was closer, Aaron could see that the man was at least as exhausted as the horse, his clothes filthy from the dust and dirt of the road, his sweat-soaked hair sticking to his forehead like damp grass. For a moment, Aaron didn't recognize him and then, with a sinking feeling of dread, he did. The man made to dismount, but in his weary state, he nearly fell from his horse, and Aaron had to step forward and catch him until he could find his feet.

"Rane, what is it?"

The messenger was struggling for breath, but he nodded, swallowing hard, "It's ... Belgarin, sir. He's ... he's on the move."

"How many?"

"Fifteen ... thousand, general," the man said between great gasping breaths, "fifteen at the least."

The man's words struck those gathered like a hammer blow, silencing the few whispered, quiet conversations that had sprung up at the rider's approach. A feeling of ice-cold dread fell upon the clearing like a heavy curtain, and Aaron himself was not immune to it.

"Get yourself and your horse to the barracks and get some shut eye, soldier," Aaron said, forcing calm authority into his voice, "you've earned it."

The messenger, too weary even to respond, only nodded and led his horse dumbly by the reins toward the troops' quarters. Aaron turned at those gathered around in the training grounds to see that it wasn't just those nearest him who were no longer fighting, but all of them. The silence was complete save for the slightly too-fast breathing of the gathered men, and their eyes searched his face, looking for something.

They look for hope, Co said, can't you feel it?

He could, but as a man who had little hope himself, he found he had none to spare. Still, they needed to hear something, some words that might give them strength. He asked himself what his father would have said, but quickly banished the thought. He was not his father and never would be. His father had been considered a hero to many, a kind and gentle man, merciful even to his enemies. Aaron was not that. His was a life of killing, of steel and blood and fire. "Alright, lads," he said, speaking loudly so that his words echoed around the clearing, "you heard the man. There's some bastards headed our way. They need killing, and we're the men for the job."

"Do you think we can win, general?" One man asked.

"There's so many," another yelled from further away.

"Yes," Aaron said, his voice carrying over the clearing once more, "Yes, there are a lot of them. You ask me, I think that's a good thing, lads. Enough for all of us. I don't know about you, but I've never been very good at sharing."

There was some scattered laughter at that, and Aaron was glad to see courage find its way onto a few of the faces of those gathered.

"But can we win?" The first man shouted again.

"Is that you, Ernest?" Aaron said, holding a hand over his eyes to block the sunlight as he peered down the field.

"Aye, sir," the man shouted back, "it's me."

Aaron shook his head, "Shit, man, I would've thought you'd believe anything's possible. I know I do after watching you. When you first got here, I would have said it was impossible that you didn't manage to stab yourself in the foot with your sword, but there you are standing tall, if not proud."

There was more laughter at that, and Aaron nodded, "Alright," he said, "this is why we're here, gentlemen. This is why we have spent our hours training and swinging practice swords and shooting bows instead of breaking our backs harvesting crops or sewing clothes..."

"My dad was a tailor," one of the men shouted, "I used to work in his shop. I hated that shit!"

There was a roar of laughter at that, and though Aaron didn't find the man's words precisely funny, he smiled along with them. Laughter was good, so long as it didn't turn into screams.

211

"I didn't buy these soft boots for nothin'" Bastion said, and there was more laughter.

"Alright then," Aaron said, looking around and meeting the eyes of the men who watched him, "Those who've been training in the woods with me, get your gear. The rest of you, meet up with your sergeants, and they'll tell you what to do. You," he said, grabbing a man nearby, "go and fetch Captain Gant, tell him the news. He'll come down and make sure everything's in order here."

"Yes sir," the man said, and then he was off, running toward the castle.

"Well go on then," Aaron said to the men still watching him, "Time to earn our pay."

***

It was nearly an hour before the men who Aaron had been training in the woods with for the last several weeks were gathered in the training grounds. Two hundred men in all, watching Aaron expectantly. There was no fear in the eyes that watched him, not among these, for they were the best of the whole army, hand-picked by Brandon and himself. They were hard men who knew their business, men who liked it a little more than was necessary, but that was good. Few had families either—they'd avoided it, whenever they could—for the job they would undertake wasn't quite a suicide mission, but it wasn't that far from it, either. "Alright men," Aaron said, his voice loud enough that they could all hear, "The time has come. This is why we have trained, why we have worked so hard. Belgarin's troops are on the march—fifteen thousand, at the least." Still no fear, he saw, and that was good. "Fifteen thousand men who plan to kill and burn whatever stands in their way. They will reach the forest in a week, maybe two, but we will already be there, waiting for them. This is your land," he said, "your homes. Let's let them know they're not welcome."

The men cheered at that, and Aaron nodded before turning and heading toward the city gate. Adina was waiting when he arrived, and she ran up to him, wrapping him in a tight hug and kissing him. "Don't go," she said, her voice a whisper. "Aaron, please."

"I have to, Adina," he said, "I can't ask these men to do anything that I'm not willing to do myself. Besides," he forced a smile, "we'll be careful."

She studied him, her eyes misting with tears, "You come back to me, Aaron Envelar. Promise me."

He kissed her on her forehead and gave her a smile, "I promise, Adina."

She nodded and with obvious reluctance backed away, giving him and his men room. Aaron saw Leomin standing at the front of the crowd that had gathered and waited on either end of the gate, cheering them. He moved toward the man and offered his hand.

Leomin took it, shaking it, "Good luck, Mr. Envelar."

Aaron nodded, "Thanks." He glanced back at Adina, hating the fact that he was leaving her, worried that she would not be safe.

Leomin must have seen something in his expression because he grinned, clapping Aaron on the shoulder, "I will look after her, Mr. Envelar. No harm will come to her unless it comes to me first. This I promise you."

"Thank you, Leomin. You are a good friend."

The Parnen's mouth worked, as if he would say something, but, for the first time Aaron had ever seen, the man seemed to have no words, so he only smiled, clapped Leomin on the shoulder once more, and then headed out of the gate, his men trailing behind him.

The road lay before them, a road that led on to fields, fields that led to forest, and a forest that led to blood and death. "Come on," he yelled behind him, picking up the pace into a jog. There was no point in waiting, in going slow. The blood and death would be there either way, waiting for them, and, as his father had told him, the sooner started, the sooner done.

CHAPTER TWENTY-TWO

He took the first soldier easily enough, creeping up behind him in the darkness of the woods and sliding his knife into his throat before the man even knew he was there. The second spun, made aware by some rustle of leaves or the quick, nearly silent gasp his companion let out as the steel went in. He was halfway turned when Aaron lashed out, more by instinct than thought, and his sword took the man in the stomach. He screamed, and Aaron let out a hiss of frustration as he stepped forward and sliced the man's throat, letting his body collapse in the undergrowth.

There was a shout from behind him, and he turned to see another soldier running out of the shadows of the trees, sprinting toward him his blade held high, a torch in the other. An arrow whistled out of the undergrowth behind Aaron and struck the man in the chest. He stumbled to a stop, staring at the length of wood sticking out of him in shock but did not fall until a second arrow flashed out of the darkness and took him in the throat. He dropped, soundless, and Aaron walked to his body, kicking dirt over the torch to smother the flame, doing his best not to look at the flickering orange light in an effort to maintain what night vision he had left.

All the fools seemed to carry torches, and he was amazed and more than a little disgusted by how easy the killing had been. Fifty men dead now, fifty, at least. Only one of his own injured, and that by one of his own men firing an arrow in the dark. Easy enough to see the men carrying the torches, sure, but not so easy to pick out a friend in the darkness.

Fifty dead. A good start, but there were many more men scattered in the trees around them, and he knew that even this was only the advanced guard, scouts and small bands of soldiers sent to check the area of the army, ensuring that it was clear. They were dying, true, but they were also doing their jobs in the process, for when they did not return Belgarin or whoever commanded his soldiers would have his answer. At first, Aaron had been shocked that these men would wade into the darkness with torches lit like beacons to give away their position, but he knew that, had he and the others not trained with Wendell as they had, they might well have made the same mistakes. These were men who were accustomed to fighting in streets or in fields, facing their enemy in the open and overwhelming them with greater numbers. These were men who killed and were killed in the daytime, with the sun shining down on them and their efforts. It was quite another thing to face such violence in the darkness, where any shadow you took to be a tree might be a man with steel in his hand and death on his mind. They were untrained. They were unprepared. And they died for it.

Two sets of footsteps came up behind him, and Aaron knew that they were his men, could hear the sounds of rustling clothing as they looted the bodies of arrows, of flint and food and whatever else would be light enough to carry. He gave a whistle then, a loud piercing sound that Wendell had taught him and the others during their time in the woods. It was the sound, the sergeant and ex-woodsman had explained, of the white-throated sparrow, a bird that had long since flown south as they were several weeks into autumn now with winter nearing. The sergeant had taught them several such bird cries. Aaron and his men had adopted them all, assigning a signal to each. The one he'd just given was to signal the all clear in that area of the woods, and he heard the answering reply of several other sets of his soldiers in the darkness.

Following those, there came a lower-toned, more rapid series of whistles which indicated that someone needed help. Aaron turned to his right, staring off in to the darkness of the trees from which the sound had come and called on his bond. He'd used it often in the day, and it was slower in responding than he would have liked, not to mention the fact that he felt himself being drained with each use. Still, it had been necessary. The torches the soldiers carried might be like beacons, but the trees were thick and uncaring of the human drama that played about beneath their boughs. Their trunks reflected lights in strange ways, so that a man might think he was walking out of the undergrowth behind an enemy soldier only to find himself standing in front of him. Aaron knew that well enough as it had happened to him not three hours gone.

The power of his bond helped him to avoid any such instances, helped to guide him and the few soldiers in his group with him to the best spot, and so he called on it now and stared into the darkness, watching as dim magenta forms seemed to materialize in the night. Two crouched and still—his men, he was sure—and then, very near them, six others, all moving close together. He snapped his fingers and then he was off, making his way through the trees as quickly as he could without risking running headlong into one, the three men with him dogging his heels.

It only took them a few minutes to get close enough that Aaron could see the orange glow of the soldiers' torches. He saw, too, that the six were walking directly at his two men, would be on them at any moment and good or not, trained or not, two to six weren't good odds.

He didn't hesitate—something he'd learned first from his father and then Darrel after him. He glided out of the shadows, the knife he held in his left hand cutting a red ruin across the first soldier's throat before the man realized he was there. He went for the next but an arrow flew from somewhere behind him, taking the man in the knee, and he collapsed, Aaron's sword missing the top of his head by inches as he did. Instead, Aaron kicked the man in the back, sending him sprawling on his stomach, and before the man could move, he fell on top of him, one knee driving into the man's lower back even as he swung his left arm down and buried the knife in the man's throat. Two figures were running toward him now, one bearing a torch, and Aaron winced, grunting as the light seemed impossibly bright to eyes accustomed to the darkness.

He backpedaled several feet, half-blinded, then a form rushed out of the darkness and tackled one of the two, and they both went sprawling. The other rushed forward, and Aaron, still seeing spots in his vision, threw his sword up on reflex, blocking a blow he felt more than saw coming. Still, the power of the blow was unexpected, and it drove him to one knee.

Instead of trying to rise, Aaron punched out with his knife-hand, and the blade took the man on the inside of his thigh. Hot blood gushed over his hand in a flood. Not finished, he jerked the blade down, digging a furrow in the man's flesh to be sure even as the arterial blood sprayed over him. He spun to see one figure on the far end of the torch's light backing away, his eyes wide in the torchlight, his hands held up as if to ward off spirits. He spun at the sound of fighting on his left and saw two men still wrestling around on the ground, caught the flash of steel in the poor light. It was impossible to tell which was his own man and which the enemy, so he rushed forward, kicking out at the one on top and sending him rolling off of his opponent onto the ground.

"Sooner started," he hissed at the man lying on his back, his sword raised waiting for a response.

"Sooner done," came the challenge's answer in a gasping croak, but not from the man beneath Aaron. Instead, it came from the one who he'd kicked, and so he drove his sword downward, and the man lying below him screamed as the steel ripped through him. Screamed and struggled and finally was still. When his struggles ceased, Aaron turned to see the remaining soldier sprinting away into the darkness. Right before he got out of range of the light, Aaron saw an arrow flash out, and the man cried out in pain, but the shaft had taken him in the arm, and he kept going.

"Damn," someone hissed from the darkness, "I'll get him."

"No," Aaron said, staring at what he thought was the figure of the fleeing man disappearing into the darkness, "let him go. If he manages to make it out of the forest without knocking himself senseless on a tree, he'll have an interesting story to tell to the man who sent him, I think."

Aaron turned back to see that the man he'd kicked was still lying on the ground, gasping for breath. "Sorry about that," Aaron said, offering his hand to the soldier who rose with a grunt of pain, and Aaron noticed that a knife protruded from his shoulder.

"No sir," the man said, "you saved my life. Thought the bastard had me there, for a minute."

Aaron nodded, motioning one of the other men forward, "Aiden, see to his wound, make sure it's patched up."

"Yes sir, general," the man said, stepping forward and peering at the wound. "This is going to hurt," he whispered, grabbing hold of the blade with one hand while he placed the fingers of the other around where the knife had entered.

Aaron heard another bird call indicating that someone else needed help. "It's okay to feel pain," he said to the wounded man, "but feel it quiet. There's more killin' to be done yet before we're through."

The man gritted his teeth, not speaking, but he nodded his head once.

"Alright then," Aaron said, "you others, with me." And then he was off and dashing through the darkness again, calling on his bond even as he ran.

CHAPTER TWENTY-THREE

Belgarin hissed, slamming his hand down on the small, portable table that served as his desk while on campaign. The wood creaked and groaned, but it held, as it had held the last six times. Soon, though, he knew he would have to either get control of his anger or get a new desk. Why do you always have to break things? The words were there, like always, a barb in his side, and he felt a brief but powerful sense of self-loathing so strong that the breath seemed to catch in his throat.

He closed his eyes, focusing on his breathing. "Another one with the same fool story," he said, scowling up at General Fannen from his seat behind the desk.

The general stood at rigid attention, his face impassive, "Yes, Majesty."

"Ghosts, they call them," Belgarin hissed. "Superstitious fools, the lot of them. As if ghosts use swords and arrows to do their killing. It's ridiculous."

"Of course, sir."

"Still, My King," said Caldwell, as he poured a glass of tea and handed it to Belgarin, "ridiculous or not, something in those woods is killing the men. What few have returned have been half mad with terror and several of those have died from their wounds. The last took an arrow in the shoulder, and since it took him the better part of three days to make it back to us, the wound had become infected. Before the pain's madness took him, he said that they were men that appeared out of the darkness like ghosts."

Belgarin sneered at the advisor but took the glass of tea he offered with the hope that it would calm his nerves. "Ghosts again. At least this one realized they were men though, and not some phantoms of the forest for the gods' sake." He sighed, sitting back in his chair and rubbing at his eyes, and he thought he detected a glint of satisfaction in the general's eyes. The man had not wanted him to come, had told him that he would be safer and more comfortable should he remain in the castle. Belgarin had reminded him, quite forcefully, that his father—considered in his time to be not only one of the finest kings who'd ever lived but also one of the best commanders—had made it a point to educate each of his sons in the art of war. Belgarin had told the general in no uncertain terms that he would come, that he would see that no mistakes were made. After all, once Isalla and Cardayum were brought to heel, the only thing standing between him and a unified Telrear would be the neutral city of Avarest. He was close now, so very close, and he would not leave his fate and the fate of his country in the hands of others.

There was another reason, too. Lyla, one of the few secrets that no one—not even Caldwell—knew about would come to visit him to let him know how the negotiations had gone. On that, at least, he need not worry. Ellemont was a coward, but he was no fool. He would see what was to come clearly enough and would throw in his lot with Belgarin. Anything else was suicide.

Still, he had expected to have had word from Lyla by now, and the fact that he had not was irksome. He would have to speak to her about his disappointment, the next time he saw her. The general cleared his throat, "Majesty?"

"What?" Belgarin snapped, realizing that he'd been so distracted by his thoughts that he'd been paying little attention to what the general had been saying.

"I asked how you would like to proceed, Majesty."

Belgarin bit back an angry retort. Things were not going as planned. He had expected resistance, of course, but he had thought he would not face it until at the city walls. "How many have we lost?"

The general frowned, glancing at Caldwell, and the advisor sighed, "Unfortunately, Majesty, there is no easy way to say for sure." He shrugged, "It has only been a few days, and there is still a chance that some more of the advanced scouting party may make it back."

"How many?" Belgarin said again, not bothering to hide the anger and impatience he felt.

The general winced, "The advanced team is made up of five hundred men. We sent them with orders to ensure the path ahead was safe and to find us the best path through the forest. It is no easy thing to move an army through such terrain, and I had thought—"

"Five hundred," Belgarin said, his tone flat and dangerous, "and how many have made it back?"

The general swallowed, "A dozen, sir, no more than that. Of those, seven have died of their wounds, and the healers believe another three will pass before the night's out."

"So you mean to tell me, general, that you sent four hundred and ninety eight men to their deaths and for what? What have we gained?"

The general swallowed, "Majesty, there will be casualties in war, it is expected. And these men of your sister's ... they do not fight as soldiers should. There is no honor in what they do."

"Perhaps," Belgarin hissed, "that is what we will write on your gravestone, Fannen. He was a worthless, stupid fool, but he was honorable."

The general froze, his face going dark red, but Belgarin did not care. He was angry. Angry at his sisters for making men suffer and die for something that should have been his already. Angry at Lyla for not having come to see him or, at the least, sent him a message. And, most of all, he was angry at the old fool standing before him.

"It isn't all bad, Majesty," Caldwell said. "The losses are an annoyance, it's true, but five hundred men are the smallest fraction of the army that you have brought to bear. This will delay your victory, no more, for however many men your sister may have hiding in the woods, it will make little difference when the bulk of your army arrives."

Belgarin stared at his advisor in disgust. "Those were my men," he said, "men who believed in the cause, who followed me. Men who shared my vision of a unified Telrear, Caldwell. You will not speak of them as if they are pieces on a board and nothing more. Those men died to set right a great wrong."

The advisor bowed his head his expression, as usual, impassive, "Of course, Majesty. I only meant to say—"

"Never mind what you meant," Belgarin hissed. "Leave me, both of you."

"But, Majesty," the general said, "I had meant to discuss—"

"Leave me," he roared, his fist slamming into the desk again, and this time the wood gave way with a crack and a snap and the table fell to the ground, the reports that had been stacked on top of it scattering about the tent.

"Very well, Majesty, as you command," Caldwell said, and the two men moved toward the tent flap.

"And Caldwell?" Belgarin said.

"Yes, Majesty?"

"Send someone to clean this up."

"Of course, my king."

Once they'd gone, Belgarin sighed, staring at the broken table. *Why,* his mother's voice said in his mind, *why must you always break things?*

CHAPTER TWENTY-FOUR

Aaron knelt beside the small creek and splashed water on his face and neck, trying and failing to wash away the blood that had dried and caked on his skin. That done, he sat, listening to the sounds of the forest, to the branches of the trees creaking in the wind, the croaks of frogs and, more than anything, his own weary breathing.

You're tired, Co said, you need some rest.

Tired? No, firefly, I left tired behind days ago. And, if you'd like, I'll send Belgarin a message—ask him if maybe he doesn't mind waiting a couple of days before he sends anymore troops, give us all time to rest. But I've got to be honest with you, I don't think he'll go for it.

There's no need to be mean, Co admonished, I only worry about you.

Aaron rose, grunting as his sore muscles made their complaints, Co, being mean is the only thing keeping me standing.

He turned and coughed, his mouth and throat feeling as if they were coated with dust no matter how much water he drank. Then he headed back toward the small clearing where his men—or what was left of them—waited crouched or seated in the grass. They looked like some dusty revenants who'd dragged themselves free of their graves, their clothes ripped and torn, bloody and covered in dirt and sap. They were weary—all of them—their eyes glazed over the way a man's got when 'tired' became a poor word to describe what he was, when it took nearly all his concentration to put one foot in front of the other.

"Sir," Bastion said, coming to stand beside him, and Aaron noted that the giant youth had blood caked on the side of his head and in his hair. "The men are assembled, like you asked."

"Thank you, Bastion," Aaron said, "now, go on and have a seat with the rest. There's little time for resting, but you may as well get what you can."

"Yes, general," the big youth said, and he jogged forward and sat in the front row of soldiers.

What it is to be young, Aaron thought. He was only in his early thirties, but he felt each year himself, felt it in the ache in his bones and the exhaustion in his muscles. He stared out at the men watching him for a time in silence, taking in those haunted expressions that were a testament to what they'd done, to the butchery that had been the week's work. They'd started with two hundred men, and with that number had fought and killed over five hundred by his reckoning. A feat any man would be proud of, at least on paper. But such things meant little when faced with the reality of blood and steel. Such things as pride were weak enough shields when the nightmares came—and they always did.

Two hundred in the beginning and now he counted a hundred and fifty men left, watching him and waiting for what he would say. "The main army's coming," he said finally, "they are entering the woods even now. Unlike the scouts whose job it was to find us—"

"And find us they did, general," one man said as an attempt at a joke, but his voice was dry and weary, and the laughter that followed was equally so.

"So they did," Aaron said. "Anyway, unlike the scouts, the main army will not be traveling through the woods, or, at least, not most of them. They'll want to take the road. It's not the safest way, maybe, but with the amount of troops and supplies they're carrying, not to mention the horses, it's the only one."

Aaron studied the trees around them as he remembered his own flight from Baresh, traveling with Adina and Leomin. For all he knew, they might have camped in this very spot, though those days—like the ones now—were hidden in a haze of exhaustion, and he could not have said for sure. He met the eyes of several of the men, "I know you're all tired—I'm tired too. But if you ever get so tired you think you can't take it, you just remember why we're here, what we're fighting for, you understand? Your women, your children, your fathers and your mothers are waiting back there somewhere," he said, stabbing a finger back in the direction of Perennia, "waiting for their fate to be decided. Over the last few days, I know some of you have lost friends, and we will lose more still before this thing is done, but that's the cost. There always is one. We're not here to defeat their army—that we'll do at the castle walls—we're here to make an accounting. To make them understand that each step they take onto your lands will be paid for in blood. That is their cost."

There were some half-hearted shouts of agreement at that, but most of the men only nodded along, agreeing but too tired to spare the breath. "Now," he said, "You're tired, but I need the best out of you for the next few days. The very best you have. There are a hundred and fifty of us left," Aaron said, "and I don't want to lose a single man that we don't have to. What we do now, we do to buy time for those whom we love." He paused, thinking of Adina then, of the way her long dark hair had spilled on the pillow the night before they'd left, the way her face had been so peaceful in sleep. He cleared his throat, "Remember your loved ones and remember, too, if you feel yourself giving into exhaustion or despair at the number of troops Belgarin commands, that what we do, we do for them. Those men out there," he said, gesturing to the far end of the forest where, even now, Belgarin's troops would be entering the road, "Care nothing for your families. They are only obstacles in their way, ones that will be removed if they deem it necessary."

The men nodded again at that, and though they were weary, Aaron was glad to see the look of defiance in their expressions. "Let's go then," Aaron said, "and if you can't run, jog. If you can't jog, walk, and if you can't walk by the gods you better crawl. We will show Belgarin that the cost of what he does is blood—so much that the bastard will choke on it."

There were more shouts then, and Aaron nodded, turning and starting off through the trees, the sound of his men behind him.

***

"Gods, I hate this place," Feddard said, glancing sideways from underneath his helmet at Bennet where he marched beside him in the column. The trees towered above them on either side of the road, and Feddard got the impression that they marked his and the other's intrusion with a strange, alien malevolence.

"Aye," Bennet agreed, hocking a gob of spit through his own helmet's visor where it landed on the hard-packed dirt of the road. "So do I, boy."

Feddard turned, looking behind him at the line of soldiers snaking through the forest, and for what had to have been the hundredth time, he remembered what the scout has said, screamed really, as he lay in the healers' tent, dying from a deep cut across his abdomen. It had been a wonder the man had made it back at all. Ghosts, the scout had said, there are ghosts in the woods. He'd said more, of course, but most of it had been inarticulate screams of agony and fear. And that was alright, for Feddard had heard enough, heard more than he wanted to in fact. He studied the woods surrounding them anxiously, searching for any sign of movement, and he noted that he was not the only one who did so. News such as what the few surviving scouts had brought traveled through an army like wildfire. He wasn't superstitious, of course, didn't believe there was such a thing as ghosts. Still … something had killed the advanced scouts.

Gods I hate this place, he thought again. His body was covered in sweat beneath the chain mail jerkin and leggings he wore—an uncomfortable weight he still hadn't grown accustomed to. He was so distracted by his own discomfort, by his worries and fears, that he accidentally walked into the man marching in front of him.

The man—Caspar, he believed his name was—stumbled, nearly falling, and turned back to Feddard, his anger clear on his face, "Watch your fuckin' step." He growled before starting forward again.

Feddard swallowed hard, following after and being careful of his feet.

"Relax, lad," Bennet said, "there aren't any such things as ghosts or spirits of the wood. The ones did for the scouts weren't nothin' but men just like you and me. Anyway, they'll be long gone by now. It's one thing to take on a few scouts, but it's quite another to fight an army of fifteen thousand men. Naw, they'll be hiding in their castle by now, whimpering and praying to the gods for salvation."

Five hundred dead scouts didn't seem like a few to Feddard, but he didn't bother disagreeing, only nodded instead. "You're right, of course." He said, wondering, not for the first time, why he was here at all. It had seemed like such a glamorous idea back in Baresh—him, a young man of no more than nineteen years, marching off to war, to victory and glory. The women in several of the taverns had also seemed impressed, and he'd been happy enough to accept their adulation and their ... gifts. Now, though, beneath the blazing sun, with the thick trunks of the trees all around him like silent sentinels, thoughts of victory and glory could not have been further away. And why was it so damned hot, anyway? It was supposed to be Autumn, wasn't it? Winter was only a few weeks away, yet he felt as if his damned skin was about to catch fire.

He looked up ahead where the captain rode his horse beside the column and felt a stab of jealousy. Why did that bastard get to ride when the rest of them had to walk?

"Wouldn't mind havin' a horse like that'n there just now," Bennet said from beside him, and Feddard looked over to see that the man had followed his gaze to the captain.

If I had a horse like that, Feddard thought, I'd just as soon turn it around and ride back to Baresh. There were worse things, after all, than being a tailor's son, than spending his days working in his father's shop, taking orders and running the counter. Dying, for one, that'd be worse. He remembered his mother and father pleading with him, begging him to stay and wondered again at how foolish he'd been, how arrogant as he'd shook his head, telling them he would do his duty, feeling braver than he'd ever felt.

But he hadn't been thinking of his duty at all, not really. He'd been thinking of Gwendolyn, the daughter of the chandler whose shop was next to their own. He'd been thinking of how she'd normally barely spoken two words to him, no matter how hard he tried to talk to her. But when she'd heard about him enlisting and going off to fight, she had come to him, talking to him about how excited she was, of how wealthy and powerful he'd be when he got back. She'd even gone so far as to kiss him, a kiss that he could feel even now if he tried hard enough. Though with each step he took, it seemed a little more difficult to remember the taste of her lips on his own, a little harder to recall the soft feel of her against him when she'd embraced him.

He'd tried to explain it to his mother and father, but they'd only frowned, his dad shaking his head in that disapproving way he had. They'd never thought much of Gwendolyn, his mother saying that the girl's vanity was much too big and her skirts much too small. Feddard had yelled then—something he rarely did and never at his parents—telling his mother that when he got back, he was going to ask for Gwendolyn's hand, and they'd be married. His father had frowned at that, but his mother had only snorted, saying it would be better to marry a wolverine, at least that way he'd have some nice fur shoes when he was forced to put it down.

Feddard frowned, remembering that last night before he'd left, remembered going to bed angry and waking up to leave before his parents were awake, his way of getting back at them. He wondered now if maybe they weren't being as unreasonable as he'd thought, if maybe some of the things they'd said hadn't even been right. Not about Gwendolyn though, about her his mother had been wrong. She was the most beautiful girl Feddard had ever seen, and she had kissed him.

He sniffed and frowned, glancing over at Bennet, "Hey, do you smell something bur—" he cut off, gasping as the bushes and dead limbs that had lain on either side of the road—evidence, he'd thought, of someone coming through recently and clearing the road, though who would do such a job, he had no idea—blazed to life. In an instant, Feddard and the column of soldiers he marched with were surrounded in either side by walls of fire as tall as he was. No, not as tall, taller. And still growing. Men screamed and shouted in surprise, and the column came to a confused halt.

"What the fuck?"

Feddard turned to see Bennet's head whipping around as the older soldier took in the flaming walls, "Bennet," Feddard said, his bottom lip quivering, and Feddard realized he was close to tears now, very close. Closer than he had been since he'd been a child, "What's happening? What is this?"

There was a monstrous crack and snap that he heard clearly even over the roar of the fire, and Feddard spun to see a massive tree, it's trunk at least as thick as he was tall, come toppling down into the road, crushing several soldiers who got caught beneath it. In an instant, what had been an orderly column devolved into chaos, as the men on the outsides of the road tried to force their way away from searing fire, pushing and shoving. Men were trampled underfoot, and smoke was suddenly filling the air, and Feddard hacked out a series of coughs, shielding his mouth and nose with his arm. "Bennet," he yelled, screaming to be heard over the roar of men shouting and crying and cursing as they fought to get away from the flames.

He turned to see that his friend, Bennet, had somehow got knocked away from the center of the column. He was pushing and struggling to get away from the flames that roared only a few feet behind him now, but even as Feddard watched, the writhing mass of people knocked the older soldier into the fire and, in a moment, he was wreathed in flame, his limbs flailing wildly, his screams of agony and terror clear even over the tumult.

"Oh, gods," Feddard gasped, hacking at the smoke filling his mouth. He spun, disoriented in the mad panic until he finally saw the captain on his horse. "Captain," he shouted, "captain what do we do?"

The captain turned, his eyes wide and wild within the depths of his helmet, then he jerked on the reins and his horse started forward. The animal had barely taken two steps when there was another deafening crash as a tree, at least as big as the first, fell across the road in front of the column, pinning several more unfortunate soldiers beneath it. Blood squirted out from underneath the tree, and Feddard gagged, his stomach heaving as puke and bile flew from his mouth.

It's not supposed to be like this, he thought, gods it's not supposed to be this way. He was pushed from the side and stumbled, barely managing to keep his feet and thank the gods for that, for he saw several men who'd fallen around him and been trampled to death by what had once been an orderly column and was now a crazed mob. He looked back and saw the captain's horse rearing up, shaking its head madly, and then dashing toward the fallen tree. Feddard watched in shock, sure that the horse was going to crash head first into the tree and break its neck, but by some miracle it's leap carried it over the fallen trunk, and he watched the horse and its terrified passenger land safely on the other side. He started toward the tree himself, thinking he could climb over it, but someone's elbow struck him in the side of the face, and he grunted, taking two lurching, drunken steps toward the fire before he could stop himself.

He looked up at the captain again with the irrational belief that if he could keep the man and the horse in sight, he would be okay. It's what they had told him often enough, during training for the last several months. Look to your commanding officer. He will tell you what needs to be done. But the captain didn't look much like he was ready to tell anyone anything as he yanked on the horse's reins again, trying to force the mad animal down the road, away from the chaos. He finally did get it righted, but the horse had barely taken two steps when an arrow flew out of the woods and stuck into the captain's throat.

The man swayed around, drunkenly, and Feddard was possessed with the wild belief that the captain was staring right at him with eyes that were mad with terror. Then, in another moment, the captain toppled from his saddle, the horse bolting off into the woods. "Oh gods," Feddard hissed, looking around him. The smoke was growing thicker now, and the line was a melee of flaming madness as far back as he could see. Several men had caught fire and stumbled their way back into the ranks and now blazes were burning everywhere, the flames searing and catching on anyone that was pushed or shoved too close like some malevolent living creatures out to devour and feast on the flesh of the soldiers.

Feddard stood there for a moment, terrified, frozen, and when he did move, it wasn't thoughts of Gwendolyn that spurred him on, but of his mother and father. He threw off his chain mail shirt then covered his mouth and nose with his own sweat-stained, linen undershirt. Before he could think better of it, he charged toward the flames, his head down, shielding his eyes with his arm.

There was a brief moment of intense pain where he felt that his entire body would be cooked down to nothing but ash, that he would be burned beyond recognition and lay forever in this forest, never to be buried, his parents never knowing what had happened to him. But then he took a few more stumbling steps, and he was through the fire, frantically patting out several spots on his clothes and hair where the flames had caught hold. The forest stood before him, the trees thick and filled with menace, but he didn't care as he began running, sprinting as fast as he could away from the fire and death that lay behind him.

An arrow flew out of the trees, so close that he heard the whistle of its passing, felt the wind from it before it stuck, vibrating into a tree trunk beside him. Unaware of the whimpering, mewling sounds that were issuing from his throat, Feddard ran on. Something struck him in the back, and he stumbled, the breath knocked from him, even as he lurched forward, not daring to stop to check and see what it was, too terrified to look. Let it just have been a rock, or a bird maybe, please, let it just be that. But his breath wasn't coming back like it should. No matter how hard he strained, it came back in tiny increments, and there was a wheezing sound that he felt all the way in his chest. Still, he pushed himself forward, one foot after the other, and was so focused on it that he only caught the faintest glimpse of a figure moving out from behind the tree in front of him.

He saw something flashing toward him, something metallic that glinted in the sunlight, and he had a brief, flashing thought of his mother, smiling at him in approval the way she had when he'd been a boy, and he'd showed her a new trick or flip he'd learned. Then something struck him, and there was only him and the darkness and, in another moment, the darkness only.

CHAPTER TWENTY-FIVE

Aaron pulled his blade free and let the body drop, looking around at the flames and the chaos. The fires had been considerably larger than he had expected, in truth, but he made a mental note to thank the scholars at the university when he had a chance. He had only visited them on a whim a week back, thinking at the time that any advantage, no matter how slight, could make a big difference when they were so outnumbered. When they had told him of the amber liquid that would help to fuel a fire, he had not thought it would do this.

He felt a stab of guilt as he took in the inferno, as he watched men burning, their arms flailing as the troops, surrounded by fire, rushed around wildly, terrified and wanting to run but having no place to go. He had to admit to himself then that he could have used half of the stuff and got the effect he'd wished, as the fire began to set alight the leaves of some of the smaller trees. He had used all that they'd given him on the road, doubting even then that it would be enough, but it had been and more.

Still, a few men had made it out, rushing through the fire looking for some escape from the flames and the smoke and the chaos. Those who had so far had been met with arrows and steel, but studying the line of troops, Aaron could see that the fire line had been broken by what appeared to be several bodies lying on top of it and that a mass of troops was filtering through it now, spurred on by the furious shouts of a man on a horse. A captain then. And how many would make it through the breach? A hundred? More? Too many, that was certain.

He gave a loud whistle, calling to those men around him, and then he started back through the woods at a jog in the direction of Perennia, careful not to trip some of the other traps he and his men had laid for the intruders as he ran. It would be several days before he and the others made it out of the forest, and he hoped that Brandon had horses waiting, as he'd promised. Aaron was wearied beyond belief. Behind him, people screamed and died, and he ran on, carrying his shame with him. It was not a pretty thing, war. But, then, it was never meant to be.

CHAPTER TWENTY-SIX

"Damnit they're making fools of us," Belgarin hissed. He was pacing back and forth in the space of his tent, General Fannen and Caldwell watching him. "How many did we lose?"

"It's hard to say for sure, Majesty," the general answered, "the fires are still going, you see, the captains still trying to gain control over their troops. We won't be able to have an accurate number until—"

"How many, damn you?"

The general swallowed, "All told? Five hundred, my king. Maybe more."

Belgarin stopped pacing and stared at the man, his body trembling with rage, "Do you mean to tell me that we've lost a thousand men before we have even seen my sister's city?"

The general swallowed but nodded slowly, "Yes, Majesty."

Belgarin nearly reached out to throw the new desk he'd been brought, but he hesitated, frowning. "A thousand men dead."

"Yes, Majesty," the general said, "but it is not all bad news. Some of the men escaped the flames and pursued the defenders."

"Oh?" Belgarin said, "then where are they, general? Where are these defenders? I want their fucking heads on spikes outside of my tent, do you understand me?"

The general cleared his throat nervously, "Majesty, the thing is ... well, they had set other ... traps. Pits with wooden spikes inside them, their openings covered up by brush and undergrowth, trees that had been tied so that, when a man broke a piece of twine, they came flying down, crushing them. Others, too..."

"You might want to hurry to the point, general," Belgarin growled, "for I am losing my patience, and I have yet to see where the good news is in this."

The general's mouth worked, though no words came, and it was finally Caldwell who spoke, "Your Majesty, those who pursued the defenders gave their lives, but they did not give them in vain. We have sent scouting parties, and each have returned. By this, we have determined that whatever force had been in the forest is there no longer. They must have been scared off when the soldiers broke through the flames."

Belgarin snorted, "Scared off? Scared off?" He shouted, "are you really so stupid as to believe that Caldwell? What are they scared of? That they would win the war so far from home that their wives and children wouldn't be able to see their glory? Is that it?"

"Majesty," Caldwell said, "I only meant that—"

"Never mind what you meant," Belgarin hissed, "only tell me how long until the army is able to move again?"

"My king," the general said, "the road is still clogged with the dead and fires still burn in some parts of it. The men are busy putting them out now and clearing it, but it is slow going, and it will be a half a day, at least, before the thing is done. The men, you see, many of them balk at the idea of going into the forest. There are whispers of ghosts and more."

Belgarin grunted, "There are no such fucking things as ghosts, Fannen. You get that road cleared, and you get it done now. In three hours, either my army is marching once more, or I will have your head on a pike. Do you understand me?"

The general's face went pale, but he nodded, "Of course, Majesty."

Belgarin studied him for several seconds then, "Well?" He said, "If I were you, general, I would be seeing to the troops just now. Now in the name of the gods get the fuck out of here."

The general bowed and left without a word. Once the tent flap had closed behind him, Belgarin turned to Caldwell, "The Knower. You brought him, as I asked?"

"Yes, Majesty," Caldwell said, "his tent is not far from here. I can lead you there, if you like."

Belgarin knew that he should, that the Knower might have some news or some information that could help him, but the thought of dealing with the monstrosity that had once been a man just now was too much to bear. "Go to him, Caldwell," he said, "ask him if he has any ideas for what Isabelle and Adina might be planning."

"The guards will not let me in, sire, not without you accompanying me."

Belgarin sighed and drew a parchment and quill from the small desk, hastily scribbling a note and stamping it with his seal. "Go," Belgarin said, "see what that creature knows that might help us."

"Of course, sire," Caldwell said, taking the note as if it was some precious gem he feared dropping, "I will see to it now."

In another moment, Belgarin was alone. He stared at the flame of the lantern sitting on the desk, thinking. A thousand men dead and nothing to show for it. He'd had other losses, of course, when fighting the armies of his other siblings, but never so many, and never without some gain. The thought made him angry, but he told himself that even a thousand lost was no great thing, not in an army of fifteen thousand fighting men. They were difficult losses, sure, but they did little to change the inevitability of the outcome. He would be king over all Telrear, as was his birthright, as the gods themselves had decreed by making him first born.

He was still standing there, staring at the flame, when a voice came from outside of his tent. "Majesty," the guard said, "may I come in?"

Belgarin sighed, "Yes, Clause, what is it?"

"There's a woman at the camp's perimeter, sir, says she wants to speak to you. She's bears a letter with your seal."

Good news, at last, Belgarin thought. "Very well, send her to me, Clause."

"Of course, sire," the guard said, and he started toward the tent's flap.

"Oh, and Clause?"

"Yes, Majesty?" The man said, turning.

"Let none other come in the tent while she is here. No one, do you understand?"

The man bowed his head low, "As you wish, my king."

Then he was gone, and Belgarin was alone with his thoughts once more. It took nearly an hour for Clause to make it back with her, having had to negotiate the camp's perimeter defenses, and when she stepped inside the tent, her head was covered with the hood of her cloak, her neck tilted down to hide her face.

Clause hesitated until Belgarin waved him away and then he vanished outside of the tent flap. Once they were alone, he rose, moving to her and wrapping her in his arms, "You came."

"Of course, my love," she said.

He held her for a moment then released her, moving back to sit behind his desk, "And my brother? Does he know that you've left?"

"Oh, he knows," she said, smiling, "He believes that I am spending my hours in prayer at a town some distance from the capital."

Belgarin grunted, "It is good to see you."

She smiled, "And it is good to be seen, my love."

"Tell me," he said, "what news of the alliance? Ellemont has refused?"

Her smile faded and died, and she met his eyes, "No, my lord. My husband ... accepted the alliance."

"What?" Belgarin said, his anger flaring, "How did this happen?"

She swallowed, and he could see tears gathering in her eyes, "Please, my love," she said, "I tried everything, I swear, but he would not relent. I had thought it would be an easy matter, Ellemont being a coward as he is, but he accepted the alliance and refused to listen to me. I tried everything—"

Standing there listening to her whining excuses, thoughts of the thousand dead men still fresh in his mind, Belgarin felt the anger rise up in him, and he reached out and slapped her, hard.

Lyla cried out in surprise, falling backward on the ground, her hand going to her face, her eyes staring at him wide and terrified.

"Majesty?" Clause said from outside the tent, "is everything okay?"

"Everything's fine, Clause," he said, "the lady was just surprised by an insect, nothing more."

Everyone, he thought, is either a traitor of a fool. I am surrounded by them. Even my brother, Ellemont, chooses our sisters over me, the first born and rightful heir. Belgarin stared down at Lyla for several seconds, his chest heaving with rage, his hands clenched into fists at his sides. Then, in another moment, the anger was gone, and the guilt came welling up in its place as he watched tears pouring from her eyes. "Forgive me," he said, rubbing a hand through his hair and crouching down beside her. "It has been a trying few days, my love, that's all. I do love you, and I am sorry. Will you forgive me?"

He saw that there was a bit of blood at the corner of her mouth, and he withdrew a handkerchief from the pocket of his trousers and wiped it away. "P-please," she said, her eyes wide and frightened like those of a child who has angered her parents, "do not be mad at me. I did try, I promise. Only ... he would not listen. There was a man there, Aaron Envelar, and both your sisters, and it was as if they cast some spell on him."

Belgarin sighed, offering his hand. She took it, and he pulled her to her feet, embracing her so that he spoke into her ear, "You have failed me," he said, "but I will forgive you, my love. I will believe, this once, that you did all that you could, that you have not betrayed me. But should something similar happen in the future," he said, tightening his grip on her arms, "I would be most disappointed. Do you understand?"

"O-of course," she said, her voice breathy and afraid, "my lord, I would never betray you. I would do anything for you, you must know that."

Belgarin considered that for several moments then nodded, holding her back at arm's length, "Then you will prove it to me."

"How can I?" She said, "Ellemont has made up his mind, and I cannot change it."

"Perhaps you can, my love," he said, pacing the room, thinking now, "and perhaps you cannot. Either way, I have a task for you."

"Anything, my love, anything. I will show you that I am yours no matter what."

"Very well," Belgarin said, "but tell me, does your husband still own that awful yellow suit of armor?"

"Own it," she sniffed, running a delicate finger along her eyes and wiping away her tears, "he thinks it the height of humor. As if being a coward is something to be proud of."

Belgarin nodded slowly, an idea taking shape in his mind. "Very good," he said, "now, I've got something I want you to do for me."

CHAPTER TWENTY-SEVEN

Lyla made her way through Belgarin's camp, her cloak pulled tight about her, her head down to hide her identity. Still, the cloak didn't do as much as she would have liked to cover her feminine form, and she was forced to endure the catcalls and whistles of soldiers from where they sat around campfires, drinking and eating their late dinners. She told herself that the men, of course, would not be so bold as to attack her, but that didn't stop her heart from thundering in her chest each time one paused to look at her or paw her as she was forced to pass close by one of the hundreds of campfires that dotted the field. She studied the faces of those that dared to be so bold, promising herself that when the war was over, and she became Belgarin's queen, she would make them suffer for their straying hands.

If they only knew who she was, what she meant to their king, they would not have dared to act as they did but, of course, they did not. To them, she was only a woman walking about alone in the night, possibly one of the many women who attached themselves to armies like locusts, offering themselves and their bodies for food and drink and some coin. The thought that she might be taken for one of those made her face heat with shame and anger. She told herself that it was important to keep her identity hidden, at least for now, but that didn't make it easier to endure the taunting and the lewd, graphic propositions that were shouted at her from the campfires as she made her way to the edge of the encampment. She wished, not for the first time, that she would have brought someone with her—there were some few of Ellemont's guards who were on her side—but with that ugly sergeant of Isabelle's snooping around, she had not dared. Bad enough that she was forced to sneak off like a thief in the night alone, but that was no great worry as Ellemont had grown accustomed to her taking trips, ostensibly for the purpose of prayer and her health.

She was finally reaching the edge of the camp and nerves that had been taut as a bowstring were finally beginning to relax when a cloaked and hooded figure stepped away from one of the last campfires she would have to go by and paused directly in her path. She tensed, waiting for the crude taunts and drunken gestures, but she did not stop. The best thing, she'd found, was to just keep moving, to keep putting one foot in front of the other. After all, there were other women in the camp, ones that would be eager enough to sell their bodies to any willing man, and the soldiers, so far at least, had not bothered to chase her down, no doubt content in the knowledge that one of the camp's followers would be along soon enough. She could hear the screams of ecstasy, after all, from many of the tents, interspersed with the drunken laughter and arguments of the soldiers as they sat around their fires, drinking and boasting about the battle to come.

But with each step she took, she grew more troubled, for the man—she felt sure it was a man by the set of his build—did not shout or speak, only stood still in the night, as if waiting for her. A quiver of fear ran over her, and she turned, cutting between two campfires and weathering the remarks of the soldiers as she did. Better that, she thought, than whatever the waiting man wanted. She hadn't been able to see his face, but she had not liked the look of him, something about the way he stood had been almost threatening, predatory.

She made it past the light of the two campfires and saw no one in front of her, so she breathed a sigh of relief, turning after she passed a tent to get back on track. Suddenly, someone was in front of her, and she gave a cry of surprise that was quickly muffled as the man clamped a hand on her face. "Ah, Queen Lilliana," a man's voice said, "it is a pleasure to finally meet you in person. I wonder if I might not trouble you for a word?"

Before she could respond, the shadowed figure clamped his hands around her arms and guided her toward the tent she'd just passed, opening up the flap and pushing her inside. Lyla stumbled but managed to keep her feet. She turned and looked back at the figure moving inside the tent, "Please, sir," she said, not having to fake the fear in her voice, "I believe you've got me mistaken with someone else. I don't—"

"Oh, no need for such dissembling, queen," the man said, "for I know well enough who you are. It is my job, after all, to know things."

"My name," he said, pulling back his hood and revealing a smile that did not touch his eyes, "is Caldwell, and I serve as King Belgarin's advisor." There was something hungry and cruel in his gaze, and Lyla felt herself shrinking away, pulling closed her cloak as it had come loose when he'd shoved her inside the tent. She wore clothes beneath it, of course, a simple dress like a thousand commoners might have worn, but something about the man's eyes roaming over her made her feel as if ants were crawling all over her body.

"Caldwell," she said, swallowing hard. Belgarin had spoken of his advisor often, told her stories of the man's cruelty, such as when he had apparently tortured a woman who had come to give him information about his sister Adina and her whereabouts. Belgarin had said the words as a king might, annoyed by the excesses of one of his subordinates, annoyed and little more than that. But standing here, alone in the darkness with the man of which he'd spoken, Lyla did not feel annoyed—she felt afraid. "What do you want?" She said, hating herself for the quaver in her voice.

The man grinned wider, "It is not about what I want, dear queen. It never has been. Each man has his master, after all, a man who requires certain ... shall we say, duties of him. My master is wise and powerful, a man of great vision, but he is not a man that is known for his mercy or his compassion to those who fail him. For such a master as that, a man will do anything that is required, anything to fulfill the tasks given him. Do you understand, Lilliana?"

The fear rose up in her, threatening to turn into outright panic. It wasn't the man's words themselves that scared her as much but the fact that he had used her given name, a demonstration no doubt calculated to show her where she stood with him, and that he cared little for the title she held. It had been intended to put her off balance, to scare her, and it had worked. "I ... I understand," she said, "but I don't see how that has anything to do with me," she said, hugging her cloak tighter about herself and taking another step back until she could feel the canvas of the tent against her.

"Oh, there is no need to cover yourself so, I assure you," Caldwell said, "I have no interest in your body. No, my interest is in your mind, and in what you will do for me and my master, when the time comes."

"Do for you?" Lyla asked, "I ... I have no power to do anything."

"Don't be so modest, my queen," the advisor said, "I think that you have more power than you give yourself credit for and, frankly, I think you know that. A power only women may have. You see, Lilliana, men fight their wars with swords and bows, with ballista and catapults. But women, like yourself, they fight their wars with words, with soft whispers in the darkness and with ... other things."

"I don't know what you're talking about," Lyla said, "please, just let me go."

"My dear queen," the advisor said, smiling, "I think you know well enough."

Lyla found her fear diminishing somewhat as her surprise at being jerked into the tent waned. Instead, she found that she was mad. No, not mad, furious. This man, this commoner, had dared to force her into a tent against her will and then proceeded to threaten her. Threaten her. "Just who do you think you are?" She demanded, "I am not some common harlot to be thrown about. I am a queen, and you are some piece of gutter trash that Belgarin decided to keep around, no doubt so that he can be amused from time to time. You are a crude beast that has somehow happened on the ability to speak and no more than that. Now, get out of my way."

She started forward, but he did not move, only smiled as she drew closer until she finally stopped, uncertainty finding a chink in the armor her anger had provided. "But, my queen," he said, his smile wider than ever, "you have not even listened to my proposal yet. And you are correct, there is no question. I am lowly born, yet my master saw enough potential in me that he chose to take me under his wing."

Lyla scoffed, "You poor fool. Belgarin saw nothing in you. He took pity on you, nothing more."

Suddenly, the man's expression twisted in fury, and before Lyla had time to move, his hand was clamped around her throat, and she gasped, unable to draw a breath. "I do not speak of Belgarin, bitch," he hissed, spittle flying into her face, "he is no more than a pawn in a game he does not understand and does not even know he's playing. Now you will stop your whore's tongue from flapping, or I swear by the gods I will rip it out."

Lyla struggled against his grip, but it was immovable, his face a rictus of fury as she tried to speak, her words coming out only as choked, dry rasps. Her vision began to darken and just when she thought she would surely pass out, he released her, and she crumpled to the ground, gasping in air that had never tasted so sweet.

"You are a whore," he said, his expression impassive once again, his voice showing no emotion, "that is all. Queen whore. Yet even whores may be useful, if they learn to listen. Even whores might be rewarded, should they choose to serve."

"What ... what do you want?"

He tilted his head, looking at her the way one might look at a confused simpleton or child, "Oh, nothing so terrible, queen, I assure you. You are a whore, but you are a whore to a king—two kings, in fact. My request is only that you watch Belgarin. He is a fool, apt to making foolish decisions, and my master wishes you and I to be his guides in the coming days. To do this, you will, of course, need to tell me whatever he shares with you after he sates his desires on your flesh. His thoughts, his opinions. You will be queen, but he will not be your king. Your king will be my master and through him, me. Do you understand?"

"You ... you would have me be a spy? A ... a traitor?" She said, incredulous.

He laughed at that, sounding genuinely amused. "Are you not already a traitor, dear Lilliana? Or should I say Lyla? You prefer that, don't you? And to answer your question, yes. You will be a traitor, a spy, a whore," he said, pausing to shrug, "and whatever else my master requires."

She rose to her feet, rubbing at her throat, "And if I refuse?"

The advisor grinned, "I would not do that, were I you, dear queen. My master has many talents and many virtues, but patience is not one of them. Nor, I would say, is mercy."

Lyla saw no way around it. There was enough noise going on in the camp that, even should she scream for help, the soldiers would think it only the feigned shouts of one of the camp followers. It might elicit some drunken laughter, maybe a comment or two, but no more than that. The man before her, she knew, would kill her if he thought it necessary. "Very well," she said, rubbing at her aching throat, "I will do as you ask."

He nodded as if he had never expected anything else. "That is good, my queen. For now, only keep doing what it is that Belgarin has asked of you concerning Ellemont. I will come to you when your service is required."

Lyla nodded, "May I leave now?"

He grinned, bowing mockingly, "Of course, my queen. Your Majesty may leave whenever she so desires."

She started toward the tent flap, letting out an involuntary gasp as he grabbed her arm, his fingers digging into it, "Just so long as you understand that you are our creature now. You may play whatever game with your husband as your lover has demanded, but remember that it is only a game. Your reality, your life, only continues so long as my master finds you useful."

"Yes," she gasped, as his fingers dug into her arm, "my ... lord."

"Oh, not me, queen," he said, letting her go and giving her a wink, "I am only a commoner."

As soon as she was free, she darted toward the tent flap, not caring, for the moment, about how she might look or about the dignity she so often strove for as queen, caring only for putting as much distance between herself and the madman as she could lest he change his mind and decide to kill her anyway. It wasn't until she was showing the letter of safe conduct Belgarin had given her to the guards at the perimeter and walking into the darkness where her horse was saddled that she truly felt safe, and the tears finally began to dry in her eyes.

Making her way through the darkness, she thought of the man, Caldwell, the man who had dared treat her like some stupid whore, the man who had dared to put his hands on her and worse, the man who had made her afraid. She promised herself that, once she became queen, the man would learn what proper respect was before the headsman's axe took his life. He would know, in that moment, how foolish he had been to underestimate her.

Soon, she thought. Soon Belgarin, her love, would be king, and she would see to it that the advisor felt the full measure of her wrath. She would tell Belgarin of what the man had done, of what he had asked of her, and she was sure that her future husband would make him suffer for his treachery. The advisor's death would come, but it would be slow and painful in the coming. The thought made her smile despite the ache in her throat. "Fool," she whispered, as she mounted her horse. "As if you could ever turn me against my love. As if anything could." She would make the advisor's treachery known to her king. But first, there was one more task in front of her, one that her king and her lover, her future husband, had asked. But it will not be long, she promised herself, glancing back at the encampment where it lay in the distance, *you will suffer for your insolence.*

CHAPTER TWENTY-EIGHT

Aaron and what was left of his men—a hundred on the last count—stumbled out of the woods after four days of travelling. They had set out at a jog, doing what they could to put distance between them and the soldiers that had no doubt been sent to pursue them, but their exhaustion had quickly made itself plain as one man after the other dropped to the ground, too tired to keep up the pace. They'd rested then, Aaron calling upon his bond to gauge the distance of the soldiers, and they'd counted on the traps they'd laid—spike pitfalls covered with brush, mostly—to slow the soldiers down. There was no running, not after so long spent in the woods fighting, catching only an hour or two of sleep each night, if that. There was only the dazed, drunken shuffle of the truly exhausted, no speaking or cheering for what they had done, no jokes or laughter. Only putting one foot in front of the other, not knowing that you could take another step until you had.

In this way, they came to the edge of the trees, and Aaron let out a ragged sigh of relief when he saw horses waiting on them. More horses, it turned out, than they needed, nearly twice as many, but better too many than not enough. He let go of the man whose arm was draped across his shoulder, and the soldier wavered then collapsed on his butt on the ground. He glanced over at Bastion, the youth smiling at him widely as he retracted his own arms, the man he had on either shoulder also collapsing onto the ground to rest.

"Thank the gods for that, aye, general?"

"Yes," Aaron said, noting that despite the fact that the giant had carried a man on either arm, he was the only one among Aaron's troops—the Ghosts, they had started calling themselves, a name derived from the screams of Belgarin's men—who didn't look as if they were about to collapse. Much further, he thought, and we would have been ghosts in truth. The men's' clothes were torn and covered in blood and ash, so much, in fact, that the regular material could hardly be seen beneath the proof of what they'd done.

It was a thing well done, Co said.

Aaron glanced over his exhausted troops, noted the relief in their faces as they emerged from the trees and took in the horses. The thoughts of their families, counting on them for protection, had taken them far, had nearly taken them to their graves, had, in fact, taken one hundred of them. One hundred men dead for over a thousand on Belgarin's side. He should have been glad of that, proud, perhaps, but he found he was only tired. The memory of those men burning and screaming for help while they were cooked alive did not stir any pride or joy, only a sadness that they lived in a world where such things were necessary. "It is a thing done, anyway," he said, his voice a harsh whisper.

My father always said, Co spoke, that any solution that calls for violence is no solution at all. Still, you must understand that you did what you had to do, Aaron. Belgarin will not stop—you know that.

Did I, firefly? He thought. Perhaps, someday, he would agree. Perhaps, when the smell of burning flesh wasn't still coating his nostrils, when the desperate screams and pleas of the dying weren't still echoing in his ears, he would be able to believe that, to take some satisfaction in the thing. Now, though, he was only tired, weary beyond anything he had ever known.

"Aaron!"

He turned at the sound of his name and before he could react, Adina was jumping into his arms. He stumbled, surprised and weak from the labors he'd put his body through, but he managed to keep his feet. "Gods," she said, pulling him so tight that it hurt, though he would have never told her so, "I'm so glad you're okay. I was worried."

For several seconds, he did not speak, content to hold her tight against him, to feel her breath on the side of his face, to inhale the scent of her. As he did, he thought he could almost feel the trials of the last few weeks sloughing away, the smell of burning flesh growing fainter, the piercing screams of the dying growing weaker and weaker. "I didn't know you'd be waiting," he said, finally.

"And not just the princess, Mr. Envelar."

Aaron looked up to see Leomin staring at him, and though his face smiled, his eyes seemed to communicate compassion, some understanding of what Aaron and those men with him had undertaken. "It is good to see you alive and well, Mr. Envelar," the Parnen said.

"And you as well, Leomin."

"Would you like me to show you to your horse?" Leomin said, gesturing toward what Aaron knew were two hundred horses behind him staked to the ground, and what appeared to be at least a few hundred troops mounted on their own chargers.

"My men first," Aaron said, glancing back at the exhausted soldiers, some lying or sitting on the ground, others standing propped against trees as if they would fall had they not the trunk's support.

"Of course," Leomin said, nodding as if he'd expected as much. He turned, "I will get the soldiers—"

But the mounted men were already moving, dismounting and leading horses forward. Many of the Ghosts could not seem to rise of their own power, and the soldiers helped pull them to their feet without hesitation, draping their arms across their shoulders even as the ones with no one to help clapped, a sound that was thunderous in the near silent day. At the sound and the kindness, some of the haunted looks left the faces of the men with whom Aaron had fought. Not all the way of course, never that, for there were some things that, when seen, could never been unseen. There were some memories that would plague a man as long as he lived, a weight that he would drag behind him until his death. Still, he could see in their weary faces a gratitude that would have been impossible to express in words, that would have sounded cheap and trite, but that was more real than anything those men had ever felt, anything that Aaron himself had felt.

It was not the recognition, as such, not the shouts of approval, but the awareness, the understanding that those who had gone out into the woods, whether now alive or dead, had given up a piece of themselves, had left it somewhere back there beneath the boughs of the trees, among the burning corpses and the screams of the dying.

"Thank you for coming," Aaron said, speaking to Adina and Leomin. "Thank you."

Adina pulled him close again, "Always," she said, her breath warm against the side of his face. "Always."

CHAPTER TWENTY-NINE

Wendell walked out of the room he'd been given to answer the prince's—king, he reminded himself, here in Cardayum, he's king—summons, brushing ineffectually at the wrinkles that had seemed to appear out of nowhere in his tunic and trousers. He'd been staying in the castle for over a week, yet he was beginning to think that the general would have been better off sending someone else. He'd tried to learn what he could of Commander Hallifax and Ellemont's queen, of course, stealing moments to speak with the castle's servants and guards, but he was not a clever man, able to elicit information from people without their knowing it. Besides, his was not a face that exactly engendered trust. One more likely to send children running and screaming, a cautionary tale to any who dreamed of being soldiers.

He had not, in fact, even been able to discover exactly where the queen had gone when she had left almost immediately following their return to the capital. When he'd asked the prince in one of their meetings, Ellemont had only waved it away, explaining that the mountain climate grew too harsh for his queen's delicate constitution at times, and that she sometimes left for a few weeks until her strength was renewed. It had seemed to Wendell that Ellemont's expression had held more than a little relief at the queen's absence.

Still, her sudden disappearance had appeared suspicious to Wendell, but there'd been no way to extricate himself to follow her as his duty—at least so far as the prince was concerned—was to coordinate their defenses with the prince's own. Not that he'd done much coordinating since he'd arrived. Unless you could call sitting in a room with the general and the prince and several members of the army's support staff, listening to them jaw on about strategy and tactics, about the formation of their army until Wendell was just about ready to fall asleep—had fallen asleep, at least two times of which he was aware—coordinating.

He made his way through the hallways of the castle, having to stop twice to ask a servant or guard for directions to the king's study as he continually got turned around in hallways that looked identical. He was not a man for castles and great halls that was all. He was a man for open spaces, for fields and forests and a drunken game of dice every now and then. He'd no sooner been led to his room on the first day after arriving than he had become hopelessly lost. Still, he finally made it to the door that led to the king's study, and the two guards eyed him dubiously.

"State your business." One said.

"How about you state yours?" Wendell said, immediately regretting the words. His ma had always told him that his mouth would get him into trouble one day, a prediction that had proven true on a number of occasions, yet he couldn't seem to stop it. "What I mean to say—" he blurted, noting the way the guards' hands had moved to the swords sheathed at their sides, "is that the pri—err, the king sent for me."

"Oh, that's right," one of the guards said, "you're the diplomat from Isalla, come to help coordinate the defense against Belgarin."

Wendell grinned, "Diplomat, is it? A promotion, then. Maybe I'll just hang around here for a while, might end up bein' king before too long, aye?"

The guards didn't smile at the joke, instead he saw that their frowns were even darker than they had been. "That is," Wendell said, clearing his throat, "I've a letter King Ellemont sent me, if you've a mind to read it." Neither of the two spoke, and Wendell hurriedly produced the letter from the inside of his tunic, handing it to one of the stone-faced guards.

The man opened it and glanced through it, noting the king's seal at the bottom. "Very well," he said, "you may enter." The two guards swung the doors open and let the scarred sergeant inside, closing the doors after he entered.

"A funny guy," the first said, grinning.

"Yes," the second said shaking his head and snorting a laugh, "be king, he said. Right funny bastard, alright."

Wendell had not been in the king's study before. The other meetings, so far at least, had taken place in the throne room or audience chamber and he was shocked by the number of shelves, all lined with books, that lined the walls. In the town Wendell had come from, few people knew how to read, let alone owned a book. Such a thing was considered an extravagance to people who spent their time farming, fishing, or hunting for food to feed their families. He started counting but realized after a dozen or so that he wasn't sure he could count that high. His mother had taught him long ago, he was sure, but he'd never really had cause to use it and certainly not about books.

"Ah, Sergeant Wendell, it is a pleasure to see you again."

Wendell turned to see the prince staring at him, along with five other people, the commander, the queen—and when had she returned, for Wendell had known nothing of it—along with three men whose faces had grown familiar to Wendell over the last week. They were the commander's highest-ranking captains, the army split between the three of them. Wendell had asked Hallifax about it, and he'd claimed that doing so made for great morale as each soldier felt himself to be part of a team, and that it also gave the opportunity for friendly competition during war games and tournaments. As far as Wendell had seen, it mostly just gave the three captains reason to scowl at each other, each of them trying to outdo the other in any way they could. Wendell thought sure that if one of the men stood up and started takin' a piss, the other two would do the same, if only to see who had the best range. Still, he wasn't a general or a prince, so he didn't pretend to know one way or the other. "I appreciate you inviting me, prince," he said, sketching an awkward bow.

"Of course," Ellemont said, grinning, "please have a seat." He motioned to one of the empty chairs at the table, and Wendell moved toward it, noticing the fine craftsmanship of the wood before he took his seat.

Once he was seated, Ellemont nodded, "I have called you all here because we've received word from my sisters that Belgarin's army is on the march. My brother's advanced scouts have already entered the Orlen Forest outside of Perennia, and apparently, General Envelar sent some two hundred men to harry their progress."

One of the general's captains scoffed at that, "Two hundred men to stand up against fifteen thousand? This general sounds like a fool."

"Like someone else I know," another one of the captains said, eyeing the first man who scowled, "Still," the second captain went on, "I must admit that it seems a foolhardy move. Two hundred men against an army in the woods?" He shook his head, "A suicide mission. One can only hope that not all of Perennia's soldiers share the same tendencies, or else this war will be over before it is truly even begun."

Wendell felt his face heat in an odd mixture of anger and shame. His place was beside General Envelar and the others, not here in a prince's study with armchairs that would have no doubt sold for more than the house he grew up in. This place was alien to him, alien and strange, and he felt as helpless as these prettily dressed fops would no doubt be if they encountered a man with a blade in his hand and blood on his mind and never mind all their talk. He shifted uncomfortably as the third captain chimed in, saying some poorly-veiled insult to the second, but Wendell was barely listening. And anyway, he was no fan of war, no lover of the chaos and violence it brought, but say this for the inevitable threat of violence—it had a way of teaching men to be, if not exactly civil, usually polite. Or at least well-armed. These men were neither of those things—the type of men who his father had called 'Armchair warriors'. Wendell had never really understood the term, but he understood it well enough now. When Wendell asked, his father had told him that the term referred to men who knew nothing of war, and yet sat around in the safety of their own homes and talked about it. Wendell had never really understood that. Sure, he'd killed men before, but it was never something he wanted to talk about. Women or ale, shit the weather in a pinch, but not that. And anyway, he thought he'd found another meaning of the term, one that, to him at least, made more sense. The men were armchair warriors on account of listening to 'em yap would tempt a man to break his chair over their heads.

"I am sure," the prince said frowning, "that General Envelar has his reasons. If you would have met him, perhaps you would understand better." He turned to his own commander, grinning, "A marvelous man, was he not, Commander Halifax?"

The general opened his mouth to speak, obviously uncomfortable with the question, but it was the queen who spoke, "Yes, yes, Ellemont, I'm sure he is a fine man, yet even fine men, I find," her eyes getting what, to Wendell, at least, seemed like a distant look, as if though she spoke of the general her thoughts were on some other man, "that even fine men can make bad decisions."

"Just so, my queen," said one of the captains, clapping his hands softly, "Just so. And even fine men can be fools."

Wendell found that he'd clenched his teeth to keep from speaking out of turn. He reminded himself that they were allies, that Aaron had sent him here for a reason—the gods alone knew what had possessed the man—and that anything he said or did would reflect on Aaron and, thereby, all of Perennia. He wondered what his mother would say, if she heard of her son—a son who'd spent the majority of his childhood trying to ride cows or other similar nonsense—having such responsibility. In truth, he thought her most likely answer would be to faint. Not that she was a fainting woman, but still ... everyone had their limits.

"It is true," another of the men said, "that only an amateur would take on such impossible odds, thereby risking the lives of all those who follow him."

Wendell frowned, truly angry now, then glanced at the prince. For his part, Ellemont looked confused and slightly embarrassed as if he did not know what to say, a man who was not used to taking charge when taking charge was necessary. Wendell's gaze moved to the queen and noted a small smile on her face. Frustrated, he turned to the commander but the man did not seem inclined to call his subordinates down for their disrespect.

"Who is this General Envelar, anyway?" The third asked, "Some whore's son from Avarest, I hear. And what, I wonder, does a born criminal know of war and how does one such as he become a general in the first place? What?" He said, snickering, "did he win his position in some back-alley card game?" He turned to Wendell as the other two laughed, apparently having called a truce for the moment in the face of a common enemy, "No offense meant, of course."

Wendell told himself to stay calm, to relax. After all, the men's' words were no more than that, and words could not hurt a man unless he let them. It was as much of a surprise to him as the others, then, when he stood and grabbed hold of his chair—the wood surprisingly heavy—and brought it crashing down against the head of the nearest, snickering captain.

Thick, hardened wood met the man's head and when one gave, it was not the chair. The man crumpled, his own chair toppling backward and spilling him unconscious onto the ground.

There were shouts of surprise from the others, and Wendell turned to see them staring at him open-mouthed, too stunned to speak. He cleared his throat and motioned to the unconscious man with his head, "Good chairs." Then he took a step toward the other two captains, and he couldn't help but feel some satisfaction as they recoiled slightly, raising their arms and whimpering. "Thing about war," he said to one, "is that it's the type of thing some fellas die in. Though I don't suspect you've any plans of seein' it firsthand yourself. And as for you," he said, turning to the man who'd called Aaron an amateur, "I understand you've some grasp of what a professional soldier is, considering how ready you are to label those who you don't think qualified. Tell me, then, how many scraps have you been in?"

The man glanced around at the others as if looking for help. The queen's mouth was working now, but no words were coming out, and the commander had risen from his chair, his hand going to the sword belted at his side but, for the time at least, he remained still. "N-none," the man said, "I don't ... sir, we did not mean any offense."

Wendell grunted, sitting the chair back down on the floor before sliding into it. "Oh, right," he said, glancing at the unconscious man, "No offense, fella."

Finally, the queen seemed to find her voice, and her words came out shrill and angry, "Commander," she hissed, "take this man to the dungeons now."

"Of course, my queen," he said, his mouth set into a hard, angry line. Wendell sighed as he watched the man come, thinking that maybe a life spent on a farm and in the woods hadn't been such a bad thing, after all.

"Commander Hallifax, wait."

The commander turned to look at his prince, and Ellemont shook his head, "You know as well as I that your man had it coming. Sergeant Wendell here did what any good soldier would do—he took up for his commanding officer. I will not see him punished for that."

"Don't be a fool, Ellemont," Lyla hissed, her face twisted with disgust, "This man came into your castle and assaulted one of your captains. He will be punished fittingly, of course." She waved a hand to the commander who started toward Wendell once more.

"You take another step, Hallifax," Ellemont said, his voice dangerous, "and you will find yourself in the dungeon before the day is out. Do I make myself clear?"

The commander recoiled as if he'd been slapped, his eyes going wide, and Wendell got the impression that the king rarely spoke to him in such a way. "Of course, Majesty," the commander said. Wendell watched the man walk stiffly back to his chair as if someone had left a tent peg sticking out of the ground, and he'd sat right on it. The commander took his seat, his face red, his expression strained.

"You cannot be serious, Ellemont," Lyla said, something like fear in her voice, "this ... this man has come into your castle and insulted you, insulted all of us. He must be punished for his insolence."

Ellemont's face twisted with anger, and he slammed his hand down on the table, the queen jumping in fear, her eyes going wider than the general's had. She stared at Ellemont in shock as if looking at a complete stranger. "Not another word about it, Lyla," he said, "I am king here, not you. As you said, it is my castle and I, at least, am not offended."

The queen opened her mouth to speak but Ellemont raised a finger warningly, "Understand, beloved, that if the next word out of your mouth is spoken in anger or in an attempt to punish a man for taking fair recompense on a pompous fool who thought to belittle his commanding officer in front of him, I will have the guards lock you in your bedroom until the meeting has finished. Be civil," he said, "or be gone."

Her mouth worked strangely for several seconds, and Wendell caught what looked like true fear in her eyes, "I … I cannot believe that you would embarrass me so, your own wife," she said.

"You have embarrassed yourself," Ellemont said, "and I've no part in it. Now, if you do not have anything productive to say—the same for the rest of you—" meeting the eyes of the two captains and the commander in turn, "then you will not say anything at all, or I swear by the power I hold as King of Cardayum and Prince of Telrear, you will regret it. Am I understood?"

"Of course, majesty," the men said, and Wendell, who hadn't been sure about the prince, decided that he liked him. His backbone might have been buried a bit, hidden, but the man had found it in the end.

"Now then," Ellemont said, turning to Wendell with a boyish grin, the stern ruler gone in an instant, "you must tell me some time, sergeant, what school of diplomacy you attended. I have never seen such tactics," he said, glancing at the unconscious man where he still lay in the floor, "but I cannot question their effectiveness."

Wendell's tunic suddenly felt much too tight, and he ran a finger under his collar, clearing his throat. He found that he couldn't think of anything to say, so the only words that came out were, "Nice chairs." As soon as the words were out of his mouth, he winced, feeling like a fool, but the prince's grin only widened.

"Yes," he said, "I suppose they are. Now, my commander and I have studied the maps, and we expect that it will take Belgarin's main force at least three weeks, perhaps more to negotiate the Orlen Forest and make it to the area outside of Perennia's walls. That gives us perhaps a week to finish preparing the army before we must depart. Did General Envelar speak to you of how he would prefer the troops' disposition?"

Wendell swallowed hard, "Um … disposition, sir?" He said, wondering if it wasn't too late to take up farming. He was in his forties, sure, and his back already ached if he slept on a bed that was too hard or too soft, but he thought maybe he could manage it anyway.

"Yes," Ellemont said, "Sorry, I was asking if you know how the general would prefer my troops arrayed, once we reach the area outside of Perennia."

"I ... that is...." Wendell was saved from having to answer as a knock came at the door and one of the soldiers who'd been guarding it stepped inside. Wendell could have kissed the man for interrupting, except he had no reason to think such a thing would have gone over as well as hitting someone over the head with a chair. Strange, these mountain people. Must be something in the air.

"Forgive me, Majesty," the guard said, "but there is a man here who wishes to speak with you—he claims to have been sent by General Envelar."

"Oh?" The prince said, his own attention so fixed on the guard, that he did not notice the worried look the commander and the queen shared. However, Wendell, who'd been taking advantage of the brief reprieve to wipe his arm across his sweaty forehead, did and he frowned, wondering.

"Yes, my king," the guard said, "he says his name is Darrell Rannion. He carries a letter bearing Queen Isabelle's seal."

"Well then by all means, let him in," Ellemont said.

The guard bowed, moving aside, and a man Wendell didn't recognize walked through the door. He was a short, older man, with long white hair, and he bowed as he came inside. "I apologize for the intrusion, Majesty," he said, "General Envelar and Princess Adina sent me to assist Sergeant Wendell in coordinating with your troops."

Wendell let out a sigh of relief deciding that, the next chance he got, he was going to burn a candle for the gods. Not only did they exist, but he thought that no matter what else they'd done, they couldn't be all bad.

"A moment, please, sir," Ellemont said, perusing the letter, apparently unknowing or uncaring about the queen who was reading it over his shoulder.

"Ah," Ellemont said setting the node aside, "my apologies, Mr. Rannion, and welcome to Cardayum. I hope that your journey was pleasant?"

"Very much so, my lord," Darrell said, bowing his head, "and if it's alright with you, Darrell will do fine."

"Very well, Darrell it is," The prince said, smiling, "now, please have a seat." He motioned to where the chair still lay toppled beside the unconscious captain. "It seems that you have chosen a perfect time for coming as one has only recently been vacated."

For his part, the white-haired man took in the scene and only raised an eyebrow.

"Ah, yes that," Ellemont said, "well, do not worry overly much for him, Darrell. I'm quite sure that Captain Bayard will be fine, if only given some time to rest. We have only recently been introduced to the sergeant here's very interesting form of negotiation."

"Of course, prince," Darrell said, giving Wendell an amused glance as he put the chair back at the table and sat.

Wendell was relieved that Aaron had sent another—no doubt had questioned his own sanity after he realized he'd sent Wendell on such a mission—but that didn't stop the flush of embarrassment that rose in his cheeks.

"Now then," Ellemont said, glancing at Wendell and all the others in attendance—at least, all those who were still conscious, "Let us begin."

***

The talk went on for what felt like hours and by the time it was done, Wendell was ready to do nothing more than spend the obligatory hour it would take him to find his way to his bedroom and then sleep for a year. He had only just taken a step out of the door, though, when he felt a hand on his shoulder. He turned to see the man, Darrell, standing there, smiling at him. "Please, walk with me, sergeant."

Wendell shrugged. If he was going to be lost, he might as well have someone to talk to. He didn't think it would benefit their cause if he ended up sleeping in the hallway, and at least the conversation might keep him awake. "Sure," he said, "lead on."

The white-haired man did not speak until they were well away from the others and the guards who had been stationed at the door and at the end of the hallway, "Forgive me," he said finally, "if I stepped on your toes back there—it was not my intention."

He offered his hand, and Wendell took it, "Stepped on my toes? No sir, I was doin' a good enough job of that already. If you would've come in any later, you'd have probably seen me passed out on the floor next to that other fool."

"Please, just Darrell," the man said, "and speaking of that fool," he said, grinning, "I did not get the entire story there."

Wendell shrugged, embarrassed all over again. "That fella in there was an ass—the other two captains were also, but," he shrugged again, "well, that one was closest. Anyway, he took to talkin' about the general, and I guess I just sort of let my temper get the best of me." He frowned, shaking his head, "Probably could have handled it better."

"Possibly," Darrell said, nodding, the grin still on his face, "but some lessons must be learned the hard way, and I think that your lesson will stick with that man for some time."

"Least a week," Wendell agreed, "I took a blow to the head once or twice, the knot'll hang around for a while, and it'll be tender for a few days after that."

To his surprise, the older man started laughing then, clapping him on the shoulder. In another minute, Wendell was laughing too despite himself. "Sir, you don't mind me askin', who are you? You ain't a member of the army, leastways, you weren't when I left."

"No," Darrell said, "you're correct, I'm not a member of your queen's army. I am a ... friend of the general's. I have known him since he was a child, in fact."

"That so?" Wendell said, "if it ain't too much trouble, what was he like?"

Darrell shook his head, remembering, "Much like he is now, I'm afraid, only smaller."

"Aye," Wendell said, nodding, "children are small. Most of 'em anyway."

"So they are," Darrell said, nodding his head sagely, "so they are."

They walked on in a companionable silence then, taking one hallway after the next, a set of stairs here and there, until Wendell thought it was likely he'd starve to death in the castle before he found a way out. Then the swordmaster came to a stop, and Wendell paused too, "Sir?" He said, questioning, but then he realized that he recognized the door they stood in front of. "By the gods, this is my room," he said.

"So it is," Darrell said, smiling, "My own is right across the hall," he paused, motioning to it.

"What is it then," Wendell said, frowning at the man, "they give you a map or somethin'?"

Darrell's grin widened, "Something like that."

"Huh. I got to find me one of those."

"You know," Darrell said with a laugh, "I think they're out."

Wendell grunted, "Figures."

Darrell glanced down either end of the hallway, making sure they were alone, "Is it just me, or is there something going on between Commander Hallifax and Queen Lilliana?"

"Well, now, I don't know about that," Wendell said, frowning, "I got to think he's at least twice her age."

"I meant something a little different," Darrell said.

"Oh," Wendell said, "like havin' to do with the way they kept glancing at each other like they'd just found out the room was on fire and neither wanted to be the one to share the bad news?"

"Right. Something like that."

"Yeah," Wendell said, "I caught on to that myself."

Darrell glanced down the hallway, frowning, "There are things going on here, sergeant. I don't know what, exactly, but whatever it is, the queen and the commander are in on it. I'd suggest being very careful in the following week. I don't think they'll be able to do anything once the army marches—too many eyes to see and ears to hear—but we are in their world, for now. There was no mistaking the queen's displeasure at our presence, and I cannot guess how far that displeasure might go."

Wendell sighed, "Well, shit. There goes my sleep for the night. See you in the mornin'."

The white-haired man nodded his head, and Wendell went inside his room, closing the door. He glanced at the bed with its many pillows and its thick, fluffy mattress, and despite the fact that he knew it'd wreak havoc on his back, he didn't think he'd ever seen anything so fine. Sighing, he headed to the room's single chair and sat, waiting for the morning to come.

***

"Won't be long now."

"No," Aaron said, turning to look at Brandon, "Not long. A few weeks, no more than that and then the fighting will begin in earnest."

The older man grunted, "You ask me, the fighting's already began in earnest for some. I've talked to some of the lads—a thousand men, they said. A thousand at least. That's a damned fine accomplishment, Aaron. I never would have thought it possible."

Aaron frowned, "A drop in the ocean, Brandon, that's all." He turned to look back at the fields and forests laid out below them, his expression troubled. "The real fighting will begin soon enough and then we'll see."

Brandon nodded and, for a time, neither man spoke. They stood on the battlements of the city's walls, staring out into the expanding fields that stretched away into the forest. The fields were empty now, the grass blowing in the wind like some painting he'd seen once, but he knew they would not remain so for long and if they resembled any painting at all, it would be one composed by some mad artist, a vision of blood and death.

It is not so bad, Co said, with Ellemont's troops—

You're assuming, firefly, that Ellemont even sends any troops.

What do you mean? She asked, he said—

I know what he said, just like I know that his wife, Lilliana, didn't seem particularly pleased, and she seemed to me like the type of person who makes her displeasure known.

But Ellemont is king in Cardayum, Aaron. Not Lyla.

He's also a coward. From his own mouth. Forgive me if I'm not comforted. Besides, firefly, even if Ellemont does show up with his troops, we'll still be outnumbered nearly two to one. We'd need a miracle to survive that. "A damned miracle," he muttered.

"I'm sorry, general," Brandon said, "what was that?"

"Nothing," Aaron said. He had his own doubts, his own fears, and there was no need to burden the captain with them. He no doubt had his own demons to struggle against.

They both turned at the sound of approaching footsteps on the battlements to see a messenger rushing toward them. "Excuse me, general," the man said, gasping, "a message for you. It just arrived."

Aaron took it, excitement rushing through him. He had not heard from May in some days now, nor had he heard from Wendell. He wondered, not for the first time, if it had been a mistake sending the man. The sergeant was clever enough, and Aaron knew him to be a capable, intelligent man, but Aaron couldn't help feeling as if he'd sent the man to his death, thrown him into a nest of vipers and asked him not only not to get bitten, but to figure out which of the snakes held the most venom. He only hoped that Darrell made it to Cardayum in time to help the sergeant.

As for May, it was troubling that he had received no communication but not particularly surprising. She would be busy about her business, whether Grinner and Hale stuck to the deal or not. She'd be spending her time either trying to convince them of the importance of fighting or trying to keep the two from killing each other. As for the city council, it was too much to hope that they would send any support. The prince's wife, Lyla, might have been an ass, and he was almost sure she was up to something, but she had not been wrong, either. There was a running joke in the Downs that Avarest's council was so slow to get anything done that by the time they decided to hold trials for criminals, they were forced to punish corpses as the men and women who'd committed the crimes had long since died of old age. It was an exaggeration, of course, but not by much. Not much at all.

An anticipatory feeling of excitement running through him, Aaron tore open the letter and unfolded it, his eyes scanning its contents, a frown growing on his face with each word he read.

Aaron,

There is still time. The enemy lurks and heals, but you would be a fool to think that he is finished or given up. He has dedicated his significant life to his goal, and he will not abandon it, no matter what or who stands in his way. If he finds those things he seeks, the entire world will be brought low beneath him. I implore you, take what little time is left and leave. I will see that your passage is safe. Of course, you may bring the princess and, I hope, the Parnen too. It is not the best way—it is the only way. You cannot kill that which is immortal just as you cannot slay a hurricane. You can only take shelter and wait for it to pass. I beg of you to reconsider your course before it is too late.

-T

The words were jagged and uneven, as if written by a child only learning the art of it, and that was no real surprise to Aaron as Tianya had no doubt written the note in that dark hole she lived in. He crumpled the note up, feeling the anger stir. Of all the messages he could have received, this was the last he would have chosen. He couldn't understand how the woman didn't see by now that he would not run. Even if he had wished to—and he did not— he knew enough of Adina to know that she would never abandon these people in their time of need. It was not in her to do so and, he found with some surprise, that it was not in him either.

There will be trouble there before it's through, Co said.

Yeah, Aaron agreed, ripping up the note until he held a handful of tiny pieces of parchment. But that is a problem for tomorrow. Today has its own, and they are large enough.

"Not a good message, I take it?" Brandon asked from beside him, and Aaron turned to see the captain studying him with his eyebrow raised.

"Good or bad?" Aaron said, shaking his head, "I don't know. And that, I think, is the most worrying bit of all." With that, he flung wide his hands, and the infinitesimal pieces of parchment scattered, carried on the wind and blown out over the city walls.

CHAPTER THIRTY

Wendell sighed as he opened up the door to his room and walked inside. The latest meeting with the prince and his staff had ended nearly two hours ago, and he'd only just now managed to find his room. He'd tried to ask some of the guards, but the men just stared at him, stone-faced like they had to take a shit, maybe, and were doing their best to hold it. Wendell didn't envy those bastards, not a bit. He was a soldier, sure, and he'd spent more than his share of time on meaningless guard duties before General Envelar had taken over and made him sergeant, but he didn't miss them and that was a fact.

He closed the door behind him and yawned, rubbing a hand over his eyes. He'd slept little, spending the majority of his time worrying about what Ellemont's wife might do, but nothing had come of it and tomorrow they would leave for the battle with Belgarin's troops. The three captains had been subdued at the night's meeting, one of them still sporting a black eye, but Wendell didn't think that was the reason. It was as if the men only just realized what they were in for, that soon they would be forced to command troops in a war, to possibly even fight themselves, to kill or be killed. Gone were their slanted criticisms and protestations of valor. Reality was a bitch sometimes—most of the times, in Wendell's experience—but at least it had a way of making fools realize their own foolishness. Wendell would have been more worried himself, if he hadn't been so relieved. He'd spent the last week worrying over Ellemont's wife, trying to uncover what plot she hid, if she hid any at all, and he'd come up empty-handed. He and the swordmaster, Darrell, had switched out from night to night, one getting what troubled rest he could—nothing kept a man awake like wondering if someone might sneak into his room and slit his throat for him while he slept—while the other went about speaking to the castle guards and servants, seeing if they could learn anything that might be useful to the general.

A week's worth of searching and the only thing Wendell had to show for it was deep circles under his eyes and a body that threatened to go to sleep if he so much as stopped walking for a moment. He was excited at the prospect of no longer having to try to look for some hidden plot in the queen's words, relieved at no longer having to wonder at the meaning of those sideways glances she sometimes shared with the commander. Sure, war was a bad thing, an evil thing, but at least it was something he understood. When the fighting started, people would be out for his life, but he'd know they were coming and if he died, well, at least he'd get to rest.

Tonight's night was Darrell's. Normally, the swordmaster would walk back to his room with Wendell. They'd sit for an hour or two and discuss anything they'd learned—short conversations, those—but this time as they left the meeting, the swordmaster had only frowned and motioned for Wendell to go ahead without him. An easy enough thing, Wendell supposed, if the castle hallways didn't all look damned identical. Still, he wondered what it was that had made the older man become suspicious—for he was suspicious, that was no question.

Wendell replayed the scene of the meeting in his head. They'd been discussing tactics, going over for what must have been the hundredth time the deployment of Prince Ellemont's troops. In truth, Wendell had only been half listening. They'd had the conversation often enough, yet he still got lost in the minutiae of it.

Wendell frowned, concentrating on the conversation that had taken place and trying to remember when exactly that look had come into Darrell's eyes. Nobody else had noticed it, of that he was sure. He wouldn't have noticed it himself if he hadn't been staring at the swordmaster and trying to guess at his age as some poor way to entertain himself.

Slowly, bits and pieces of the conversation came back. The commander had been going over the gear they'd need to take, had made some mention of how they could, at least, not be overly concerned with taking extra blankets for the soldiers as the year had been unseasonably warm.

And the prince ... damnit what had the man said? Wendell closed his eyes, rubbing at his temples fiercely as if he might somehow physically dislodge the knowledge he sought. Then, in an instant, it was there. The prince had said, 'If it grows any warmer, my queen may not even have to leave us again this year in search of warmer climes for her fragile constitution." He'd laughed when he'd said it, but it was not the laugh of a man who found something funny. It was more a sad laugh. The queen had spoken little since Ellemont had last reprimanded her, but hers had been a cold presence despite that, and whenever he spoke, the king glanced sideways at her as if expecting to be reminded of his own foolishness. She said nothing though, and there was only that cold, frigid silence.

Then Darrell, Wendell remembered, had said something, making some offhand mention about how he himself preferred the warmer climes, had even gone so far as to inquire from the queen about where she enjoyed going.

The woman had sniffed—she often did that, Wendell had found, and he was beginning to think she really might have a problem with her constitution, always walking around with a cold, like she did—and at first it had seemed as if she didn't plan on answering then, reluctantly, she had, "Not so far," she said, "mostly, to pray for our people in these troubled times." She'd paused then, and it seemed to Wendell that she only just managed to keep herself from turning and staring at her husband in what he thought would have been recrimination, as if Ellemont was personally responsible for all the world's woes. "To pray and seek guidance as I have done since before Ellemont and I were wed."

The prince had nodded and though he smiled, Wendell could see the bitterness hidden beneath the surface, "Oh yes, my wife is most pious. You would not believe just how much."

Lyla's face had colored at that, and Wendell thought he could see well enough how it had gone, could see, too, why it was that no little princelings or princesses were running around the castle, sneaking treats and making nuisances of themselves. The queen, it seemed, had been ready enough to take her share of the king's wealth, but had been much stingier with her own. Cruel, maybe, but it was not enough to show that she was some conspiring criminal. Still, as far as Wendell was concerned, he'd prefer a nice roll with a working woman any day. Better their warmth than this ice queen's frigid beauty. And anyway, when a man hands over coin, he can pretty well guarantee he'll get what he paid for.

Wendell forced his thoughts away from the distraction and back to the conversation. 'I am a praying man myself,' Darrell had said, 'may I ask, my queen, what city and church is it that has the honor of hosting one such as yourself?'

Wendell frowned, trying to remember what the queen had said to that and, at first, nothing came to him. You damn fool, he scolded himself, the general sends you here to do one thing, and you were too distracted and bored to even pay any attention.

Sighing, he sat down on the bed and pulled off his boots, tossing them to the side. He laid back in the bed, promising himself that he would not go to sleep, would only rest his weary body for a few moments. Maybe he'd even be able to better remember what had been said if his sleep-deprived body wasn't complaining every few seconds.

Then, just like that it came to him. 'As a praying man,' the queen had said, 'you must know as well as I that the place does not matter, only the intent. The gods listen to the wise and the foolish alike, to the rich and the poor, whether they send their entreaties up from the lowliest hovel or the finest castle, it matters not to the gods. Only a heathen and a blasphemer would think that the place matters more than the prayers and the earnestness of those who pray them.'

'Oh, come now, Lyla,' the prince had said, 'we're all friends here.' He'd turned to Darrell then, 'please forgive my wife, Darrell. She is very pious, as I believe I have said, but it is no secret that her visits most often lead her to the town of Arandoc some week's travel away from here.'

'Ah, Arandoc,' Darrell had said, smiling, 'I know it well. A fine place and a fine people. Fisher folk mostly, but no less pious for all that.'

Wendell had thought the queen might have thawed some small amount at the swordmaster's compliment for the place in which she spent a lot of her time, but her frown grew deeper instead. 'You seem to be quite well traveled, sir. In just what capacity do you serve Queen Isabelle?'

Darrell had grinned at that, 'My apologies, queen, but I did not intend to mislead you. I do not bow to Queen Isabelle. I am only a friend of General Envelar, and he asked me to assist Sergeant Wendell in whatever way I might.'

'You speak much,' the queen said, 'for one who is an assistant only.'

Darrell had only shrugged at that, the smile never leaving his face, 'Forgive me, my queen, but I'm afraid it is one of my faults. And, if I might be so bold to inquire, is Arandoc where your most recent journey took you?'

The queen opened her mouth to speak, but Ellemont had spoken first, 'So it is, Darrell,' he said with a laugh, 'I swear those priests see more of my lady wife than I do myself. If those old men were not sworn to celibacy, I might even find myself growing jealous.'

'Ellemont,' the queen had scolded, 'that is no way to speak of your queen to … to visitors.' Wendell had been distracted during that part as well, but he'd have had to have been deaf to not hear that 'visitors' had not been the word the queen had wanted to say. Bastards, maybe.

'Alright, I'm sorry,' Ellemont said, holding his hands up, 'I only jest and meant nothing by it, my love. Still, Darrell,' he said, winking at the man, 'you know how women can be. It seems some days that nothing I do is right no matter how hard I try.'

Darrell though, didn't seem to hear the princess's words, so focused was he on the queen's face. He was smiling affably enough, but it seemed to Wendell that there was determined intent in his unwavering gaze. 'A fine place, is Arandoc.' He said again, 'fine people. And with what priest do you discuss your prayers, if I might ask, queen?'

She snorted at that, 'Everyone knows that the only priest worth seeing is High Priest Lerifan.'

Darrell nodded at that as if in appreciation, 'You are as wise as you are beautiful, Queen Lyla, and Lerifan is a fine man of the gods indeed. Or was, I'm sad to say. You no doubt heard of his accident."

"I ... that is, of course," the queen said, "a most unfortunate incident. Still, I find that Arandoc is as fine a place to worship the gods as any.'

'So it is, my lady,' Darrell said, smiling, 'so it is.'

With that, the conversation had gone on to different topics, the war in particular, and Wendell had thought nothing of it. Now though, thinking back, he thought that maybe there had been a strange look in the swordmaster's steady gaze from then on. It was something she said, wasn't it? He thought, something that didn't sound right to you. Wendell had no idea himself as he spent little time with priests and the like. It wasn't that he didn't believe in the gods—there was a whore in Isalla that'd make any man believe in them if he had the coin—it was just that he'd never felt comfortable around holy men. Always had to stop and check about a hundred times to make sure he hadn't somehow forgot to put on pants.

As for Arandoc, he'd never been, hadn't even ever heard of the place before tonight. Still, the more he thought of it, the more he became convinced that something in the queen's words had bothered the swordmaster. Never mind, he thought, he'll tell you when he comes back. All you've got to do in the meantime is wait.

Just stay awake and wait. And that wasn't really such a hard thing. He figured an hour, maybe two, and the swordmaster would be back, and he'd tell Wendell whatever it was that had put his back up at the meeting. He was exhausted, and the bed was soft, but that was a good thing, his aching body needing the rest. He just wouldn't go to sleep, that was all, wouldn't close his eyes.

As he lay there, he thought of Ellemont. The prince was a funny character, but despite his self-professed cowardice, Wendell found that he liked him. The prince was what he was, and he made no attempts to appear otherwise. Wendell had never seen a man so ready to accept the mantle of coward without a fight, but the prince had. According to what the man had said, he'd even gone so far as to make a suit of armor painted yellow. The yellow prince, he'd called himself.

Wendell shook his head slowly from side to side in wonder. There really was no understanding people. And then this same prince, this same man who called himself a coward intended to wear that armor onto the battlefield, into the war. Wendell was sure that the man would have plenty enough guards around him to make sure he didn't do so much as stub his toe, but he was still surprised to find that the prince was going, had expected him to stay back at the castle and the relative safety it afforded. Then when the prince mentioned offhandedly that he was coming, the three captains present had tried to talk him out of it. Wendell had expected the queen to scold Ellemont on how foolish he was being, tell him that a king had no place on the battlefield. To his surprise, she had said nothing and in the end the prince overruled those few worried captains who—to Wendell at least—seemed much more afraid than Ellemont himself.

Wendell shook his head slightly again and realized that his eyes had somehow closed, and he hadn't noticed. Ah well, he thought, that's alright. My eyes need a rest just as much as the rest of me. I just won't sleep, is all. Anyway, if someone did try to come, I'd hear them long before they got the door open. It's fine. Just don't go to sleep. Which, of course, is exactly what he did.

***

A familiar sound jerked Wendell from sleep. It was the sound of steel slicing through the air, impacting on flesh, and he let out a scream to call the guards down even as he rolled to the side. He was brought up short as one hand gripped his arm in a vice-like grip, spinning him back before letting go only to clamp down on his mouth, muffling his screams.

"Relax, sergeant. It's me. Please, stop screaming."

Wendell grunted, gave a single nod and the older man let him go. "Just so's you know," Wendell said staring up at him, "that weren't no scream. It was a battle cry."

The older man grinned wide, "Of course."

Wendell sighed, sitting up. "Shit. What are you doin' here anyway? I was thinkin' someone had come into the room, and I was about to get my throat cut for fallin' asleep like some fool."

Darrell winced, and for the first time, Wendell noticed that there was something red on the man's face. "You've uh ... you've got something," Wendell said, pointing at the crimson spot, "right there."

Darell wiped at his face with his free hand then nodded, his expression sober now, "Blood," he said, "but not mine."

Wendell frowned, "Don't guess as there's any chance you maybe decided to visit the healers, help them work on some patients, and maybe that's where you got that."

Darrell shook his head slowly, "About how you said you thought I'd broken into your room and that you were going to die."

"Get my throat cut, I said. And yeah, what of it?"

Darrell stepped to the side, and Wendell stared in shock at the two corpses lying on the ground, naked steel clutched in their dead fists.

"I don't suppose those men just come by to sing me happy birthday, wish me a good one?"

"It's your birthday?" Darrell said.

Wendell sighed, "No, gods help me, no it ain't. And anyway, I ain't never seen anybody celebrate a birthday by skewering somebody on a sword." He shrugged, "Not that kind, anyway." He levered himself into a sitting position, "Well, shit. Why don't you tell me what's happened and why it is I got two dead men lying in my floor."

"Back at the meeting room," Darrell said, "do you recall me asking the princess about Arandoc?"

"Sure," Wendell said absently, unable to pull his eyes from the dead men. "You said it was a nice place, nice people."

"And that might even be true," Darrell said, "but I must confess that I've never been."

Wendell frowned, pulling his eyes away from the men and the swords they still clutched in their fists—swords that had been meant for him—and meeting the older man's eyes, "If you hadn't ever been, how in the shit would you know about that one priest's accident? Unless..." he cut off as realization struck. "Oh. Damn."

"Right," Darrell said, glancing back at the open doorway, a bloody sword still in his hand, and when he spoke his words were fast and hurried, "I had no idea who this 'Lerifan' was that the queen spoke of, but what's more interesting is that she had no idea I was lying when I said he'd been in an accident. Instead, she only agreed with something she'd have known for a lie if she had actually been there on her recent trip, as she claimed."

Wendell shook his head, rubbing at his eyes in an effort to rouse his drowsy mind, "So if the queen didn't know you were lying, that means she never went to Arondac at all."

"Right," Darrell said, "and I think I've got a pretty good idea of where she did go. But, sergeant, listen, we have to go and fast. If I'm right, Ellemont is in serious trouble."

"Fine," Wendell said, snatching a sword from one of the dead men, "lead on."

***

Wendell followed the swordmaster through the castle at a run, dodging out of the way of surprised servants until they finally came to an abrupt halt at the entrance to the hallway that led to the king's chambers. The two guards watching the hallway drew their blades, "What is the meaning of this?" One of them demanded, stepping forward.

Wendell was just about to comment how that wasn't exactly polite when he remembered that he and the older man were both holding bared blades.

"Listen," Darrell said, "I've reason to believe that someone is going to make an attempt on the king's life. Now, I need to know where he is."

Instead of answering, the guards rushed him, their swords swinging. The swordmaster stepped out of the way of the first blow, bringing the handle of his sword down on the man's helmeted head. The unfortunate guard crumpled and before he hit the ground, Darrell had knocked the other man's blade wide and had the tip of his own poised at the man's throat.

Wendell, who had only managed to take a step with the intent of helping, stared in shock. "What the fu—"

"Tell me where the king is," Darrell said, "I swear by the gods, major and minor both, we do not mean him harm. We've come to save him, but we need your help."

The man was staring wide-eyed at the blade at his throat, but he nodded slowly, apparently deciding to believe Darrell. Funny really, Wendell thought, the kinds of things a man would believe if it kept him breathing a little longer. "His Majesty's not here," the man stammered, "he went ... went with Commander Hallifax and his captains. They came asking him to accompany them for a final meeting of strategy before the army departs tomorrow."

Darrel nodded and started away, Wendell following when the guard spoke, "Sirs, please. If you really are here to help, like you say. Protect the queen. The queen, you see, she's ... she's with them."

Darrell frowned, "I do not doubt that. Where exactly did they go?"

"Sir," the guard said, "they ... they said something about going to the courtyard. I meant to go with the king, I swear, but the commander, he—"

"Never mind that, soldier," Darrell said, "it's not your fault. Now, tell me where this courtyard is."

Soon, they were off and running again, barreling down castle passageways as they followed the hasty directions the guard had given them. It wasn't long before they came upon the door the guard had indicated, and Darrell barely slowed as he lashed out with one foot, striking the wood of the door beside the handle.

The wood cracked and gave beneath the blow, and the door swung open. The swordmaster rushed inside, and Wendell, gasping for breath, followed after him. Flowers and bushes of all shapes and sizes bloomed within the courtyard and well-trimmed and maintained grass lay on either side of the pebbled stone path, and the path itself led to a fountain at which Wendell could see several men standing.

He followed the swordmaster as the man barreled down the path, and the first thing Wendell noticed as they drew closer to the fountain was Prince Ellemont's unconscious form—at least, he hoped it was unconscious, gods don't let him be dead—lying in a heap at the fountain's base. The second thing he noticed was the fact that he had no shoes. "Damnit," he hissed, wincing as he lifted his foot, knocking off several of the sharper pebbles that clung to the bottom of it.

Darrel spun, raising his sword as if expecting that Wendell was under attack, "What is it? What happened?"

"Forgot my boots," Wendell said by way of explanation.

Darrell raised his eyebrows as if to say that they had bigger concerns than his boots just then. "Thing is," Wendell said, "I got sensitive feet."

Darrell stared at him for another moment before turning and running on, directly at the figures standing over the prince's body. Wendell sighed. Clearly, the swordmaster had never suffered from sensitive feet. If he had, he'd have been a damn sight more understanding than that. Wincing in anticipation of the pain to come, Wendell darted after the swordmaster.

The sound of the fountain's water must have obscured the sound of their approach, for by the time the figures finally turned, Darrell and Wendell were no more than ten feet away. There were seven in all: The commander, his three captains, two guards who Wendell did not know and, of course, the queen herself. "What is the meaning of this?" Darrell demanded.

They turned, fear on their faces, but after a moment, the queen's expression turned to a sneer, "You fools. You'll die for meddling in something that's none of your business."

"The assassination of a king in his own castle while I am a guest of the same king is my business," Darrell said.

"Right," Wendell said, wanting to help, "and it ain't right, besides."

The queen sneered again, waving the two unfamiliar soldiers forward, "Kill them."

Wendell stepped forward, intending to help Darrell, but the thing was done before he'd drew close enough, the two soldiers lying dead on the path. Apparently, the swordmaster's mercy did not extend to would-be assassins of their liege. "How long have you been Belgarin's creature?" Darrell said, turning to stare at the queen, his breathing not even labored.

The queen stared in shock at the two dead men then looked back at Darrell, her face twisting with anger, "I am not his creature, you stupid common brute," she said, "I am his queen. Or, at least, I will be, just as soon as you and your pathetic little rebellion are done away with. He is the fistborn. He will be king, and I his queen."

Wendell walked up to stand beside Darrell, facing off against the commander and his three captains who had their own blades clutched in their hands. "Commander," Wendell said, deciding to give it a try himself, "you don't have to do this. What type of soldier betrays his king, anyway? There's still time for you to fix things, to set them right."

The commander scowled, his face growing red, "And what do you know of it? I tried to tell the king that we could not fight such an army, but he would not listen. Well, I will not watch my city burn, will not watch my family die all because the Coward Prince decides he wants to be a hero. The people of Cardayum deserve better than that. They deserve better than him," he growled, kicking the prince's unconscious form. *Please let him just be unconscious.*

"And you feel that you are qualified to make such a decision for them?" Darrell asked.

The commander shrugged, "Somebody had to. A soldier learns early on that the job ain't always easy, but it's the job anyway. War's not a business for people that have weak stomachs or faint hearts."

"And what of you three?" Darrell said, turning to look at the captains whose faces were pale, their hands shaking where they held their swords, "Do you hold with your commander? Would you be as willing to die for your beliefs as he is?"

"I ... I don't—"

"Shut up, fool," the commander hissed.

Queen Lyla only laughed, "Oh, I'll admit that you are good, old man, but just how good are you? Enough to take on two guards sure, but what of ten?" As if on cue, Wendell heard the ringing footsteps of armored men and turned to see four more guards approaching on the path behind them. *Not ten, at least.* Still, that made the odds eight on two not including the queen. *Plenty enough to get the job done.*

"Alright then you bastards," he growled, "let's go."

Before he could think better of it, Wendell charged forward, swinging his sword two-handed at the nearest guard with all the strength he could put behind it. The man stopped, throwing his blade up in time, but he hadn't expected Wendell to charge— frankly, Wendell hadn't expected it either, not until he'd done the fool thing—and the guard wasn't prepared for the force of the blow that knocked his own blade aside before striking his helmet and crushing the metal of it inward.

The guard screamed, stumbling backward, but Wendell didn't have a chance to pursue him as another sword was flashing at his face. He got his blade up in time, but barely, and he stumbled backward under the force of the blow. A lucky stumble as it turned out, for two more swords flashed in the area where he'd been only moments before, the other men attacking from the side. Had he still been there, he would have been skewered.

Not that there's not plenty of chance of it still happening, of course. Wendell had always considered himself a competent fighter, no more than that. The type of fighter that served well enough in a shield wall or on the line, where he was flanked by his fellow soldiers, but not the kind that would ever duel for the sport of it so that rich men and women could have a little blood with their meal. And most times in an army being competent was good enough. Now though, he wasn't so sure, and he continued retreating slowly as the three men closed in, confident and why not? Sure, maybe Darrell could take such odds, but Wendell was no swordmaster. If he tried to move like the older man had he'd just as likely end up tripping over his own feet, and if he was going to be killed he'd just as soon not make a fool of himself in the bargain.

"Look here, boys," he said, "how's about we call it square? I'm sure your king will be lenient, if you help me now. Shit, I'll even put in a good word for you. How'd that be?"

The men didn't answer, only continued closer to him, and Wendell sighed. "So it's like that then." He glanced over at Darrell to see that the swordmaster was currently engaged in a fight with the commander and one of the captain's, his blade flying back and forth with incredible speed, yet still only just managing to deflect the combined efforts of the two men. The other two captains lay on the ground, dead or unconscious. Darrell would be done with his work soon enough, Wendell thought, but not so soon as to save him.

Sighing, he set his feet and waited for the men to come on, which they did willingly enough. The first moved in, swinging his blade, and Wendell knocked it aside, stepping back to avoid a blow from the second man's sword. He saw the third sword coming and turned his head away, though not fast enough to avoid the steel slicing a thin line across his cheek. Grunting, he kicked out with his foot sending the man tumbling back into his comrades. The three men fell in a mass of flesh and steel. Wendell stepped forward, stabbing down into that writhing mass and was rewarded with a scream of pain.

He stabbed down again but one of the soldiers, still on his back, knocked his blade aside with his own and grabbed Wendell's wrist in a vice-like grip. He tried to pull away, but the man was too strong. The guard gave his arm a jerk and suddenly Wendell was falling on top of him. They rolled around then, hissing and biting, both trying to get a good hold on the other, but the soldier was stronger than Wendell and soon he found the man's hands locked around his throat. Gagging for breath, Wendell struggled, but the man's grip didn't loosen

"Bastard," he hissed, spittle flying from his mouth as he tried and failed to push the man off of him. He felt himself blacking out, knew that it would be the death of him but was helpless to stop it. Then there was a rush of movement and suddenly the hands that were choking him—and the man who owned those hands, and wasn't that a trick—were gone, flying off of him.

Wendell wheezed in a breath, blinking at the dark spots in his vision and felt around on the ground, half blind, searching desperately for his sword. The man must have fallen or something, but he would be back in a moment and if Wendell wasn't ready... "Are you okay?"

Wendell looked up to see Darrell standing over him, offering his hand. Grunting, he rolled to look in the direction of where his opponent had rolled and saw the man lying crumpled on the ground in a pool of spreading blood. Not coming back then, not now or ever. Wincing as he rubbed at his throat, Wendell took the hand the swordmaster offered and was pulled to his feet. "Wish you ha..." he paused, hacking before continuing, "wish you hadn't stopped me. I was just about to make my move."

"Oh?" The swordmaster asked, his eyebrow raised.

"Well," Wendell grunted, dusting himself, "Dying's a move. Don't know that you can say it ain't."

Darrell grinned, but the expression quickly turned into a wince, and Wendell noticed for the first time that the man was bleeding from a cut on his upper left arm. "Ah, the bastards pinked you."

Darrell nodded grimly, "Nothing serious, but I find that the older I get the less I'm able to shake off such things."

Wendell grunted, "Old, is it? Well. Suppose that'd explain why you're so slow in a fight. Anyway, can't be helped, time gets us all, the bitch. Now, let me see the arm."

Darrell shook his head, "We really don't have time—"

"We really ain't got time for you to be bleedin' to death either," Wendell said, bending and tearing off a length of one of the dead men's shirts. It wasn't as if the bastard was going to need it anymore. "Now, let me see that arm."

With a sigh, the swordmaster held his arm out, and Wendell pulled the knife from his belt. He groaned as he realized he should have pulled it while fighting the man, but finally decided that having the life choked out of you had a way of messing with a man's thinking. He cut away the sleeve of the swordmaster's shirt and grunted, grabbing some water from the fountain to clean the wound before wrapping the bandage around it. "You ought to be ashamed of yourself," he said as he worked, "A swordmaster who can't even handle seven men in a fight. Pitiful, really, but don't you worry none. Your secret's safe with me."

"Three, I'm afraid." Darrell said, wincing as Wendell pulled the bandage tight.

Wendell frowned, "Three? There were these four here," he said, gesturing around them at the corpses lying scattered on the pathway, "then the commander and the three cap—" his words cut off as he turned to look back at the fountain. The three captains were lying on the ground unmoving, as was the king himself, but there was no one else in sight. "Now just where in the shit did they go?"

"I'm afraid Hallifax got away. He's wounded though. So there's that."

Wendell groaned, rubbing at his eyes, "And the queen?"

Darrell sighed, "Gone too, I'm afraid." She slipped away while I was fighting the general and once I saw the four men you were fighting—"

"Well," Wendell said, pausing to spit, "I 'spose you could call it a fight, though I think that's a bit generous. Anyway, do I mean to understand you left off taking them down to help me?"

Darrell hesitated then slowly nodded, as if not knowing how Wendell would react. What he did, of course, was clap the man on the back hard enough to send him stumbling a step, "Well, by the gods I can't fault you for that. I appreciate it friend, truly I do. I ain't never done it before, but I got it in mind that dyin' would be a real bitch. Though that means we've got no traitor queen or traitor commander. I can't expect General Envelar will be particularly happy."

Darrell nodded, "But, then, when is he ever happy?"

Wendell barked a laugh, "Seems you are the general's friend, after all. Now then—" he grew silent at the shouts and ringing footfalls of what sounded like a hundred men at least, and he looked up to see guards flowing into the courtyard, their swords bared.

"The king!" One shouted, "They've killed King Ellemont!"

"Now, just hold on a minute there," Wendell said, raising his hands only to realize he was still holding the knife he'd used to cut Darrell's shirt. He swallowed hard and let it fall to the ground, "I can see how this might look bad, what with the king lyin' there, but I'm middlin' sure he ain't even dead and—"

"You'll die for this, bastard!" Another shouted, and the guards started forward.

"Alright, Alright," Wendell shouted back, "I'm middlin' to fairly sure, he ain't dead, that better? Now if you boys would just hold on a moment ... see, it was the queen we was after, not the king. And anyway—"

"The queen!" another guard shouted, "What have you done with her, assassin?"

"What?" Wendell said, backing away as the guards—surrounding them now—drew closer, "look, fella, that ain't what I meant. She got away is all, but we still got time to find her—"

"No you don't, murderer," still another guard said, "you've only got time left to die. Now—" Abruptly, the man went silent and all of the soldiers froze.

Wendell, who'd been doing his level best not to piss himself, let out a sigh of relief. "Well, alright then. It's good to know you boys are willin' to see reason, after all, now as I was saying..." he turned as a hand grasped him on the shoulder and let out a gasp of surprise as he saw Ellemont standing there. Blood was caked to the side of the king's face from what appeared to be a powerful blow to the head, but his gaze was steady, almost amused—gods what crazy bastards these royals were—as he nodded to Wendell.

"I'll take it from here, if it pleases you, sergeant."

"Well I'll be," Wendell said, "you ain't dead, after all."

Ellemont gave a pained smile, "Not quite yet, I'm afraid. Now," he said, turning and taking in the guards with his gaze, "these men are not my assassins but my saviors. If not for them, I would have been murdered outright. I want men searching for Commander Hallifax and Queen Lilliana." A pained look came over his face, but he went on, "They are traitors."

The guards stared in shock and soon they were whispering to each other. "None of that now," Ellemont said, his voice strong and sure, and Wendell was glad to see the man finally sounded like a king. And all it took was for him to get a good whoppin' upside the head. Well, why not? Wendell thought, it was one of my ma's favorite methods of education.

"The traitors have a lead on us," Ellemont was saying, but he paused, all of them turning at the sound of moaning to see one of the captains moving weakly on the ground. "Alive then," Ellemont said, grinning. He motioned to two of the nearest guards, "Take this man to the healers and then the dungeon and make sure he doesn't die. We'll have some questions for him very soon."

"Yes, Majesty," the men said and then they were hauling the man away.

Wendell glanced at Darrell and shook his head disapprovingly, "Swordmaster indeed."

The swordmaster grinned as the prince continued speaking to the gathered guards, "As for the others, we might still catch them before they escape the city, but we must move now. All of you, go! I want men posted at every gate out of the city. The commander and my wife will be taken but not killed. I want them questioned. Now, let's move. I want this dealt with tonight, gentlemen, for tomorrow we ride to war."

There was a thunderous clanking of armor as the men saluted and an even more thunderous sound as they ran to do their king's bidding. Once they were gone, Wendell took his hands from his ears and glanced at the prince, "You don't mind me sayin' so, prince, but perhaps it ain't the wisest idea, you goin' to war with your head half caved in."

Ellemont grinned, "Oh, it's not so bad as all that, sergeant. You're correct though. It might not be the wisest idea, yet I am going anyway. The queen and the commander let slip their plan as they were taking me. They had intended to carry me into the city and stage an assassination there, some unfortunate soul no doubt playing the role of the dead assassin, slain moments after taking my life. Then the general was to take my armor and lead the men to war pretending to be me." He sighed heavily, shaking his head, "My wife, it seems, has struck some deal with Belgarin."

Wendell sighed, clapping the prince on the shoulder, "Tries to kill you then betrays you to your brother," he said, shaking his head, "that's why I never married myself."

"Oh?" Darrell said, "that's the reason?"

"Well, anyway," Wendell said, "maybe not, but it'd be a good one."

"Yes," Ellemont said, nodding, his gaze distant, "yes, sergeant, I suppose it would. Now, if you two are ready, I think a visit to the healer is in order." He glanced at the swordmaster's wounded arm, "It appears that I am not the only one who was injured in the fighting."

"Lead on, Majesty," Darrel said, bowing his head in respect.

"Yeah, sure," Wendell said, "just one thing though."

The two turned back from where they'd started walking to look at Wendell, "Sergeant?" Ellemont said.

"That fella there," Wendell said, nodding at one of the corpses before glancing down at his own bare feet. "What size boot would you say he wears?"

CHAPTER THIRTY-ONE

Aaron stood on the city walls, Adina, Leomin, and Captain Gant beside him as they watched Belgarin's army emerge from the distant woods, thousands and thousands of men, so that it seemed there was no end to them.

"Gods," Adina said beside him, "there are so many. I knew but..." She trailed off and no one said anything as they all knew how she felt, were feeling it themselves. It was one thing to hear that the enemy commanded an army of fifteen thousand men. It was quite another to see that army materializing before you, to see the fifteen thousand not as individual men but as one great heaving mass that would swallow up anything in its path.

Aaron had felt pleasantly surprised by the strength and size of Isalla's walls, when he'd first inspected them. He did not feel so now. Considering the size of the force that approached them, he would have been happier had they been twice as high and twice as thick. And while we're at it, why not wish for twenty thousand well-trained soldiers behind them?

Aaron wanted to say something to comfort Adina, but found that he had no comfort to give. He had his own worries, ones that she no doubt shared. It wasn't just the nearly fifteen thousand men marching toward them—though, admittedly that was a part of it. Equally troubling, he'd still heard nothing from May or from Wendell and Darrell. For all he knew, he'd sent the sergeant and the swordmaster to their deaths.

They will be fine, Co assured him, Wendell and Darrell are both capable men—they can take care of themselves.

That's the thing, firefly, Aaron thought, none of us can take care of ourselves. If we could, we'd be at home with our feet up, drinking some hot tea and yelling at our children to quiet down instead of preparing for a battle in which thousands will die, and more likely than not, us along with them.

Well ... the Virtue responded, you might die. I'm not sure that I can.

Not helping, firefly. He sighed, rubbing at his temples where a headache was beginning to form, then a hand was on his shoulder, and he turned to see Adina staring at him. "She'll come Aaron, you'll see. May is one of the most capable women I've ever met, and she'd do anything for you."

He nodded slowly, thinking of Hale and Grinner, men who had both tried to put him in the ground at one time or another, men who would no doubt jump at the chance even now, and he'd sent May to somehow convince them and a city council that was notorious for its inability to commit to anything not just to fight, but to fight for Aaron? It seemed that it had been his year for putting people on impossible tasks. "Might as well ask 'em to fly over Belgarin's army and drop some rocks on them," he muttered.

"Aaron?" Adina asked, clearly confused.

He sighed again, "Nothing, never mind." He turned to her, taking her hands in his, "Adina, there's still time. You could get on one of the ships in the docks—there were still a few left, last I checked—and get out of here." He leaned close so that none of the soldiers that lined the walls to either side of him would hear, "There's no point in you dying along with the rest of us."

Adina leaned in and kissed him then, and when she pulled away, she shook her head. "We've been over this, Aaron. I won't go, and you can't make me go, so that's that. Whatever happens, I will be here for it. Besides," she said, winking, "someone has to watch out for you and make sure you don't do anything stupid."

Aaron gave her a smile, but it was a poor, weak thing, so he turned back to stare over the crenellations of the wall, out at the enormous army that was still pouring out of the forest. The first of the soldiers had already begun erecting tents, and he could see men busily chopping down trees for lumber to warm their campfires. Keep me from doing anything stupid, huh? He thought as he stared out over that vast army full of men who wanted little else but to kill him and his friends as quickly as possible. Too late.

***

Captain Savrin was not happy. They had walked all morning through the woods, and it seemed to him that every thorn in the entire forest had decided to stick itself into his clothes and flesh. The skin of his hands and arms was scratched in a dozen places from where he'd been forced to push his way through the dense underbrush on too many occasions to count. Only a savage, he thought, would live in such a place as this. He was a man built for cities, for tournaments and dueling circles and the cheering of the crowds when his blade struck home. Still, he told himself he should be thankful for the excuse to leave the cave.

He'd spent the last several weeks there, leaving only long enough to bring back food for his master—an enormous amount, it had to be admitted as his master had explained that he needed sustenance to heal more quickly—and those trips were far too short. He'd grown to hate that small cave, to hate the smell of rotting flesh and blood as his master's body slowly reassembled itself, hated the way his master insisted it remain dark, so that the only company he had inside of it was his master—a man not prone to idle chatter and not one that Savrin would have engaged in conversation with even if he were—and the ever-present smell.

Still, there were worse things than darkness and blindness. He'd learned that too, during his time spent in the cave. There were some things no mortal man should ever see; things that would threaten his very sanity. He had caught a few glimpses of his master over the last weeks, and had lost his stomach, vomiting out what food he'd managed to keep for himself while assuaging his master's impossible hunger. Even now, he felt his gorge rise at the memory.

There was something to be said, he supposed, for being immortal and never being able to die, for being able to heal from any wound, but a man who'd fallen from the top of a castle was still a man who'd fallen from the top of a castle. Such things made themselves known on a person, incredible healing powers or not, and they had made themselves known on Savrin as well. At first, his master had been little more than a pile—more of a puddle really, if he was being honest, but his stomach could only take so much truth at a time—of shattered bones, torn flesh, and seeping blood. Boyce Kevlane had not died when being thrown from the castle by this man, Aaron Envelar—a name he'd heard cursed often in the last weeks—but, if Savrin had been in his place, he thought he would have wished he had.

"Ah," his master rasped beside him, and Savrin couldn't help but cringe at the inhuman sound of it mixed with the smell of rot and death that the words carried. "It seems that things proceed according to plan. Wouldn't you agree, captain?"

Savrin turned to his master. The man had healed much over the past weeks, was even able to stand after a fashion, though he was forced to lean heavily on the wooden walking stick he'd made Savrin make him. Still, magic healing or not, the cloak he wore did little to hide the freakish shape of his body as several bones still jutted out at angles that were very, very wrong. The hood that covered most of his face did not manage to hide the disfigurement of his features, features that looked as if someone with a particularly strong cruel streak had taken a mace to them until there was little left that was recognizable as human at all. There was no nose, for one, only empty holes in the man's face, and his chin sat at an impossible angle since his throat hadn't fully formed back correctly. This was also the reason for the inhuman sound of his voice. Savrin realized that he'd been staring for much too long and nodded, clearing his throat, "Yes sir," he said, "as you say. Still, those are good walls, sir. A lot of lives will be lost before the taking of them is done."

His master smiled. The movement made his whole face shift and writhe, and Savrin's stomach lurched threateningly. "We can hope," his master said, hunger in his tone. "Still, wall or no walls, Envelar and the other will die here and, when they do, I will take back what is mine. With such power, I will make this entire world fall to its knees, will watch it bleed out at my feet."

Savrin couldn't think of anything to say to that—didn't know if there was anything a man could say—so he only remained silent, reminding himself that by doing as this creature bid him, he was protecting his family, his sister and nephew. "Tell me, captain," his master was saying, "as you have some knowledge of war, when do you believe the attack will begin?"

There was a gleeful, hungry tone to his master's voice that he didn't like, but Savrin turned to study the army, happy for an excuse to look away from the twisted form beside him. He studied the army in the distance, "If it were me," he said, "I'd wait until first light. The men will be tired from the road and a good commander would know to give them time to rest and recuperate."

"Yessss," the creature beside him hissed, "we all do need time to, as you say, recuperate. Now, go and fetch us lunch, won't you? All the excitement has got me quite hungry."

"Of course," Savrin said, swallowing. He turned to walk back into the woods, drawing the bow from his back as he did. He'd only taken a few steps when he heard his master speak.

"Your death comes for you, Envelar," the creature hissed, "for you and all those you hold dear." There was a terrible sound then, one that was somehow grating and rasping and thickly wet all at the same time. It took Savrin a moment to realize that it was what passed as laughter to the shattered thing he served, and then he set off into the woods at a jog, heedless of the thorns and briars that snatched at him as he ran through the undergrowth, wishing only to get away from that sound—and the thing that made it—as quickly as he could.

CHAPTER THIRTY-TWO

Aaron ripped his sword free of the dead man and let the body fall to the stones of the battlements. Then he spun and rushed to the side of the wall in time to catch a soldier trying to climb over the top of the stone crenelations. He lashed out with his sword, and the man toppled from the battlements. His mouth was open in a scream as he fell, but Aaron couldn't hear it over the furious roar of the battle going on around him.

For the moment, his section of the wall was clear and a glance out at the fields below showed him that, for now at least, no more soldiers were coming. His chest heaving with his ragged breaths, he studied the walls around him where his soldiers were finishing off the remnants of the latest attack and rubbed an arm across his sweaty forehead. Two days. They'd been at it for two days, yet it felt as if he'd been fighting on this damn stretch of wall for his entire life.

The stones of the wall were coated in blood and worse and not all of it belonged to Belgarin's soldiers. For the last two days, he'd sent only light infantry, keeping his cavalry and heavy infantry in reserve. The men had charged forward carrying tall sieging ladders they'd cut using the wood of the forest and no matter how many men Aaron's defenders took down with their arrows before they reached the wall, it seemed that there were always a dozen more to take their place.

"Where the fuck is Ellemont?" Aaron growled.

"There's been ... no word."

Aaron turned to see Brandon standing beside him. There was a bandage wrapped around one of the captain's arms, and his face was haggard and exhausted. The man looked as if he was about to collapse but then, they all did. "No fucking word," Aaron said, shaking his head, "I don't like this, Brandon. Not at all."

The captain grinned but there was no humor in it, "What's not to like?"

Aaron grunted at that and turned back to study the battlefield. Corpses littered the field, arrows sticking out of their dead bodies, and the normally green grass was stained red with blood, yet it seemed to him as if they hadn't diminished Belgarin's forces at all. A horn blew in the distance, and he held a hand up to block the sun from his eyes as he watched a fresh wave of soldiers rushing toward the walls. "Well," he said, "looks like rest time's over."

"Just as well," Brandon said, though Aaron saw the wince as the man stretched his arm, "I was getting bored."

Thank gods Adina's not here for this, at least, Aaron thought. The princess had been trained in healing, and she and Leomin had volunteered their services at the healer tents that were already nearly filled to capacity with the wounded. Aaron knew the healers would need all the help they could get. The last time he'd checked on them during one of the all too brief reprieves, the healers had looked even more exhausted and ill than the soldiers they tended.

"Archers ready!" Aaron shouted. His voice was hoarse from many other such shouts over the last two days, but soon the call was taken up all along the wall. Slowly—much slower than Aaron would have liked—the exhausted archers stood and prepared their bows.

He looked back, gauging the approach of the enemy until they were in bow distance, "Fire!" He bellowed and arrows fell among the attackers like droplets of rain. Where they fell, men collapsed and screamed and died. There was a scream from Aaron's right, and he turned to see an archer who'd gotten greedy or careless and leaned too far over the wall for his shot stumble back with an arrow through his chest. The man closest to him grabbed him and laid him down, tearing his shirt open to look at the wound, but did not go any further as the unfortunate archer's chest rattled out one final, wheezing breath and was still.

Another loss then, and one they could ill afford. Already, there were empty spaces in the walls that had once held defenders, and the ones remaining were having to roam further and further to defend the parts of the wall that were left unoccupied as ladders were thrown up and men began to crawl over. Aaron felt more than heard motion beside him and cursed himself for being distracted as he spun, his sword coming up just in time to block a blow that had been aimed at his head. The unexpected blow knocked him off balance, and he backpedaled, nearly slipping on the blood coating the stones beneath his feet.

Seeing his advantage, the enemy soldier—a big, bearded man—grinned and rushed forward, swinging his sword again. Aaron lunged to the side, sliding more than stepping, and the soldier spun to strike him. As he did, Aaron kicked him in the leg, a glancing blow that normally wouldn't have done much, but coupled with the slick stones, it was enough to make the man stumble, and he let out a yell of surprise as he fell face first on the ground. Before he could right himself, Aaron leapt onto him and drove his steel through the man's back.

Ripping the blade free, Aaron turned to see another man hoisting himself over the wall. He rushed at him and made it to the soldier just as he landed on the stone, barging his shoulder into him and sending him tumbling back over the side. Aaron swung his sword at the next man trying to make his way up the ladder. The man jerked out of the sword's reach but as he did his hands came free of the ladder and he plummeted after his comrade onto the ground below where soldiers swarmed like ants. A quick look showed Aaron at least half a dozen more men scaling the ladder. He tried to heave it backward, but it was too much weight, and he turned to see Brandon just delivering the final blow to his own opponent.

"Help me!" He yelled, and the captain rushed forward. Together, grunting with the strain, they managed to push the ladder away from the wall and the men clinging to it crashed to the ground pinning several of their comrades beneath them.

Panting, Aaron stared down as still more men came on, "Thanks," he said, turning to Brandon.

The sergeant nodded, "Had nothing better to do," he said. He tried for a smile but his exhaustion caused him to come up short. "I reckon he's got to be running out of ... troops, any time now. Don't you think?"

Aaron stared across the fields where the bulk of Belgarin's army still waited. His cavalry—at least five hundred and possibly as many as a thousand, it was hard to tell at this range—sat on one side while his heavy infantry and still a significant number of light infantry stood waiting. "Not quite."

A horn sounded and another section of Belgarin's light infantry broke off and started toward the walls at a jog. They'd only made it a few steps, though, when a series of horn blasts rang out from the north. Attacker and defender alike paused, turning to look.

Daring not to hope, Aaron glanced toward the sound and breathed a heavy sigh of relief. An army had appeared on a large hill north of the city and even from this distance, he could make out the yellow armor of what must have been Ellemont riding at the fore with what appeared to be a few hundred horsemen of his own.

"Well, it's about damn time."

"Yellow armor," Brandon said beside him, "the prince ... knows how to make an entrance. I'll give him that much."

"He could have come buck ass naked for all I care," Aaron said, "just so long as he came." He shaded his eyes from the afternoon sun and tried to make out Darrell or Wendell among those soldiers riding with Ellemont, but the distance was too great to identify any specific figures, and if they were there, Aaron could not see them.

A different call was raised from the horn on Belgarin's side, ringing in what felt like a deafening silence filled only with the sounds of the wounded weeping and screaming as they died on the wall and in the fields below. Aaron frowned as he noted that the soldiers in the field did not move and, for a moment, nothing seemed to happen. Then, there was an answering horn from Ellemont's side, and Aaron's frown grew deeper still.

***

Belgarin watched, a satisfied smile on his face as his brother's army lined up on the northern hill at what was nearly a straight line from his traitor sister's northern gate, a smile that grew wider as the signal they'd prearranged was given and reciprocated. His brother's army, yes, but not led by his brother, not anymore. And another sibling dead, he thought. Well, it was an unfortunate occurrence, but Ellemont had been warned. The man should have listened to reason. "Still though," he said, "I must admit that they have shown up right on time."

"Majesty?"

Belgarin waved the man's question away, "How much heavy infantry do we have, general?"

"Three thousand in total, Your Majesty," Fannen answered. Belgarin smiled at that. "Very well. Send half to the area outside the northern gate and tell them to prepare. We will attack both gates at once and end this today."

"M-Majesty?" The general asked, obviously confused, "but ... forgive me, your brother's troops—"

"Never mind my brother's troops, general," Belgarin said, "only do as I say and now. Else, I will find someone who will."

"O-of course, my king," the general said, then waved a hand at one of the messengers standing nearby waiting for orders. The man came forward at a run, "Yes, general?"

"Take word to Captain Burrow. He's to send half the heavy to the northern hill in preparation for a dual assault."

"General?" The messenger asked, his face surprised, "but the northern—"

"I know what's there, boy," the general snapped, "now, do as your king has commanded."

"Of course, sir," the messenger said. He threw a hasty salute and then he was off and running.

Belgarin smiled to himself as he watched the heavy infantry start toward Ellemont's line. He glanced back at the city, wishing he could see the shock and terror on his sisters' faces when the army they thought had come to save them turned against them instead.

***

Aaron watched in confusion, a feeling of dread rising in him as what appeared to be half of Belgarin's heavy infantry marched directly toward Ellemont's lines, not seeming to be in any kind of hurry. An idea, one that he did not like at all, began to creep up into his mind.

"What is he doing?" Brandon asked from beside him, "never mind if Belgarin has the largest army or not—Ellemont has enough troops to cut those infantry down. A foolish move."

Aaron wanted to agree, but found that he could not. He had seen Belgarin's work, and he knew that the man was many things. Unfortunately, a fool didn't appear to be one of them. If he was sending half his heavy infantry to Ellemont's army, then he had a reason. He watched, the feeling of dread growing stronger and stronger as Belgarin's heavily armored soldiers drew closer to Ellemont's own army. His hands knotted into fists at his sides as he willed Ellemont to sound the attack, but no horn blew, and Ellemont's soldiers only stood still, seemingly unconcerned about the approaching troops. There was only one reason Aaron could think for them to act like that, and it wasn't a good one. "Damnit," he hissed.

"What?" Brandon asked beside him "What's the..." he trailed off as Belgarin's heavy infantry came within a few dozen yards of Ellemont's forces then closer still. Instead of attacking, Ellemont's forces only slid to the side as if to make room and soon Belgarin's forces were interspersed with Ellemont's own infantry. "Oh gods," Brandon said, "it ... it can't be."

"But it is," Aaron said, feeling the last flickering spark of hope he'd had for the city die. "It is."

***

"You see, general?" Belgarin said, turning and feeling a deep sense of satisfaction at the dumbfounded expression on the man's face, "perhaps, next time, you would do better to do as you're told than question your king."

"Of ... of course, sire," the general said, still gaping at the spectacle, "only I had not known..."

295

"No and you were not meant to." Belgarin said, "Now, prepare our own heavy infantry. We will—"

There was the sound of a horn blowing then, followed by screams that could be heard even from so far away, and Belgarin snapped his head around staring. "No," he breathed, "no, it can't be."

***

Boyce Kevlane watched, his disfigured face twisted into a mockery of a grin as Belgarin's heavy infantry merged with Ellemont's forces. "Ah, you have done well, Caldwell. I had almost doubted. You will have to be rewarded for this." Kevlane looked back at the city of Perennia and its walls. Somewhere, within that city, Aaron Envelar was only now coming to realize the full depth of his doom. "I told you that you would suffer," he hissed, "now you will se—" he cut off, frowning as a horn sounded from Prince Ellemont's ranks. He turned in the direction of the sound in time to see Ellemont's ranks explode into motion as it seemed as if each man turned against the other. Steel flashed in the sunlight and even from this distance he could just make out the sounds of surprised screams as the soldiers killed each other.

Frowning, he concentrated on his bond, drawing the power from it as he had so many times before. It was slow in coming, the wounds he'd suffered turning what had once been an ocean of power into a dribble but, slow or not, it did come. He cursed each wasted second but in less than a minute, his eyes had changed to something not human at all but to something similar to the eyes of a bird of prey, creatures known for their long distance vision. He concentrated, narrowing his gaze, and rage flooded through him at what he saw. Ellemont's soldiers were not killing each other at all. Instead, they were cutting down each and every one of the heavy infantry that Belgarin had sent to them. The men fought for their lives, but they were surrounded by more than twice their number, taken unawares and unprepared and the thing was over nearly before it was begun.

Fury more intense than Kevlane could remember feeling in a thousand years roared through him, and he screamed, a great, terrible scream of inhuman rage. "Noooo!" It was not supposed to be like this. The man, Envelar, was supposed to die, was supposed to have been betrayed by a man he thought was an ally. Caldwell had told him as much. The advisor, though, was another matter — he would be punished in time.

"Master, is everything okay?"

Kevlane snapped around to see the captain, Savrin, staring at him, a question in his eyes and two rabbits held in one hand. Kevlane nearly killed the man right then, was moments away from doing it when he got some control over his anger. "Give them to me now," Kevlane said.

"O-of course." The captain tossed the dead rabbits in Kevlane's direction, and he snatched them out of the air, tearing into their still warm flesh with what few teeth had grown back, savoring the hot blood as it gushed into his mouth for with it came strength and with strength, power.

In moments, both rabbits were little more than bones, and he tossed their carcasses aside, staring back at Ellemont's troops. "No," Kevlane said, "you will not survive this day, Envelar. This I promise you." He turned his twisted body back to stare at the captain, "Stay here. I will return."

The captain said something, but Kevlane was not listening as he was already sprinting down the hill he'd been using as an observation point, calling on the last bits of his strength and the bond to work the changes that he would need.

***

Aaron stared at the spectacle, speechless, as the last of Belgarin's heavy infantry were cut down by Ellemont's men. Whatever the prince who would be king had expected, this certainly had not been it. Slowly, he found himself grinning, "Darrell and Wendell, you sons of bitches."

"I told you Ellemont would not betray us."

Aaron turned to see Adina walking up beside him. There were dark circles under her eyes, and he could tell by the way she moved that she was exhausted, swaying on her feet as if half asleep already. The simple tunic and trousers she wore were both stained with blood from her work in the healing tents, but exhausted or not, bloody or not, Aaron was still struck by how beautiful she was. "Yes," he said, smiling, "you did."

"So," she said, "what now?"

Aaron turned and gazed back out over the fields at the army that still outnumbered them two to one. "Now," he said, "we stand a chance. Not a good one but a chance all the same." He found himself thinking of May again, hoping that she and the others were alright.

"She'll be okay, Aaron," Adina said, "she'll be here."

Aaron nodded, gazing around at the defenders on the wall on either side of him, men whose exhausted faces were showing something they hadn't shown in days—hope. They were still outnumbered, terribly so, and the situation was still grim, but they had allies now, friends, and Aaron knew from personal experience that such things mattered a great deal. They were not alone. All along the wall, soldiers stared at Ellemont's forces as if an army of the gods had come down and landed on the battlefield to aid them, cheering and giving shouts of appreciation. We may still die, he thought, but at least we'll have company.

CHAPTER THIRTY-THREE

Belgarin stood and watched his fifteen hundred heavy infantry—fully half of the heavy infantry in his army—massacred, a white rage building inside of him. His hands were clenched at his sides and as they began to ache he glanced down to see that blood was running from them where he'd squeezed his nails into the meat of his palms in his anger.

Once the thing was done, the knight in the yellow armor raised his visor and even from this distance, Belgarin thought he could make out his brother's face, imagined him staring at him, a smile of satisfaction on his lips. "You'll die for this," he said, his words coming out in an angry hiss.

"Majesty," the general said, his own voice weak and confused, "I don't understand—"

"Not another word, general," Belgarin said, "unless you want to join those men in death."

A soldier approached at a run, "My king, forgive me but I have a message."

Belgarin turned, and his rage must have been plain on his face, for the messenger cringed back, clearly frightened. "What?"

"There's a woman here, Majesty," the messenger said, his face pale with fear, "she ... she says she wishes to speak with you."

"A woman?" Belgarin asked, his eyes narrowing, his body trembling with barely contained rage.

"Yes, my king. She says her name is Lyla."

"Bring her to my tent. Now."

***

Belgarin was pacing his tent, his anger and agitation far too great to even consider sitting, when two guards escorted Lyla inside. They turned to go, and Belgarin held up a hand, "Stay," he said, and the two men took up position on either side of the tent flap.

Frowning, Belgarin studied the woman before him. She looked exhausted. Her clothes were ripped and torn, covered in dust, and it seemed as if she was barely able to stand up straight. "My love," Lyla exclaimed when she saw him, and then she was running toward him, folding him in an embrace.

Belgarin only stood there, not hugging her back and after a moment, she released him, staring up at his face. "My love, is something the matter?"

"Fifteen hundred of my best men are now dead, Lyla." He said, "All of them dead because I trusted you. Tell me, did you go and warn my brother, your husband of what we planned? Is that it? What reason did you have to betray me?"

"What?" She said, recoiling as if he'd struck her, "My King, I would never betray you. You must believe me!"

He felt something twisting in him, the love he'd felt for this woman in front of him turning sour and bitter. He took in her filthy, cringing form and the rage was there again. "If you did not betray me," he said, "then why are my men dead, Lilliana?"

The queen's face grew pale, and she began to tremble. "My love, I tried my best, I swear it. I spoke with Ellemont about ending the alliance, but he would not hear of it, no matter how strong my pleas. And then ... I did as you asked. I lured Ellemont to a secluded place in the castle, and Commander Hallifax and I knocked him out. We were going to stage the assassination in the city, as you commanded, but two men serving Aaron Envelar came, and we were forced to flee."

Belgarin studied her then, saw the adoration and desperation mixing in her eyes and some part of him hated her, hated the need he saw when she gazed at him. And was all that a lie, then? Was she only manipulating him to serve her husband? Fury beyond anything he'd ever known bloomed inside of him and before he knew what he was doing, his hand lashed out, striking her in the face. She gave a cry of surprised pain, stumbling and falling to the ground. Belgarin stared down at her, his body shaking with rage. "Fifteen hundred men," he growled. "Because of you. Because of your betrayal."

She held up her hands as if to ward him off, "Belgarin, my king, please," she said, her voice shaking with her tears, "I would never betray you. I only tried to do what you asked. Please, you must believe me."

"Must I?" Belgarin hissed, jerking her to her feet so that her face was only inches from his own, "must I?"

"W-wait," she said, "p-please. You can ask Commander Hallifax. He'll tell you, my love, he'll tell you the truth of it, I swear."

Belgarin released her in disgust, shoving her away from him. "And where, pray tell, is this Commander Hallifax?"

Lyla's face grew paler still, "I ... I don't know, my lord." Belgarin started forward again, and she raised her hands as if to ward off a blow, "He was with me when we reached your camp," she blurted, "but I was taken here and he ... I don't know where he is."

Belgarin looked to the two guards, "Well?"

"Majesty," one said, bowing, "The man who accompanied the lady was taken to a private tent by order of Advisor Caldwell to be debriefed."

"Very well," Belgarin said nodding, "bring the commander to me."

The guard nodded and started toward the tent flap. He'd only taken two steps when it was thrown open from the outside and Caldwell walked in followed by a thickly muscled, gray-haired man. One of the man's arms was in a sling, and if anything his appearance was even rougher than that of Lyla. His clothes were torn and bloody, his complexion as white as milk, and he wavered on his feet as if at any moment he might fall. "My king," Caldwell said, "forgive me for the intrusion, but I have only just finished speaking with Commander Hallifax here, general of Prince

Ellemont's armies. He has quite an interesting story to tell, and I thought it best to let you hear it from his own mouth."

"Go on," Lyla said, her voice breaking with tears, "Tell them, Hallifax. Tell them the truth." She turned to Belgarin, "You'll see, my love. I would never do anything do displease you. Please, Hallifax, only tell him," she said to the commander once more, "tell him that I did all I could to sway Ellemont and when he would not be swayed, you helped me try to stage his assassination."

"Well, commander?" Belgarin said, "is what she says true? Were you involved in trying to assist her in persuading Ellemont to break the alliance or, failing that, to do what needed to be done?"

The commander blinked, his gaze unsteady as if he didn't realize he'd been addressed at all.

"Well?" Caldwell said, "tell the king what you told me." The man glanced at Lyla for a moment before turning to Caldwell. "Go on then," the advisor said, holding the man's gaze.

Finally, the commander breathed in a heavy breath and turned back to the king, "Majesty, forgive me, but I know nothing of any plot against Prince Ellemont. As for the alliance, the prince was ..." he paused, glancing at Caldwell who only stared back at him, his face an expressionless mask, "the prince was reluctant," the commander finally said, each word seeming as if it pained him, "to enter into an alliance with Queen Isabelle and Princess Adina. In the end, it was Queen Lyla who convinced him that allying with Isalla was the only hope for his kingdom, who then came to him with a plan to betray you."

"Liar!" Lyla screamed and before anyone could react she lunged at the commander, her fingernails raking bloody furrows down his face. Hallifax cried out in surprise and pain, stumbling backwards under the vicious assault until one of the guards stepped forward and jerked Lyla off of him. Moaning with pain, the commander brought his hands to his face, and when he took them away, Belgarin saw that they—and his face—were coated in blood.

"Quickly," Caldwell snapped at one of the guards, "take him to my tent and summon a healer." The guard glanced at Belgarin who nodded dazedly, stunned by the savagery the woman had shown and soon the guard was escorting the groaning, stumbling commander out of the tent.

"My love," Lyla said, turning to Belgarin, her voice desperate and hoarse from screaming, "you must see that this … this snake lied, that he forced the commander to say whatever story he wished of him. Please," she said, holding her bloody hands up to Belgarin as if in supplication, "he is trying to poison you against me, surely you can see that. I would never do anything to bring harm to you, my king, never. I gave up everything for you."

Belgarin stared at her, standing there in her torn and dirty clothes, her hands covered in blood, weak and frail and ugly in her fear. Then he frowned, turning to his advisor, "Why did you not bring the commander to me immediately, Caldwell? Why did you, instead, choose to meet with him yourself?"

Lyla turned to look at the advisor, and Belgarin did not miss the look of satisfaction on her face as the advisor suddenly looked uncomfortable. "Majesty," Caldwell said, "I only thought it prudent to interrogate the commander as quickly as possible, to discover whatever I could that might aid you. And it is a good thing that I did, for it was the commander who told me of what I might find in the queen's saddlebags under a hidden flap." He reached into his tunic and withdrew a folded piece of parchment, stepping forward and offering it to his king.

Belgarin frowned at Lyla who stared at the parchment in bewilderment as if she'd never seen it before, then he took the paper and unfolded reading through the first note.

Good luck, my love

Please be careful. Belgarin is not a man known for his mercy.

I know you have sacrificed much for Cardayum and its people, for me, but after this it will be finished.

Remember, when it is done, work your way to the edge of the encampment and give the signal—I will send men to get you.

Yours in love,

Ellemont

Belgarin felt his face heat with anger and shame both, and he turned to Lyla, holding the piece of parchment up in a clenched fist, "Is this true?"

"My king?" She said, a confused expression on her face as if she'd fallen asleep only to find herself in some place she did not know surrounded by people she did not understand.

She said something else, but Belgarin wasn't listening, his attention focused on the second note.

My love,

My sacrifices have been small enough for the love I bear you. I would do much more than this, would sacrifice my life for you, if it required. I will see that the ambitious fool breathes his last then give the signal as you ask.

Until I am in your arms once more,

~L~

Belgarin stared at that signature, his body trembling with rage. It was the same signature that she used when writing him the letters for their secret rendezvous, the same stylized 'L' that had once sent excitement running through him. "Forgive me, my king," Caldwell said, "but it seems that she was unable to send this second note for whatever reason. I suspect she was in a hurry to complete her mission which, to me at least, seems clear was to get close to you and then assassinate you when your guard was down."

Belgarin stared at Lyla as if seeing her for the first time, full of rage and embarrassment and pain. "Ambitious fool," he said, his voice hoarse with emotion, "I loved you more than anything else. How could you do this to me?"

"My king," she said, "I don't know what you're talking about, I'd never—"

He threw the notes at her then, and shaking, she picked them up from where they'd fallen on the ground reading through them, her eyes going wide with terror as she did. "I had meant to make you my queen," Belgarin said, an inexplicable pain in his chest, "had meant to rule over all of Telrear with you at my side."

"My love," she said, staring up at him, tears leaking from her eyes, "you have to believe me. These ... these are not my letters."

He moved forward then, snatching the letters from her and holding them inches from her face, his hand shaking with his rage. "It is the same 'L', Lyla," he hissed, "Gods, I can even smell your perfume on them." He turned to the remaining guard, feeling numb and empty, "Take her and throw her in a cage. She will be executed for crimes against the crown upon our return to Baresh."

***

"No!" Lyla screamed as the guard started toward her once more. She ran to her love, throwing her arms around him, "I would never hurt you, Belgarin," she sobbed into his shoulder, "please, you have to believe me. It's your advisor. He caught me the last time in one of the tents, tried to turn me against you, but I refused. Please, I would not harm you! You're the fa—" her words turned into a gasp as the blade bit deep into her heart, Belgarin screaming in a sob of pain and anger. She stumbled back, staring at him in shock and disbelief as a spreading stain of crimson blossomed on her shirt.

"I trusted you," he said, his voice cracking with emotion, "I loved you, and you would try to kill me?"

She stumbled back another step, bringing her hands to her chest and in moments they were covered in blood. She felt the strength drain out of her legs and she collapsed to her knees, her blurry eyes locked on her king's. "My ... love," she said, her voice little more than a faint whisper as she forced the words out. "Your ... son..." What little strength she had left her then, and she fell to the ground.

The advisor, Caldwell, knelt in front of her, his back to Belgarin, and he grinned a cruel, vulpine grin as his hand reached out and cupped her neck. "Did you really think you could hide your secrets from me?" He whispered, his eyes dancing with dark amusement, "you really should have done what was asked of you."

Lyla struggled to speak, to warn her love of the man's treachery one more time, her mouth working as she summoned whatever strength her failing body might have left.

***

Belgarin stared in shock at the woman who'd been his lover as she bled out on the ground of the tent. Caldwell crouched beside her, reaching out to feel her pulse. Her mouth worked desperately, as if there was something she wished to say, but no sound came

305

out, and Belgarin could only watch her helplessly. Then she wheezed one final breath, falling backward and onto the ground and spoke no more, her dead eyes staring blankly at the roof of the tent.

Belgarin looked down at her, shaking with rage and terror at what he'd done. "What?" He rasped, "what did she say, Caldwell? Did she say ... a son?"

"No, Majesty," the advisor said, "only the incoherent ramblings of the dying, nothing more."

The knife dropped from Belgarin's numb hands, and he stared at the woman whom he'd loved lying dead at his feet. "Leave me," he said, his voice a grating whisper, raw with more pain and heartache than he'd thought possible.

"As you wish, my king," Caldwell said, bowing his head. He motioned to the remaining guard, "Grab her feet—I'll get her hands."

"Do not touch her," Belgarin growled, and the two men hesitated.

"My king," Caldwell said, "it will do you no good to be left here with ... this. You did what you had to do, of course. Please," he said, "let us take her away. I will see to the burial." He started forward again, and Belgarin let out a vicious growl more akin to an animal than any sound a man might make.

"You will die, if you touch her, Caldwell. You have my word on this. Now leave me." Still the two men hesitated, "Leave us!" Belgarin screamed in a shrill, not quite sane voice, and finally, they did, disappearing outside of the tent flap.

Once they were gone, Belgarin fell to his knees in the dirt beside her, grasping her hands in his own. "My love," he moaned. "Oh gods what have I done?"

Why? Why must I leave a trail of broken things to mark my path?

He wept then, great heaving sobs of pain and despair. Your son, she had said, he was sure of it. The words thundered in his mind, and he felt a great, terrible weight of grief and regret settle on him, so that he thought he would be crushed beneath it. Hoped he would be.

Only the incoherent ramblings of the dead, Caldwell had said. "Was that true, my love?" He sobbed, "Was it no more than that?" She did not answer, would never answer again, and he felt his mind slipping as some madness threatened to overtake it. He knelt there for a long time, his grief wrapped around him like a cloak, until her fingers grew cold in his, until there were no tears left in him, only the grief and the fear that as bad as his crime had been, it was more terrible by far. Son, she had said. He needed to know for sure. Had to know. He rose, lifting her up with him, heedless of the blood that stained his tunic as he cradled her against his chest. There was one way, he thought, to be sure. One way to know.

CHAPTER THIRTY-FOUR

Aaron grunted as he slammed against the gap in the crenellations of the city wall, hissing and spitting as his attacker's hands pushed and tore at his face, trying to force him over the side. "No ... you don't. Fucker," Aaron gasped, feeling around his waist with one hand while the other fought to knock away the soldier's grip. The soldier was a big man, and his mouth was twisted in a strained grin as he forced Aaron closer to the edge inch by inch.

Finally, Aaron's fingers found the handle of the blade at his side, and he slid it from its small sheath, driving it into his attacker's stomach with all the strength he could muster. He was off balance and had no leverage, but the man was light infantry and so wearing no armor to protect him. The blade went in smooth, and Aaron grunted with the strain as he jerked it up, tearing through the man's internal organs.

The man's body went rigid, and he stumbled backward collapsing onto the walkway. "Damn," Aaron croaked, shuffling away from the wall, kneeling and jerking his blade free of the dead man, cleaning the blade as best he could on the corpse's filthy tunic before sliding it back into his sheath.

Gasping for breath, he rose and peered over the wall at Ellemont's forces. They had not yet moved to aid Aaron and the others, and the reason was clear enough when Aaron turned to look at Belgarin's army. Belgarin's cavalry—five hundred horses, at least—had maneuvered to the side nearest Ellemont. If the prince sent his troops to aid Aaron and the others in the castle's defense, they would be caught between the attackers at the wall and the cavalry behind, would be cut down before they could be of any help. The only good thing to be said for it was that Belgarin could not engage his own cavalry for the fear of leaving himself open to Ellemont's counter attack. A standoff then with Aaron and all of Perennia caught in the middle.

"Ships approaching!" Someone yelled, and Aaron and Adina spun to see vague forms in the distant ocean, dozens of them. Hundreds.

"Allies!" Another voice shouted, "Allies from Avarest!"

All along the wall, soldiers that had been nearly too tired to breathe let alone speak took up the call, shouting in excitement. Aaron stared, not quite believing his eyes as the lead ship came into view enough for him to make out the flag of Avarest flying from its mast. "She's here," he said. "I can't believe it." He turned to see Adina smiling widely at him, laughing with the joy of it, and soon he was laughing too. They were still outnumbered, still with their backs against the wall, but if those ships were even half full of fighting men, then their chances of surviving the week had just increased dramatically.

Cheers erupted from along the wall as the ragged, exhausted defenders rejoiced, and Aaron could hear many men whispering of 'miracles' as he wrapped Adina in his arms, lifting her off her feet. She laughed again at that, hugging him back, and he spun her in a circle, finally feeling like they might have a chance after all. A small one, true, but a chance nonetheless. He sat her down then, still hugging her tight against him and took in the cheering, laughing soldiers, their faces alight with new hope. All, that was, except for one.

He stood on the wall near the Eastern Gate. He was too far away for Aaron to see clearly, but he could make out enough of the man's face and his form beneath the hooded cloak he wore to see that there was something wrong with him. His features seemed deformed somehow, and his body looked strange even hidden as it was by the cloak, as if whatever god had made him had created him out of left-over pieces that didn't exactly match. While the other soldiers were staring at the ships and at what very well might be their deliverance, this soldier was staring directly at Aaron, his eyes intent.

Even as Aaron watched, the soldier smiled, a smile that Aaron recognized, and a shiver of fear went through him. "No," he breathed, "it can't be."

Aaron, it's him, Co said, her voice frantic and scared, it's Kevlane.

"Aaron, what's wrong?" Adina asked from beside him.

Aaron watched as the grinning soldier turned and started down the steps on the inside of the wall toward the eastern gatehouse. "Shit," he growled. Then he was running.

"Aaron, what is it?" Adina called after him.

He spun, raising a hand to her, "Stay there!" And then he was off and running, no longer thinking of the blood slicked stones beneath his feet or how easy it would be for a man to slip and fall over the edge, thinking only of that smile the soldier had given him, of the cruelty he'd seen in the man's eyes.

"Stop that man!" He shouted. Soldiers on the wall turned and looked, trying to figure out who Aaron meant but already the grinning soldier was out of sight down the steps.

Aaron ran on, finding a new surge of energy in his fear despite the days spent fighting on the wall. He was halfway to the steps the soldier had gone down when he risked a glance over the edge of the stone walkway and saw the man making his way toward the gatehouse, apparently in no hurry. Aaron forced himself to run faster, knowing he wouldn't get there in time even as he did it but having no other options. "Stop that man!" He yelled again, and although the soldiers around him heard, they couldn't seem to figure out who he was talking about.

The man paused at the gatehouse door long enough to turn and look back. A shiver went up Aaron's spine as he saw his own face staring back at him, a too-wide grin creasing features that were twisted and deformed but most definitely his. He watched, helpless to do anything as the soldier—not soldier, Kevlane, and you know it—knocked on the gatehouse door. Fearing treachery after the many betrayals within the city, Aaron had left orders at the gatehouse for the men not to open the door for anybody, citizen or soldier. Anybody, that was, except for him.

Cursing himself for his own foolishness in not seeing such a thing coming, Aaron was still running, watching in horror as the door to the gatehouse opened, and the twisted version of him disappeared inside, closing it behind him. Even over the raucous cheers and celebration of those men along the wall, most of which remained oblivious to what was happening, Aaron could hear the screams. Sharp, splitting screams of pain and fear that seemed to reverberate within his chest.

He dodged around the men on the wall when he could and knocked them aside when he couldn't until finally he made it to the steps. He leapt down them three, four steps at a time and soon he was at the gatehouse. He rammed into the door with his shoulder, the screams still sounding from inside, but the wood was strong and thick, chosen specifically for the purpose, and it did not budge. "Open the fucking door!" He yelled.

The only reply was the screams as those inside suffered and died at the hands of a man who should be dead. Aaron struck the door again, but the wood didn't show the slightest signs of giving. He spun to see a dozen soldiers who'd apparently followed after him staring in confusion. Bastion was among them, the youth looking at him in bewilderment. "Break it down!" Aaron yelled.

A soldier stepped forward with an axe, and Bastion took it from him, hurrying to the door. Aaron moved out of the way and the giant youth raised the axe above his head and brought it crashing down against the door. The steel bit through the wood, but the door held firmly, and Bastion grunted as he pulled the axe head free and swung again. Suddenly, the air was full of the metallic, clanking sound that he'd feared, and he spun to see the eastern gate rising until, beneath its frame, he could make out Belgarin's forces on the other side. A horn sounded in the distance, and the entire army save the cavalry started toward the gate at a jog.

Aaron turned to take in the faces of those soldiers around him, their expressions full of fear now, the hope that they'd held only moments before nowhere in evidence. They all knew what it would mean, if they could not get that gate down. The ships carrying the might of Avarest were still miles off shore, and it

311

would take them time to dock and for the troops to disembark. Time that, should the gate stay open, the city of Perennia did not have.

He spun back to look at Bastion, the youth grunting and sweating with the effort as he brought the axe down again and again. Faster. Faster damnit. The youth swung the axe with the strength of three men, but the wood of the gatehouse door was firm and solid and it took him at least a dozen swings before the wood cracked enough that he was able to push it open.

As soon as he did, Aaron shouldered the weary Bastion aside and charged through the doorway, his blade held at the ready. Four bodies lay scattered on the floor of the small gatehouse, the table that had sat in the center of it lying shattered in two pieces on the floor. Aaron took in the scene in a moment, noted that none of the soldiers had even so much as been able to draw his blade before his death was on him and there, standing on the opposite side of the guardhouse, grinning at him, was Boyce Kevlane. He did not wear Aaron's face any longer, but his own. The face had a twisted, melted look to it that didn't belong on anything living, but Aaron knew it just the same.

"Ah, General Envelar," the thing that was Boyce Kevlane said, its voice coming out dry and cracked, "I told you that you would pay for what you did. Surely, you did not think you would be able to defy me and live." The wretched face twisted into that strange, alien grin. "I told you that you and those you cared about would suffer for what you did, for the choice you made. Just as your father suffered for his choice. And your mother."

Aaron glanced at the spoked wheel that was used to raise and lower the gate and saw that it had been turned all of the way. Normally, the mechanism took at least two strong men to turn, but this creature had done it himself. He noted too that a sword had been jammed into the catch, the metal twisted around it. Even as he watched, two soldiers tried to push against the spokes, straining and cursing with the effort, but the wheel would not turn. He stared back at Kevlane, fury rising in him. "Why won't you just die, you son of a bitch?" He said.

Kevlane cocked his head, the smile still well in place, "Gods cannot die, Mr. Envelar. Now, I think I'll be going—don't worry.

I'll come back to collect what's mine once the prince's army has destroyed everything you care about. As you watch those you love die, Aaron Envelar, know that it was I who brought their doom upon them, upon you." Something shifted beneath the creature's cloak then, and it turned and charged through the thick wall of the gatehouse as if it was made of paper. The wood cracked and splintered, and the creature screamed as long thin shards tore into it, but it did not slow.

"No!" Aaron yelled, running after it and through the opening. Someone jerked at his arm trying to stop him, but he shoved them away and ran through the hole to see the creature sprinting for the wall, its legs changing even as it did, growing thicker, more muscled, its arms shifting, melding into the hooked appendages that Aaron had seen before when it had tried to assassinate the queen. Aaron charged after it, knowing what was going to happen before it did and knowing too that he would not catch the intruder in time. So, at the last moment before the creature's feet left the ground, Aaron drew one of the blades from his waist and threw it with all his strength. It caught the creature in the back as it was leaping. Boyce Kevlane screamed in agony even as his jump carried him halfway to the wall where the hooked appendages lashed out and found purchase between the stones.

"Archers!" Aaron shouted, and several arrows flew from the bows of the terrified bowmen along the walls. Most, shot in haste and fear as those who fired them stared at something out of nightmare slithering up the wall, rebounded from the stone around the creature, but some few found homes in the thing's flesh. It screamed in pain and rage as each arrow went in, but it did not slow and soon it had gained the top of the wall. It spared a moment to turn and stare at Aaron, its wasted face twisted with unspeakable rage, its eyes dancing with insane fury, then it leapt over the wall and was gone.

His own rage rising in him, Aaron stared after the creature, his chest heaving with a wrath that demanded to be spent.

"General!"

Aaron turned to see Bastion and several other members of the Ghosts, standing watching him. "General," Bastion said again, his own chest rising and falling in great gulps of air, his skin coated in sweat, "Belgarin's army. It's coming."

Aaron bit back a curse, "Which? Cavalry, light infantry?" he asked, afraid he already knew.

The youth swallowed, "All of it, sir."

"And the gate?"

"Captain Gant has an engineer looking at it, sir, but the man said something about counterweights and mechanisms," he shrugged helplessly, "I'm not sure what all, but he said it would take some time to fix."

More time than we've got, Aaron thought, glancing at the faces around him and the faces on the wall staring down at him, the realization of what they faced reflected in each of their expressions.

"That's it then," one of the soldiers said, "those ships won't be here in time. By the time they unload, they'll arrive just in time to stare at our corpses. It's over."

Aaron considered that for a moment, the rage still bubbling close to the surface, not willing to be put down easily now that it had been awakened. "No," he said, "it's not over. Not yet." He turned to Bastion, "Gather all the Ghosts and tell them to meet me at the eastern gate. You have five minutes."

"Sir," the youth said, "many of the ghosts are resting, some recovering from their wounds, they—"

"They can rest when they're dead," Aaron said. "They're the best we have. Get them, now."

"Yes sir," Bastion said, then he and the others were off and running.

Aaron started back to the gate, and Brandon stepped out from where he'd been haranguing the man working on the mechanism. "It's not good, Aaron," he said, even as he followed Aaron to stand in front of the open gate.

Aaron nodded, staring out at the fields as, some distance away, men flooded the plain, heading straight for the city, straight for the open gate in which he currently stood. They were too far away to see specific features right now, but the ground shook with their coming, and he knew that he would see more than he wanted to soon enough. "You take the walls, captain, and see that the engineer hurries—give him whatever help he needs. We'll buy you what time we can."

He turned and met the captain's eyes and an understanding passed between them. "Very well," Brandon said after a moment. He opened his mouth as if he would say something more, but cleared his throat instead. "Good luck, Aaron."

Aaron nodded, "You too, Brandon."

The roar of the approaching army was growing louder now, not the voices of thousands of men raised for battle but one voice, the thundering call of some mad god of blood and death that drew closer to them with each passing moment. Brandon hesitated, but Aaron only nodded again, "It's alright, Brandon. We all do what we must."

"Aye," the captain said, his voice full of emotion, "so we do."

Then he was gone, barking orders to the men along the walls, and Aaron was left at the gate, staring at the army drawing closer, bringing with it their deaths. "Aaron!"

He turned to see Adina running to him, a bow in her hand and a quiver of arrows slung over one shoulder. "I'm here to help."

Aaron was shaking his head even before she was finished, "No, Adina. Your place is at the castle now. Belgarin might be kind and spare you and Isabelle, should the worst happen, but these men who come won't know you for who you are. They'll cut you down like they would any other."

"No," she said, "I'm staying with you."

"Damnit, woman," he growled, "Go! Don't you understand that I can't do what I need to do, I can't be what I need to be, if I'm worried about you? Now go, please," he said, meeting her eyes, "please."

She studied him for several seconds then stepped forward and ran a hand along his face, "I love you, Aaron."

He started to run a hand through her hair—so beautiful and long—but he stopped himself. Now was not a time for soft things and soft words. Now was a time for steel and blood. "Then do what I ask," he said.

She stood studying him with tears in her eyes, her face twisted with grief as if he was already dead, but finally she turned and left.

By the time she did, the Ghosts were gathered, a hundred men who had already done much, but he would ask more of them. They stood in a semi-circle at the gate, staring at Aaron. He tried to think of what he could say to these men, what words he could use

315

to lift their spirits, to convince them that the suicide mission he asked of them would be worth it.

Then he felt within him a burgeoning power as the magic of the bond responded to his need. Co? He thought, feeling strange at the unexpected power rising in him.

It's alright, Aaron, the Virtue responded, let them know how you feel. Make them feel the same way as you.

Without knowing how, Aaron reached out and grasped the power that was rising, formed and shaped it by instinct more than anything else, then he turned to meet the eyes of those soldiers gathered before him. "The gate will not be fixed in time," he said. "That army will be here soon, and it's going to be our job to buy the engineer the time he needs."

The men frowned, glancing at each other uncertainly. "I won't lie to you," he went on, "there's little chance that we'll survive this, but I intend to keep the promise that I made." He called on the power of the bond then, investing it with all of his rage and anger, his desperation to protect those he loved, and each word he spoke landed with the power of a thunderclap, "Belgarin will pay in blood for each step he takes on your lands. He will know our anger, our wrath, for we will show it to him." The soldiers rocked as if struck by a physical blow and their expressions of fear and uncertainty slowly changed to ones of rage and fury. Suddenly, they raised their weapons in the air as one, their voices rising in an unintelligible roar of emotion and deadly promise, and Aaron felt his own fury rise to meet that call. When he turned back to look at the approaching army, the anger, the wrath, looked with him, and he watched them come with a smile of anticipation on his lips.

CHAPTER THIRTY-FIVE

"Oh gods be good," May breathed as she watched the whole of Belgarin's army moving toward the castle. She said a quick prayer for Silent, Adina, Leomin and all the rest. She normally wasn't the praying type, but she thought that maybe, just this once, it couldn't hurt. Thom put a hand on hers where they were clasping to the side of the ship so tightly that her knuckles ached.

"Nothing to worry about yet, love." He said. "I only met your friend Aaron the one time, but it was enough for me to know that the man's good at killin' and killin's what's needed just now."

"He's the best I've ever seen at it," May admitted, "still, Thom," she said, lying her head against the first mate's shoulder, "there's so many of them. Silent might be good but nobody's that good."

"Maybe not," the first mate admitted, "but he's not alone either. Best not to yell sharks 'till you see their fins. All the worryin' and panic in the world won't stop 'em from coming, it'll only steal your breath with all the shoutin'."

She nodded distractedly, knowing he was right but not feeling that he was. They were only a few hours away from docking, but they might as well have been days. She wanted to shout for the second time—well, if she was being honest with herself, probably the tenth, tenth at least—that Prince Ellemont should send his forces forward. On the last time, however, Thom had explained it to her, had told her that so long as Belgarin's cavalry sat on their flank, Ellemont was forced to wait and watch or risk being caught between two enemy forces.

She glanced around at the ships surrounding her own, dozens of them, hundreds. Grinner and Hale and all their men, even the city council had been convinced to send troops—no easy thing that. And now it looked as if it would all have been for nothing. No, she thought, I won't let it. "I think I'll go speak to the captain again."

Thom sighed, "As you will, love."

Captain Festa was standing near the ship's wheel, frowning through a looking glass at the distant city as May approached.

"Captain?"

Festa replaced the looking glass into a sling on his belt that was made for the purpose and turned. When he saw that it was her, he sighed, "Yes, May, what can I do for ya, eh? Don't 'spose you've come bringin' ale or whiskey with ya, have ya?"

"No, captain," May said, "I've come to ask if there isn't any way to go faster."

"Well," the captain said, "considerin' as this is what, the fifth time you've asked me now, I 'spose I'll give it due consideration." He furrowed his brow in mock concentration, "Well, let's see. I suppose we could always lighten some weight."

"Perfect," May said, "that'll be gr—"

"Thing is," Festa went on, "anythin' that ain't nailed down or breathin' was thrown out days ago—the third time you asked, as I recollect. Course, I suppose we could start throwin' some of these soldiers—and I use the word loosely mind, as I wouldn't let a one of these thugs close to my daughter, if'n I had one—overboard. There's some of 'em that weigh considerable. I'll tell you this much, club owner, a life of crime must pay pretty damn good for some of these bastards to be able to eat like they obviously do. Makes a man reconsider his job, I can tell ya that much. Either way, I hesitate to do that on account of I suspect that once we got to the city, you might like to have some troops to do the fightin', seein's as its why we come."

"But surely," May said, staring back at the city and the army that swarmed to it like ants from the world's largest anthill, "there must be somethin' we can do."

"Aye," Festa said, and he must have heard the worry in her voice or seen it in her face, for his tone softened, "there is, lass. We can go as fast as we can—which we are, mind—and we can wait."

"That's it?" May said, "You're telling me that all we can do is wait?"

Festa shrugged, "If you got prayers to say, I reckon I'd be sayin' em about now."

I already have, May thought, but as she turned back to gaze on the city, she said another. After all, it couldn't hurt.

CHAPTER THIRTY-SIX

Aaron and his Ghosts were lined up and waiting when the first soldiers came charging to the gate, the relatively small opening it provided making it impossible for the enemy army to bring the full strength and weight of its numbers to bear. Archers rained arrows on them from the walls above killing dozens, hundreds, but their numbers were so great that it made no noticeable difference, barely even slowing the army. When one man fell, his comrades trampled him underfoot, eager to get into the city and put an end to the war as quickly as possible.

Aaron looked at the faces of the men as they charged, his own anger building and building in him until he felt that his skin would catch fire. These men had come and attacked innocent people, people who only wanted to go on about their lives in peace. They had come and brought steel and death with them. If they broke through, they would destroy everything that Aaron had grown to care about in a lifetime spent caring about nothing. Leomin, Brandon, Isabelle. Adina. His muscles tensed at the last, and the bond's power flared even brighter, the familiar rage sweeping through him like wildfire. The feel of it, normally terrifying, was welcome just now, and he fed the fires as much as he could, stoked them and tended them until they grew into a towering inferno. Then he screamed in a wordless, inarticulate cry of rage and fury, and power floated along that cry, carried itself to each of the men standing with him until they lifted up a roar that seemed to shake the very walls of the city. In another moment, the soldiers were on them.

The first man to come within Aaron's reach was busy climbing over a fallen comrade, but Aaron didn't hesitate, his sword lashing out. The man's head flew from his shoulders in a shower of hot blood, and Aaron reveled in the feel of it against his face and hands. "More," he said, but it was not his voice alone that spoke, but Co's and the wrath's too, the three of them glorying in the bloodshed to come.

The second man was ready, swinging his sword, but you could not slay wrath, could not make anger bleed, and Aaron flowed around the cut, feeling the steel pass within inches of his face as he drew his remaining blade from his belt—the other was stuck in the back of the fleeing Kevlane last he'd seen it—and rammed it up and into the soldier's chin. The man's eyes snapped open, impossibly wide, and Aaron laughed as blood coated his hand, his Ghosts around him laughing along as they cut down those fools who had dared come against them.

The third man was ready for him, as was the fourth, but it made little difference. Ready or not, they died the same, and the steel drank its fill, glutting itself on the blood and the pain and the death that followed in its wake. Aaron ripped his sword out of the fifth soldier's stomach, twisting it and pulling it out at an angle, so that the man's entrails spilled onto the ground in front of him, a grizzly proof of his own inadequacy. "Yes," Aaron hissed as the man collapsed to his knees, "yes."

For a time, he knew nothing of the city around him, forgot about its people or those he cared about that lay within it. He did not even remember Boyce Kevlane or Belgarin. His world was a world of steel and flesh and the cutting of the flesh, the opening up of it, and there was nothing else. He was an artist painting his masterpiece in blood and bone and spit, and there was nothing but his fellow artists beside him and those men, those stretches of canvas in front of him on which he carved his work. Some, appalled by his ferocity and the ferocity of those with him, tried to turn and run, but they died like all the rest, a blade cutting a man from behind as well as it ever did from the front.

His sword was stuck in the chest of one man—the dying bastard gripping it with both hands—even as another came upon him, and that was alright. Aaron used his free hand and pulled the man close, ramming his forehead into his nose again and again, breaking it then shattering it, then shoving what remained deeper and deeper into the man's skull with each impact. When he was done, he let the corpse drop to the ground, shaking his head to clear it. Something—a piece of bone, maybe—was stuck in his forehead, and that was alright too, for it was all part of it, all a piece of the work. Their pain and his pain, their fear and his rage all mixed together to form the color with which they painted. It did not matter how they died only that they did. And they did. By the score they did.

After a time, he and the Ghosts were able to push the approaching army out of the gate leaving a trail of the dead and dying behind them. Some small, quiet part of Aaron's mind knew that they should stop there, should take advantage of the funnel the gate opening provided, but they did not, could not. The rage demanded more, needed more, and so they pushed on, driving toward the beating heart of the army that stood before them. When they saw the scope of it, the numbers that swallowed up the fields around them, they did not fear but rejoiced, for more deaths were demanded, many more, and here, here were those who would give them.

Aaron bellowed a laugh as he pushed forward, his sword and knife lashing out and taking their price in equal measure, and the Ghosts laughed behind him, a sound both terrible and wonderful at the same time, and that, like all the rest, was as it should be, as it had to be. They pressed forward, the point of a spear driving into the enemy ranks, slaughtering as they went. They did not worry or concern themselves with those enemy soldiers that surrounded them on either side, for they were too far away to die, and should they venture closer they too would become a part of it, a part of the masterpiece that Aaron and those with him were making.

Some Ghosts were cut down, but it was not unexpected, and those remaining did not mourn their passing, for it too was a part of the thing, and those who died knew their place in the grand work, did not fear or regret their passing but went to it with bloody smiles on their faces. Soon, they were through the ranks of armorless men and upon soldiers in full armor, their visors down, and Aaron's only regret was that he could not see the fear dancing in their eyes as he and those with him barreled into them.

**

"By the gods," Ellemont said, staring out at the gate of the city, watching in shock and wonder as a force led by General Envelar, a force that couldn't have consisted of any more than a hundred men, charged into the full weight of Belgarin's army and, to his astonishment, Belgarin's army faltered. "It's ... it's magnificent," he breathed. "He is magnificent."

Wendell and Darrell shared a troubled look with each other from where they sat their own horses beside the prince. Magnificent it may be, but they both knew well enough how it would end. Whatever spell the men with Aaron worked under, it could not last forever. Each man with them might fight like ten, even a hundred, yet still it would not be enough. "I should be down there," Wendell said, "it ain't right for the boys to take on so, not without me present. Right selfish, is what it is."

"Aye, sergeant," the prince said, grinning, his yellow visor raised, "we all should. To be a part of something such as that," he shook his head slowly, unable to take his eyes from the battle below, "it would be a grand thing."

"A grand death, anyway," Wendell muttered, but if the prince heard, he gave no sign.

Ellemont glanced across the field where Belgarin's cavalry sat their horses, waiting. "Bastards," he hissed, "no good cowardly bastards." He turned back to the battle below, watched as Aaron and those with him forced their way forward, deeper and deeper into Belgarin's army. Some of Belgarin's forces were still trying the walls with scaling ladders, but as far as Wendell could see, that still left more than enough to deal with Aaron and the others. "They're going to be killed down there," Ellemont said as if only now realizing it. "I wonder, why did they open the gate?"

Wendell glanced at Darrell who only shook his head, "Something must have happened to the gate. I can only imagine sabotage. No doubt they'll be working to fix it, but there's no telling how long such a thing might take."

"Time," Ellemont said, and it was clear that he was not speaking to Wendell or Darrell now but to himself. He seemed to make a decision then and turned to the troops behind him, "Sergeant!"

A man came running forward from the front line of infantry, "Yes, Majesty?"

"You are now in command of the infantry," Ellemont said, and once more Wendell noted that he had the voice of a king. "Engage as soon as you feel that it is safe to do so—whatever happens, we must not let the city be taken, am I understood?"

"Of course, my king."

"Very well," Ellemont said. He hesitated, glancing around at all the men, cavalry and infantry alike, who stood watching him. "You are all good men, and it has been my pleasure and privilege to lead you," he said, and Wendell and Darrell shared a frown before looking back at the prince. He turned to them then, speaking in a low tone so that the other troops might not hear, "If anything should happen, know that I have left orders with my chamberlain to bequeath rule of my lands to my sister, Adina."

"Wait a minute," Wendell said, "what do you—"

"You mean to go down and meet them," Darrell said, and it took Wendell a moment before he realized what the man meant.

"Aye, Darrell," Ellemont said, grinning and looking somehow more alive than any other time Wendell had seen him, "so I do. You two will stay with the infantry."

"Prince," Darrell said, "with respect, I would prefer to come."

"Me as well," Wendell said, "it ain't right, the lads down there without me."

"I'm afraid, gentlemen," Ellemont said, "that that is an order. Sergeant." The man he'd spoken to earlier stepped forward again.

"Yes, Majesty?"

"If these men attempt to follow, you've my permission to chain them down until this is done."

"Of course, my king."

Ellemont nodded, smiling at the two men, "Oh, don't look so glum. Besides," he said, his smile slowly fading, "you two need to tell Aaron of what happened with ... my wife. Tell General Envelar I wish I had known him better and tell my sisters ... tell them I love them," he said. "Very much."

Wendell tried to speak, but found that there was a lump in his throat. Luckily, Darrell took the lead, bowing low, "Of course, Majesty."

Ellemont winked, "Alright men!" He shouted at the cavalry surrounding him, "those are our allies down there, fighting for their lives. Are we to leave them to their deaths?"

"No," a chorus of voices shouted back.

Ellemont nodded, "Very well then will you follow me, your king?"

There were shouts of agreement at that then Ellemont snapped his visor closed and gave his horse a kick, drawing his sword as he did. In another moment, he and the other cavalry went charging down the hill in a roar of hooves and shouting men as they raced toward the massive sprawling army in the field below. Wendell watched them go then turned to see Belgarin's cavalry starting forward to come up behind the prince's horse. "They'll be pinned in," he said, his voice hoarse and full of emotion.

"Yes," Darrell said, "they will."

Wendell cleared his throat, wiping a hand across his eyes, "He said it right enough, did the prince. They're magnificent."

CHAPTER THIRTY-SEVEN

Aaron heaved in a desperate breath. There was a sharp pain in his side—from a blade or only exertion he did not know and there was no time to check—but he fought on, roaring as his sword cleaved through steel and flesh and bone. There was no time to be tired, for the rage demanded more, always more, and there was no denying it. Now that he was fully within its grip, he found that he did not want to. Still, his attacks were growing weaker, his parries slower, and he bled from several shallow cuts on his arms and one on his leg where a stray sword had caught him a glancing blow in the ferocious melee.

His throat was dry, coated with dust, and his roar now was little more than a choked wheeze as he fought on. He would die here, he realized, and that was alright. There were worse things than dying fighting for what you believed in, protecting those you cared about. There were no more than thirty of his men left now, and they fought in a ragged circle, the army pushing up against them from all sides, a tide of steel and flesh, only to be pushed back time and time again. Still, it would not be long now. He found a brief reprieve as the tide receded and glanced around to see that the men with him looked weary beyond belief, coated in blood and sweat, but they did not weep or show fear, only studied the army around them with determination and a rage that could not be slaked no matter how many fell beneath their blades.

Aaron bared his teeth at the enemy, his own rage not diminished in the slightest for all the men he'd slain, and the looks of fear on the enemy soldiers sent a thrill of joy through him. "Come on then!" He screamed, the power of the bond carried on his words and seemed to radiate out from him in a shockwave that sent the soldiers nearest him and the other Ghosts reeling as if they'd been struck. Those closest gasped and whispered to each other, their eyes wide and full of terror, but they did not come closer.

"General," said a man beside him, and he turned to see Bastion staring back at the city, "look." Aaron did and he saw that the gate had been fixed, that the men on the walls were even now motioning them back.

Some part of Aaron felt cheated somehow, and he shook his head, "It doesn't matter. We aren't going back—we never were." Not that they could have, even if they'd wanted to. It would be an easy enough thing, should they turn to run, seeking the shelter of the city and its walls, for the men surrounding them to cut them down, and Aaron had no intention of dying like that. A quick glance around at the remaining Ghosts assured him that they knew the truth of the thing, that they felt the same as he. That left only one thing to do.

He met the eyes of each remaining man in turn then bared his teeth in a savage grin that was answered by each of those staring back at him. "Alright then, lads," he said, "let's keep our promise." With that, he turned and, bellowing a cry of rage, charged the soldiers closest to him. In a moment, the Ghosts gave their own cries and followed behind him.

The first man Aaron came on tried to shy away, but his comrades were blocking him in at the back and sides, and there was nowhere for him to go. A mistake then, but not the real one. The real one had been him coming at all, and Aaron's blade taught him the truth of it as it whistled through the air and sent his head flying from his shoulders in a fountain of blood. Blades lashed out from the enemy line, more out of desperate fear than any attempt to engage with him. He blocked two swords, sidestepping a third and driving his blade into its owner's throat. He jerked the blade back, grinning at the surprise in the dying man's face, then lunged to the side, not quite fast enough to avoid a sword cutting a ragged, bloody furrow across the upper part of his left arm.

He did not cry out, barely even felt it at all, for the rage was everything, filling him up and leaving no room for anything else, and he was on to the next man. His blade lashed out in a cut across the man's chest, but the deadly steel slid off armor, and Aaron was forced to sidestep—not retreat, for the rage would not allow it—to avoid the man's counterattack. Then, before the man could bring his blade back around, Aaron barreled into him, his shoulder leading as he let out a roar. The impact sent a shock through his whole left side, and his arm went numb, the knife he held dropping from nerveless fingers, but even this was a minor thing, and the armored man went sprawling on his back, knocking several of his comrades stumbling as he did.

Aaron followed him down, hammering the handle of his sword into the helmet. The steel warped and compacted under the savage blows, and the man screamed, but Aaron brought the hilt down again and again until blood leaked from the insides of the ruined, twisted remains of the helmet, until the man's screams had gone silent. He called on the bond and a web of power spread out around him connecting him to each soldier, to their thoughts, their fears. A vicious dizziness swept over him and, for a moment, he thought he would lose consciousness, but he slammed his teeth together, biting his tongue in the process, and the pain forced the shadows that had been clinging to the edge of his vision back. Suddenly, with the bond's power, he understood these men, knew them better than they knew themselves, and he tilted his head back and laughed.

He knew what move the men would make, what shape their attacks would make even before they knew it themselves. He waded into them, shifting and gliding around their blows as if he was a ghost in truth, but this ghost was not of the dead—not yet. Not of the dead, but a maker of them. He was a musician whose only instrument was the sword, whose melody was one of steel and screams. He charged into the soldiers leaving a river of corpses in his wake as he played the only song he knew, the only song he cared to know.

He wasn't sure for how long he fought, or how far his steps had taken him, but eventually he came upon an armored giant, the man at least a head and a half taller than he was himself. The man stood still, a mace in his hand that most men wouldn't have even been able to lift, and he was covered from head to toe in thick armor. The other soldiers around them backed up a few steps, and Aaron's grin widened. He glanced behind him and saw only the dozens of dead he had left in his wake, no sign of Bastion or any of the other Ghosts. He turned back to the big man, "Alright, you big fucker," he growled, "it's only me and you."

"You've no cha—" Aaron was charging forward before the big man had finished saying whatever he'd planned. He swung his sword at the big man's arm with all the force he could summon, but his sword rebounded from the armor, and nearly flew from his hand at the impact. He got in two more strikes—both as ineffective as the first—before the giant grabbed his mace in both hands and swung it in a blow that would have knocked down a building. Aaron ducked beneath the swing, grabbed his sword in two hands, and brought it crashing down into one of the big man's wrists.

The giant grunted, that was all, and then the mace was coming back, cutting a line through the air toward Aaron's head. Aaron leapt backward, leaning his head back farther than the rest of his body, and he felt the wind off of the mace's passage as it flew within inches of his face. Before the man could bring it back around, Aaron lunged forward and brought his blade down on the big man's wrist again in the same spot as he had before. The enemy soldier bellowed in pain as the mace slipped from his fingers and crashed to the ground.

The giant made to reach for it, but Aaron was already moving, slamming his sword into the joint of the armor where the man's knee was. Once, twice, three times, and the giant staggered and fell to one knee. The man swung his left fist at Aaron—a blow that would have sent the sellsword's broken body flying no matter the giant's awkward position—but Aaron was already spinning away, around behind the giant and to his other side.

The man turned his head just in time to see Aaron ram his sword in the unarmored part directly underneath the giant's arm, and it stuck to the hilt in the big man's side. The man groaned at that, and Aaron tried to jerk his blade free, but it had stuck on something, and he was still trying to rip it out when the giant's arm rushed out in a wide swing and struck him in the chest.

The air exploded from Aaron's lungs as he hurtled backward, landing on the ground half a dozen feet away and rolling until finally managing to come to a stop on one knee. Pain lanced through his chest, sharp, stabbing pain, and he knew without checking that the man had broken some of his ribs. Still, the grin did not leave his face, and he looked up to see the giant on one knee as well. For a moment, the two men seemed to study each other then the giant toppled face-first onto the grass and was still.

Hissing in pain and fury, Aaron levered his way to his feet, his left arm still numb below the shoulder, his chest aching terribly. His sword was gone—still sticking from the giant's side—but just now it didn't seem to matter. "Come on then!" He yelled at the soldiers surrounding him as he dropped into a fighting stance, his good arm extended out to the side and at an angle to the ground, "Who dies first?"

The soldiers started forward then, and Aaron watched them come, watched his death come, yet he was not afraid. Not afraid, only regretful that he could not have taken more with him, that the grand dance of steel and blood was coming to an end. Then, when the nearest soldier was no more than ten feet away, the air was split with what sounded like thunder from somewhere in front of him, and the very ground beneath him shook. At first, he couldn't see what was making the noise for the rank after rank of enemy soldiers that stood in his way, but then men further back were screaming, and he saw their line buckle and bend as if under attack from the other side. Abruptly, the line of enemy soldiers was not bending at all but broken and men on horses were charging through them, swinging their swords to either side of them as they tore into the enemy soldiers from the rear, cutting them down like so much chaff.

A horseman wearing armor that had been painted completely yellow reined up beside Aaron, flanked by several other soldiers on horses. The horse the yellow knight rode was armored too, yet still bore several deep cuts along its flanks, and the horseman looked little better, his armor battered and bloody. Aaron bared his teeth, preparing to launch himself at the man—whoever he was—his animalistic fury pushing out all logical thought. He crouched low and was just about to pounce, when the man raised his visor. His face was soaked in sweat, his breathing nearly as hard as Aaron's own, but he was grinning widely. "General Envelar," the man said, "it is good to meet you once again."

"Do I know you?" Aaron asked in a dry rasp, his voice not just his own, but Co's and the wrath's as well.

The man frowned, a troubled look on his face, "it's me, general," he said, "Prince Ellemont."

The name meant nothing to Aaron, and he took a step toward the man, thinking that, perhaps, his work wasn't done after all. "You remember me," the man said again, "we met in the castle. I am Adina's brother."

Aaron froze at that, his muscles going rigid. That name. There was something about that name and suddenly he heard a woman's soft voice in his head, 'You are not a monster, Aaron.' Something in him recoiled at that like a serpent protecting its territory, hissing even as it did.

"A ... Adina," Aaron said, and with the speaking of the name, he felt some part of himself return, felt some fraction of the anger subside.

"That's right, a friend," the man said, and Aaron realized it was Prince Ellemont after all, was amazed that he hadn't recognized the prince in the first place.

Aaron's face twitched, and he hesitated, uncertain. The rage inside of him demanded that he kill the man, that he tear and rend his flesh until his body was nothing but a corpse, and he would have, he wanted to. But that name. Adina. He took a slow, deep breath, forcing the rage down as much as he could, "Prince Ellemont," he said, and this time it was only his voice that spoke, "what are you doing here?"

The prince grinned at that as, all around them, men on horses fought with the enemy infantry. They were giving better than they got, but Aaron noted one man being pulled from his saddle, saw a group of soldiers surround him, burying their blades in his twitching body. "Saving you," Ellemont said.

Aaron stared blankly at the man for several seconds as the battle raged around them, finding it difficult to comprehend what he'd said. "Saving me?" He asked finally, "Prince, it is too late for that. Far too late. The gate has been sabotaged, and I will fight as long as I'm able to buy time for the ships to make it into the shore. There is nothing else I can do."

"Ships, you say?" Ellemont said, gesturing, "do you mean those ships?"

Aaron turned to where he pointed, and stared in shock. The docks of Isalla's capital city had apparently not been enough to accommodate all of the ships and many were anchored a short distance away from the shore, men in smaller boats paddling forward even as he watched. "They've ... they've landed," he said, stunned. It had felt as if he'd been fighting for fifteen minutes, half an hour on the outside, but clearly that was wrong. Two hours. Two hours at the least. He turned back to Ellemont, "It doesn't matter," he said, "they still need more time to work their way to the gate, and I'll buy them what time I can."

"And take all the glory for yourself?" Ellemont said, shaking his head, "and what of your men, general? Will you take them to their deaths as well? Don't you believe that they have done enough today?"

"My men," Aaron said, his voice harsh, "are dead, prince."

"Oh?" Ellemont said, "then who, I wonder, is that?"

Aaron turned to look behind him and saw what appeared to be about fifteen of the Ghosts shuffling toward him. Several had lost their weapons and bore wounds—some serious, some not—but all were coated in blood and worse and clearly exhausted, barely able to stand under their own power. Bastion walked at their front, and he alone did not look as if he was moments away from collapsing.

"Go then," Ellemont said, "back to the city. We will hold them as long as we can."

Aaron stared up at the prince on his horse, "You will die, then."

"Yes," the prince said, "we will die. But the last week has taught me that there are worse things than death, General Envelar. I may be a coward and a fool, but this, at least, I will do." He grinned, "the yellow prince must have some use, after all."

The man seemed very different from when Aaron had first met him. Gone were the timidity and the anxiety, as if he felt that he'd be called out any moment for a fraud. He was regal there, sitting upon his horse, his bloody blade in his hand. He was a king. "You are no coward, Ellemont," Aaron said, "whatever else you are. The yellow prince will be talked about for years to come. You are a hero."

"That means much," the prince said, "coming from a man such as yourself. Now, will you go?"

Aaron turned to look back at Bastion, "Take the men back to the city, coordinate with Captain Gant. I will remain here with the prince."

"Gods man," Ellemont said, "but why? Haven't you done enough?"

Why? Aaron thought. Because she was wrong, prince. I am a monster, and the best thing a monster can do is die killing its own. "Never mind that," Aaron said, "my reasons are my own. Thank you for coming prince," he said, "it will be a pleasure to fight beside you."

Ellemont shook his head, glancing over Aaron's shoulder, "Can you carry him?"

"Yes sir."

Aaron turned to look back at Bastion, frowning, "What in the—"

"Forgive me, Aaron," Ellemont said, "it was a pleasure." Aaron spun, suddenly sure of what was coming, but he was too slow. The hilt of the prince's sword crashed into his head, and he knew nothing more.

CHAPTER THIRTY-EIGHT

Aaron roused to wakefulness, his head pounding. The rage was gone now, and he felt empty, used up. He rubbed at the ache in his head gingerly, wincing at the tenderness of the flesh beneath his fingers. There was a sharp pain in his chest also, and his left arm didn't seem to want to obey his commands. Then the memory came back in a flash, and he remembered Ellemont. Looking around, he found that he'd been propped against the city wall, and he jerked to his feet, stumbling and nearly falling until strong hands reached out and grabbed him.

"Easy, sir," a voice said, and he turned to see Bastion standing beside him. The big youth was covered in blood, his arms sporting a dozen small cuts, but he stood well enough.

"Good gods, man," Aaron said, "you've got blood all over you. What did you do, bathe in the stuff?"

The youth's mouth stretched in a grin, "You're not looking your best yourself sir, you don't mind me sayin' so."

Aaron grunted at that, "Soldier," he said, remembering the question Ellemont had asked, 'Can you carry him?' "Am I to understand that the prince knocked me out and you—"

"Aaron!"

Aaron turned to see Adina running toward him, followed by Leomin and another figure, and his eyes went wide, a grin spreading on his face, as he recognized May, the club owner, her flaming red hair trailing behind her as she ran.

"Adina—" He started as she drew close, but cut off as she threw her arms around him and hugged him tight.

"Thank the gods you're okay."

Aaron grunted in pain at the pressure on his broken ribs, and she took a step back, letting him go. "Aaron, you're hurt."

"I'll be fine," he said, his expression sobering, "but Adina, Ellemont—"

"I know," she said, her smile fading, "I saw."

The club owner was on him then, and Aaron winced as he was pulled into another tight hug. "Easy, May," he grunted, "you're going to kill me."

She laughed at that, but she let him go. "I'm beginning to think that nothing can kill you, Silent."

"I feel half dead now, if you want to know the truth. But there's no time for dying just now. Tell me, how many were you able to bring?"

She smiled wide, "All of them."

Aaron frowned, "What? All of Hale's men or Grinner's?"

"All of them," she said again, "and the council sent the army of Avarest as well."

"Envelar!" Someone shouted.

Aaron turned to see Grinner and Hale walking toward him from further into the city, hundreds of men spread out behind them and following in their wake. "Ah shit," Aaron muttered, "I've had nightmares that start this way."

Leomin patted him on the shoulder, "From what May told us when we met her at the docks, I have a feeling this nightmare may have a different ending."

Aaron, cognizant of all of the abuse his body had taken in the last few hours, only shrugged with his one good arm, "I'm not so sure, Leomin."

The Parnen opened his mouth to say something more but then the two crime bosses—the most powerful men in the Downs— walked up, the captain, Festa, not far behind.

"Ah, Silent," Hale said, booming a hearty laugh as he took in Aaron's ragged, exhausted state, "I've hoped to see you this way many times before though, admittedly, under very different circumstances."

"On that, at least, we can agree," Grinner said, the older man nodding slowly. "Now, Envelar, where do you need us?"

Aaron grunted, hardly able to believe what he was hearing and seeing as more soldiers—these not criminals at all but well-armed and well-armored, clearly members of Avarest's standing army, emerged from within the city. "We'll need more men along the walls," he said, "ask for Captain Brandon Gant—he'll know where you're needed most. You'll find him on the eastern section of the wall, I'm sure."

Grinner nodded, smoothing his gray eyebrows with one long, thin finger, "Very well." He turned to his men and raised a hand in a beckoning gesture, "This way!" And with that, he and his men were off, marching toward the wall.

Hale shook his head, the big man folding his arms across his thick chest as he watched them go, "Bastard always has to be first. Well," he said, turning back to Aaron, "no matter. From what I've seen, there'll be plenty of killin' for all of us." He clapped Aaron on the back with a blow hard enough to stagger him then barked a laugh before leading his own men after Grinner's. Aaron watched them go in disbelief, half-convinced that he'd died already and was experiencing a final dream brought on by his death.

"General Envelar, I presume?"

He turned to see a man that looked to be in his forties approach in armor that gleamed in the afternoon sun. "I'm Aaron."

"My name is General Yallek, and I represent the council of the city of Avarest. My army is at your service."

Aaron stared blankly at the man and for several seconds he couldn't seem to speak. Then, finally, "I had not expected the council to send any men."

"Not any men, General Envelar," the older man said. "All of them."

"All of them?" Aaron asked.

"Yes, well," the older man said, smiling as he turned to May, "You have some very persuasive friends."

Aaron looked at the club owner who beamed happily then grunted, "I guess I do."

The general nodded, "Where would you like us?"

Aaron sent the general and his men to spread out along the wall, strengthening those gaps that had been created as the defenders had fallen in battle, and he stood watching them go, shaking his head in wonder. "It's a damned miracle," he muttered.

"A miracle," boomed a familiar voice, and Aaron turned to see Festa walking up with Gryle beside him, a frown on the captain's face that was belied by the amused sparkle in his eyes. "It's a miracle that we made it here at all, and I can tell you with confidence that there's not a single thing of any value left on my ship." He shook his head, "I half expected the bastards to start ripping up the deck when they ran out of shit to steal."

Aaron laughed and then Gryle was moving forward as if to embrace the princess.

"Eh!" May scolded as if she was speaking to a dog, and Gryle froze, embarrassed. "What did we talk about, chamberlain?"

Gryle sighed heavily, "No touching, I know, I know." He bowed low to Adina, "It is a great pleasure to—" the chamberlain's words cut off as Adina ran forward and pulled him into an embrace, his own arms held stiffly out to his sides.

Aaron glanced at May, raising an eyebrow, and she grinned. "It seems that you're not the only person I know who's got one of the Virtues. The chamberlain here happened upon the Virtue of Strength just sitting around waiting to be picked up."

"Really?" Aaron said, "but ... Aster Kalen had the strength Virtue. Melan wasn't it?" He glanced at the chamberlain who stared at his feet, his face red with embarrassment.

Festa frowned at the chamberlain's back, "Half of my ship broken—I don't think there's a door left in the place. It's a wonder we made it here at all."

"Yes, well," May said, the amusement heavy in her tone, "Aster Kalen happened to get trampled by a horse."

"Trampled by a horse," Aaron said, his voice dry. "I think I'm going to need to hear this story."

"Later," May said, patting him on the shoulder, "Right now, we've a city to save."

CHAPTER THIRTY-NINE

The Knower's tent was on the edge of the camp, as far away from the campfires and tents of the other soldiers as possible, and Belgarin walked there with his dead love's body cradled in his arms, her blood coating his tunic and chest. Several soldiers moved forward, most likely to ask if he needed help, but he looked at them, his grief and rage plain on his face, and they backed away.

Four guards stood stationed outside of the Knower's tent, as still and unmoving as statues, and as Belgarin approached, they bowed low. He walked by them without seeing them, his mind in a haze of fear and shame. The stench inside the tent would have been unbearable normally but, just then, Belgarin found that it barely registered, so terrible was the pain roiling inside of him.

"Ah, my king," the creature rasped from the bed, and Belgarin studied him in the light of a lantern sat on the ground. The loose white linen shirt the man wore was coated in blood and vomit, but he did not seem to notice or care if he did. "And who, I wonder, is this that you have brought me?"

"I think you know," Belgarin said in a dead, emotionless voice, "you seem to know all other secrets."

"Very well," the Knower said, a disappointed expression on his ruined, hollowed-out face, "I had only thought that you might wish to introduce us—as much as you were able, anyway, with one of us a corpse and the other nearly so."

338

Belgarin looked at the foot of the bed where the young girl—Sarah, he thought her name was—stood silently. He noted that there were deep cuts around her eyes and on her cheeks. By their look, it was clear they'd been done by fingernails and by the spacing he suspected they were self-inflicted. Normally, he would have wondered at that, would have been curious as to what terrible knowledge the Knower had shared with her to cause her to give herself such pain, but his love was dead in his arms, dead by his hands, and he found that he did not have the curiosity to ask. "Leave us."

The girl looked at him with eyes empty and devoid of any life, as if she were no more than a puppet that obeyed the pull of its strings. He stared back at her, his own gaze lifeless and cold and after several seconds she turned and left the tent without a word.

"Ah," the Knower said, staring at the tent flap after the girl had left, "but she is a special one, truly. She has lasted longer than any of the others but, then, I believe that the time grows close now. For both of us."

Belgarin bent, gently laying Lyla's body on the ground before looking back at the creature. "I ... I have a question."

The Knower grinned displaying his few remaining, rotten teeth, "Oh, it is knowledge you seek. And here I thought you enjoyed my company."

"This woman," Belgarin said, "is—"

"Queen Lilliana," the creature said, "oh, yes, I know of her, My King. I know, too, that you have been meeting with her in secret. Your own brother's wife, no less." He made a tsking sound, "Such a sordid love affair for one who would be the king of all of Telrear."

"She said ... that is, I want to know..." Belgarin hesitated, scared of finishing the sentence, as if by doing so he would somehow make it true, would, in those words, make himself a killer not just of his lover but of his unborn son as well.

"If she was with child?" the Knower said, his grin wider than ever.

Belgarin swallowed hard, staring at the body of his love lying on the ground, and he felt tears pouring down his face. Do not ask the question, some part of him pleaded, do not. For so long as it remains unasked, it cannot be made true or untrue. It will only be a memory of something she said as she was dying and even that will fade in time.

But he knew that it would not, knew that he would remember the way the knife had slid into her so easily for the rest of his life, knew that he would remember the feel of her blood on him, the shocked eyes that stared at him as she breathed her last breath. And had there been love in those eyes, even then? Yes, he thought there had. Gods, Lyla, he thought, his chest hitching, why did you betray me? Why did you make me do this?

And on the tail end of that thought came another, not in his voice but in his mothers'. Why do you always break things?

Please, the voice tried once more, do not do this. Do not.

"Yes," he said, "I want … I need to know, if she was pregnant. Is there some … examination you can do? Some … test?"

"There are such tests, of course," the Knower said, "but there is no need for those. Just as well as I do not have the strength to perform them. Still," he said, his smile wide and without mercy, "are you sure, Majesty, that you wish to know the truth of this? I told you once before, remember, that all knowledge comes with a price. For small things, the price is small. But for great things, things such as this, the cost might very well be more than even a man as rich as you can afford."

Belgarin hesitated, suddenly uncertain. What good would such knowledge do? Either she was or she was not. Knowing would not change anything. Whatever life she carried within her would have vanished along with her own. "Yes," he heard himself say, his voice empty and strange in his ears, "I would know."

The Knower grinned that macabre grin as if pleased, "Very well. Yes, my king, the queen was pregnant with your child. A boy, too, it would have been, had it but lived."

A sound somewhere between a sob and a moan escaped Belgarin at the man's words, and he collapsed to his knees beside the body of his lover. "It … it cannot be."

"Oh, but it is, My King," the Knower hissed, "and in the answer you have your knowledge and your price too, I think, for you look much to me like a man who has paid more than he can spare. Your son, your heir, dead by your own hand."

"Shut up," Belgarin sobbed, his voice cracking, "please I beg you."

"Would you like to know how far along she was?" The creature said, ignoring Belgarin's desperate plea, "how long it would have been before you had seen your son? He would have been strong, this one, I think. Strong and healthy. A worthy heir. "

"Stop, damn you," Belgarin said, his heart thundering in his chest, his hands shaking as he reached out and grasped the corpse desperately, as if somehow he could take the knife's kiss back, take it all back.

"Oh, but I cannot, my king," the Knower said, "for the question has been asked and the knowledge has been given. He would have been a fine son, and she a fine queen. She loved you, you know—truly."

Belgarin let out a howl of rage and pain and before he knew it, his hands were clamped around the creature's throat, his fingers digging into the wrinkled, sickly flesh.

The Knower only grinned at him as his face turned a deep red, "A ... true ... heir," the man croaked, and with a cry of anguish, Belgarin tightened his grip even more, and then he was screaming, not words at all, only the wailing, wrenching cries of a man who has suffered a greater loss than he'd thought existed.

Still screaming, he began to shake the man so that his body flailed around like a broken rag doll. He screamed until his voice was nothing but a dry, hoarse croak, squeezed until the man beneath him was still.

He looked down and saw the man's dead eyes staring up at him in what looked like amusement, his purple, mossy tongue flopping grotesquely out of his mouth. The worst, though, was the grin that still stretched the man's face, even in death.

Suddenly repulsed, not just by the dead man, but by himself, Belgarin found himself whimpering. He stumbled back, and his foot caught on Lyla's body. He tripped, collapsing to the ground and knocking over the lantern. The glass shattered, and the flame died leaving him—and the two corpses—in darkness. He heard a voice then, the same one he'd been hearing since he was a child, but it didn't seem to come from his own memory, not this time. Instead, it was as if someone spoke from only a few feet away.

"Why, Belgarin, must you always break things?"

No, it can't be. It can't. Whimpering in terror and grief, he lurched to his feet, his hands held out in front of him. As he did, a cold certainty washed over him, a certainty that, at any moment, he would feel cold, clammy skin against his fingers, would hear that voice speak again. The voice scared him more than the rest, for he knew without question that if he heard it again he would go mad. Sobbing, he stumbled in the direction where he thought to find the tent's opening. For several terrifying moments, his fingers found only the canvas of the tent then he let out a cry of relief as he felt the split in the fabric. Moaning, he staggered toward it, sure that he would feel a hand grasp his ankle before he made it out.

Nothing happened though and, in another moment, he was outside of the tent, turning and backing away from it, his hands still held up defensively in front of him.

"Majesty?" Someone asked, "are you okay?"

Belgarin spun at the voice, and the man must have seen something of the madness in his eyes, for he swallowed hard, taking an involuntary step back. Not just a man, Belgarin realized as he took in the man's armor and sword. A soldier. He studied the man for several seconds, his fevered mind unable to understand the man's presence. Soldiers, he thought wildly, soldiers mean death. Death like that of my queen. Of my son.

No more. The thought rang in his mind, pushing its way past the madness that wanted him to do nothing but lie down and scream until there were no screams left in him. Instead, he turned and started toward the observation point where General Fannen would be waiting, the soldier staring after him with fear dancing in his eyes.

Belgarin stumbled and fell several times as he struggled up the hill, a greater exhaustion upon him than any he'd ever known. The last time, he could not find his feet, yet urgency drove him on and so he crawled the last dozen steps to where Caldwell and General Fannen stood surrounded by several soldiers, the general peering through a looking glass at the battle raging below. They did not notice Belgarin's approach until he was nearly on them, then both men turned.

"My King?" The general gasped, rushing to him and pulling him to his feet, "are you ... alright?"

Belgarin did not answer, only stared out over that vast field as battle raged. Tears still streamed down his bloody face, but he did not know it, so focused was he on the still, dead forms that lay scattered about the field. He could not see their faces from here. To his fevered mind each form was his son, dead and him to thank for it, or his lover, Lyla, also slain at his own hand. The blood that stained the ground was her blood, hers and his, all of it proof of what he'd done, a testament to his mistake.

Why must you always break things?

"Their reinforcements made it to the city, Majesty," General Fannen said, "but they are still outnumbered. In time—"

"Call them back."

The general hesitated, turning to Belgarin, "My King? We will have the city 'ere long—the extra troops will make it take longer, but we still have the numerical advantage. We will—"

"I said call them back!" Belgarin screamed, his voice raw and thready, wavering dangerously on his feet, and he would have fallen had the general not been holding him.

Caldwell moved close to him, his face displaying its usual passivity. "My King," he said, "I am truly sorry for what happened, for what you were forced to do, but you must understand that Queen Lilliana—"

"She was with child, Caldwell," Belgarin said, his voice sounding hollow and empty. A stranger's voice. "My child."

The advisor nodded slowly, leaning close so that none but the king might hear, "The Knower told you this, your grace?"

Belgarin stared at his hands, coated in dried blood. They were his, he knew that, but they seemed strange to him, the hands of some other man. A man who was cruel and cold and given to violence. A man who killed his own son. "The Knower is dead."

Caldwell's normally placid expression slipped at that, but he quickly regained his equanimity, "It is a loss, made worse by the fact that we know not where the Virtue will have gone, but we will find it again, Majesty, I assure you. As for the rest, I know that the price may seem high now, but you are so very close to achieving your aim. Soon, the city will be yours—all of Telrear will be yours."

Belgarin stared at the man, "The price?" He rasped, "You speak to me of the price?" Before he knew it, his hands—those stranger's hands—reached out and grasped the tunic of the bald man, jerked him closer. "I have lost everything," Belgarin hissed, spittle flying from his mouth as he shook the man, "everything." Why do you always break things? "I don't care about Telrear anymore, Caldwell, don't you understand? There has been enough blood now, enough killing." He shoved the advisor back and the man stumbled and fell. Belgarin looked down at him, his face twisted and wretched in his grief. Some part of him knew that he was losing his sanity, that with each moment he inched closer toward a precipice, a fall from which would send him spiraling into the darkness. A part of him knew that. Knew it and welcomed it. "There has been enough bloodshed already. Enough for a man to drown in," he said, "for the world to drown in."

He turned to the general who watched him warily, as if he was some feral animal that might, at any moment, bare its fangs and attack. He was not wrong to do so. "Call them back, general," Belgarin said again, "now. We march to Baresh tonight."

The general hesitated then finally bowed, "Aye, Majesty. It will be done."

Belgarin was no longer paying attention to either man though, as he turned back and stared out over the fields, at the corpses in their hundreds. Corpses put there by his hand even if he wasn't the man who'd wielded the blade. His legs wavered again and suddenly gave out beneath him, and he found that he was falling into darkness. He did not know when it would stop, did not know if it ever would.

***

As the fool general ran off shouting for a healer, Caldwell pulled himself to his feet, staring down at the unconscious king lying on the ground. Fool, he thought. You cannot stop the killing, cannot halt what is coming. You fancy yourself the creator of it, but you are no more than a pawn just like all the rest, and you will learn the truth of it before your time comes.

CHAPTER FORTY

"Call me a fool, but it appears as if they are ... leaving."

Aaron glanced over at the Parnen. They were standing on the city walls, he, Leomin, Adina, May, Balen and, of course, Gryle. The chamberlain hadn't gone more than five feet from the princess since their arrival as if he expected her to fall at any moment and wanted to make sure he was there to catch her when she did.

Aaron saw his own surprise mirrored on the faces of the others, and he turned to look back over the wall at the departing army. "Yes," he said, "it seems so."

"But why?" May asked, the club owner frowning as if she'd just eaten something she didn't like, "even with Avarest's forces and the prince's combined, his army was still considerably larger. It's like watching a bear run from a rabbit."

"Oh, do give us some credit, ma'am," Leomin said, "a small dog, at least. Still," he gave his own frown, "I'm glad, of course, that they're leaving but..."

"But it doesn't make any sense," Adina said, shaking her head. "He's not likely to get a better chance than this. What could possibly have made Belgarin decide to abandon the battle?"

Aaron only shook his head, thinking. Whatever it was, he did not think that it boded well. The storm had been postponed for now but storms—as Aaron knew—grew worse the longer they had to build.

They watched until the last of Belgarin's forces either disappeared into the forest or were cut down as they tried to flee—those they fought against were criminals, after all—then Adina let out a sigh. "The healers will be going out soon to see if there's anyone that can be saved. I'm going to go with them."

Aaron watched her go then turned back to the battlefield as his own troops returned through the gate. The blood-coated fields were empty save for the dead and dying numbering in their thousands. He glanced up at the sky. It was clear now, the sun low in the sky and not a cloud in sight as evening drew on and night approached, but he felt no comfort in that. The storm was coming—he could smell it in the air. And when it did, it would be all the worse for the wait.

CHAPTER FORTY-ONE

"Majesty."

Belgarin turned, looking on his advisor with dead eyes. "What is it, Caldwell?" He said, having trouble finding the energy even to speak. It seemed to him that nothing mattered anymore, that all of his hopes and dreams had been a house built on sand, destined to shift and crumble at the slightest sign of pressure. He had wanted to do something good, had believed that and still did, but intentions meant little in the face of reality. I killed my lover. I killed my son. He sat in his throne room in Baresh, miles and miles from where the battle had taken place, where his lover and unborn son were now buried, but he could see her face clearly just the same, could hear her voice whispering, "Your ... son." The voice followed him wherever he went, even into dreams that were troubled and dark.

"Please, My King," Caldwell said, "you must order your troops back. The war might still be won, for yours is by far the greater army even now. If given time to prepare, to heal, then Isalla will be all the more difficult t—"

"Enough," Belgarin said. "The war is over, Caldwell. As for healing," he laughed at that, a high-pitched, terrible laugh that was far too close to a scream, and he thought he saw the four guards stationed two on each side of his throne cringe, "some wounds can never heal."

"But Majesty, your dream, your goal—"

He finally turned to look at the advisor then, finding some anger in his emptiness, after all. "Dreams," he hissed, "my dreams are turned to ash. Do you know, advisor, that my mouth tastes of it no matter what or how much I drink. Wine, water, the taste remains either way. We have done much, have united much of the country, and it will be enough. It has to be, for I am done with war. I have killed my own brothers, my own sisters, even my own son. I am finished."

"Then you are a fool," Caldwell spat.

Belgarin recoiled as if slapped, turning and rising, his hands clenching into fists at his sides, "What did you say to me?"

"Yes," Caldwell hissed, "you are a murderer. You have slain your family, have seen the lives of your brothers and sisters snuffed out by your command, so why, then, do you balk at the murdering of a lover and an unborn child?"

Belgarin's face heated with shame and rage, "It was different with them," he said, staring at the bald man as if seeing him for the first time, "my brothers and sisters, Ophasia, Eladen, all the rest, they tried to kill me. But my son ... he did nothing."

Caldwell laughed, and the strange, cruel sound of it echoed in the nearly empty throne room. "You are such a fool," he said, "have you ever really thought yourself king? You are nothing," he hissed, "nothing but a puppet that jumps when his strings are pulled." The bald man shook his head in wonder, "Your brothers and sisters never tried to kill you, Belgarin. It was all a lie. Many lies, in fact, and each one a pull on your strings to make you dance the way I wanted. The way my master wanted. You murdered nearly your entire family," he said, "and you did it for nothing."

Belgarin took an involuntary step back at the unexpected fury and disgust in the man's voice, "You lie," he said, his voice breaking, "that ... that can't be true."

"Oh, but it is, king," Caldwell said, "just as it is true that your lover, Lilliana, never betrayed you."

The room seemed to spin around Belgarin now, and he put a hand to his head, closing his eyes, "You ... you're wrong. The note..."

"Was something that I wrote myself," Caldwell said, "and what, king? Did you really think you'd be able to keep something as big as a sordid affair with your brother's wife a secret from me?" He laughed again, stepping closer to Belgarin with something like hunger in his eyes, and Belgarin found himself retreating from the man, stumbling backward.

"N-no," Belgarin stammered, "the commander—"

"Was manipulated easy enough," Caldwell said, shrugging, "I needed only a few minutes of his time to convince him of his only true option. Yes, Belgarin, you are a murderer of innocents, of your own son, but this is not what I hate the most," he said, his expression turning into a sneer, "you are also a coward. More than your brother ever was."

Belgarin screamed then, a sharp, desperate outcry of grief and despair, and he collapsed to his knees. His heart hammered so hard in his chest that he thought surely it would burst free in another moment. "Guards," he tried to say, but his voice came out in a dry croak, and he swallowed hard, trying again. "Guards, kill this man."

The guards did not move, and Belgarin felt fear clutch at his racing heart. "You heard me, damnit!" He bellowed, "Take him!"

Still, they did not move, and the only sound was that of Caldwell's building laughter, and he turned to see the advisor grinning at him, "Oh, king, but you are a pathetic, stupid man. Did you really believe that these men here were yours?" He shook his head, "They have been mine since the day I stepped into the castle. Before that."

"You," Belgarin said, his body shaking not just with sobs now but anger, "You're responsible for this." He rose to his feet, "Why?" he said, "Why would you do this to me?"

"Me?" Caldwell said, "Oh, no you've got it all wrong, Belgarin. It isn't me who is behind your misfortune." He grinned widely, glancing over Belgarin's shoulder, "It's you."

Frowning, Belgarin turned and came face to face with something out of nightmare. The man's face—if it was a face at all—was twisting and shifting like clay until finally, it settled on a face. His own. Belgarin stared at his own features, at the grin spreading across them, and he screamed until his voice broke and cracked, and he was left coughing.

"Relax," the other version of him said in a soothing voice, "you will still rule. At least, in a way."

"In ... a way?"

The other version of him grinned and stepped forward, surprisingly quick. Belgarin tried to back away, but he was too slow, and he felt something strike his chest. He stumbled then and looked down to see a blade sticking out of him, blood seeping from the wound. He stared back at the thing, his eyes wide, as the strength left his body. "Mother ..." he rasped, "I'm sorry." Then he was falling into nothing and the nothing reached out and swallowed him up, and he knew no more.

Boyce Kevlane stared down at the dead king, a smile on his face, then walked to the throne and sat. "Check on the army," he said, "I want us to attack Perennia as soon as possible. Aaron Envelar and his friends must die."

"Of course, master," Caldwell said, bowing low, and his face was not impassive now but smiling widely. "Still though," he said, his expression growing serious, "we will need more troops."

Boyce Kevlane grinned at that, and the face he wore, the face of a king, grinned with him, "Thousands of years ago, my friend, Aaron Caltriss, ordered me to stop my experiments and I did. For a while. But, then, it has been a long time, and I have needed something to occupy me." He glanced at the bald man, "Do not worry, Caldwell. You will have your troops and I..." he paused, fingering the wound at his back that had still not fully healed from where the bastard Envelar had thrown a knife into him as he'd climbed the wall, "I will have my revenge."

***

They sat around the table in Isabelle's audience chamber, nine of them in all and for the first time since Aaron had seen her, Queen Isabelle was not sitting at the head of it—in the position of power—but was instead sitting near to Adina, the two women holding and comforting each other over the loss of their brother.

Gryle sat a few feet away, wringing his hands nervously, his mouth opening repeatedly as if to offer some words of comfort but closing again a moment later. Aaron was sorry for Adina's sadness, but he found himself glad that, for once at least, she seemed to have a real sister, one that she could share her grief with.

Darrell, Wendell, and Captain Brandon Gant all sat across the table from Aaron, sneaking looks at him when they thought he wouldn't notice. They tried to be subtle about it, but Wendell in particular was about as subtle as a sword to the face. Aaron supposed he might not have noticed the man's stolen glances if he'd been blind ... or dead, maybe. He probably wouldn't have noticed them if he was dead.

He sighed heavily, refilling his empty glass with wine from a silver pitcher on the table and draining it in one swallow. He wasn't normally a fan of wine but ever since the battle at the gate, ever since they'd seen Aaron and his Ghosts charge Belgarin's army, the three men—Wendell most of all—treated him as if he was some kind of god come down to earth. The soldiers of the army, of course, were even worse, and Aaron had heard more than one rumor about his having slain a thousand men by himself. Foolishness, of course, stupidity. The blade would have broken long before then and, even if it hadn't, he would have. Still, soldiers were notorious for their penchant for tall tales and exaggeration, and anything he said to try to quash the rumors had only made them worse, so he had stopped saying anything at all. Instead, he drank.

Give it a week, he thought, *and I will have sprouted wings and killed those men with nothing but a word or maybe a waving of my hands.*

Wings would be nice, Co said.

You can already fly, lightning bug, he thought, *what the shit do you need wings for?*

Yes, I can fly, Aaron, but wings are majestic, she responded. She tried to force humor into her tone, but they both knew it for what it was—whistling in the darkness—for what the stories didn't mention was the need that he'd felt, that they'd both felt. The need to kill, to bathe in a river of blood.

351

Still, there was nothing to be done about it—nothing but drink at any rate as the stories weren't nearly as bad as the truth. He didn't remember everything from when the power of the bond had taken him, and he and the Ghosts had charged Belgarin's army—from what he'd heard, the Ghosts remembered little as well—but what he did remember was enough. Steel and blood and death. The truth was, he didn't want to remember. He remembered the rage, the need to kill, and he could not be sure, even now, that his blade had not found an ally in that bloody chaos. Gods, he'd been only seconds away from attacking Ellemont who had come to save them, who had given his life in the doing of it. Luckily, the prince had mentioned his sister, had said her name, and something in it had acted almost as a talisman against the wrath, bringing Aaron back from the brink. Yet even that was little comfort.

He may have pulled it back this time, may have managed to leap over the pit, to scramble up its side, but that did not mean he would be able to tomorrow or the day after. Still, he consoled himself with the fact that the stories were not only of him but of all the remaining Ghosts—fifteen in all now, the rest ghosts in truth. Each man's name was shouted and cheered when they walked down the street as if they were some visiting king. Bastion had even been invited to this dinner, but had only shook his head, grinning bashfully as if he was ten years younger than his nineteen years, saying that he would only make a fool of himself in such company.

And that makes two of us, Aaron thought, filling his glass again and leaning back in his chair.

"Forgive me for saying so, Mr. Envelar," Leomin said from beside him, "but your thoughts seem troubled." The Parnen, luckily, had been in the healers' tents when the gate had come down and so, like May and the others who'd arrived in the city moments after Ellemont's charge, had not witnessed what some fool bard had taken to calling the 'Ghosts' Harvest' in a song that was quickly making the rounds in the city.

Aaron stretched, wincing as his wounded ribs protested. The healers had done a fine job on them, but there was still pain. Not that he minded, much. Pain, after all, was not the worst thing a man could feel. "I was just wondering about Belgarin's army again," Aaron lied because the last thing he wanted was to talk about that damned charge again, "trying to figure why he would have retreated and what it means."

The Parnen looked at him doubtfully, as if he understood well enough the direction of Aaron's thoughts, but he shrugged, apparently deciding to leave it alone, "I suppose it could have been many things. Perhaps, Prince Belgarin decided that it was not worth it, after all. Maybe he has decided to become a farmer instead. Or a tavernkeep. I do so love tavernkeeps. Listen, did I ever tell you all about the time—"

"Yes," May said, rolling her eyes, "you've told us 'about the time' about a thousand times." She turned to Aaron, "And anyway, you ought to be grateful for a break regardless of the reason instead of sitting here moping like a child who just lost his favorite toy."

Aaron frowned, "I'm not moping."

May sighed, "I swear, Silent, it's like the only time I don't want to strangle you is when you're busy fighting for your life."

Aaron smirked, raising an eyebrow, "Speaking of fighting for your life, where's Thom?"

The club owner blushed, clearing her throat, "I'm sure I'm not the man's mother. It's not my job to keep up with his whereabouts."

Aaron turned to Leomin, and they shared a smile. "So you're saying you don't know then?"

May hesitated, fidgeting. Finally, she scowled, "Fine. He's gone with Balen and Festa to see to the ships. The captain was mumbling something about having to repair some broken furniture." She glanced meaningfully at Gryle, and although the chamberlain never looked away from Adina and Isabelle, his neck seemed to disappear a little further into his shoulders. "And anyway, since we're apparently talking about anything, just now, I wonder," she said, smiling cruelly, "if someone will tell me once more about the 'Ghosts' Harvest.' Oh, but I do so love a good story."

"Happy to ma'am," Wendell said, "it was the most wild thing I ever saw, I'll tell you that much, and when I was a kid I once saw a dog tryin' to err ... mount a horse."

"Oh," May said, "that crazy, is it? The poor horse."

Wendell grunted, "Poor dog. That horse was a fella, you see, and he didn't much care for the dog's attentions. Anyhow, this is how it happened—" conversation in the room cut off at the sound of breaking glass, and they all turned to see the chamberlain, staring sheepishly at the shattered remnants of a wine glass in his hands.

"I ... that is..." the chamberlain swallowed, his face heating, "Sorry. I was thirsty."

May shook her head with a sigh, "Alright, open your mouth then," she said, and before Gryle could protest, she was pouring wine from her own glass down his mouth, and he was forced to drink or drown. "Oh, don't stop on my account," she said, turning back to Wendell, apparently oblivious of the chamberlain's frantic gulping.

Wendell glanced at Darrell, and the swordmaster grinned, nodding his head. "Alright," the sergeant said, sitting forward in his chair, "this here's how it went..."

THE END

BOOK THREE
OF
THE SEVEN VIRTUES

BY JACOB PEPPERS

I hope you enjoyed visiting with Aaron, Adina, and the others again in *A Sellsword's Resolve.* To stay up to date on the next release and hear about other great promotions and giveaways, sign up to my mailing list at www.jacobpeppersauthor.com.

For a limited time, you will also receive a FREE copy of *The Silent Blade,* the prequel novella to The Seven Virtues, when you sign up!

Thanks for reading *A Sellsword's Resolve.* You can continue your journey with Aaron and the others by picking up your copy of *A Sellsword's Resolve,* the third book in The Seven Virtues series.

If you enjoyed the book, I'd really appreciate you taking a moment to leave an honest review—as any author can tell you, they are a big help.

If you want to reach out, you can email me at JacobPeppersauthor@gmail.com or visit my website at www.jacobpeppersauthor.com

Note from the Author

Well, dear reader, we've come to the end again. I hope you've enjoyed spending some more time with Aaron, Adina and the others. I also hope you were as surprised by some of the book's revelations as I was. As always, the book you've read would be much worse (picture a dozen wadded up page 1's, and you won't be far off; also, they'd probably be on fire) without the help of several people, so I'd like to take this opportunity to thank them now.

Thank you to my wife, Andrea, who sacrifices a lot so that I can sit around in house shoes and make things up. Thanks to my mom, dad, and brothers who never complain that nearly every conversation we have starts with me talking about people and places that aren't strictly real. Thank you also to my newborn son, Gabriel. I'm not sure how he helped with the book, but I'm sure he did and, anyway, he makes sure I get my exercise. What can I say? The little guy keeps me on my toes.

Thank you to all of those beta readers who took the time out of their busy schedules to share this dream with me for a time—the book is better for it. A very special thank you to Morris. Above and beyond, sir. Above and beyond.

And the final thanks? Well, I've saved that for you, dear reader. If it's been slightly gummed, I apologize. Gabriel tried to run off with it, but he's a baby and doesn't know any better, so I ask that you forgive him. Anyway, he didn't make it far. You see, he can't run yet. Or walk. Take it from me though, he's got the intense stare mastered. He reminds me of it every time I consider putting him down to work on my next book.

I am glad you took the time to visit with Aaron and the others. Aaron probably won't say it—truth is, he can be a bit of a jerk—so I'll say it for him. Thanks. And until next time,

I hope you find some wonderful worlds to explore,

Jacob Peppers

About the Author

Jacob Peppers lives in Georgia with his wife, his newborn son, Gabriel, and three dogs. He is an avid reader and writer and when he's not exploring the worlds of others, he's creating his own. His short fiction has been published in various markets, and his short story, "The Lies of Autumn," was a finalist for the 2013 Eric Hoffer Award for Short Prose.

Printed in Great Britain
by Amazon

28147878R00205